REYoung

ZOL

where even the sun sweats

ZOL

By REYoung

This book is available in print and electronic format at most online retailers.

ISBN 978-1-7334461-2-9

TageTage Press

REYoung-author.com

BOOKS BY REYOUNG

UNBABBLING
MARGARITO AND THE SNOWMAN
INFLATION
THE IRONSMITH

ΓΙΑ ΣΕΝΑ ΑΓΑΠΗ ΜΟΥ

OH MARGARITO! It was a song on the radio, *el éxito número uno!* It was the sun's golden rays on the petals of a daisy, *mira qué bonito!* It was a people's cry for freedom, *escucha mi grito!* But *Margarito?!* Isn't that some kind of *baybeedo?* Tequila, Grand Marnier, crushed ice, salt on the rim, a teaspoon of sugar and the juice of a *limoncito?* No, not margari-*ta* with a feminine *uh!* but Margari-*to* with a decidedly masculine *oh!* Ohhhh ... you mean Marga*reeto* the bandeeto with drooping mustachios and a marijuana cigarreeto clenched between his teeth-o? The picture postcard Margarito in a serape and floppy sombrero leaning *ay-ay-ayyyy!* against a spiny cactuseeto? Margarito *el guapo* serenading his latest swoon with a plinky-plunk guitarrito? Margarito in toreador costume waving his red cape in the bull ring (*¡Olé, Matadorito!*)? Margarito the revolucionario splashing across the Frio Grande on horseback in a blazing shootout with the federales (*¡Viva Zapatarito!*)? Margarito squeezed, distilled and desphinctered out of a thousand screaming childhood Saturday afternoon matinees of grainy, crackling and popping Technicolor big screen adventure? *That* Margarito? No, *not* that Margarito. Another Margarito, in another time, in another place, somewhere south of the border, down old Mexico way and beyond in a land ruled forever under the kingdom of the sun and called from ancient times in the ancient tongue by the single word *Zol.* Margarito whose ancestors led young men and women, warrior princes and virgin princesses, naked, terrified, maybe even in a drugged euphoria, up steep stone steps to the top of temples in the sky. Who bent them backward over stone altars, cut open their heaving chests with an obsidian blade, and in an ecstasy of blood tore out the beating heart with their bare hands and thrust it up to the rising sun while the now useless body fell to the ground, its mouth gaping in a silent scream, like the hot yellow light slicing across the green jungle canopy where birds of a thousand colors sang and life went on.

1
Touchdown

PITCH DARKNESS. A sound that could either be crickets chirring or the great squeaky wheel of the universe turning. Then movement, shadows and silhouettes. The smells of hot coffee, cigarette smoke (of course the audience can't smell this but they can see the gleam of coffee mugs, the glow of cigarette ashes). There's a sense of an encampment stirring to life, maybe military, a team of special ops preparing for insertion into hostile territory, or a bunch of bedrolled cowpokes waking around the smoldering coals of a campfire, farting and yawning and thinking about getting up to pee or take a dump. In the eastern sky membranous layers of lavender, violet and robin's egg blue peel apart from each other like silk shrouds interspersed with odd tatters and swirls of Paris green and blood red. Shadow and silhouette withdraw into form and substance. Light stands, camera dollies, sound equipment, black coaxial cables snaking over the rocky, sandy ground. It's a movie set. Crew members stand around, smoking, sipping coffee, talking in low voices. A tractor trailer, a step van and a pair of silver-skinned Airstream trailers are parked on the perimeter of the set like prairie schooners circled against the slings and arrows of dyspeptic Native Americans. A silver gleam, a flash of incandescence, the door in one of the Airstreams opens and all noise and motion cease, a cigarette freezes inches from a pair of parted lips, a rubber bathroom slipper hangs off a foot in mid-step, the pull tab on a can of carbonated beverage (Red Bull?)

hovers micro millimeters from releasing its gaseous admonition *shhh* as that master of the no-holds-barred B-grade movie, Boone Weller, appears on the set looking every bit the eccentric director in a brown silk mandarin robe with black frog buttons and embroidered gold dragons, pencil-thin mustache stenciled above his upper lip, ebony cigarette holder clenched between his teeth, and, even at this crepuscular hour, a pair of antique sunglasses, oval, with smoked lenses, perched on his narrow nose (some have suggested a William Burroughs resemblance, others, Hunter S. Thompson). He glances toward the horizon where a dusty orange halo has just begun to appear, removes the cigarette holder from his mouth and points it at the camera assistant, who raises a black clapperboard on which is scrawled in white chalk *Scene: Snowman at church, take one.* And it's Lights! Camera! Action!

Quiquiriquiiiiiiii! A proud prince of a rooster resplendent in iridescent crimson and orange, emerald and turquoise feathered finery stands tall on a split rail fence and proclaims his feudal reign over the dynasty of all within hearing. A pair of black metal bells on a timeworn Towcester wind-up clock clamors in alarm as the hour and minute hands on its staid moon face announce the passing of another sixty units of existence. A sonorous voice, old, wise, slightly bemused, intones, Time to wake up, Snowman, hats off to dreamland, goodnight moonbeam, the sandman's gone away. Come on, Snowpal, it's a new day, a new way, rise up and shine! In the spreading cellophane yellow light we now see a vintage and venerable coal-black Coupe du Jour, shark fins in the rear, Cheshire grinning chrome grill in front, classic (and also bald) whitewall tires, parked behind a ruin of crumbling adobe and naked roof poles that once may have been a church. The camera slowly pulls in to show us a man (the *Snowman* mentioned on the clapper?) slumped in the front seat on the driver's side. His head hangs partway out of the open window. His dirty blond hair is matted with dust and dried sweat. He's got two-three days of beard stubble. His face is oily, sallow. The camera pulls in tighter and in his glazed, bloodshot, arctic blue eyes we see the crimson ball of the sun rising in the side mirror. A small trickle of drool from the corner of his mouth suggests he's still in the borderlands of sentience, although it's not hard to imagine that at this moment the question, still inchoate, colloidal, is forming in his mind, *Where the fuck am I?* Like the Frankenstein monster recovering from a bad case of rigor mortis, he (the presumptive Snowman?) pulls himself more or less erect in the seat, fumbles with the buttons of a faded orange and green (pineapples and philodendrons?) Hawaiian shirt, which is open to his navel, exposing reddish-blond chest hairs and a not precisely buff belly, color some extreme of white between codfish and alabaster, finally gives up the effort, pushes open his door, painfully (judging by his grimace) extracts stiff muscles and aching joints from the Coupe and staggers toward a dead rattlepod tree. The sun has fully risen above the horizon. Bright yellow sunlight illuminates ochre mountains, flares up in sand crystals, pieces of broken glass, hundred-year-old brass bullet casings. His back to the camera, the Snowman (let's agree it *is* the Snowman) unzips his faded jeans and takes a disconcertingly long and poisonously orange pee that splashes heavily onto the sandy, rocky soil between his dirty gray sneakers, raising up a ragged bulwark of mud and dislodging a scorpion from a piece of dead scrub brush, sending it scuttling across the baked earth like a tiny arachnid backhoe in search of other shelter, which is how he notices the odd stumps of stone and wood sticking up out of the ground around him, some with words in Spanish … *nuestra hermana Tilapia … gracias a Santa Agave.* Grave markers. He's standing in a fucking cemetery. By now it's already hot, trembling waves of heat have begun to rise around him, but a shudder wracks his body and he utters aloud an involuntary *nyaahh!* Has he desecrated sacred ground? Brought a curse down upon his head? Shading his eyes with his right hand, he glances heavenward where he notices now a pair of small black specks turning in lazy circles in the pale blue ether. *Buzzards?*

He staggers back to the Coupe, devours the remaining Kay Milagro cupcake (he has no memory of eating the other five last night, nor of the last hundred miles or so of switchbacks and hairpin turns navigated in pitch blackness and somnolent insobriety), licks oddly chemical tasting chocolate icing from the wrapper (*We put the lead back in your tank*), washes it down with lukewarm coffee from the thermos he fishes out of a balene pod of empty beer bottles under the front seat, as a chaser he extracts the bottle of tequila sticking out from beneath the grungy midnight blue parka crumpled up in the back seat, which, squint-eyeing the contents, he can't help but notice is nearly empty, and, yeah, sure, *Snowman*, maybe a leprechaun did drink it, but let's not kid ourselves, okay? And while this truth-telling to self might suggest a resolution toward abstinence, yet another in a lengthy (say it—*laundry*) list, the greater truth is he's simply bemoaning the paucity of booze as he raises the bottle overhead and the final two-three jiggers of smoky liquor pour down his throat like strawberry soda. He scratches a strike anywhere kitchen match across the dash, takes a couple hits from the half-smoked joint wedged behind the chrome knob of the radio tuner, lights one of these annoyingly cloyingly sweet (even worse after the cupcake) oval cigarettes he bought on a guess, takes a couple puffs and, disgusted, stubs it out on the dash, once again pulls himself more or less erect in the seat, turns the key in the ignition and the ever faithful Coupe roars to life before settling into a low, four hundred sixty-seven horsepower rumble. And just like that, groggy, groaning like a peg-legged pirate with lumbago, not entirely arrived yet at a state of what might be medically defined as consciousness, he's back on the road again, the hot air roaring in the open windows, his hair whipping around his face, his body already locked in that forward leaning, fists gripping the steering wheel, let's get serious now posture, his eyes fixed beyond the bug-spattered windshield, beyond the ochre sprawl of sandy rocky soil and olive drab patches of cactus and scrub as if he could actually will himself across the gravitational and inertial restraints of time and space to his destination, which, not entirely unlike Zeno's paradox, grows ever nearer if still no clearer.

There's a small colonial city called *Chopahuac* circled in black magic marker on the wrinkled road map of Mexico he's carrying in his back pocket, and somewhere in the vicinity of this city, somehow overlying, infusing, permeating this city, and yet always on its periphery, is a place called Zol, which he has not been able to pinpoint on his map, nor to locate anywhere within the familiar realms of topographical and political boundaries in any encyclopedia, geography, history or guide book he has consulted. Nor could he ever get a straight answer when he pointed at said map and asked Margarito in his best friendly used car salesman voice, So where'd you say this Zol is again? To which Margarito, black eyes gleaming like the sun emerging from a solar eclipse, bristly black mustache twitching like a tree asp, invariably gave him that trademark *bemused* look, like, C'mon, *Snowdude*, you're trying to illuminate the moon with a flashlight. This cartological conundrum is overshadowed by another, slightly more existential question he's been asking himself with increasing frequency and, therefore, anxiety, not just *where* but *why?* Why is he driving through a barren stretch of desert somewhere in the heartless heart of Mexico on a tank of gas that should have been empty a hundred and fifty miles ago on this mission or quest or whatever the fuck it is to find this guy Margarito who, let's be honest, *Snowman*, you hardly knew at all? Was there something, an unspoken bond or sense of camaraderie or, who knows, maybe even something more you can't or don't want to acknowledge? In his mind (projected on the big screen for the viewing audience's convenience), he sees a figure bent over the engine cowling of an odd-looking vehicle, both futuristic and anachronistic, kind of a cross between a rocket ship and Santa's sleigh. Despite the puffy, midnight blue parka and coveralls this figure is wearing, he can see, stares at, involuntarily, doesn't want to, the ass, taut, round and, yes, attractive. He hears a voice, yes, Margarito's, full-throated, melodious, tunneling its way through an icy blast of wind-driven snow, *Come geeve eet a try, Snowman.* But maybe it's something else altogether, not nearly as complex or scary (sex with another *man?*) but equally as heavy, i.e., your own desperation, *Snowman?* This totally delusional notion you picked up God knows where that this dude who is essentially a stranger and by US government edict an *alien* is going to welcome you into his home for an unannounced and possibly extended stay simply because he said once, *You must come veeseet me sometime, Snowman?* And by the way, *Snowman*, you're doing it again. What? You know ... talking to yourself?

His misgivings seem to be reflected in the intestinal twists and turns this narrow winding road is taking him on as he continues to climb higher and higher into the steep, rugged mountains, dodging boulders that have crashed down onto the pavement from the weathered cliffs above, swerving around sinkholes that have swallowed large chunks of asphalt. Shaley red, yellow and bluish-green strata of exposed anticlines undulate like lapidary serpents. A dry gulch gouged next to this tortuous track is strewn with huge uprooted tree trunks, suggesting torrential rains in a wetter season. The air has turned much cooler and his ears pop painfully as he begins to pass through a bleak landscape. Everything is scorched, blackened, the undergrowth, the tall dead pine trees draped in ragged orange shrouds which he notices first with curiosity and then, his spine tingling like a glass armonica, alarm. Something's wrong here. He pulls over and climbs out of the Coupe for a closer look, an atavistic mix of awe and fear rising from his lizard brain as he realizes that these orange shrouds are actually sheaths of butterflies, monarchs, he guesses, *millions* of them, clearly dead, and somehow adhered to each other as if glued, perhaps by pine resin, their laminate wings illuminated by the sunlight like stained-glass windows in a burned-out cathedral. Clearly some cataclysmic event has occurred here. His (mostly) rational mind seeks a rational explanation among the usual suspects like, oh, you know, global warming, or the overuse of pesticides, herbicides and other such cides. But what if it's something else, some *force majeure* beyond human or at least *his* understanding driving before it a terrible plague or devastating storm? An even more disturbing thought smacks him in the middle of his forehead, yes, implausible, paranoid even, but what if he himself is the harbinger of this catastrophe? A shiver convulses his body. Despite old Sol's golden face beaming down upon this surreal landscape, both apocalyptic and Dalían, the air has turned sharply colder. A twig snaps, perhaps beneath the infinitesimal weight of an ant going about its business, but that's all it takes to send him hurrying—okay, walking quickly—back to the Coupe pursued by various unidentified haints and spooks. He briefly considers pulling on the parka in the back seat but the idea's about as appealing as wrapping himself in a wet dog blanket and besides, tromping the gas pedal and swerving back onto the road, he feels the temperature quickly rise as he descends into a steamy bowl-shaped valley beneath a blue ceramic dome of sky. Pungent vegetative smells assault his nostrils. The steep hillsides are lush and almost preternaturally green with tropical foliage. Patches of cultivated corn suggest a human attempt to impose order on this verdant chaos. He begins to pass a series of still lifes (interestingly, *dead nature* in almost every language but the more euphemistic—or pusillanimous, take your pick—English) that appear to have been stolen, er, *borrowed*, from a *National Geographic*. He sees clusters of Indian women with copper faces and Asian eyes wearing red woven shawls over boxy white dresses embroidered with bright red and yellow flowers, the tips of their long black braids tied together in back with pink or green or red ribbons, most barefoot, a few in pink plastic slippers. He sees copper-faced young boys in coarse, black wool jackets and white cotton pants, all barefoot, marching single file as if they're part of a religious procession. He sees old men with machetes in canvas scabbards at their sides, hurrying along in short, quick steps, some wearing huaraches, some barefoot, their thick calves exposed by short white trousers, their backs bent beneath huge loads of firewood, their brown, weathered faces, tomahawk noses and prognathic jaws Paleolithic. He notices barely discernible paths plunging into the jungle, marked with a red ski pole stuck in the ground or a large yellow satin bow tied to a stick or a pink vinyl purse hanging from a tree branch. A man, incongruous in a fedora, suit and tie and briefcase at his side, stands at a trailhead as if he's waiting for a bus, which is probably exactly what he's doing, but the Snowman's immediately suspicious. Does this guy really live somewhere back in the jungle in a bamboo hut with a thatched roof? Or is he actually an international spy like James Bond, suave and debonair even on assignment in the sweltering tropics? Sure, that'd make perfect sense, right? Which is precisely why *Boone*, as his (few) friends and select associates call him, shaking his head in disbelief and muttering *fucking ignoramus*, is hesitant to relinquish the narrative, even for one second, to this *idiot Snowman* who, in fact, *was* just about to go off on a long and improbable tangent about some big global conspiracy that, naturally, involves *him*. Although, second thoughts, Boone patting down nearly nonexistent strands of hair on the back of his head, what if the Snowman's character *did* encounter Mr. Bond? Easy enough to rip off some old footage, a little airbrushing, pixilation and … we hear Henry Mancini's immediately recognizable twanging surf guitar and blaring brass as the camera now follows the putative Bond back into the jungle toward what does indeed appear to be a bamboo hut with a thatched roof, which, wouldn't you know it, at this precise moment explodes in a cloud of smoke and flames, sending bamboo shards and presumed body parts flying everywhere and snapping the Snowman out of this divagation just in time to slam on his brakes and avoid crashing into the back of a banged-up, rusty white Isuzu pick-up truck exhumed from the primordial muck of the 1980s, which is creeping along in front of him at about twenty kilometers (a turtle-like twelve miles) per hour, the bed packed with a dozen mostly thin, shabbily dressed, dark-skinned men, women and children jammed among sacks of garlic, potatoes and chayote squash bristling like bright green hedgehogs, some of them clutching chickens under their arms like feathery white piñatas, most of them staring glumly straight ahead, which means backwards, disconcertingly at *him*, keeping in mind that this antique vehicle's about a quarter the size of the average SUV plying today's highways, i.e., not much bigger than a refrigerator, and still it stops again and again and more people pack themselves in with their sacks of fruit or vegetables, babies in slings and wing-flapping chickens. His antennae go up again when he spots a couple of young boys seated on a stone ledge turn and watch him pass. Neither of them appears to have an EyePhone® but he has the distinct sense they're reporting his presence to *someone* and, hmm, this is interesting, because just now he's come to a blinking yellow light over an intersection where, set back from the road, a military post has been established, crude log watchtowers, barbed wire, sandbagged bunkers, heavy machine guns manned by boyish-looking soldiers with Indian features and hostile expressions that suggest a readiness to shoot and kill another human being at a simple command *fuego!* He can see a soldier inside a bunker, shirt off, shaving. Another is talking to a village girl at the entrance, almost certainly a violation of regs and, who knows, maybe setting himself and his comrades up for disaster. On cue, the Snowman hears shouting and a group of men run forward, waving him off the highway with sharp, impatient gestures, and then something really crazy—a house built out of raw pine boards with a corrugated tin roof lurches toward him and past like an ancient war machine carried by thirty, forty men, their bare brown torsos running with sweat, their muscles straining, and yet they're all laughing and shouting drunkenly—indeed, he still feels a little drunk or hung-over or something because now it's like he's seeing everything through a camera lens smeared with Vaseline or wrapped with gauze, a kind of Hallmark picture of poverty, scattered tin and adobe and board shacks, naked children playing in dirt yards, mangy, scabrous dogs, a barefoot woman in a shapeless pink dress hanging damp laundry on a line. A turkey, bald-headed like a little old man, ragged tail feathers spread like a tattered Venetian fan, struts among a flock of scraggly chickens. Spiny prickly pear cactus and rubbery-looking red and green kalanchoes grow out of terra cotta roof tiles. On one rooftop he spots a small brown donkey nonchalantly chewing dead yellow grass, and, yes, he is reminded of Chagall but also of a high school classmate with a heavy panhandle drawl reading Lawrence Ferlinghetti's poem "Don't Let That Horse ..." Cracked pots of pink and red geraniums fill windows, doorways. Mounds of pink, purple and red bougainvillea explode next to cracked adobe walls. Acrid black smoke rises from smoldering piles of garbage. The conflicting savory and rancid smells of roasting and rotting meat pour in the Coupe's windows. Everything the Snowman passes seems to exist in an otherworldly celluloid dimension. He sees the green of the jungle and the bronze and terra cotta faces and the incongruous Hollywood floral displays erupting out of the dirt and the poverty, and it's all real and unreal, like he's watching a movie or riding in some kind of Jules Verne time machine. Occasionally people stop and stare at him with startled expressions as if they too recognize this wrinkle in time. Of course it's the Coupe, right? How often do you see a Motown classic like this outside of Cuba? More likely it's that odd solitary Joe Bftsplk black cloud hovering directly above the Coupe, from which a squall of fluffy white snow flurries continuously sifts down and immediately evaporates in the steamy atmosphere. Which is what—Boone's new special effects guy going for, well, effect? Or simply the Snowman's paranoid imagination, like maybe he really is some malevolent force propelling itself across scorching deserts and over tortuous mountain passes all the way down into this tropical clime and the rustic lives of the indigenous population like an unwelcome emissary from the frozen reaches of the North Pole? Something's clearly troubling these folks. They quickly lower their heads as he goes by and—surely this is his imagination—

he hears a panpipe's shrill, breathy voice playing a melancholy and familiar tune that he associates with a curiously named American pop duo from the 1960s. A minute later he passes a little old woman dressed entirely in black whom he's almost certain he has passed at least two or three times in the last couple of hundred miles. Doña Hermosa? Is that you? I thought they buried you yesterday. *Eh? What did you say? Dead? Me? Of course I'm not dead!* (For those who missed it, here Boone has inserted a subliminal, split-second clip of a squinting, hook-nosed (prosthesis), black-garbed, witch-like Doña Hermosa cupping her hand to her ear.) No, not dead, nor quite alive. Resurrected maybe, revived—*reanimated*, that's it. The studio keeps her in mothballs between shoots. She's practically a mainstay in Boone's movies, and she hardly costs a dime. None of which the Snowman's privy to. He simply assumes she's part of the slightly skewed space/time fabric he's been traveling through ever since he crossed the riparian border of the Frio Grande.

Now he's bouncing over a narrow cobblestone street crowded in on both sides by a chalk box arrangement of pastel red, yellow, blue and green stucco houses jammed shoulder to shoulder against faded, mildew-stained colonial buildings with Moorish arches, heavy stone lintels over doors and windows, inlaid blue tiles and wrought iron balconies. Music emerges from dark pockets, cooking smells, laughter, voices on TV *Acuérdense, un pueblo informado es un pueblo cálido*—which, after a lapse of several seconds, translates itself more or less accurately in his brain as, *Remember, an informed populace is a warm populace.* He smells raw leather and then a sweet yeasty aroma as his eyes register the words *Zapatero, Panadería.* He spots picks, shovels, hoes in the doorway of a *Ferretería.* He passes a public health clinic with a sign in shaky, hand-painted red letters advertising treatment for *ANSIEDAD.* A line of men and women in everyday work clothes, faces afflicted by tics, twitches and grimaces, hands confusedly wringing and praying, feet performing neurotic little *I gotta pee* dances, stretches out

the door and down the block, suggesting both a large population
of very anxious people and, that creepy tingling in his spine
again, a cause for such anxiety.

He relaxes his grip on the steering wheel, rolls his head on
his shoulders with a disturbing mix of liquid and crunching
sounds. It occurs to him that he's been nursing a childish
expectation most likely spawned by some Hollywood
abomination of saccharinity that any second now he's actually
going to spot Margarito standing on a street corner and, who
knows, maybe even some kind of reception committee behind
him cheering and waving signs, *Welcome to Chopahuac,
Snowman!* Finally he parks on a narrow side street where a
bright-eyed, floppy-haired boy of about nine or ten assures him
with a vigorous nod that the Coupe will be okay here. (Boone
had considered developing the kid, to be played by his
gardener's son Mateo or Martín *or whatever the fuck the little
wetback's name is* (*sic*) (he's Filipino, actually—the fact check
guy. Oh, it's a *girl* now?), as a kind of Tag*alog* sidekick who
accompanies the Snowman around town, showing him the
sights, explaining the indigenous culture to him, occasionally
playing third-world, underclass tricksterish tricks on him
(scorpions in his backpack, some kind of medicinal herb that
also happens to be a powerful laxative). But that plan fizzled
after Boone received unspecified threats from a child protection
agency (*Madres Con Machetes*) that had apparently gotten wind
of some of the (in)famous director's less savory propensities).
Setting off on foot, the Snowman soon finds himself strolling
through the zócalo among throngs of tourists and locals alike
beneath a canopy of towering Royal palms, vibrant purple
jacaranda and incandescent flamboyant trees with large
vermillion flowers (taxonomy also thanks to the new fact check
girl—*welcome aboard!*). He pauses in front of an elevated
bandstand with an antiquated zinc roof that looks like the nose
cone of a Victorian rocket ship (it's Trumpian history) where a
small orchestra is playing a lively arrangement of *La
Cucaracha*, and judging by these guys' sleepy-eyed grins, it's

pretty obvious *no les falta marijuana que fumar*. One of them even gives him a conspiratorial wink, or no, maybe he's just got a bug in his eye. Vendors hawk helium balloons, piñatas, dolls, toys, post cards, candy, trinkets, religious icons. Indian women in bright red huipils sit on straw mats, selling woven blankets, serapes and hammocks, bundles of spices and herbs, baked goods, triangular mounds of mangos, papayas, guavas. Indian girls hold out reed baskets piled with what the Snowman assumes at a glance are dried red chiles, but upon closer inspection he's pretty damn sure are actually roasted grasshoppers, an insect he hasn't seen a living representative of since his childhood. Old men sit like bookends on iron benches beneath which scabby, mangy mongrel dogs lie, tails flat, floppy pink tongues lolling out. A hideously deformed young woman, face twisted like a rubber glove, gnarled hand held out for donations, is led around by her mother, who says to someone in Spanish, Oh yes, her great misfortune! She is our fortune. She earns five times more than my poor Pablito, everyone is too ashamed not to give. Which the Snowman misses completely as he jams a five hundred peso note (a lousy twenty-five cents at most—he hasn't figured out the exchange rate yet) into the deformed hand. Little beggar girls and boys put on sad-eyed puppy dog faces for passing tourists, then skip away, laughing and clutching in their hands coins and paper currency in pesos and yanqui dollahs. Barefoot seven- and eight-year-old boys in dirty ragged shirts and pants with earnest little old man faces sell *chicles* and ballpoint pens from old cigar boxes or else they carry around makeshift shoeshine kits. The Snowman can't shake the feeling he's watching all of this on film rather than experiencing it *en vivo*, like there's a button to push or a switch to throw or even a damn remote that'll bring it all into focus and make it *real*. Everything, the quotidian, commonplace, the normal day to day existence of these people seems not just unfamiliar but alien and even a little threatening, which, sure, seems silly until he spots this female tourist—it's Betty Louden from Cincinnati, Ohio, nice lady, church-going, conservative in politics and appearance (but a heart of gold), she's wearing a vintage fifties blond bouffant, black cat's-eye glasses with rhinestones in the corners, modest outfit (matching yellow skirt and top), she'd never guess she's about to make the biggest mistake of her life when she buys a woven cloth belt from an Indian woman in an embroidered black wool vest and red huipil and—*abba cadaver* (that's how the Snowman heard it as a kid)—it's like magic, suddenly Betty is surrounded by a whole crowd of women and children. It's like she's become the designated tourist, the human ATM. A tentacular flurry of hands grabs at her, disembodied voices demand that she buy another belt exactly like the one she just purchased or a beaded pocketbook or a bouquet of flowers, or give me some money, *por favor, señora, un dólar!* The Snowman can see the uncomfortable smile on Betty's face (of course he doesn't know her name is Betty—he suspects it might be Margaret or LuAnn or even Kay) and then desperation as she looks for escape, for someone to save her, she wants to scream *Help! Help me!* but she feels so, yes, *silly*, and—too late, there's a sound of ferocious eating and presto! just like that, everyone scatters and it really is like a magic act—all that remains is Betty's bouffant, a wig after all, lying on the ground like an expired golden Pomeranian, which disappears in the twinkling of an eye, snatched away by an anonymous hand in a classic feat of legerdemain. Hmm, the Snowman's starting to think more in terms of survival than sightseeing when he notices a young greenghost couple sitting cool as cucumbers on a bench, talking to some Indian kids. The woman seems perfectly fluent in Spanish, the man, *meh*, passable (like the Snowman would know any better). There's something familiar about them and then he remembers. It's the young couple he saw broken down on the mountain outside of Saltillo yesterday morning, which already seems like a year ago. Although why does he think of them as young? The man's probably his age, early-mid-thirties, dark hair, athletic build and, yeah, sure, kinda handsome. The woman, true, is somewhat younger, maybe still in her late twenties, sort of waif-like, nymphish, with wispy blond tresses and wearing a loose red hippie dress embroidered with flowers and small round pieces of mirror—very pretty. She and the man talk excitedly as they study a map. They seem happy to be here, happy to be together. Only after they get up and walk away holding hands like total high school lovebirds does he realize he's been staring at them like a complete loser jerk, because of course now he's thinking of Judith, like, why doesn't he remember the two of them happy and doing things together or even once going on vacation or even taking a fucking day trip, for crying out loud? And why is that, *Snowman?* Because you really were a fucking snowman? Welded to the same spot from winter solstice to vernal equinox and straight on through summer and autumn, 365 days a year frozen in place in that eternal hibernal clime? Mister don't do nothin', don't go nowhere, old stick-in-the-mud, bump on a log, spinning your wheels, barely treading water *glub glub glub?* And, sure, easy enough to blame himself because there usually was a reason to blame himself, e.g., juvenile outbursts of anger and jealousy—a shrink would say something about acting out repressed behavior, delayed or protracted adolescence, to which *he'd* say bullshit, and then, after a couple minutes of sulking, he'd have to admit, well, okay, *maybe.* But there were two of them, after all, two ones joined in a union of possibilities that dwindled into the realm of irreconcilable differences (not limited to cruelty, adultery, felony conviction, abandonment, and confinement in a mental hospital (see below*)—had, that is, they been *married* rather than simply(?) living together). How is it possible to inhabit the same space as another person but exist in a different dimension? Is it some function of quantum mechanics? A new interpretation of feng shui? Something to do with extraterrestrials? Judith, whose ethnicity, country of *oreegin,* even her planetary provenance (that androidal intelligence flickering in the cobalt blue lenses of her eyes, for example), he was never able to ascertain. And carry on like that five, six— *seven?* years, long enough to colonize Mars or even one of

Jupiter's dozens of moons and return to Earth traveling via electromagnetic propulsion? And by the way, Snowman ... why are those people looking at you? And why *are* those people looking at him? Could it be because all this time he's been talking to himself out loud and in public like some kind of mental case (see above*)? Which in itself should be reason enough for him to break down and buy a damn EyePhone® as cover. *Hey, Fred, I gotta run—talk to you later!*

Before anybody has a chance to call the cops, the white coats, the attaché from the American embassy (you're making a public disgrace of yourself, *Mister* Snowman, you're an embarrassment to your nation, do you want everyone to think Americans are a bunch of loudmouth ignoramuses who don't respect other cultures?), he slinks off into inconspicuousness, relatively speaking (cadaverous looking white guy in grungy green and orange Hawaiian shirt), and begins to peregrinate through the crowded streets, his mind's eye superimposing an altered reality upon the existing reality of everything he sees. It's like he's in another country—because you *are* in another country, dumbass. Truth is, beyond a brief border crossing in his college days for some largely unremembered initiation rites into manhood that left him with a two-day hangover and a couple weeks' worry about STDs, he's never been out of the US before and everything's, well, *different.* He passes a butcher shop, in the doorway haunch and hoof hang from steel hooks, blood brown meat and greasy white fat swarm with flies, an anatomy lesson for a column of schoolchildren, boys and girls, two by two, in white shirts and black pants or skirts. A pair of Indian men in white cotton shirts and trousers and leather sandals squat over a broken patch of sidewalk, inlaying a mosaic of colored tiles with trowels and cement. A car with gray metal loudspeakers mounted on its roof blasts urgent, reverberating political messages *¡Adelante con el mejor candidato para nuestro futuro!* He passes a wall plastered with the various parties' red, white and green political posters, PAIN, PRIX, PARD, PAST, PDDT, but he can detect no compelling signs of honesty and integrity or even the opposite (lying, cheating scumbag) in the candidates' somber, unsmiling faces. Alternating smells of frying onions, raw sewage, roasting meat, rotting meat, diesel fumes and pine-scented disinfectant flood his nostrils. He sees kids five-six-years-old carrying stacks of newspapers or cardboard on their heads or pushing wheelbarrows containing propane tanks or firewood or lugging jugs of water. A naked baby boy splashes in the dirty water running down a gutter. His mother (presumptive) washes clothes in it. A dog drinks from it. (Boone seems intent on piling on the local *color*. That or it's the Snowman searching for clues to something he can't name but is pretty certain he'll recognize when he sees it. Is there a GPS for that?) Muttering under his breath *get the fuck out of my way you fat pigs* (add latent sociopathy to the list), he pushes through a throng of mostly obese, floppy-hatted American tourists—oh, and apparently a couple families of Canucks, pretty hefty meat and potatoes types themselves—loaded down with umbrellas, water and soda bottles, daypacks and bags of snacks. They're waiting to board a line of tour buses outside a large modern hotel from which a refreshing blast of cold air wafts over him when someone pushes open the double glass doors. The Arctic evaporates and the heat and humidity close in on him again as the cobblestone street leads him inertially down a steep hill toward a wide, shallow river demarcating the edge of town. At various spots along this fast-moving and surprisingly crystal clear stream men and women stand or sit or kneel in the water, washing clothes or bathing, some unabashedly naked (move along, folks, nothing to see here). A narrow concrete span without guardrails carries him across to the other side—well, okay, he walks under his own power, but some strange force does seem to be drawing him forward voodoo zombie-like. A sign's green arrow directs him up a steep winding road toward something called Monte Blanco, described as *ruinas Mayas*, which, in addition to the promise of exotica, also seems to exert a strange magnetic attraction of its own. After a short cigarette break, only his second of the day, which, yuck, tastes awful, dry, musty and way too sweet, he begins to climb, not taking into account that it's now high noon, not a cloud in the sky and the mercury's already topping one hundred. The blazing sun beats down on his completely unacclimated bare head, he's shedding buckets of sweat. He hasn't even hiked a hundred meters and he's starting to feel dizzy. Maybe it wasn't a good idea to smoke that last cigarette. And, yeah, he probably should have bought a bottle of water somewhere. And now this line of goddamn tourist buses is grinding up the hill, inundating him in waves of hot diesel exhaust. Faces at the window stare at him like he's a donkey foraging for grass on the roadside, some are aiming EyePhones® at him. At this very instant a fifteen-year old kid at the back of his English class in Guangzhou, China (the fact check girl's still verifying the time difference) is saying to his neighbor, ha ha, look at this idiot (except in Cantonese, which is why he should pay more attention to his teacher, a well-meaning young American woman with deep Christian roots named LuAnn Louden—yes, it's Betty's daughter, she'll learn of the tragedy via text message in one, two, three *ding!*). By the time the Snowman reaches the top of this small mountain where a marker informs him the altitude is four hundred meters, not nearly high enough to cause oxygen deprivation, he's nevertheless wheezing and gasping for breath. The hot air burns in his lungs. Blood pounds in his head. He's completely soaked with sweat. He looks slightly deranged. A woman sitting in a small wooden ticket booth talking to a man in a security uniform barely glances at him—she's seen tons of crazy tourists. The entrance fee is a rather steep ten thousand pesos but he figures since he's already made this effort he might as well go in and—*yeow!* He's seen stuff like this in the *National Geographic*, his bible of natural and manmade wonders, although usually years out of date (rare trips to the dentist), but real, live, in person, it's fucking incredible. It looks like a Martian city the way he imagines a Martian city (Bradbury? The *Chronicles?*), but built out of giant limestone

Lego blocks. Palaces, stairways, truncated pyramids, a clunky circular construction that resembles the key cylinder of an enormous deadbolt lock but turns out to be an astronomical observatory. Uniformed guards stationed here and there keep an eye out for any untoward behavior, climbing, graffiti, public urination (okay, admittedly, he was looking for a secluded spot, maybe in that dark corner, hurry, hurry, *shit*, here comes somebody), but otherwise he's completely free to roam around these structures with the other tourists and right now he's gotta admit he is just another pop-eyed, drop-jawed, gawking tourist, minus a hundred and fifty pounds of extraneous blubber, floppy hat, umbrella and water bottle—the last three of which, to be honest, he'd like to have right now. He gets another of those creepy spine tinglers (okay, Vincent Price, I said it) when he places his hands on a block of stone hewn two thousand years ago by another pair of hands directed by a mind inspired by visions of God or gods entirely alien to any theological dogma he has ever been indoctrinated in or repudiated in his lifetime, images of which (the alien gods) he sees everywhere, carved in stone walls, over entranceways, zoomorphic monsters, giant serpents, crocodiles, jaguars with huge square teeth and human heads emerging from their mouths. He reads a plaque in Spanish and curious English (*noteworthy is how the intercourse of stones gives pleasure to the eye*), which informs him that, through an ingenious feat of engineering, rather than laboriously hauling blocks of stone up the mountain, the original inhabitants quarried the mountain down into this hilltop citadel. A roar explodes overhead and he looks up just as the orange and blue fuselage of a jet plane passes so low he can see the passengers' faces in the windows. He half expects the cabin door to open and a bunch of overly zealous tourists wearing wingsuits to jump out. An odd glint catches his eye and his gaze travels higher still and he sees something like a huge buzzard soaring across the sky, but it's not a buzzard, it's another jet plane painted exactly *like* a buzzard, and not some dopey, ragged-winged cartoon buzzard crawling with fleas and mites, but a super buff buzzard that hits the weights in the gym five days a week and munches anabolic steroids like candy. He shudders as he again hears panpipes, haunting and melancholy, but again the rational part of his brain dismisses it as nothing, a teenager's ear buds turned up too loud or the wind blowing through holes in a metal flagpole. And there is wind. A refreshing breeze has sprung up, cooling his face and drying his sweat. Spirits and appetite revived, he decides to head back into town, grab a bite to eat, but he's hesitant to leave. He senses something here of vital importance, his magnetic compass is spinning out of control, it's like he's an iron bar sitting on top of a mountain of lodestone. Does it have something to do with his search for Margarito? Could he be receiving messages from outer space? ☆▲ ▼✳❂▼ ✳✱○✾ ✧❑▢▼✝ ✱✳▲✾ ▼✳✱ ✳■❑◗○❂■ (*Is that him, Gort? Yes, the Snowman*—rough translation by Dr. Yoodi Bambang, Director of advanced SETI research on the remote Indian Ocean island of Zapfdingbats.)

Both exhilarated and, true, a bit discombobulated by this unexpected side excursion, he trudges back down the hill, which is certainly easier than hiking up, but by the time he reaches the bottom and starts into town he's soaked with sweat again and he's feeling wiped out. He could probably use about sixteen hours of sleep, he's hungry, famished actually, he hasn't eaten anything since that damn cupcake this morning and his blood sugar's low, he's woozy from the heat, and maybe for all those reasons he hears a strange sloshing sound in his ears. But wait, maybe there is balm in Gilead, he thinks as the smell of cooking meat enters his nostrils, savory and, according to reputable sources, pleasing to God. An old woman is selling tacos from a stand outside the gates of a factory (*kitchen appliances?*). He feels like he could probably eat a dozen right now, he even starts to ask for a more moderate *dos, por favor*, but glancing at the meat on the grill he has second thoughts. Sure, maybe it is beef, maybe goat, but also maybe somebody's pet dog or cat. Then he notices the ice chest full of canned Cokes. The old woman follows his glance. *¿Quiere Coca, güero?* she says.

(*Güero* is pretty much equivalent to *whitey* or *white guy* and isn't intended as a racial slur in this case—Eduardo, Foreign Language and Cultural Editor, but you can call me *Eduardito*—if you're good.) Sensing salvation, he nods enthusiastically, but rather than simply give him the can of soda, the old woman officiously pops the top, pours the contents into a clear plastic cup, says more as a statement than a question, *¿Le pongo una piedrita de hielo, güero?* and before he can say yay or nay, she digs her hand in the cooler, scoops up some ice cubes and dumps them in his soda. He stares at the woman's rough, worn fingers, and then at the ice floating like used flashcubes in his drink, in which he also sees now or at least imagines he sees tiny black specks, which could be anything, dirt, human hairs, insect legs, mitochondrial traces of bubonic plague—indeed, the old lady gives him what he perceives as a malevolent wink and says, or so he thinks, *¿Sabe que trae bichos, güero?* And then— he's not a hundred percent certain about this, maybe it's the heat, this strange dizzy spell—she adds, in *English*, You know, *germs, microbes, bacteria?* Which immediately sets off alarm bells or ships' bells or even bells of glad tiding because, yes, he remembers now, he's heard these very words spoken before. Of course, it's a message from Margarito. His hopes buoyed like a helium balloon, he practically shouts at the old woman, Where is he?! How do I find him?! Now it's her turn to act confused. She wrinkles her brow and squints at him, *¿Está loco, señor?* Uh-oh, he senses that one false word and things could go horribly awry. He completes his transaction (a thousand pesos) and waits until he's out of the old lady's sight to dump the questionable Coke in the gutter, then conscientiously looks about for a garbage can to dispose of the plastic cup (sorry, eco-fans, no recycling bins in this burg), which is when he spots a large blue stucco building. A bunch of people with cheap suitcases and bulging plastic bags are waiting outside to board idling buses, some of them modern, air-conditioned *ejecutivos*, some nothing more than beat-up old school buses hauled all the way down here from Osberg, TX, the Snowman's hometown, in a feel-good exchange of repurposed vehicles and home appliances arranged by the ladies' auxiliary of the Rivenbundt Church of Christ Warrior Redeemer, under the personal supervision of the renowned orator and servant of God Reverend K. James Fallible *our obsolescence is their future.* The camera—there's always a camera somewhere—zooms in on one bus in particular, a battered, banged-up blue and white hulk with the words *Confía en Cristo* in white plastic applique across the top of the rectangular windshield, followed by a smash cut to this same bus rumbling across the desert in a cloud of yellow dust. The camera moves inside and—ha, there's the Snowman again, for some inexplicable reason dressed in a magenta silk shirt and cream-colored linen sports jacket and pants that scream *Halfinger* and *Armoani.* He's jammed between a pair of fairly large and very sweaty *campesinos,* the seats are all packed, the air's hot and stuffy, chickens squawk, a miasma of garlic and bean farts floods his nostrils, his bladder's seriously beginning to hurt because he really has to pee but he's not going back *there* again—and, poof, just like that, he's right back where we left him, standing outside the bus station. But why, the audience wonders (a few more people have wandered in, *Hey, down in front!*), is the Snowman so intrigued with this bus station? Answer: because he also remembers now that Margarito once said he worked in a bus station. Inside, people are slumped on plastic chairs. Some lean against the mildew-stained walls in various states of somnolence. Large wooden fans turn overhead like airplane propellers. The sweet, cloying smell of wood polish rises from the gleaming floorboards. A chubby, middle-aged woman in a starched white blouse that bulges over the waist of her black wool skirt and a pair of dumpy, middle-aged men in black ties, sweat-stained white shirts and black polyester trousers, one with a noticeably torn fly, look at him with varying degrees of disinterest from behind a wooden counter. Dreading the effort this will take, he asks in more or less intelligible Spanish if perhaps they know a certain Margarito who once worked here. Disinterest turns to suspicion.

The three exchange glances bordering on horror. *Noooo, señor*, one of the men shakes his head, there ees no Margarito here. The woman makes a scornful face. *¿Margarito? ¡No hay aquí!* The man with the torn zipper winces as if he has a toothache and also starts to say no, then lifts his eyebrows. Wait! Deed you say Margarito? *Sí*, there *was* a Margarito. *¿Sí?* The other two look skeptical. *Siiií*, he insists in a kind of chainsaw whine, the fonny leetle fat guy with bad teeth? Oh *sí sí sí*, the others agree, *that* Margarito. But no, he shakes his head, *not* that Margarito.

Disheartened, he leaves the bus station and starts back in the general direction of the zócalo. His spirits sink even further when he passes a couple of rough-looking hombres, one short, stocky, studs in his eyebrows, barbed wire tattoo around his neck, the other tall, lean, straight black hair tied back in a ponytail. A black patch over one eye partially obscures a jagged scar that runs from his forehead to his jaw. Hmm, he's pretty sure he remembers seeing these two in a little pueblo he passed through yesterday, so what are they doing here now? Even more disconcerting, these dudes have him on their radar and that ain't exactly love light in their eyes. He tries to pick up his pace without being obvious but his energy levels have dropped to near zero and his ass is dragging like he's pulling a plow behind him. His legs feel like logs, he's broken out in a cold sweat, he's feeling dangerously light-headed. (Here Boone is playing with some jerky handheld camera work to recreate the Snowman's state of mind, a decision that, along with a growing number of issues, will occasion continued bickering among the crew until the end of the production.) He also feels a desperate need to eat something, preferably sweet. Providentially, he wanders into a huge covered market—surely they sell food here. It's kind of like a department store bargain basement, stall after stall of clothes, boots, shoes, baskets, pottery, kitchenware, electrical appliances, hardware, and finally, yes, there is food, huge burlap sacks of dried beans and grain, produce stalls packed with heads of cabbage, cauliflower and broccoli, potatoes, peppers and onions. A meat market displays plucked chickens, pigs' heads, cow tongues, bins of—*insects?* And that's clearly what they are, grasshoppers, crickets, some kind of worms, roasted a shiny lobster red or root beer brown. Man, that's not doing much for his appetite. He exits the market feeling defeated, but just when his mood's about to pack its bags and head (farther) south, his spirits soar like a Saturn 5 rocket (too hyperbolic?) as a sweet yeasty aroma fills his nostrils and he spies a bakery on the corner. With a renewed sense of determination he beelines toward it, practically throws himself through the open door and—look at all this treasure! His eyes roam over a table laden with pink and yellow, red and green frosted sugar cookies and even better, he doesn't have to say a word, just grab the metal tongs, load up half a dozen of these beauties on a brown plastic tray, hand them over to the lady behind the counter who, yes, perhaps a little brusquely, places them in a white paper bag and, yes, perhaps a mite curtly, says, *Mil pesos*, which by now he understands is like fifty cents, but who cares how much it costs, right? This is an emergency. Ten, twenty, a hundred bucks—take my whole fucking wallet, just give me the damn cookies. He hurries outside, plops down on a low stone bench outside a park and begins to gobble one cookie after another, grimacing and making animal-like growling sounds and dropping crumbs on the ground until all the cookies are gone. But now, through some inverse algebraic equation he vaguely remembers *seeing* in a high school textbook (as opposed to actually studying, much less learning), the pleasure he has derived in gorging himself turns to distress. His stomach feels like he's eaten a sack of wet cement, his mouth is coated with a greasy, lard taste, his head has begun to ache. He's also feeling despondent again. This is not at all the way he imagined things. That bucolic little Margaritoville he accumulated and spliced together out of all the other towns and villages he passed through on his journey here—a fake, fantasy, fraud of his own imagination? I mean, did you really think you'd just pull into Nazareth and say, Howdy folks, I'm a friend of Margarito's, and that'd take care of everything? Of course! You must be the Snowman! We've been expecting you! Come this way! Um … you're doing it again, Snowman. Doing what? You know—talking to yourself. Not that any of these *campesinos* gives a shit, just another crazy greenghost, right? Just make sure your chickens are locked up at night? Oh yeah, and your wife, your daughter and your national assets? Uh-oh, someone's getting testy. Experiencing some of that shoe-on-the-other-foot thing? Stranger in a strange land?

(Although still early in the game, fans of Boone's previous release *The Abominable Snowman of the North* are getting impatient. Where's all the action? The special effects? What happened to the car chases? The monsters from outer space? Has Boone really hung up his shooting ironies and transformed his existentially challenged (anti-)hero into a petty, sniping flaneur gadding about a foreign locale? Boone's mostly young, mostly white, mostly male, hipster crew *Dude!* are especially upset. They didn't sign on for some G-rated family affair about Bambi and Buffy running off to join ISIS. They wanta see Boone's legendary razor's edginess in action. As for Boone, he'd love to regale these young punks with tales of *his* Indie days surviving on Campbell's pork n' beans and Wonder Bread sandwiches and selling his blood as often as FarmCorps allowed him on the gurney, pale as a ghost, barely able to stand on his feet, just so he could afford a cartridge of super eight. But what's the use? Just inviting more abuse. *Save it for the nursing home, Old School!*)

Well, there's obviously some confusion (and resentment) among the cast and crew about what they're doing here and tempers are running pretty high, Boone's not the least. His eyes flicker like lasers behind his smoked glasses, he mutters something that sounds like *barada nikto!* and with a vicious snarl that loosens more than a few bowels in attendance, he calls for quiet on the set and aims his ebony cigarette holder like a blowgun armed with a curare-tipped dart at the DP (yes, Jeffrey—*director of photography*). The lights dim and the camera draws in until the Snowman seems to be enclosed in a little box set off from the rest of the world. A mix of street and foley sounds crashes around him, the rumble of buses and trucks, car horns, children's screams, vendors shouting, pigeons cooing, a bicycle bell chiming—he hears none of it because, you know, it *is* a movie, you just turn off the sound and then— it's like the Twilight Zone, same setting but everything's *different*.

2
Hotel Caulifornia

THE HOUR GROWS LATE, the shadows long, the dusty red ball of the sun has just sunk behind the municipal building where the clock centered in the oblique triangle of the pediment discreetly informs us that day has passed into evening. A man sits like Rodin's thinker (albeit clothed) on a low stone bench in a small colonial city in the interior of Mexico, the world around him reduced by fatigue and a profound sense of displacement to an impenetrable babble of tongues. Of course it's our Snowman, but as distant as he feels from humanity, at least in its current manifestation, he feels equally distant from himself. It has dawned on him that he'll have to get a room but the thought of speaking to anyone, of asking directions, much less seeking a recommendation, in *Spanish*, Excuse me, sir, you wouldn't happen to know of a nice, clean, *cheap* hotel in the vicinity, would you? Oh, really? And you say it's only three and a half blocks over on *Avenida Chichinautzin,* just make a right at *Mi Caballito Rosa*—it's a restaurant? there's a pink horse on the roof, you can't miss it?—and then a left at the School of Engineering and Advanced Technology, and after that go straight until you come to the new construction site where that German consortium, International Colors Are Us, is building an automobile paint factory?—the thought of all that, or, more likely, wandering aimlessly until he finally stumbles upon a place, most likely way overpriced—further enervates and prevents him from taking action even though he knows, admonishes himself, you have to *do* something, Snowman, you can't succumb to this paralysis or things will fall apart, completely, irrevocably, forever. Which is when he spies the young couple again, strolling along like before, cool as cukes, no trouble at all navigating this burg. He instinctively pulls himself up from the bench and follows in their wake like a lurching zombie *brains!* A few blocks later they enter a courtyard adjoining a two-story, flamingo pink stucco building with balconies, wrought iron railings, leaded windows and pots of pink and red geraniums everywhere. A mass of purple bougainvillea sprawls against an exterior staircase. An ancient, forest green station wagon loaded down with rocks, logs and giant bones is parked in the circular, brick-paved drive near the entrance over which a creamy white neon sign says *Hotel Caulifornia*, simultaneously evoking in the Snowman's mind a waxy, white, broccoli-like inflorescent vegetable and a murderous, time-travelling cyborg who in another dimension is governor of a very large and notoriously ditzy state on the west coast of North America. The hotel lobby is dim, baroque, brocade sofas and chairs, wainscoting, electric candles glow in brass fixtures over gilt-framed oil paintings of stern-faced men and women in eighteenth century Iberian costume. Behind a polished wooden counter stacked with Mexican and foreign newspapers, maps, guidebooks and tourist brochures sits a desk clerk who, the Snowman can't help noticing, looks a heck of a lot like a young Peter Lorre, in fact, he's wearing a name tag that says Peter Lorre, and when he bats those long-lashed psychopathic puppy dog eyes and says in that unctuous, wheedling, chillingly familiar nasal sibilance, Of courssse I'm not *that* Peter Lorre, *hnn, hnn, hnn,* he sounds exactly *like* that Peter Lorre. He also speaks perfect English, and yes, there is a room available, and it's even pretty reasonably priced, although it's upstairs in back and doesn't offer a street view.

After divulging practically his entire life history in the guest ledger (nationality, place of birth, passport number, driver's license and license plate number, mother's maiden

name, blood type, food preferences and shoe size), the
Snowman spends another half hour hunting down the Coupe,
which he has foolishly assumed all along is parked *right over
there*, and another half hour navigating the labyrinth of narrow,
crowded, mostly one-way cobblestone streets (there's a kind of
Cabinet of Dr. Caligari feel here, chiaroscuric shadows and
light, sharp angles, a sense of malevolence and constriction—
the DP's got a pretty strong idea of the ambience *he* wants to
see) until at last he finds his way back to the hotel. He parks the
Coupe in the street out front and lugs his bag up a steep,
winding staircase with a burnished maple bannister and wrought
iron railing and down the hall to his room, which is about the
size of a sleeping compartment on a passenger train. He sits on
the bed (gratefully, it's firm, but he wonders at the wool
blanket) and stares at the hot plate on top of the mini-fridge, at
the faded black and white print on the wall of a man dwarfed by
an enormous prickly pear cactus, at the darkness gathering
outside the lone window through which he can see dense jungle
foliage. He feels totally beat. He feels grimy, grubby and
disgusting. The smell of his own sweat reeks in his nostrils. He
tells himself he should get cleaned up but right now all he wants
to do is lie back on the bed and close his eyes for a second. And
just like that he's falling through empty space. His whole body
jerks and he gasps awake. Groggy, disoriented, he sits on the
edge of the bed. Maybe a shower will help. The bathroom is
small, cramped, but clean, and the hot water works. This is the
best thing that's happened to him all day. His sighs of relief and
pleasure are practically orgasmic, or at least that's how they
sound through the wall to his neighbor, a beautiful blonde from
Munich, who, initially intrigued, glances away discreetly when
she sees the newly squeaky clean and nearly phosphorescent
Snowman emerge from his room a short while later in yet
another Hawaiian shirt, one of a closetful inherited from his
father (white kukui and pink hibiscus flowers).

His spirits and appetite again revived (the discovery of a
frosty mini-bottle of platinum tequila in the mini-fridge helps),

he heads out to get some chow and it looks like his fortunes have begun to change for the better because right around the corner he finds a brightly lit, totally packed cyber café. Shouting, laughter, screeching chairs, bustling wait staff, pounding techno music, fragments of Italian, German, French, Russian, Spanish, English, Japanese, Chinese. Mostly twenty and thirty somethings (i.e., more or less his *cohort*, except they're not) bend over screens, chat with neighbors, nod their heads to music. Behind a long wooden counter, young artsy types (tats, piercings, rad hair—oh, you know, red, yellow, green, chopped, shaved, lawn-mowered, spiked) take orders for coffee, tea, beer, wine, soups, salads, lactose, gluten and peanut free-ranging certified organic vegan dishes. Glass cases offer pies, cakes, cookies, cupcakes, chocolate fudge brownies, empanadas, super stuffed deli sandwiches. Prints and posters cover the walls and ceiling. Corkboards are crammed with xeroxed fliers, advertisements for yoga and tai chi classes, music groups, massage therapists, Spanish lessons, Swedish, French, German and Russian lessons *learn to speak in only two hours! Zwei Stunden! Dva Chasa!* Sticky notes and torn out journal pages are scribbled with silly, profound, urgent messages in pencil, ink, felt tip, crayon and maybe even blood, *Ursula! Wo bist du?* Beneath that, *Pax! Vobiscum?* Beneath that, a pair of cartoon eyes and a Jimmy Durante nose peer over a picket fence inscribed with an existentialist *Kilroy wasn't here*. The Snowman orders the most normal-sounding, meat-related item on the menu, a soy-something mock brisket sandwich packed with a bunch of healthy green stuff he'd happily have done without and a bottle of dark beer he can't do without. He finds a tiny wooden table not much bigger than the stool under it in a relatively quiet corner and wolfs down his remarkably tasty faux meat sandwich between gulps of a delicious hoppy, molassesy beer while examining the montage of humanity like an animal watching out of the woods.

Hunger satisfied, spirits further on the rise, he returns to the Hotel Caulifornia and, to his surprise, finds a dozen or so people engaged in a fairly lively conversation over drinks in the lobby, most of them in their sixties and seventies, except for the young couple (YC), whom he notices hovering on the periphery, and who also, by their expressions (ambivalent?), seem to have noticed him. Turns out the hotel is the nexus for a fading colony of American and European expatriates, exiles, artists, writers, aging new-agers, anthropologists, archaeologists, ethno-musicologists, high-dudgeoned unapologists, including professors of literature, languages and linguistics, as well as a dapper if somewhat dissolute-looking sixtyish gentleman in a tweed jacket, who gives off an aura of spydom. Apparently these evening colloquiums are a regular event (tonight's topic: the demise of the classical Maya civilization), although the atmosphere seems more combative than collegial. Aloof, disdainful, the participants openly smirk and snort in derision at each other's comments. *Reahlly*, Rutherford? Comparing coprophagy to anthropophagy? Oh come on, Pinchley, take the cork out of your ass! Until, that is, someone says, What do *you* think, Professor Simianovsky? At which all eyes focus on the renowned (somebody said) professor of Pre-Columbian studies Gregor Simianovsky. (*Professor* to all, Gregor to none, and most definitely not Sy, *ever!* You may call him the learned, the esteemed, the eminent, the distinguished, but Prof, Doc or, most egregious, P.S.? *Never!*) Extremely hirsute, his face almost entirely carpeted in orange fur, kind of like a bespectacled yeti or a beard wearing glasses (rectangular steel rims), the professor says in a melodious baritone, more or less to the tune of Rudolph the Red-nosed Reindeer, Well, you know the Toltec and Olmec, Mixtec and Aztec, the Zapotec and Yucatec, Tzotzil and Tzeltal, but do you recall the most famous Mexican dynasty of all? And here the Snowman's ears perk up as the professor hums a few bars, ending with a wobbly falsetto *Zoltec!* And just who were, or rather *are*, I should say, as their descendants still live among us, or, *ahem*, more accurately, we live among them, these Zol-*tec?* The professor's voice snaps like a door latch on this second syllable before he answers his own question, clearly rhetorical. Scientists! Mathematicians! Astronomers! They studied the stars in the heavens at night. They observed the plants and animals in their habitat. They translated the world around them into an extremely complex cosmology, built magnificent temples, astronomical observatories more accurate than anything in the western world, cities equal to any in Europe. The question we must ask ourselves today, ladies and gentlemen, is what caused this great civilization to fall? Professor Simianovsky glances around as if he has an auditorium full of rapt listeners. Auditorium, no, rapt, yes. His gaze lingers on the Snowman and in the narrow blue gleam behind his glasses he seems to be thinking, hmm, do I know this guy? He adjusts his specs and proceeds. Many theories have attempted to explain the collapse of Pre-Columbian Maya society, one of the principal being a swollen leisure class whose sole purpose was to consume without producing anything. Not much different from today, eh? *Hear! Hear!* his audience, mostly a bunch of old lefties, responds. Professor Simianovsky continues his catalogue of causality: drought, famine, internecine warfare—all candidates for the ruin of empire. The final tragedy? The arrival of the Spanish *conquistadores* and with them slaughter, disease and possibly worse—the professor scans his audience but only a slight *sniff* of dissent is heard when he exclaims with obvious disdain—their missionaries! *Go therefore and make disciples of all the nations, baptizing them in the name of the Father and of the Son and of the Holy Spirit* (Matthew 28:19-20). Huh? The Snowman glances around with a puzzled expression that seems to ask—did anybody else hear that? The professor continues, a tone of resignation in his voice. (One can almost hear the tolling of a heavy iron bell—or no, there actually is a bell. *Vespers?* Never affiliated with any faith or religion, the Snowman can only guess.) What the invaders didn't destroy succumbed to the vegetative anarchy of the jungle, to be plundered later by looters, vandals, thieves. Not all is lost, however. Much of the history and culture of this ancient civilization has been recovered thanks to the tireless efforts of the indigenous people themselves, with the support of the World Heritage Fund, as well as scholars in multiple disciplines from around the globe. Professor Simianovsky makes a self-ingratiating flourish and flutters his eyebrows, well, pretty much his whole forehead, á la grouchy Marx, and like a snake oil salesman conning a bunch of hayseeds, casually mentions a remote Zoltec archaeological site he has been investigating, interested parties are welcome to accompany him tomorrow morning. This invitation is received with a great deal of hullabaloo but few takers. Whether it's too much Indiana Jones in his adolescence or a whiff of destiny, the Snowman rashly signs on. Fact is, Professor, he says in a Big Tex cowboy drawl that surprises even himself, I'd kinda like to know more about the origin of these Zoltec fellas I used to work with, which draws another curious glance from Professor Simianovsky, a hearty clap on the back from one of his orange-furred paws, and a smoker's phlegmy laugh in which the Snowman detects a nodule of—what? Mischievousness? *Malevolence?*

The night air is damp and surprisingly cool and he's glad to have the wool blanket. Despite his fatigue he can't sleep. He lies awake, twisting and turning, questioning again his motives for coming here. Did he make a terrible mistake? Confuse fatalism with fate—the act of bodily moving himself from one location to another with actually getting somewhere? Now he's too warm. He gets up and opens the window. What is that smell? It's sweet and cloying, a little like the scent of the heirloom roses he remembers growing in his mother's garden, but intimating madness, putrescence and death. It must be coming from those large white flowers he notices now, luminous and moon-like against the dark tropical vegetation. He returns to bed and lies there, listening to the sounds of wings flitting and things creeping and water dripping. And then he knows he's asleep because now he sees a very large cat with black and orange spots that he thinks is a jaguar trot toward him through the dense green jungle. An enormous snake drapes over a tree limb. Monkeys swing from leafy vines. A full moon is rising behind an enormous stone pyramid on top of which a Maya warrior wearing a feathered headdress, knee-length loincloth and jade ankle and wrist cuffs, dances and twirls, his winged arms spread like an eagle in flight while drums beat and flutes shriek and bodies bound in fetal positions tumble down the pyramid's steep stone steps, making sickening thumping, smacking sounds as spines fracture and arms and legs snap. This is followed by a volley of severed heads that bounce down the steps like basketballs. Grimacing, eyes staring wildly, skulls cracked open, noses broken, teeth shattered, they hit the ground and are immediately met with the thick callused feet of pelota players in loincloths and bright red and blue body paint, whose hard, sweeping kicks planted squarely in the face send the heads flying downfield like soccer balls. How the Snowman acquired these details of Maya dress and culture is unclear. Perhaps through the telepathic medium of dreams. Perhaps through the subliminal accumulation of cultural referents—posters of Maya warriors on the walls of his favorite Tex-Mex restaurant in Osberg, for example. Or maybe he simply read a pamphlet on the Maya people while he was exploring Monte Blanco and Boone neglected to show us this detail. (By the way, get your balls straight—basketball or soccer but not both—Edmund Farrell, Professor Emeritus, University of Texas at Osberg, but you can call me Ed.)

3
The Expedition

A BLAST FURNACE ROAR brings him wide awake. The morning light is gray, misty. The savage green of the jungle seems to crowd in the window, which he doesn't remember opening last night. To his horror he spots a man in a black monkey suit crouched in a tree no more than a few feet away from him. But wait, it's not a man, it actually is a monkey, a very large monkey. It stares directly into his eyes with its own very human and hostile brown eyes, opens wide a set of very human choppers, releases another blast furnace roar, and then it's gone.

Still processing these totemic visitations, real and oneiric, he performs various G-rated ablutionary functions in the bathroom (shave, brush his teeth, comb his hair), pulls on a t-shirt, faded jeans and worn sneakers and heads downstairs to the lobby where five other guests from last night's colloquy have gathered, including the YC in cargo shorts, t-shirts and Tevas, a pretty fit looking older couple, maybe early-mid sixties, also dressed in cargo shorts, t-shirts and Tevas, a rather dour lady— *Miss* Flossiter—probably about seventy, wearing an approximation of a safari outfit that includes pith helmet and elephant-eared (Indian) riding jodhpurs. There's also a heavily tattooed (vivid red, green and blue knights, dragons, wizards) young hipster dude sporting a wispy Van Dyke, straw fedora with a plaid hatband, pink tank top, madras shorts and baby blue rubber bathroom slippers, who looks vaguely familiar (the cyber café?). And finally, Professor Simianovsky, himself in full khaki explorer regalia, floppy field hat, multi-pocketed vest over a long-sleeved poplin shirt, cargo pants, and a well-worn pair of hiking boots. They're all chowing down at a table laden with pastries, hard boiled eggs, whole-grain toast, fresh butter and jam, bowls of granola, yoghurt and sliced fruit, and steaming cups of coffee so aromatic the smell alone increases the Snowman's wakefulness by a factor of six. Ah, there you are, my Snowman friend, Professor Simianovsky greets him warmly, waves a furry orange paw over the breakfast spread and encourages him to help himself. And so he does. It's only after he has single-handedly polished off pretty much everything on the table, laid claim to the last boiled egg, piece of toast, spot of jam, dollop of yoghurt and slice of papaya, and is stuffing the final bite of strawberry and guava Danish down his throat, that he notices everyone else staring at him with something just short of horror, with the exception of the dour *Miss* Flossiter who has opted not to partake of this sumptuous repast with a polite (but pinched) smile. *Moreover when ye fast, be not, as the hypocrites, of a sad countenance: for they disfigure their faces, that they may appear unto men to fast* (Matthew 6:16). What the heck? There's that voice from last night. Apparently the Snowman isn't the only one hearing things. Professor Simianovsky, too, glances around with a puzzled expression that furrows his brow like a bunched up carpet.

This awkward moment is followed by a lot of hemming and hawing, people start crumpling up napkins and getting to their feet, checking their pockets for wallets and sunglasses and shouldering daypacks. And then everyone's out the door and piling into Professor Simianovsky's (it turns out) ancient station wagon, now empty of artifacts, and off they go, creaking, bouncing and banging over increasingly primitive roads into ever denser jungle until there's no road at all. Professor Simianovsky parks the station wagon in a small clearing and his passengers get out yawning and stretching as if they're about to take a peek at some mildly entertaining local roadside attraction

(*Is it really a two-headed donkey? Can it really speak Spanish?*)
before heading back home for lunch and a nap. Little do they
know. Professor Simianovsky flashes a fiendish smile, the white
slash of teeth and thin blue gleam behind his rectangular glasses
about as reassuring as a rogue AI insisting *you go on home now,
I'll finish up here*, and taking the lead, he and his troupe begin
to pick their way through the steamy jungle foliage along a
ragged suggestion of a trail. Giant ceiba and ficus trees tower
over them, their heavy limbs overgrown with pothos ivy,
philodendrons, bromeliads and orchids, their huge roots
undulating outward like the dorsal fins of enormous prehistoric
eels. Iridescent blue Morpho butterflies as big as human hands
flit around them. Red and blue, green and yellow macaws
squawk and flap in the trees. A flock of toucans with short
stubby wings and bright orange, red and green outsized beaks
flies over like a formation of WWII fighter planes (once again
all thanks go to the fact check girl for filling us in on the
taxonomy of the tropical flora and fauna). The Snowman hears
a familiar blast furnace roar and looks up with everyone else as
a troop of large black monkeys swings through the treetops,
baring their teeth and roaring at the interlopers below. *Howlers*,
Professor Simianovsky says as if he's referring to the trailer
trash side of his family, even as an unmistakable spray of urine
rains down on them. The explorers step over shimmering black,
liquid-like trails of ants, climb over mossy boulders and logs,
one of which turns out to be an enormous brown and green
snake that seems to be so engorged with some other large
creature that it completely ignores the intrepid Junior
Woodchucks. It's still early but the air is already hot and
extremely humid and the Snowman's almost completely
drenched in sweat. Flies and mosquitoes buzz around his head,
biting and stinging his face and neck. This is possibly the first
time in his life since his early and largely unremembered
childhood that he has been bitten by a mosquito. The bites itch
and burn and scratching only makes them worse. The others
also seem to be engaged in their own ground/air combat. Both

the older couple and the YC swat and slap incessantly at these winged pests. *Miss* Flossiter, in addition to her protective safari garb, has been regularly administering an aerosol insect repellant that makes an imperious *hssst* with each application. *I will say to the Lord, "My refuge and my fortress, my God, in whom I trust." For he will deliver you from the snare of the fowler and from the deadly pestilence. He will cover you with his pinions, and under his wings you will find refuge; his faithfulness is a shield and buckler. You will not fear the terror of the night, nor the arrow that flies by day. Though a thousand fall at your side, though ten thousand are dying around you, these evils will not touch* you (Psalm 91:1-7). There it is again, that voice, considerably more long-winded this time. The Snowman briefly locks eyes with Professor Simianovsky, who, other than sticking a finger in his ear as if trying to dislodge the source of an odd buzzing sound, seems to be the only one unfazed by this aerial assault, protected by the thick orange pelt pushing out of the neck and cuffs of his khaki shirt. Worst off is the lightly dressed hipster dude (HD). Swarmed by flying insects that have clearly recognized a banquet in their midst, he appears to be cursing into his EyePhone®, which is probably why he alone seems destined to tumble blindly into the enormous sinkhole that suddenly opens before them, at the bottom of which they can see a murky green pool. It's a cenote. Professor Simianovsky, who, without missing a beat or a breath (and unnoticed by everyone except the Snowman), has, with extraordinary dexterity, just snatched the HD from gravity's fatal attraction at the last second and deposited him safely and still yammering into his phone on terra firmer, now explains that these sunken, spring-fed pools served the Maya as both a source of water and a spiritual center, which included tossing in the occasional sacrificial victim. Oh yes, it's true. Divers have found the skeletal remains of men, women and children in this very pool. A family affair, eh? Professor Simianovsky or rather his beard smiles jovially. Certainly makes a good case for fluoridation.

The explorers now push onward through the dense vegetation toward a small mountain looming ahead of them. This topographical feature seems oddly incongruous with its surroundings, an observation corroborated when we hear on the soundtrack an ominous passage from the brass section *bwa-Bwaw-BWAAWWW*, a brief rumble of tribal drums *Boom-ba, Boom-ba*, and we see the silhouette of—a giant ape? *It's not that movie!* a voice hisses and the camera returns to the Snowman's face as it dawns on him that this mountain is not only a manmade structure but a *fucking pyramid!* He glances around to see if he said this aloud, but everyone else is staring at this thing with pretty much the same goggle-eyed reaction because it really is a pyramid fully worthy of *National Geographic*. Barely discernible beneath a heavy green carpet of jungle growth, a steep stone stairway rises well over a hundred feet into the pale blue sky. Nothing like that tourist-ridden Mount McMaya in Chopahuac, Professor Simianovsky scoffs and immediately begins to scramble up the steps with the doughty band of aspiring Eagle Scouts gamely following after him. Lizards dart everywhere, huge iguanas with leathery green, black and blue hides crouch rigid and alert like sentinels, an enormous black scorpion scuttles into a deep crevice. Climbing the stairs is both difficult and treacherous. The moss-covered stones are damp and slippery, the treads very narrow, maybe six inches deep at most, the risers very tall, well over a foot, forcing the climbers to lift their knees high while placing their feet at odd, sideways angles. A misstep invites disaster. The Snowman's neck is stiff as a rusty hinge from watching his footing, his thighs burn from the Stairmaster aerobics, his breath rasps in his throat like a rake through gravel in the garden paths of a Buddhist monastery. Both the YC and the older couple (OC?—only if they stick around, and the general sentiment is they won't), who, the Snowman notices now, bear an eerie resemblance to each other except for the age difference, are panting but otherwise managing pretty well. *Miss* Flossiter is stoic and erect. *For I, the Lord your God, will hold your right hand, saying to you, 'Fear not, I will help you'* (Isaiah 41:13). The Snowman stops climbing. There's that voice again. It's like some sort of low frequency radio wave, like somebody's trying to call him on the telephone but the reception isn't very good. Oh, wait, it's not for him he sees now as Professor Simianovsky, who has been bounding hand and foot up the stairway with an athleticism not generally associated with academe, pauses with a *Yes? Hello?* expression on his face that immediately turns sour, suggesting he's not interested in accepting this call, although his refusal is more polite than one might have suspected. *One general law, leading to the advancement of all organic beings, namely, multiply, vary, let the strongest live and the weakest die* (Charles Darwin, *The Origin of Species*). This message, which the Snowman catches enough of to recognize the Professor's voice, appears less a rebuttal to *Miss* Flossiter and more a warning to the EyePhone® hugging HD, who's faring the least well of the lot. His rubber bathroom slippers slip, slap and slide on the damp, mossy stones. At every step he flails wildly as if he's going to tumble back down the stairs. *Yeah, but you just can't take your eyes off that damn phone, can you, jackass? Look, shithead, I don't give a rat's ass if you do a swan dive off this rock pile, just don't take me with you.* The Snowman's muttering under his breath and struggling against a murderous urge to give the HD a little nudge, but what he really wants right now is to get to the top of this damn thing and have a smoke.

The intrepid adventurers finally arrive at the pinnacle of the pyramid gasping for breath and then gasp again at their vertiginous view of the jungle spreading out below like a nappy green carpet. They're more or less standing in the middle of the sky on a rectangular stone platform about the size of a tennis court, in the center of which is a low stone altar sculpted in the form of a male figure reclining on his elbows. His ghoulish face, made more so by wind and rain erosion, is turned sideways as if he's lying on a couch watching TV. On his head he wears something that looks like a giant wing nut, or a bullfighter's montera cap, which Professor Simianovsky explains is actually a pair of very large ornamental ear flares. In his lap he holds a stone bowl. Popcorn! the professor laughs and is met with blank stares. It's a *Chaac Mool*, he adds, as if that explains everything. You know, the Maya rain god Chaac? More puzzled looks. I thought it was Mickey Mouse, the HD says with disarming or, more accurately, alarming sincerity, eliciting groans from all the *adults*, except the Snowman who, well, yeah, thought *maybe*. Professor Simianovsky releases a deep sigh and for what is probably the thousandth time (he *is* a professor) launches into a lecture about the Zoltec's propensity for human sacrifice, out of which the Snowman only hears certain words and phrases *the great god Tlaloc … the high priest leads the victim …* because at the same moment he's also having disturbing aural and retinal flashes that remind him of some bad experiences on acid. He hears a flute's shrill whistle, drums beating, he sees a man lying on his back naked, watches in dream-like horror as a gleaming black blade slices open the man's upper abdomen. Crimson blood gushes everywhere as a bare human hand reaches inside the man's chest cavity, makes a twisting, tugging motion, extracts the still beating heart and raises it up to the rising sun. The hand then places the heart in the bowl the Chaac Mool holds in his lap and shortly after an eagle descends, clutches the heart in its talons and begins to tear it apart with its beak. *How*, you might ask, are these sacrificial victims procured? Professor Simianovsky's voice calls the Snowman back to the here and now. The question seems directed at him. Indeed, Professor Simianovsky gives him a stern look that says you really should be paying attention, *Snowman*, because this will be on the test. Then he's off again, his lecture made more colorful by Boone's intervention. On the screen we now see a large party of Maya warriors attired in bizarre costumes, an outré Halloween array not just of bird and animal fangs and feathers, claws, teeth, talons, skins and skulls, but shrunken human heads, leg and arm bones, fibula, tibia and humerus. Their faces and bodies are covered with tattoos and

painted in bright colors, red, blue, green, orange. They're armed
with spiked war clubs, spears, bows and arrows, gleaming black
obsidian knives. Apparently they're preparing to attack a large
village enclosed by a palisade of pointed logs. We hear screams,
see smoke and flames. The warriors swarm through the
compound like rapacious beasts, slashing and gouging, cutting
throats, raping and slaughtering women, old men, babies,
dragging off in bonds young men and women, princes and
princesses, their lives once to be intertwined in marriage, great
dynasties, now they're captive, trophies of war, stripped naked,
beaten and taunted, made to suffer horrible torture. In the
background, Professor Simianovsky's voice begins to expand
on a catalogue of atrocities Boone wisely skips over but the
Snowman, prisoner of his own imagination, isn't spared. He
hears bloodcurdling screams, he sees faces in extreme torment,
people, human beings, spitted and roasting alive over fires, men
and women being immersed in cauldrons of boiling liquids,
garroted with raw hemp rope, he sees objects (red-hot, barbed,
sharp) being inserted in body cavities, he sees bodies
dismembered, mutilated, vivisected, he sees the traumatic
amputation of limbs, genitals, facial features, ears and nose
sliced off, chunks of flesh gouged out of cheeks, tongues
excised, the lower jaw torn from the face—in general, the
systematic dismantling of the human corpus. Those who
survive, or, rarely, are spared this ordeal—Professor
Simianovsky has picked up the narrative again—have
something else in store, the aforementioned open heart surgery.
In a final ignominy, after the excision of the heart the bodies
and sometimes decapitated heads will be tossed down the stairs.
At which all eyes present tumble back down the stairs they have
just climbed, more or less bearing the same image, essentially a
manifestation of the Snowman's (precognitive?) dream last
night: heads and bodies bouncing off stone steps, bones
breaking, blood spurting everywhere. So much for the
misbegotten notion that the ferocious, blood-lusting Maya were
a gentle, peace-loving people living an Edenic idyll, eh?

Professor Simianovsky grins fiercely as if challenging, indeed, *mocking*, any such misbegetters among his audience. And don't think for a second that the Maya were just about hurting the other guy. The professor glances around to see if any fool of this stripe is in attendance. They also indulged in auto sacrifice, particularly bloodletting. Most popular, the piercing of the tongue or the genitals—penis, scrotum, labia, that sort of thing—often with a stingray spine, the *holy perforator*, and then drawing a knotted cord through the hole until the individual passed out from the pain, the object being to induce hallucinatory visions of the gods. Professor Simianovsky has been approximating these various acts with fairly graphic hand gestures, but now he shoves an accusatory and disconcertingly hirsute finger at his startled audience. *Blood*, ladies and gentlemen! They worshipped blood! Lord have mercy! *Miss* Flossiter exclaims with equal but contrary passion. *Save us, O God of our salvation, and gather us together, and deliver us from the heathen, that we may give thanks to thy holy name, and glory in thy praise* (1 Chronicles 16:35). The Snowman, who, by now, has come to suspect (correctly) that *Miss* Flossiter is a bit of a religious zealot, and who is also trying his darnedest not to eavesdrop on this telepathic discourse developing between her and Professor Simianovsky, rolls his eyes like, *oh brother*. On the other hand, the professor, who also knows his Bible, although as a historical document rather than divine word, stares in defiance at *Miss* Flossiter. *Surely I will require your lifeblood; from every beast I will require it. And from every man, from every man's brother I will require the life of man* (Genesis 5:9)! Odd, wouldn't you agree, he concludes without a trace of irony and apparently unaware of the nervous glances the rest of his troupe have been giving each other, that a civilization so advanced in architecture and engineering, in agriculture, animal husbandry, tool making and art, exhibited such barbarism?

The group now begins to descend the pyramid, and going down, they discover, is even worse than going up. The most popular means of descent is a backwards, hand and foot, crab-like motion with only occasional vertigo-inducing glimpses of blue sky above and green jungle below. Everyone finally arrives safely at the bottom, rolling their eyes at each other and letting out sighs of relief *whew, glad that's over*, until, that is, Professor Simianovsky throws a sloppy roundhouse air punch, barks *C'mon!* like a Marine sergeant leading his men out of the trenches, and marches forward, clambering over mossy rubble, up and down crumbling stairways of partially buried temples and palaces, his increasingly ragged pack of adventurers stumbling along behind, the HD cursing every time he stubs a toe or gets his foot stuck in a crevice (the Snowman's pretty sure he just heard him say *Fuck you, Boone!*), Professor Simianovsky, oblivious to his entourage's discomfort, blithely pointing out objects of interest, for example, a row of huge stone phalluses that elicit juvenile, jejune and jaded ejaculations of jocularity, as well as an almost orgasmic *Oh!* from *Miss* Flossiter (the Snowman'd be pretty darned shocked if he were privy, as Professor Simianovsky's just-stuck-his-finger-in-an-electrical-outlet expression suggests *he* is, to her most private thoughts), *remembering the days of her youth, when she played the whore in the land of Egypt and lusted after her lovers there, whose members were like those of donkeys, and whose issue was like that of horses* (Ezekiel 23:19-20). Which may explain why *Miss* Flossiter, attempting to restore her decorum, points primly at a small limestone building topped with a piece of architecture that all present agree looks very much like a church steeple and at the pinnacle of that steeple an object that, yes, certainly does resemble a cross. Ah yes, Professor Simianovsky nods, the Temple of the Exfoliated Cross. Ever since the Spaniards arrived, people have tried to make an issue of the Christian symbolism. *Sniff!* Conspicuously ignoring *Miss* Flossiter's nasal criticism, the professor explains that for the Maya the cross represented the great ceiba tree of life at the center of the universe—yes, my Snowman friend (he didn't say anything), much like the Norse Yggdrasil. Of course the

Spaniards, and especially their pious religious brethren (Professor Simianovsky, who has marched off again, rolls his eyes heavenward), dearly desired to disabuse the Maya of their pagan beliefs, and undertook to do so with both spiritual and physical inducements, keeping in mind that back in ruff-collared and mantilla-veiled "Old Spain," where the Inquisition was well under way, those good church fathers had already proven themselves as adept at mortification of the flesh as the Maya. *Miss* Flossiter's nose crinkles furiously and, who knows, maybe at this very moment she *is* imagining red-hot tongs applied to nipples and clitoris, for all we know she may even be wearing bizarre undergarments and appurtenances specifically designed to inflict excruciating plea—*pain* to all those rebellious sensual organs and orifices that would betray even the most pious, chaste and chastity-belted penitent *but I chastise my body, and bring it into servitude, lest by any means, having preached to others, I myself may become disapproved* (1 Corinthians 9:27). By the way—the professor spins around, causing his followers to pile up against each other—and almost as an afterthought, he says, I wouldn't want you to get the idea the Maya were only about pain. You've all heard of *God L?* Uh ... by the looks on their faces, apparently not, but their eyes meet in a quick colloquium and it's tacitly agreed that mum's the word. P.S.—oops—*Professor* Simianovsky gestures at a detailed wall carving of a gnarly, gnome-like old codger with a jaguar ear and an owl perched on his head (vigilant cineastes will see a reference to Johnny Deep in Sid Ney's overlooked little gem *Tonto Flies Solo*) who is gleefully puffing on what looks like a fairly large spliff. The smell of raw tobacco penetrates the Snowman's nostrils and then deep into his brain where that neurotic little on/off button is screaming *On! On! On! On!* as it releases rapid-fire pulses of the monoamine neurotransmitter 5-hydroxytryptamine ($C_{10}H_{12}N_2O$), or serotonin, the *pleasure hormone*, to various—what else?—pleasure receptors all over his body. Professor Simianovsky has extracted from his shirt pocket a crude twist of chocolate brown leaves very similar to the panatela God L is enjoying. *Nicotiana rustica,* he says, digging a lighter out of a cargo pocket. A bit stronger than the commercially sold cancer sticks. He winks at the Snowman as if they're in on a private joke. *Fumar para ver más claro,* no? (more or less, *Have a smoke and get a better perspective on things*—Eduardo.) Aztecs believed it anyway. The Maya too. Priests and nobles smoked this stuff ritually. Or they ingested it with other botanical substances, inducing both hallucinations and, especially for the uninitiated, projectile vomiting. Any takers? Hmm? My Snowman friend? The Snowman, who only discovered at the top of the pyramid that he was out of cigs and, therefore, hasn't had a smoke since some time yesterday, would like nothing more than to suck an entire cancer stick down into his lungs in one breath, but the projectile vomiting puts him off. He's also just a tad creeped-out by this conspiratorial tone Professor Simianovsky has adopted with him. Oddly, the professor is giving *him* a perplexed look, as if he too is getting mixed messages. No? Well I don't mind if I do. Keeps away the mosquitoes. The professor lights up and, puffing away like a steam locomotive, leads his not entirely willing followers toward a sooty, mildew-stained, white limestone building with an intricately tessellated and reticulated façade that looks like it's woven out of cotton yarn rather than carved from stone. The roof is caved in, the walls are crumbling, the floor is strewn with rubble and shards of ceramic pottery. The Prof (*don't* … he didn't notice) gives a light kick to an intact terra cotta pot that seems to have been placed strategically on the floor like a film prop and launches into another lecture. The vandals who ravaged this site were searching for gold, priceless artifacts. A plain piece of pottery held no interest for them. Much the same way, I imagine, the knights of the Round Table may have overlooked the true holy grail in the misguided belief that the son of God could only enjoy his wine in a jewel-studded atrocity of bad taste. *Miss* Flossiter, neither an imbiber nor an iconoclast, makes a sound as if she has just been stabbed in the heart. *But the cowardly, the unbelieving, the vile, the murderers, the sexually immoral, those who practice magic arts, the idolaters and all liars—they will be consigned to the fiery lake of burning sulfur* (Revelation 21:8)! In response, the professor sends a cumulus cloud of highly toxic tobacco smoke *Miss* Flossiter's way. *I am not afraid of any god in the universe who would send me or any other man or woman to hell. If there were such a being, he would not be a god; he would be a devil* (Clarence Darrow)!! And yet, he continues for the telepathically challenged, it was in this very spot that I discovered *this*. And with, yes, a magician's flourish, he pulls from one of his many pockets a crude paper pamphlet—a *codex*, he calls it—and holds it up so all can see. It's completely covered in Maya hieroglyphs that, to the Snowman anyway, look something like Play-doh® faces squashed up inside children's alphabet blocks. But there's also this Rorschach blot of ink on a hand-beaten square of paper tacked to the wall of his shivery little shack back in the permanently frozen climes of *el Norte* and a storm cloud of black hair framing a somehow alien, possibly even extraterrestrial female face and a pair of androidally bright cobalt blue eyes that suggest levels of intelligence beyond any normal human range, and on top of that something weird's happening, his whole body's tingling and there's this strange electronic interference in his brain like overlapping radio frequencies. He sees streams of red and green symbols, like squiggly Christmas ribbon candy, and there are sounds, *words*, but either he can't hear them correctly or he can't articulate them in his own language. *Ha!Ha!Ha!* A burst of laughter returns him to the present. Apparently Professor Simianovsky has just made a witty comparison between the codex and kids' comic books. Still tingling from his *petit mal* aphasic episode, the Snowman agrees something funny's going on but it doesn't have anything to do with cartoons. Nor does the HD seem particularly amused. *Frustrated* beyond any slight or humiliation he's suffered since kindergarten by all this—what else to call it but *abuse?*—he utters an imperious, May *I* see it, *please?* and grabs at the booklet and—*riiiiip!*—tears it in half. A collective gasp is followed by stunned silence. Eyes dart back and forth, terrified by the imminent explosion they know must come and when it does they're even more startled. *Ha!Ha!Ha!* Professor Simianovsky laughs again, even louder. *It's a facsimile!* It's almost like a comedy routine, like the HD was in on it all along, except that, cool completely blown, he's gone crimson in the face and he's sputtering like a Vespa. Rule number one, the professor, still chuckling, digs it in. Never let an amateur handle the merchandise. To the HD's further humiliation, he then relates the cautionary tale of a colleague in the English department who allowed students in his Joyce seminar to personally examine his prized first edition, uncut folio of *Finnegan's Wake*, but only after repeatedly and explicitly warning them *not* to cut or tear the joined pages—yes, they're meant to be that way—and then watched in bespectacled horror as this hayseed hillbilly country bumpkin from God knows what pig farm in western Pennsylvania deftly pulled out a bone-handled carbon steel Barlow knife that had been in his family since the Revolutionary War and—*zip! zip! zip!*—with a Zorroastrian flourish undid the barbarously conjoined parchment. Professor Simianovsky extracts the torn half of the codex from the mortified HD's clutches. The original, dating back to about 900 AD, was inscribed on bark cloth made from the wild fig tree and is one of only perhaps a dozen in existence. Apparently the Spanish priests were not great fans of literature. What they did not destroy disintegrated in the tropical clime. The obvious anger and, yes, grief that constricts Professor Simianovsky's voice causes all present to shrink into themselves with varying degrees of assumed guilt. Even the unforgiving *Miss* Flossiter seems to empathize. *Even though I was formerly a blasphemer and a persecutor and a violent aggressor, Yet I was shown mercy because I acted ignorantly in unbelief* (1 Timothy 1:13). Oh well, the Professor says, reappraising *Miss* Flossiter with a mite or a mote of interest or curiosity or *something* in his eye. All is not lost. With the help of his graduate assistant Washington-Irving Li Zhou, he has nearly completed translating this document, which—and here Professor Simianovsky visibly trembles with excitement— refers to a giant *fire breathing* feathered serpent, or *quetzalcoatl.* Yes, yes, I know, he raises his hands against the anticipated protests of a largely adult audience, for the most part non-superstitious, *Miss* Flossiter excepted (*What?! Me?! SuperFUCKINGstitious?! Sorry, Jesus, I really meant to say SuperCALIFRAGILISTIC!*), and sick to death of CGI flying dragons, the HD excluded (he's suddenly all bright-eyed boy). However, the professor continues, the fire-breathing attribute may not be as farfetched as one might suspect. Recent research has demonstrated that, due to an odd configuration of certain dinosaurs' alimentary systems, they belched powerful streams of methane gas. In other words, Professor Simianovsky practically shouts with sophomoric exuberance, *they farted out of their mouths!* The long-suffering *Miss* Flossiter emits another sniff of disapproval *really, there's no hope of saving that man,* which the professor pointedly ignores (his curiosity, however, more piqued). Paleontologists have subsequently discovered an even odder feature unique to these creatures, specifically an osseous and cartilaginous mechanism inside the beak that resembles the flint and spark wheel of a cigarette lighter. Professor Simianovsky takes out his lighter again and holds it up for all to see. By clicking their tongues, these oversized proto-chickens were able to ignite the methane gas they belched, sending out a powerful flame. The professor makes a slight adjustment, then flicks his Bic and *whoosh,* shoots a seven-foot flame over his listeners' heads. Eyes dart sideways like frightened cockroaches searching for the nearest exit. For the first time suspicions arise that the learned professor may be more than just eccentric, that or it's the *Nicotiana rustica.* Sensing some pushback from this crowd, Professor Simianovsky seeks to alleviate their skepticism by drawing parallels with European legends of fire breathing dragons— keeping in mind that folks across the pond generally considered these beasts to be evil, minions of Satan, that sort of thing (aiming a piercing?—*playful?*—eye at *Miss* Flossiter). Grendel, Beowulf's great nemesis, for example. And, of course, St. George's dragon—to be honest, a fairly pathetic-looking thing in most paintings. Same with Saint Michael. *The great dragon was hurled down—that ancient serpent called the devil, or Satan, who leads the whole world astray. He was hurled to the earth, and his angels with him* (Revelation 12:9). *Take that, buster!* Certainly nothing like the much more grandiose *and* benevolent *simurgh*, a mythical giant flying creature of the deserts of North Africa and the Middle East, stories of which European knights brought back with them from the Crusades. Professor Simianovsky takes off his glasses and cleans them with a white handkerchief, for a discomfiting moment resembling nothing other than a myopic beaver. Of course, most scholars (and here he makes a palms upward shrugging gesture, like, what can you do with people like that?) believe the quetzalcoatl referred to in Zoltec and other Meso-American myths is probably based on fossil remains early people discovered of *Quetzalcoatlus northropi*, a two-hundred pound, four-legged, hammer-headed, toothless, clam and worm eating, leather-winged flying dinosaur commonly known as the pterodactyl, which lived during the late Jurassic Period about one hundred fifty million years ago, as you may recall from your sixth grade science class—those of you, that is, who weren't home-schooled for religious reasons. *SNIFF!! Where were you when I laid the foundation of the earth? Tell me, if you have understanding. Who determined its measurements—surely you know! Or who stretched the line upon it? On what were its bases sunk, or who laid its cornerstone?* (Job 38:4-6.) Momentarily nonplussed by this counterattack (there is something compelling about *Miss* Flossiter's rhetoric), Professor Simianovsky stabs his finger at a row of glyphs in the codex. *However*, according to this document Ms. Washington-Irving and I are examining, in terms of size, the Zoltec quetzalcoatl was probably more akin to the recently discovered

Dakotaraptor, a very large winged but flightless Dromaeosaur that sprinted at speeds up to forty miles an hour and tore its victims to shreds with nine and-a-half inch claws! Now imagine if such a beast could not only fly but also possessed fire breathing capabilities—you'd have something like a primitive fighter jet. Fighter-*bomber*, I should say, considering the size of the loads it dropped. Allowing this idea to sink in (you can see noses twitching, foreheads wrinkling, eyes squinting as everyone gets the picture), Professor Simianovsky now adds the real kicker (no shit!). Some scholars, myself included (keeping in mind that *some* can mean as few as two, which the good prof doesn't specify), think it possible that a large number of these great winged, fire-breathing creatures—a species I have dubbed *Quetzalcoatlus ignisraptor*—survived into the era of humans. In fact, it is my fervent belief that the last of these *fire-breathing dragons*, if you will (the HD certainly will, he's nodding his head like a puppy dog begging for its kibbles), retreated to this very valley in Mexico. Interestingly—and now everyone *is* interested, they're hanging onto the professor's every word, everyone, that is, except the HD who, attention span about the length of a carrot, has already returned to his EyePhone®, deconstructing a language that has taken tens of thousands of years to evolve into a sophisticated system of grammar, syntax and meaning back into rudimentary chicken scratches with his opposable thumbs *tap tap tap*. (Question: will fingers devolve into vestigial appendages? Atrophy and disappear completely, leaving our species all thumbs as it were?). Now where was I? Apparently the professor is having some trouble (early onset dementia? the wacky tobaccy?) maintaining his own train of thought. Oh yes, I was just about to say that the Zoltec Codex would appear to confirm the conjecture that the ancient Zoltec coexisted with the *ignisraptor*. *Miss* Flossiter's eyes gleam brightly with an *I knew it* expression. Even this man of science admits humans and dinosaurs lived at the same time, not anywhere near a hundred and fifty million years ago, of course, more like five or six thousand according to scripture as she understands it. The professor grimaces like that's not exactly what I said and points to another set of glyphs in the torn replica, and once again something weird's happening to the Snowman, huge quantities of data begin to flash through his brain, except it's all in Martian or the way he imagines Martian would look, red, green and black dots and bars, loops and squiggles, but this time he isn't just seeing this stuff on the screen or hearing it in his head, he's speaking aloud, in tongues, or at least a tongue not his own, and everybody's staring at him, not the least *Miss* Flossiter, whose rapturous gaze suggests she's having a vicarious Pentecostal moment *For anyone who speaks in a tongue speaks not to men but to God* (1 Corinthians 14:2), but most of all Professor Simianovsky, whose eyes narrow as if he's thinking to himself, ah-ha, so it's true, whatever *it* is. For those of you who don't share our Snowman friend's gift for languages, he says, the text describes an interesting Zoltec ritual. Once a month at sunrise the high priest and his entourage climb to the top of the pyramid with a sacrificial victim and make an offering of a human heart to these great flying creatures, which then go out to patrol the mountains, jungles and barren desert for signs of the return of the golden-headed god foretold to come and restore the Zoltec people to their destiny. The Snowman, who's still recovering from this latest fugue episode, glances around to see if anyone else noticed that Professor Simianovsky has been speaking in the present tense, but the others seem oblivious to this grammatical distinction, especially the HD, who is indeed all thumbs *tap tap tap* (and, boy, if that *is* Boone he's communicating with, the director's getting an eyeful).

Disclaimer: Boone's fact check girl hasn't weighed in on some of this science stuff yet. Nor has Boone chosen to deal with certain issues that must have occurred to the discerning viewer, so it's entirely up to Professor Simianovsky's troop of Junior Woodchucks to accomplish at their own propitious moments, in whatever privacy they may find, their various bodily functions. Also, it seems that the benevolent prof, who provided his guests with such an abundant repast at breakfast, has neglected to bring along so much as a bag of Skittles (although he was seen at different times by various members of his party nibbling on the native flora) and, not having been informed this was going to be an all-day event, his followers have brought very few provisions themselves. So that by the time the expedition returns to the Hotel Caulifornia that evening, they're hungry, exhausted, covered with scratches and bug bites, disheveled, streaked with mud and green herbaceous smudges, and it's every man and woman for his, her or their self. The exceptions to this motley crew are Professor Simianovsky, who looks positively blissed out judging by his loopy Cookie Monster grin (Still feeling the *Nicotiana rustica*? Or ... ?), and *Miss* Flossiter, who looks just as starched as when they set out, other than an odd damp stain around the, um, crack of her ass, oh, and a missing button in her poplin blouse whose dangling threads suggest some sort of physical struggle (caught on a branch?), and one does wonder about those furtive glances the Professor and *Miss* Flossiter exchange before they separate.

(Apparently Boone was forced to cut a scene with the professor and *Miss* Flossiter engaged in furious intercourse on the subject of Christian-primate sensibilities that the board of censors found morally reprehensible but which, thanks to a gross oversight in the editing process, we can judge for ourselves—Ed.) *And God said, Let us make man in our image, after our likeness: and let them have dominion over the fish of the sea, and over the fowl of the air, and over the cattle, and over all the earth, and over every creeping thing that creepeth upon the earth* (Genesis 1:26). *Whilst Man, however well-behaved, at best is but a monkey shaved!* (Charles Darwin, *The Origin of Species*.) *Get thee behind me, Satan!* (Matthew 16:23.) Ah, you wish to make *the beast with two backs* (Shakespeare, *Othello*)? Despite the ardor of this debate, it apparently resulted in an equally satisfying accord for both combatants *Do not deprive each other except perhaps by mutual consent and for a time, so that you may devote yourselves to prayer. Then come together again so that Satan will not tempt you because of your lack of self-control* (1 Corinthians 7:5). Cigarette?

4

Clues

REVIVED BY A HOT SHOWER and, frankly, relieved to be free of *that* crowd, the Snowman heads to the cyber café for a bite to eat. His appetite's enormous after today's adventure, for which he fancies himself quite the explorer and infinitely superior to all these loser *tourists*. Perusing the menu, he spots an indigenous dish that seems perfectly suited to his adventurous state of mind called *pollo asado con mole de xocolatl,* which the waitress, a young woman with an accent, not Spanish (Russian?), explains is roast chicken served in a very rich sauce, or *mole* (she pronounces it *moh-lay*), a primary ingredient of which is *xocolatl*—Nahuatl for chocolate. Sounds great, he says, I'll have that. Oh, I am sorry, the waitress says, we are not having thees dish anymore. Unfortunately, now he's really got a hankering for this stuff. He wanders all around town in search of the famous chocolate mole, which, in a bit of subliminal linguistic wizardry, he has inadvertently conflated with *Chaac Mool*, the sacrificial altar Professor Simianovsky pointed out (at least one film scholar will argue that here Boone is suggesting the Snowman is seeking his own death, an idea that may have occurred after a re-reading of *Under the Volcano*). His appetite grows into a ravenous, mouth-watering craving as he encounters one restaurant after another that purports to offer this dish, only to discover they no longer serve it (or, more likely, judging by the eager to please but confused expressions on their faces, the wait staff don't understand why this greenghost is asking for

Chaac Mool, which, not helping, he has begun to pronounce *Chalk Mule)*. He's about to give up and grab a burger at a McDonald's that he's pretty sure wasn't on this corner an hour ago when he spots a tiny, dimly lit cafe—really it's just two or three small tables in the front room of a house in an alley, but a chalkboard outside says *Abierto* and inside it has a welcoming charm, colorful serapes on the walls, a candle burning at each table next to a black ceramic vase of marigolds, the musky pungence of which penetrates deep into his brain, stirring up a latent childhood memory of his mother smiling at him over her shoulder as she worked in the garden on her hands and knees, one of the rare times, he realizes now, he ever saw her happy. Momentarily immersed in this memory both bright and melancholy, he'd never guess this fiery orange and red flower is yet another symbol of death among the indigenous culture (maybe that film scholar was onto something). He sits down and opens the menu, which, rather eerily, lists a single item: *pollo asado con mole de xocolatl*—the famous *Chaac Mool* he has been searching for. Almost as eerily, a man and a woman in matching black mariachi outfits, minus the hats, and almost identical in appearance, sixties, leathery brown faces, raven black hair (dyed?) and mustache (the man, although in the dim light the woman looks as if she may have one too), appear in a shadowy archway and, shoulder to shoulder, march to the Snowman's table, nod to him in unison, and the man says, What will the *señor* have this evening? Ah'll have the chicken in chocolate *mole-lay*, and a bottle of *cervaysa oscooro* if you got it, the *señor* says in this Big Tex voice he seems to be cultivating. The man and woman's eyes lock and nodding their approval, again in unison, the woman says, Excellent choice, *señor*, and they march off, returning not more than two minutes later bearing a covered silver platter, a brown ceramic dish containing fresh corn tortillas wrapped in cloth, a glass and a bottle of dark beer, which the man opens and pours for him to taste, and it's delicious with hints of chocolate, molasses, sassafras and raspberry, which doesn't obscure the fact that this plate of chocolate mole stuff the woman has uncovered in front of him looks pretty much like runny diarrhea (he has a graphic flash of himself squatting in an alley, pants around his ankles, flames shooting out his ass, that Boone judiciously skips past). The man and woman, meanwhile, are hovering over him like a pair of morticians just itching to get to work on this new stiff as soon as he takes a bite of the poison apple. The stiff responds by raising a cautious forkful of chicken smothered in reddish-brown sauce to his mouth and—*yeow!* It's delicious! Absolutely the best chicken he's ever eaten in his life. Chocolaty and spicy and succulent. How can something look so foul and taste so good? This must be what shit tastes like to a coprophage. Satisfied with his reaction, the husband and wife (he's guessing) mortuary team depart and he quickly consumes his meal like a savage, chewing every succulent morsel of chicken flesh from the bones, sopping up every spicy, chocolaty drop of mole with soft corn tortillas, squeegeeing invisible traces of sauce from the plate with his finger and licking it clean, and washing it all down with a final palate cleansing swallow of rich, dark carbonated hops and barley malt.

Body and soul nourished, he starts back to the Hotel California, the musky, pungent odor of marigolds lingering in his nostrils, and no wonder. When he paid his bill, the female half of *los mariachis* stuck a bright orange flower in the top button hole of his shirt, her mouth tightened into a rictal smile and she whispered in a hoarse smoker's voice, *Cempazuchitl*, which he misheard as *siempre tu something*, probably means *you're always welcome here*, he figures (wrong). Clanging steel and flashes of firelight draw his attention to an open wooden shed. In the orange glow of a fiery hearth, he spots a bare-chested, powerfully built man, black with soot and dripping sweat as he pounds a piece of red-hot metal with a heavy iron hammer. Some viewers will jump to the conclusion that this is yet another allusion to death, foreshadowing the Snowman's subsequent descent into Hades (cf. Dante, Orpheus, et al.). Boone, however, was hoping these numbskulls would get the more obvious reference to Vulcan, Roman god of the forge and also, as his name implies, *volcanoes*, another potent symbol, as we shall see later. A deep-throated whistle blows like a Samuel Clemens steamboat coming up the ol' Mississip' and a black-barreled barbecue pit on four spindly metal wheels rolls onto the set, pushed by a man who looks a hell of a lot like Jackie Gleason in the heart-rending role of Gigot (mute, simple-minded janitor befriends young daughter of prostitute—Edna, Editorial Assistant, and you can call me *Edna*). Bumbling, overweight, a hangdog expression on his fleshy face, Yaqui Glisón yells out every few steps, *¡Camotes!* (actually, he opens his mouth and holds up a cartoon speech balloon on which is scrawled in childish letters *¡Camotes!*). The guy looks like a complete slob, overweight, stained t-shirt, baggy pants tied up with a piece of rope, but with a sad, gentle smile he places a roasted yam on a piece of newspaper and offers it to the Snowman and even though he's thoroughly stuffed with that delicious chalk mule (he's forgotten again) and fresh corn tortillas, he just has to have one of these, and *yummm*, it's also delicious, just as caramelly sweet and creamy as it smells, which, he surmises, probably satisfies some southern cuisine gene inherited from his crazy old ma. *I yam what I yam.*

The following morning, feeling more rested than he has in years, body and soul unburdened by an enormous and enormously satisfying dump (no visuals, thank you, *TP*), he strolls to the zócalo for a breakfast of huevos a la mexicana and an ice-cold bottle of Sol at a crowded outside café inserted in the stoa of a six hundred-year-old colonial building with arched colonnades and wrought iron balconies, the kind of touristy place he'd normally avoid like the city morgue but today he feels like mingling with the public, who, he's pretty sure, must be aware by now of the great explorer in their midst, and, who knows, maybe *somebody* (read *young woman*) will even inquire about his latest adventure and he'll say, *Well, it started like this* … Apparently, however, the word hasn't gotten out yet (*What? Sir Hillary? Here?*). After his meal he orders coffee and lights up a cigarette (he's trying the *Tigres*, chosen based entirely on the packaging *grrrowwwl!*). It's only then that he notices the YC sitting at the table right next to his, apparently commenting on the other tourists with some amusement, but rather than acknowledge his presence—and surely they've noticed him—they seem to be scrupulously avoiding eye contact (for the seasoned traveler, the repeat encounter is a known hazard). In return the Snowman makes an even bigger point of not acknowledging them, which becomes so stressful and outright ridiculous that he finally stubs out his cigarette, leaps up from the table and hurries off as if he's just received an urgent call from the Pentagon (Air Force One is on the way—we need you back here immediately, Snowman!). Despite its awkwardness, this non-encounter with the YC triggers a nostalgic yearning for the intimacy he now remembers, or at least imagines, he and Judith once shared. He buys a postcard of an emerald green iguana yogically posed on an unnaturally yellow rock and scribbles a quick note in smudgy blue ink *in the event I never see you again ... those happy times ... love ...* which sounds like a total cheap shot when he reads it over, saccharine, obsequious, and unduly ominous. But what the heck, it's basically a message in a bottle he's tossing into the endless black sea of the universe via the Mexican Postal Service, in a local office of which he unexpectedly suffers further humiliation and discouragement standing at the counter sputtering and stuttering like Daffy Duck (Porky Pig?) B-b-b ... cor ... cor ... cor-ray ... thbbb-thbbb-thbbb. Finally the guy mercifully says, in English, *Air mail?*

He spends the rest of the day wandering the city in search of that something without a name (hasn't anyone patented that damn GPS device yet?). Well, okay, it's not like he really expects to bump into Margarito right here in the street, but it'd be great if he at least had a clue. Which he seems closer to finding when he returns to the hotel and actually does bump into—not Margarito but a gentleman in black western boots, ankle-length black leather duster and black felt Stetson with

flashing silver bangles around the crown. He introduces himself
with a bone-crushing handshake as Sam Steele (not sure how
we know there's an "e" on the end) and with a steely gleam in
his gun metal gray eyes invites the Snowman for a drink, which
turns out to be a bottle of eighteen-year-old single malt scotch
(Mister Steele buying), over which he and Steele engage in a
conversation that gradually reveals to his increasingly peat
smoky brain that Steele's profession is, if not exactly illegit, at
least questionable—fact is, I'm a bounty hunter—and even
more alarming, he, too, seems to be searching for Margarito,
although throughout this *tête-à-tête* Steele continues to repeat
"bounty hunting is illegal in Mexico, it is illegal to carry arms
into Mexico," all the while suggesting through various tantric
yogic grimaces and the isometric squeezing together of his very
large and callused hands that he is nevertheless capable of
inflicting great *distress* on the individuals he pursues. After all,
Mister—*Snowman*, you said?—these are very bad hombres who
have done very bad things, murder, torture, rape, extortion,
grand theft, meddling in presidential elections—you get the
picture (pouring more scotch). However, through bureaucratic
fuck-ups and more often greased palms, these perps have
escaped U.S. jurisdiction. Steele's eyes narrow like, what else,
gun slits. Keeping in mind that Mexican nationals are only
rarely extradited to the U.S. Also keeping in mind that Mexico
doesn't have capital punishment, at least in principle. As a
result, the victims or their relatives often hire people like *me* to
come down here and, shall we say, settle the score? At which
point Steele finally gets down to brass knuckles—er, tacks. Just
to be sure we're on the same page here, *Snowman*, this
Margarito—funny little fat guy with bad teeth, right?

   This encounter leaves a nasty taste in the Snowman's soul,
as if Satan has been licking this nebulously located organ with
his oily black, bifurcated tongue, an unpleasant sensation that
increases as the effects of the scotch wear off, replaced by a
mild hangover and the return of his anomie, which might
explain his next action. He enters a church. It's this massive

stone cathedral he has passed near the zócalo. Its elaborate façade looks like a macabre wedding cake baked out of bone flour with arches and columns, statues of saints and prophets in niches or carved in bas relief. Not really an atheist, agnostic maybe, certainly no papist tendencies, it's doubtful the Snowman's ever seen the inside of a Catholic church. Everything is a mystery. The flickering votive candles and smoldering incense sticks in the vestibule, the glass case of *milagros*, the little silver or gold or tin arms or legs or hearts or other afflicted parts of the human body for which—if he understands correctly—parishioners are asking God's intervention. The nave is like the inside of a giant jewel box. Tall stained glass windows, flickering sconces and candelabra, ornate gold, silver and crystal chandeliers, wooden pews gleaming like the carapaces of huge brown beetles, statues and gilt-framed oil paintings of prophets, saints, Biblical scenes, an elaborately carved wooden pulpit with a balustrade that reminds him of a seventeenth century sailing ship's forecastle. Contrasting this lavishness and luxury—carved wooden effigies of martyrs, hideous Baroque monstrosities, naked, scourged, burned, mutilated, arrow-pierced, blood-splattered. A similarly conceived Messiah, face tormented beneath a bloody crown of thorns, torso torn and emaciated, el Greco-like limbs sinewy and elongated, bloody hands and feet pierced with iron nails, hangs on his eternal cross over the altar. Winged angels and diaphanously clad cherubim smile benevolently upon this glut and excess from a pastel blue sky painted on the vaulted ceiling. The screech of shoe leather on the tiled floor returns the Snowman's attention to the temporal realm as a dark form with a bony face, membranous bat-winged ears and eyes burning like coals suddenly appears out of the shadows. *Nosferatu!* No, wait, it's an illusion, just the flickering candlelight, a trick of perspective, not some gothic monster at all but a man, square-jawed, formidably built, eyes gleaming brightly, but still just a man. In the ambiguous tone of a police inspector, the man says in an odd accent the Snowman can't peg, I see you are interested in church architecture. It's a *lay* interest, he replies, playing his cards close to his chest (he's not wearing a vest). The man, who, he sees now is wearing a simple black priest's cassock, smiles at this (unintended) pun and introduces himself as Father Juan Patricio O'Jalajan. Folks call me the *Snowman*, he responds in his recently acquired Big Tex cowboy drawl and adds, This is quite a church you got here, Padre (to his no small embarrassment, the Snowman will learn later that, despite his modest garb, Father O'Jalajan is bishop of the Chopahuac diocese). The good Father, who, in an amazing linguistic feat, speaks English with a Spanish accented Irish brogue (*chooorrrch* for church, for example), explains that much of the artwork and statuary are artifacts from the earliest missions in the New World six hundred years ago, as well as gifts from wealthy patrons over the subsequent centuries. *Quid pro quo,* no, Mister … *Snowman?* Bribes, annulments, very expensive indulgences for very guilty consciences? Father O'Jalajan points at a stone column. The Spaniards built this church out of stones from the Zoltec temples they destroyed. They waved their crosses in the air while they tumbled the mutilated bodies of the indigenous people into mass graves and justified their bar*barrrr*ity as a holy war against the heathen. That sounds kinda cynical for a man of the cloth, Padre, the Snowman continues in his Big Tex drawl. Father O'Jalajan's gaze, ardent, incinerating, penetrates him to his soul, searing the pointy ears and tails of the multitudes of petty demons peering out from behind this immaterial organ which his equally multitudinous (but mostly minor) sins have leased to them. I serve God and God is *trrrruth*, Mister Snowman. The truth is in the stones. Each stone contains the soul of its maker. If you place your hand on a stone you feel his cries, his torment. This church is a palimpsest. Beneath each layer of paint you scrape away is another. Beneath portraits of kings and queens, beneath great palaces and cathedrals and bucolic still lifes, you find pictures of peasants laboring in fields, factories and mines, their faces distorted by hunger and suffering. Scrape away that layer and you find a painting of mausoleums, of crypts and ossuaries filled with bones. And beneath that—you find God, or at least someone's concept of God. The world is changing very rapidly, Mister Snowman, but it is still filled with the same pain and suffering. Every prayer I offer, every baptism, wedding vow, eulogy, is in honor of that suffering. Please, if you wish to stay for mass, you are most welcome. I must go now. Peace be with you, Mister Snowman.

Intriguing as this encounter is (it's pretty clear Boone, who has just appeared on the set in an uncharacteristically silly looking floppy hat stuck with trout fishing flies and Largemouth Bass lures, is angling for some sort of plot here), Big Tex, er, the Snowman, figures he'll pass on the mass. He's starting to feel antsy, a sense of urgency has overtaken him, like he's in a little sailboat swirling around a drain in ever tightening circles, the axis of this vortex a completely unknown entity—yes, Margarito, but which Margarito? The uncertain Margarito of his memory, who, over a matter of days, weeks, months, morphed from illegal immigrant, crew member, workmate to *friend?* Were they friends? Were they something more or less than friends? Is it that Margarito you're searching for, *Snowman*, the more or less friend you knew, thought you knew at that time in that place? Or is it the Margarito here and now, a Margarito as alien and unknown to you as this, *his* country, homeland, the place of his birth? It's also getting late, he's wasted another day wandering around like a lost mutt. He decides to grab dinner at the cyber café and ponder his next move. As he enters, he glances at the message board and reads in emerald green ink in what he's pretty sure is a female hand, *Snowman, mientras tú buscas, ¿quién te busca a ti?*—which he translates correctly if woodenly as, *while you search, who's searching for you?* And beneath that, in the same green ink but in English, *Look for the answer at the end of November.* His first thought, accompanied by an icy breath on the back of his neck, is *uh-oh*, somebody besides Sam Steele knows he's here and they also seem to know why he's here. His second thought is, *November?* So what—I gotta wait another month and, uh, twenty-three-four days? Something like that? (Don't try to do the math on this—as usual, Boone's chronology is all over the map. Don't be surprised if it starts snowing in August.)

Too agitated now to sit down and eat, he takes off again like a gumshoe hot on a new lead, his mind churning through the murky waters of plausible possibilities. What if it's a red herring? A trap? It *was* a woman, right? Who wrote the message, I mean? But who would that be? A name comes to his mind, *Maria*, and with it the face of a young woman with hair as black as a raven's wings, eyes flashing like obsidian, lips like red silk rose petals—that, anyway, is the face he has assigned to this Maria, whom he has never met in person, never seen in a photograph, whom, in fact, he has most likely conflated with an actress who, he's pretty sure, actually was Mexican and who starred in a movie classic of lovelorn, unbearable longing, oh yeah, and a bunch of gunfights, soldiers and bandits splashing across the Frio Grande on horseback in flickering, grainy, Technicolor he watched on the big screen at the Saturday afternoon matinee, him and a bunch of buddies, eight, nine, ten-year old kids wide-eyed and amazed, the world outside, school starting next week, some kind of *health issue* mom's having and something called the *atomic bomb* hanging over their heads like the sword of Damocles, all forgotten for these two or three hours of movie magic. But now what? Lost in his thoughts, he's become equally lost in a labyrinth of unfamiliar shops, markets and plazas. The shadows are growing longer. Thin lemon yellow light gleams on terra cotta rooftops, wrought iron staircases, TV antennas, a street sign that says *Calle 30 de Noviembre,* but other than pondering the Mexican propensity for naming streets after days of the month, he doesn't get the significance until an old man in white cotton shirt and pants appears out of the growing crepuscular gloom like a numinous presence, lifts his grizzled, beard-stubbled face, which, hmm, does look vaguely familiar, points a gnarled finger at the street sign and with a nearly toothless grin says as if delivering the

punch line to a forgotten joke, *¿Fin del mes, no?* Ohhhhh …
now he gets it. Still grinning, the old man proceeds to deliver a
cryptic message in Spanish that he once again more or less
understands. Drive east out of town—the old man makes a one-
handed chopping gesture to indicate where east lies. When you
pass the man plowing—the old man holds out his hands as if
he's driving a motorcycle—look for the feathered serpent—he
flaps his arms like wings, bunches his fingertips together like a
snake's head and goes *sssssss!*—then turn onto the road to
riches—*huh?*—and look for the *casa azul*—that one's easy.

5
La Casita Maria

HE WAKES THE FOLLOWING MORNING with an erection straining against the bedcovers and Maria's face, the face he has concocted for her anyway, lingering in his mind, except that it's Margarito's eyes he sees staring back at him. This is disturbing for a couple of reasons. One, he's been fantasizing about a fantasy who happens to be his buddy's significant other, and two, he has again crossed into ambiguous sexual territory. After checking out of the Hotel (Oh, Missster Snowman, I'm so sorry you are leaving us, *hnn, hnn, hnn*—Peter Lorre rubbing his hands together as if he's anticipating a good strangulation), he drives east out of town through a narrow cleft, kind of like a key slot, in the jungle-covered mountains, sucking on a sizable roach he discovered stuck in a gap in the steering column and trying to untangle conflicting strands of reason and paranoia, including the distinct possibility he's going down a very deep rabbit hole. What if the old man's crazy? What if he's in cahoots with bandits and they're waiting to dry-gulch him in some arroyo ahead? What if this is his only chance to find Margarito and he blows it? Lush green jungle evaporates into barren, sun-blasted desert. Choking heat pours in the Coupe's open windows. He swerves around the flattened remains of an armor-plated creature with horns and jagged teeth. A metallic gleam engulfed in a cloud of dust catches his eye and he finally makes out a man walking behind a steel share plow drawn by a large black ox. Shortly afterward he passes an oddly solitary mountain, its rugged yellow slopes dotted with dark green cactus and yucca. Near its summit he can see an enormous winged creature with a coiled serpent tail, which, in a neck-wrenching double take, he determines to be an unusual outcropping of stone. About a kilometer farther he passes a large clump of prickly pear cactus on which is perched a raggedy, moth-eaten buzzard with a dead rat snake clutched in its beak. A weathered wooden sign points to *Las Riquezas* thataway and thataway he goes on a rocky dirt road. He begins to pass abandoned board and adobe houses, then a partially ruined church, its bell tower empty, its arched entrance cracked, its yellow adobe walls crumbling in places, exposing mud brick and termite-riddled timbers. Next to the church is a small cemetery behind a rusty wrought iron fence and, okay, that icy tingling in his spine again, there's some heavy duty déjà vu going on here because he'd swear on a stack of cordwood he's seen this cemetery before. Curiosity piqued, he pulls over for a closer look. The iron gate creaks open at his touch. Prickly pear cactus and dead brown weeds crowd among wooden and cement crosses and doghouse-size brick and mortar shrines embedded with colored pieces of glass and tile and decorated with weathered plaster statues of the Madonna and Jesus, tattered pink ribbons, garlands of faded plastic flowers and multi-colored lava flows of candle wax. Behind small dirty glass windows he can see curling, moisture-stained photographs of the deceased. Baptisms, grammar school, communions, weddings, soldier boy home on leave, maybe the only photograph they ever had of him. There's one in particular, a young man, handsome face, laughing eyes, boyish mustache— Margarito, that's who it reminds him of, a younger Margarito he never met, barely out of adolescence. And then, maybe it's the hot sun beating down on his head or Boone's fucking with him again or, more likely, it's the roach he smoked, because there's this surreal footage inside a limestone vault, spider webs, moss, a rotting wooden coffin, glimpses of moldy cloth, luminous white bones. *Nyaah!* He squeezes his eyes shut, opens them again, slowly, his brain trying to decide if the data the optic software is sending it is cause for alarm or totally benign, because only now does he notice the fresh mound of dirt, which, by its shape and size, clearly connotes *grave*, and then another mound and another. He hears a sound like a single chord on a pipe organ, or maybe it's just a shrill gust of wind swirling across the desert. The sun moves a notch higher in the sky and a shadow falls over him, cast by the church's empty bell tower, on top of which he notices now a stone cross, each branch of which ends in a carved fleur-de-lis so that it looks like crossed leg bones, femur and tibia. Rising behind and above this cross, perfectly aligned with its vertical member, he sees the peak of that rugged yellow, strangely solitary mountain. Spooked by these omens or premonitions or whatever messengers they are of the paranormal realm, he returns to the Coupe with a whole hive of those icy tingler things running up and down his spine and an urgent need to get back on the road and shake the dust from his feet. But following a script predicated upon expectation and delivery, he immediately slows again when he spies marching toward him a peasant army bristling with picks and shovels, women in faded, work-stained, ill-fitting skirts and blouses, pink plastic slippers or worn black pumps, men in torn, sweat-stained cotton shirts and polyester trousers, shod in work boots or huaraches or even barefoot, their big peasant toes coated with yellow dust or crusted with dried red clay, in their solemn faces, in their lambent eyes a grim determination and, yes, anger that initially causes him a panic inducing *uh-oh* moment. Has he defiled sacred ground? Violated some taboo? Are they coming to *kill* him? The throng swarms around him and past, carrying on their collective peasant shoulders a simple yellow pine board coffin, like a little wooden dinghy cast upon a stormy sea.

His doubts return. What if he got it all wrong? What if this trip was a complete mistake? What made him think Margarito would be happy to see him? What if he knocks on the door and Margarito greets him with surprise but not the good kind? You

really came, Snowman? Why did you come? Maria, look who's
here. It's that greenghost I told you about. All right, come in,
Snowman. There's a pail of water by the door if you want to
wash up. There might be some cold tortillas if you're hungry.
And this fabled Maria—will she laugh at him, hate him? Her
face, features, the red scar of her lips, the high, severe
cheekbones and flashing, obdurate black eyes crush into a gelid
smile that extracts from him in return a smile so painful it
makes the back of his head ache? Of course she'll hate him.
He's the accursed—nay, say it—the *abominable Snowman* who
forced Margarito into the unnatural act of making snow. And
now he's come here to *seduce* him, draw him back into that
frozen hell again, get him drunk and crazy with dreams of
power and money from the bottle he's brought especially for the
occasion, the drop or two that's left, anyway, *a drink for old
times' sake, Margarito?* And then what? Margarito, glancing at
Maria, You know I don't drink, Snowman, and Maria almost
audibly whispering to him with her eyes, *Why did you invite
him here, Margarito? Can't you make him go now?* And
Margarito, dutifully, relieved of the responsibility, Don't you
think you better get going, Snowman? You know what they say
about driving after dark? And then what? Climb back in the
Coupe and drive off into that great big nothing with his tail
between his legs like an old mongrel mutt with nowhere to go
and not a friend in the world? Aww, but Snowman, Snowman,
that's just you again, just your usual hang-ups and insecurities.
Always trying to chess masterly figure out every move so far in
advance you're caught off guard by things happening in the
moment. You gotta learn to relax, Snowboy, take life as it
comes. And by the way … yeah, yeah, I know …

And like a big screen Technicolor epiphany—sunlight
bursting through the clouds, the Berlin Philharmonic breaking
into the final movement of Beethoven's ninth symphony and
the Mormon Tabernacle choir screaming *Alle Menschen werden
Brüder*—he roars up out of an arroyo and into a panoramic
picture postcard. Against the backdrop of that odd (and

peripatetic, apparently) yellow mountain he sees nestled a blue
stucco cottage with a terra cotta tiled roof. A small herd of goats
bleats like a roomful of politicians and trots away as he pulls up
the long flint and gravel drive. Chickens flap up into the bare
branches of a dead rattlepod tree, clucking like indignant
washerwomen as he crunches to a halt next to a mud-splattered
dirt bike that looks like it's been rode hard and put up wet.
Images of Margarito roaring across the desert like T.E.
Lawrence flash through his mind, accompanied by the moody,
melancholy and then soaring string section of Maurice Jarre's
dramatic movie score. He (the Snowman, not Maurice Jarre)
climbs out of the Coupe like a rodeo cowboy rearranging his
body after a bad fall and shuffles up the flagstone walk, which
is bordered on one side by a surprisingly lush green vegetable
garden, at the back of which he notices an array of solar panels
on top of a small barn and smiles to himself at these obvious
signs of Margarito's handiwork. The house, however, is some
misinformed scriptwriter's concept of a bucolic Mexican
residence. Pastel blue stucco walls, a rustic patch of exposed
orange brick in one corner, heavy stone lintels over the door and
windows that suggest the simple but enduring architecture of
centuries past. Terra cotta pots of pink and red geraniums fill
the window casements. A straw broom leans against the
doorpost. There's even some kind of rusted bicycle contraption
half-buried in a fuchsia mound of bougainvillea to add an air of
antiquity   or—Boone   foraying   into   mystery?—intrigue.
Anxious, almost giddy, he reaches out to knock on the heavy
wooden door, in his mind seeing the door open and Margarito's
surprised expression—and then his own surprise when the door
does open and suddenly he's staring into the face of someone
familiar, maybe even famous, *Mariiii-aaa, I just met a girl
named Mariiii-aaa*, because he does know this face, he's seen it
on the big screen of his imagination a thousand times, a young
woman with long black hair that shines like raven wings in
flight, lips like red silken rose petals, eyes flashing like
obsidian, in a red cotton dress and bare peasant feet. And it is

that face, but different, the black hair chopped short and ragged with slashes of purple and henna, a jade stone in the wing of the left nostril, a silver bead gleaming like a tiny starburst above her right eye, and not a dress—specifically a plain red dress—but retro hippie-grunge checked flannel shirt, untucked, charcoal gray jeans, fashionably torn knees revealing glimpses of perfectly smooth skin, and not barefoot but big black *don't-fuck-with-me*, lace-up-the-front, shit-stomper Doc Martens, each part synecdochally acquiring for the Snowman the value of her whole being, which is what, an attractive, all right, *pretty*, young woman with an alternative lifestyle? But pretty suggests fragility, softness, and while there is softness, curves, a sense of her female body under the grunge garments, there's also a hardness in her eyes, in her cheekbones, in the line of her slightly aquiline nose and the way she compresses her lips like an archer's bow. Despite this tough edge, she seems excited, as if she has received very good news. *¿Sí?* she says, this simple interrogative opening the door, as it were, for him to ask or answer any one or all five of the cardinal questions of an increasingly obsolete journalism, who? what? where? when? and how? (Or is it why?) He tries to speak but he stammers like a bashful schoolboy, more accurately like a chimpanzee just down out of the trees trying to communicate in the King's English or in this case the Queen's Spanish, *¿S-s-s-sabe d-d-d-dónde está M-m-m-margarito? Yo soy su amigo, el S-S ... Snowman?* the young woman finishes for him with another interrogative and a bemused smile that also seems familiar, then introduces herself as, yes, Maria, and, yes, of course she knows who he is, Margarito spoke of him often. And just like that *raaaaaa!* a radiant burst of positive energy floods his brain. His spirits sink again when she informs him that Margarito isn't here, he's taken a job in another town. Oh shit (he doesn't say). Now what? Go off on another wild goose chase? Go back to Chopahuac? Go *home?* But wait, Maria is saying, no, please, stay. Margarito should return later this evening. And up, up, up, his beautiful balloon soars again. In the meantime, come, I'll show you around. The house is small, two bedrooms, a living area, a dining area, a bathroom and kitchen. And yes, maybe he was expecting rustic furniture, cheap prints on the walls, a shrine to Santa Agave, so he's a little thrown by the shelves packed with books, the computers and electronic equipment, the holographic TV. Maria leads him outside to the garden and it's a 4-H'er's dream. Watermelons and *calabacitas* (that's zucchini to you, Snowman), *berenjenas* (eggplant), tomatillos, jalapeños, string beans, rows of corn, the savory and medicinal herbs cilantro and epazote (he'll figure that one out later on his own *braaap!*). His eyes leap here and there, but it's not the blue ribbon vegetables that cause him to stare. It's the shaggy Christmas tree shapes with unmistakable clawed leaves and thick, resinous buds. My magical sisters, Maria says, feline-lowering her eyelids and wrinkling her nose like a witch casting a mischievous but not hurtful spell. You know, *Snowman*, the magic of organic gardening, composting, natural fertilizers, friendly bacteria? Soooo … he rethinks his initial impression … the garden is Maria's work, not Margarito's? And by the way, how long have they been speaking English? And—obliquely, discreetly, sideways sneakily giving Maria another glance—is this really the unsophisticated country girl Margarito described? And, who knows, maybe she really *is* a witch and she knows *exactly* what he's thinking because suddenly she laughs and her teeth are sharp and white and for just a second there's a wildness in her eyes like an animal escaping human bonds. Just as quickly she returns to picking vegetables, which she has been doing with the precision of a commercial produce buyer, and placing them in a woven reed basket, zucchini, bell peppers, ripe red tomatoes that actually have that musty, tomatoey smell he faintly, maybe, *thinks* he remembers from the faraway place of his childhood. Again Maria seems to read his thoughts because she cradles the basket of produce in her arms and smiles a wide friendly smile like she's doing a TV commercial for a universally known spaghetti sauce whose brand hearkens back to a more bucolic existence when barefoot maids in caps and aprons with ankle-length skirts raised playfully, flirtatiously but mostly (yes, *Edna*) for practicality's sake above their knees, stomped tomatoes in big wooden vats, while behind them men in rough peasant garb swung scythes in fields of golden grain. Carrying her harvest into the kitchen, Maria asks if he'd like a beer and before he can answer she pops open two bottles, and then, while she hovers over the sink, the stove, the countertop, washing and chopping, putting on a pot of beans to simmer, sautéing onions, jalapeños and bell peppers in the sizzling, crackling black cast iron frying pan, and in between taking swigs from her bottle of beer, he sits at the heavy wooden table, sipping at first and then, following her lead, gulping his beer, a very good, full-bodied, hopsy brew, and examining the terra cotta tiled floor, the flowered tiles over the windows and door frame, the heavy iron spigot shaped like the head of a Chinese dragon over the sink, the gleaming copper and stainless steel pots and pans and cast iron skillets hanging over the stove, the odd bundles of herbs, roots, bark, dried poblano, ancho and chile peppers hanging from hooks on the walls and ceiling, the shelves packed with jars and bottles of spices, herbs, condiments, oils, vinegars and extracts, the large blue ceramic vase containing big wooden and metal ladles and serving forks—everything and anything, that is, except Maria's taut round butt playing peekaboo below her untucked flannel shirt, which he'd desperately like to stare at boldly, unabashedly, for one full second (or two) and which his eyes mutinously keep returning to, unfortunately at the precise moment Maria glances over her shoulder or turns to say something, exactly as if she expects *witch?* to catch him in the act *or simply feminine wiles?* (*C'mon*, Edna, loosen up.) But if she's offended she doesn't show it, in fact, she seems inordinately happy, whistling and breaking into a somewhat dated pop hit in surprisingly melodious, full-throated Spanish *Te quise tanto* (he hasn't a clue). Only when he offhandedly mentions the peasants carrying the coffin does her demeanor change. Her face darkens, the earlier hardness in her eyes returns, and in a strained voice she informs him that the villagers, in defiance of some judicial ordinance, have begun to bury their dead in the old cemetery again. Just as quickly her darkness passes and she smiles and seems happy again as she dishes out steaming plates of food and opens another beer for both of them, her mere physical presence, her proximity, her arm brushing against his shoulder, even the touch of her lumberjack flannel shirt on his skin, shooting barrages of warm and tingly subatomic particles through his entire body. The meal is hot, spicy, and so delicious he doesn't even notice the absence of meat. Between bites, he asks Maria about everything, how do you say this in Spanish? and what are those called and what's that? Until she lets out something between a scream of frustration and a strangled laugh. *Snowmaaan, stop!* Then apologizes, sort of. I forgot that you ... that Margarito said you eat words. Taking this as a compliment, he asks how she learned to speak English so well. She starts to reply, then raises her forefinger, signifying *wait*, gets up from the table and returns with a bottle of *El Residente* brandy (the camera zooms in on the label and the familiar logo of a man climbing out of the Frio Grande on the American side with a red sash across his chest that reads *I'd rather be a resident in the U.S. than president of Mexico*) and two glasses, which she fills to the brim. Offering him a *salud*, she tosses down her drink and when he follows suit, pours another and this too she downs in a single swallow, almost, he thinks, as if she's fortifying herself for an unpleasant task. You see, Snowman, my mother and father died when I was young. There was a ... sickness. *I was on the roof repairing the tiles when I saw the column of black SUVs speed up the highway. I don't know how many, ten, fifteen. I was making tortillas when the men came. They went from house to house, there wasn't time for anyone to escape, I don't know why they let me go, maybe because they were hungry. I was at the pigpen slopping the hogs when I heard the screams and the gunfire. After the noise died down Genaro and I went across the arroyo to see. And the girl?* She went to live with her aunt and uncle. They were good people but poor, ignorant and very superstitious. Her future looked bleak. It's an old story, Snowman. You've seen the movie. *Oliver Twist, The Little Princess, Jane Eyre.* Let's just say I'm a poster child for rural education. Art, music, literature—she loved it all and all of it she abandoned with her admission to the university where she applied herself to the sciences, agronomy, engineering, medicine. Why waste time learning pretty words when people are dying, know what I mean, *Snowman?* The way she says this sounds to his ears like an insinuation if not an outright accusation, the result most likely of low frequency echoes of a more idealistic time in his own past and his painfully convoluted justifications for dropping out of the higher echelons of academe, which had something to do with fraud, hypocrisy (*theirs*, of course) and, to unequivocally state his case, direct or indirect participation in warmongering capitalist adventurism. And how did he act on those noble intentions? Join a door-to-door campaign to collect food for the poor in the cantons of East Osberg? Go on a mission of Christ's love to build public toilets in some steaming, disease-ridden, fourth-world shithole President Ronwald DeBoche has declared persona non grata? Surely you jest, bro'. More like wasting ten years of his life in a dead-end blue collar job whose specific purpose was to make everybody else's life miserable while devoting the precious little time he had outside that job to a drug and alcohol soaked self-pity party. Which is probably why he has only been half-listening as Maria describes the very real suffering she deals with, not just the normal everyday issues like, oh, bubonic plague, tuberculosis, dengue fever, but grinding poverty, ignorance, centuries of oppression and neglect. The *pinche gobierno* makes promises, but it doesn't matter what *hijo de puta* is in office, nothing ever changes. The anger that has entered Maria's voice is a little scary. Also familiar. He's heard Margarito express these same sentiments. Maria shrugs, a little sloppily, the brandy probably. Perhaps she was naive, she thought it was possible to end this cycle. She returned to Las Riquezas, helped set up a health clinic, a community organization to improve sanitation, agricultural practices. Her tone swerves back into positive territory and she says with a goofy 4-H'er grin that's almost certainly the brandy, I guess I'm just a *campesina* at heart, *Snowman*. You kin' take the girl out of the country but ya can't take the country out of the girl, he says in his Big Tex voice, which is supposed to sound self-consciously corny but mostly comes across as obtuse.

During this exchange Maria has been meticulously picking apart a miniature Christmas tree that actually looks like it's covered with lights, tinsel, ornaments and artificial snow, but instead of a pungent pine scent, the Snowman detects lemon blossoms, sandalwood, musk, cloves, cinnamon and—*apple pie?* It's a cannabis bud, of course, a thick, emerald green inflorescence bristling with tiny white and gold hairs and laden with sticky, crystalized resin. With rapid, precise movements Maria rolls an exemplary joint (the classic fuel pod or "bomb" shape with ends perfectly crimped), grabs the bottle, and they move outside where, sipping brandy and passing the pot, they watch the day go out in a blaze of glory, and it is glorious, made more so by the cannabis, as Maria says, repeating a phrase he's heard before, *Fumar para ver más claro, ¿no, Snowman?* Gleaming gossamer threads stretch back to their source as Old Sol settles his golden glowing butt down on the horizon, illuminating the cactus-studded mountainsides with a shifting palette of dusty pink, yellow, orange and red light. Gray and purple shadows spread across the desert like stealthy inland seas. The sky turns nacreous, then indigo, then black. Stars twinkle like diamonds, fireflies, glass beads (hard to decide stoned). The warm night air smells of dried herbs. Maria and the Snowman are sitting very close and without either of them understanding exactly how this has happened they're staring into each other's eyes. Maybe, okay, probably, it's the pot and the brandy, but there's clearly some chemistry (physics?) going on here, the air's full of electricity, excited subatomic particles bounce back and forth between male and female poles. Who knows where this might lead. They're right at that presynaptic moment when—*what the fuh* ... *?* In another of those disturbing *déjà vu* episodes, it's no longer Maria's eyes he's staring into but Margarito's. What is it? Maria asks. Nothing, he says, a mosquito bite. And then, so abruptly he surprises himself, he says maybe he should go now, it doesn't look like Margarito's returning tonight. Maria objects, it's late, he's in no condition to drive. Which is definitely true, although he almost blurts out, heck, I do it all the time (unfortunately, also true). But before he can say something so stupid, Maria, in what seems like a totally uncalculated move, takes his hand and leads him back inside to a small room with a single bed, but just when he and the viewing audience and even most of the crew on the set believe this is going to turn hot, steamy and triple XXX, she turns to leave. And just as suddenly turns back and embraces him. I'm so glad you came, *Snowman.* The warmth and softness of her body against his and the smell of her hair and her warm breath produce the immediate stirring of an erection. He feels an almost overwhelming desire to lift her face to his and kiss her, he even senses she wouldn't object. Unfortunately, that little goody two-shoes Snowman angel of (self-) righteousness sitting—where else?—on his right shoulder is practically shouting in his ear, And then what, *Snowman?* You end up in bed together and five minutes later your *friend* Margarito walks in the door? And then what? Angry words? Fists, knives, gunshots, somebody dead? But no need to worry about that narrative playing itself out because there are two minds at work here. Maria abruptly pulls away, apologizing profusely, Margarito has told her so much about him, she feels as if she knows him, Margarito will be so happy to see him, she's going to bed, goodnight. And what a fucking idiot he feels like now, right?

Without bothering to undress, he falls asleep (okay, passes out) on the bed in an alcohol and cannabis-induced swoon as his subconscious sneaks off into dreamland and various scenarios involving him and Maria in somewhat murky states of nakedness and physical embrace. He wakes from this reverie an hour or two later, a piss hard-on suggesting two alternatives, one essential, and, compelled by an inexplicable Y chromosome thing, stumbles outside to take a leak rather than use the perfectly functioning and in fact quite modern indoor toilet. And somehow ends up lying in a hammock afterwards, his body swaying gently in the warm air to a chorus of chirring crickets, the sound they make oddly like the regular *jink, jink, jink* of a horse's sleigh bells in winter, an association that probably comes from a fondly remembered Hollywood classic rather than his personal experience (the snow, yes, the sleigh, no). He falls back asleep staring at the white splatter of stars across the violet sky. A little later he sees the moon has risen like a luminous yellow egg yolk. Later still a rooster crows and through the narrow grillwork of his eyelashes he watches the horizon paint itself in a wistful watercolor wash of pink, red and orange with iridescent streaks of turquoise and aquamarine, like the feathered finery of a much larger rooster.

6
Margarito?

HE WAKES AGAIN AND IT'S LIGHT. He cocks an eye at the rooster perched in the branches of the dead rattlepod tree directly over his head and immediately recognizes the danger he's in, especially when the rooster cocks an eye back at him in furious defiance. (Boone had intended to develop this preening chanticleer as the Snowman's arch nemesis. He's always devising ways to kill the damn bird. Maria'll come around a corner and find him with his hands around the rooster's neck, or just about to chop off its head with an axe. The rooster's squawking, in *English*, in a strangely inflected voice Boone's sound mixer put together from samples of Woody Woodpecker and Donald Duck, *Mom! Mom! Help! He's trying to kill me!* The Snowman's smiling a sheepish, shit-eating grin like *who, me?* Unfortunately, a misunderstanding among the kitchen staff led to a horrible discovery at the cast's dinner table one evening, as well as hard feelings that will linger to the end of the shoot. And right here Boone performs another of his trademark sleights of hand. Violating grammatical boundaries, he skips the closing parenthesis and ties this past cast repast directly to the sound of pots and pans banging inside the house. Sure enough, as the Snowman gradually comes to his senses, we can see from his expression that right now he's picturing Maria preparing breakfast (yes, chauvinistic—it's Boone's ~~chau~~ show). Fragments of last night, inchoate, unattached to meaning, flash through his brain—swilling brandy with Maria, the two of them staring into each other's eyes, an unexpected embrace, the warmth of her body against his—enough that he decides it wise to formulate some kind of game plan (he's a guy, it's a game plan). How should he greet her? Casually? Like, oh man I was so fucked up I don't remember a thing— how *you* doin'? What if she gives him an affectionate hug and in that brief embrace reveals everything—or nothing?

Well, at last you are awake, Snowman! The voice is familiar and the face but it's not at all what he was expecting— the twinkling brown eyes and the shining black mustache and the wide open smile and—*Margarito?* Yes, it is Margarito, laughing and shaking him by the shoulder, Come on, *Snowman,* get up! The SnowBile ees waiting! We gotta make some snow! Groggy, blinking against the bright light, he tumbles out of the hammock like a drunken sailor, crouches like a gunslinger ready to draw his shooting iron and sticks out his mitt for the classic male handshake (consult manual: four up and down pump handle movements in quick succession). To his surprise, Margarito throws his arms around him and says with oven-fresh warmth and affection *Ayyy, Snowman, I'm so happy to see you!* and for about three and a half seconds they hold each other, closely, but it isn't Margarito's embrace he feels, not Margarito's eyes he's staring into, but Maria's arms and Maria's eyes and their embrace last night. His body stiffens and he gives Margarito a couple of quick Norwegian bachelor farmer pats on the back. Not oblivious to this emotional tectonic shift, Margarito reciprocates, his body stiffens, and he and the Snowman separate awkwardly, hands in their pockets, aw shucksing and flatfoot shuffling like a couple of West Texas bubbas who are mighty glad to see each other after such a long spell but not *that* glad. He can also see now that Margarito's had a bit of a night himself, he looks disheveled, shirt untucked, eyes bloodshot, mustache crusty, ungroomed, even kind of askew. *Bad mustache day?* Margarito explains that a friend dropped him off on the highway late last night and he walked in. You were sleeping so well, I deedn't want to wake you. And

Maria? he asks, trying not to sound too guilty quilty. Margarito shrugs. She has already left for the clinic on her motorcycle—deedn't you hear? Which, hmm, debunks another of his preconceptions (we again hear the soaring string section of Jarre's famous score, cut short by the sound of a Wurlitzer organ crashing to the floor).

This information presents him with an unexpected conundrum. He and Margarito have reunited at last, to his relief Margarito's obviously glad to see him, they've apparently got a full day ahead to hang out and catch up, Margarito's even a pretty good cook, the breakfast is almost as delicious as Maria's dinner last night, huevos rancheros, black beans, corn tortillas, fried plátanos, papaya with yoghurt, whole grain toast with guava jam, and rich black coffee with an indulgence of fresh cream and raw brown sugar. There's another similarity. Throughout the preparation and serving of this meal he finds himself in an awkward reprise of yesterday evening, that is scrupulously avoiding staring at Margarito's ass passing back and forth between the table, the sink and the stove more or less at eye level. There's also this unsettling sense of disappointment—and it is disappointment, isn't it?—that now it's Margarito he will spend the day with and not Maria. Margarito, on the other hand, seems in an unusually jovial mood. What do you think of my Maria, Snowman? She's very nice, he says. *Ha!Ha!Ha!—nice?* Ees that all you can say? Don't you think she ees beautiful, *Snowman?* Well, heck yeah, I guess. I mean, what are you supposed to say when a guy asks your opinion of his girlfriend, especially when you've developed a raging crush on her? She isn't exactly the country girl you described, he says. Margarito laughs again. But eet's true, Snowman. She ees a girl and she ees from the country. Which sounds pretty much like what *he* said to Maria last night.

After breakfast Margarito rolls a joint, which, the Snowman notices, he does with the same fastidious precision he observed in Maria, a fact he attributes to their close relationship, traits they've acquired from each other, there's even a kind of sibling resemblance, but let's not add incest to the equation, *Snowmund*. They pass the joint back and forth while drinking another delicious cup of coffee, which has somehow become the current topic of conversation, Margarito having just remarked that the brew they're enjoying comes from coffee beans grown in the mountains around Chopahuac, leading thence to a discussion of the comparative qualities of coffee from around the world (Brazilian, Vietnamese, Colombian, Indonesian, Ethiopian, etc.), a subject Margarito seems surprisingly knowledgeable in (did you know Brazeel alone produced almost eight billion pounds of coffee last year, *Snowman?*) and quickly devolves into the kind of meandering, stoned discourse that sounds brilliant to the participants but like total ~~gibbonish~~ *gibberish* to an outside listener, although there's a brief and disturbing seismic shift in the mood when Margarito by some association the Snowman completely missed begins talking about knives, in particular the comparative virtues of carbon steel and the more primitive obsidian employed by the indigenous Zoltec people, for example, their facility in severing muscle and bone, at that moment placing on the table a large knife with a carved wooden handle and an oddly scalloped but extremely sharp-looking blade that appears to have been made (*knapped* is the correct term but the Snowman doesn't know that—Edna) out of a shiny, black, glass-like material. Margarito's eyes meet his and in one of those freakish, THC-induced bouts of sudden and extreme paranoia, his entire nervous system lights up like a supermax prison under lockdown and, completely paralyzed in his seat, he watches Margarito's face transform into a monstrous mask, dragon-like in shape, with a fiery red and orange mane of feathers and scales, vertical serpent eyes and huge fangs, and even wilder, another face is emerging from its mouth, a fierce warrior's face, like Margarito's but not exactly, covered with tattoos and studs made out of sharks' teeth and human finger bones, and his mouth is open too, in a scream of pain or anger or both. The moment passes just as quickly as it came when Margarito shrugs and admits the point's moot because I—that is *we*, Maria and I—are vegetarians. *What?* he almost shouts in disbelief and not a little relief, and then they're off again on another bullshitting roller coaster, paleo diets, vegan, meatless, gluten-free … No wonder they're both absolutely famished by lunchtime, which is a much more slap dash affair, basically a communal platter of nachos that he and Margarito initially pick at civilly before giving in to a furious neck and neck race to the finish, washed down, of course, with ice-cold cervezas. So it's already well into the afternoon before they broach a practical plan of action for the day, which, of course, involves more beer—Margarito says he knows this little place.

No matter what direction you come from, north, east, south or west, across the sandy rocky desert on foot or along the lone highway via car, truck or bus, the village of Las Riquezas seems to haphazardly assemble itself out of a scattering of weathered wood and adobe shacks and corrals and then one-story stone and stucco houses gathered around a tiny plaza, more or less rectangular in shape and bordered by narrow beds of mostly dead roses, which is boxed in by a shabby-looking bakery, a miniscule mini-mart with a partially lit green neon cross in its dusty window that also identifies it as a pharmacy, and something that looks like a combination butcher shop and hardware store. In the center of the plaza a woman in a white cotton blouse and black wool skirt and not a drop of sweat visible on her porcelain painted face sits at a small desk inside a sunbaked and yellowed plexiglass kiosk, where, Margarito informs him (he asked), she operates a fax, copier, internet and telephone service for villagers at a few pesos per transaction. A narrow and deeply rutted cobblestone street leads out of the village and up a small, steep hill on top of which he can see the white bell tower of a church. At Margarito's direction, he parks the Coupe outside a rudimentary-looking cantina named *Mi Sedecita*—really, it's just some wooden posts, a thatched roof, a couple of tables, a makeshift bar and a widescreen TV. And look who's here.

7
Los guys

IT'S THE SNOWMAN'S OLD WORK CREW, *los guys*. They're all laughing and clapping him on the back, buying him beers and shots of tequila. The mood is merry, the conversation light (to the extent he understands what's being said). They talk about football (i.e., soccer)—there's a game on the TV right now, Nico is neurotically pacing back and forth in front of the screen, aiming his tomahawk nose, prognathic jaw and darting ferret eyes sideways at the camera while combing his shiny black pompadour into greater heights of perfection and puffing on a crooked, hand-rolled sheath of tobacco very likely of the *rustica* variety as he argues some arcane point of the world's most popular sport with Raf-I-el in a two-cycle chainsaw whine, *Nooo güeyyy* (sounds exactly like *No way*—Eduardo), that *eesn't* how it works! Raf-I-el, who makes a pretty convincing fakir with his short henna dreads, heavy applications of kohl around his eyes, and a gold ring in his right ear, has been *af*-fecting the lidsy-eyed enlightened look of a veteran yogi with a heck of a lot of ayahuasca, muscaria and peyote under his belt while attempting to create the *eef*-fect that he's levitating by sitting on a wooden stool with one foot tucked under his butt, un-yogically replies in an annoyed, nasal Hindi-Mexican accent (Brando in *Candy*?), *I know perfectly vell how it verks, cabrón. Goallll!* the announcer shouts and Raf-I-el, who can't keep up the pose, lets out a shriek and topples over *crash!* against Xuan, a possibly fatal mistake because, for those who haven't already met him, Xuan is one scary dude. Wearing a fashionably revealing faded denim vest open across his chest, he looks like a totemic giant, a Marvel Comics hero of *anti*-ness. He's about seven feet tall, four hundred pounds of solid muscle, biceps like bowling balls, armor plate abs, pecs like the stone slabs Moses carried down from Sinai. Plus those *scars*. His face looks like it's been raked by the claws of a lion or other very large cat, that or he's wearing grotesque war paint. Even that odd crooked grin, at first glance friendly, conveys a vague sense of menace, enhanced somehow by the blue sapphire gleaming in his left front tooth like a dwarf star in a Magellanic cloud galaxy. His massive right arm shoots out like a striking python and in the same motion he knocks Raf-I-el upright in his seat, grabs Nico by the scruff of his neck, picks him up as easily as if he were a papier-mâché piñata and deposits him in a plastic chair with an admonition as thunderous as a coal mine explosion *EH-STOP!* They talk about the weather (hot). They talk about fixing a tractor and planting corn. The brick shithouse-built Carroteeno's lumpish, sweet potato face brightens at the mention of anything agricultural (and if it looks like he's wearing an orange mop on his head, he is—kind of resembles Moe Howard, not sure if this is a personal tic or Boone's doing.) He's also been smiling at the Snowman fondly, yeah, sure, nostalgic for old times' sake, believe in that kind of fondness if you want, but he also looks suspiciously like a Papua New Guinea cannibal envisioning a hearty evening meal. On the same subject, they talk about eating—Bombástico, bouncing up and down in his seat like a tethered weather balloon, his face round as a pumpkin, his eyes wide with *oo! oo!* child-like excitement. Ees anybody else hongry because I could probably eet a donkey right now eef you cook heem up for me? (For those of you unfamiliar with Boone's *oeuvre*, broken English is meant to convey spoken Spanish for the benefit of the mostly monolingual American audience—Ed.) (*Most of these people are so goddamn stupid they wouldn't know Spanish from Mandarin*—Boone). They exchange anecdotes about the snow business and their old boss Gastreaux and—uh-oh, that's all the rope Boone needs to go off on another of his (in)famous tangents.

First there's a classic fade. We see the Snowman's eyes go glassy as he stares at the foam on his beer, followed by a total white-out on the screen. Dark hooded forms begin to emerge from this blizzard like a tribe of yeti. The camera moves in for a close-up and we see now that it's the Snowman and *los guys*, largely unrecognizable in their goggles, face mics, midnight blue parkas and knee-high, faux reindeer skin mukluks. The SnowBile looms behind them like a giant white jumping spider, its flashing lights sending a kaleidoscope of multi-colored patterns crashing against an unassuming two-story wood frame house, which, he notices immediately, has no snow on the roof, the yard's bare—clearly scofflaws. Oh yeah, it's that job they did out in Sleepy Hollow, one of the earliest subdivisions in the hill country west of Osberg, back when it was nothing but hardscrabble ranchers, cedar choppers and hunting camps. Irony of ironies, now the interlopers are the interloped. Huge McMansions and Post-Modern Industrials breathe down the necks of once quaint or bucolic or sentimental or nostalgic but now rather tacky Cape Cods and Victorians, Swiss Chalets and Georgian. The wind howls, snow blows around them. Bombástico, huge butterscotch pudding belly bursting out of Velcro restraints, Carroteeno, bulldozer-like in his movements and Xuan, cannon ball biceps bared (in violation of company regs he has torn the sleeves from his parka—too *pinche* tight, he says), completely unrealistic in this boreal clime, of course, but Boone's shooting for the effect and fuck veracity—think Rambo, the Rock, etc., begin unrolling hoses and offloading the bazookas. Meanwhile the Snowman, Raf-I-el and Nico have strapped on three-gallon backpacks, they're adjusting their torches, firing off pencil-thin streams of Icine that expand against the black night sky like feathery white boas. A smattering of chatter erupts over the headsets. Carroteeno, muttering malevolent-sounding incantations that seem to involve cumulonimbus clouds and potatoes., Nico and Raf-I-el, continuing what seems to be a long-running comedy routine. Hey, Raf! Sí, Nico? What do you call a Mexican who crosses the Frio Grande back into Mexico? I doan know, Nico, what do you call heem? *Loco!* To the Snowman's ears it rings like gallows humor, which is appropriate for tonight's job. It's been months since he's done a refusenik. He doesn't even know who the fuck these people are. All he *does* know is that Gastreaux has sent him out here to take care of this nasty business on Jippi Jaime's route, ostensibly because Gastreaux thinks the perennial flower child's too soft to handle the job himself, but more likely (and accurately), he surmises, it's because he's earned himself a place on Gastreaux's shit list again. Whatsa matter, *Snowman*, college boy like you can't figure out this simple equation: Just do what the fuck you're told, okay? And, yeah, sure, he can— *does*—rationalize what he's about to do. All these dumb motherfuckers were so hot to live out here in the tony phony burbs, now they gotta pay the piper because the law says they gotta have snow so *let it fucking snow*, right? He glances at his sleeve screen, who is it this time, the Clampetts? Yeah, he can see them in there, fucking losers are peering through the blinds, probably can't believe it themselves, *Look, Pa, what's that dadburn snow truck doin' out front?* Truth is—and here his mouth twists into a vindictive sneer—he takes special pleasure in meting out justice to deadbeats like this. He figures they've got plenty of dough, they're just being cheap, trying to get by with enough drift from their neighbors' yards to meet the minimum. Or maybe it's some Tea Potty types, rugged individualists who don't believe in contributing their fair share to the common weal. Scumbags'll change their tune pretty damn fast, won't they, *Snowman?* He's in full aggressor mode now and it's on with the show. *¡Vamos!* he says into his mike. Xuan, Carroteeno and Bombástico move up the walk with their bazookas, lobbing lumpy white turds that expand into snowflakes the size of bass drums and slam against the roof, the front door and windows. Glass shatters. A rusty hinge lets out a squeal of protest and a shutter crashes to the ground. An already sagging gutter collapses with a loud clatter. The roof has actually caved in near the chimney and only now does the Snowman notice the patches of missing shingles and bare wood showing through torn tarpaper. And, hmm, that's interesting—as the menthol smell of Icine spreads through the frigid air, and he, Raf and Nico turn a bay window completely opaque with layer upon layer of intricate lacework (snow queens, ice castles, reindeer), he also sees that some of the window panes are cracked, the glazing missing, the frame unpainted. He turns his attention to the car parked in the drive and, man, it's just an old junk heap, one of those early hybrid models that came off the assembly line with more built-in obsolescence than planned. And, boy howdy, those Culture Commission-approved yard ornaments (a white, wire-framed Holiday Tree and an inflatable Snow*person*) are shabby, saggy and falling apart. No wonder the neighbors are complaining. All this time the Clampett family has been cowering in the living room. Ma's having conniptions. How in tarnation did we get in this mess, Jed? We done everything expected of us. We always spent beyond our means. We accrued more than our share of debt. Big sis is crying, practically suicidal at the prospect of facing her peers' unmitigated cruelty in school tomorrow. The boys, near tears themselves, are staring in disbelief as Pa paces back and forth, smacking his fist into his hand with an angry tormented look on his face as if *he* might cry. Why doesn't he *do something*? It's pretty obvious these folks are just hanging on by a thread and the wolves are at the door. And what are they gonna do now, spend the night in this ruin? Go to a motel—can they even afford that? Get in the car and drive somewhere, if the car'll start, that huge battery dead as an asteroid sailing off into deep space? End up on the side of the road, the heater blowing increasingly colder air, the lights beginning to dim? And then what? Does the answer to that question have anything to do with the loaded pistol Pa placed under the front seat this evening? So now it's not just Boone who's almost at the end of his rope but this wretched Clampett family, and here *he* is, the Snowman, with the coup de grace, the big kibosh. But why? He's just a fucking peon himself, the bearer of bad tidings, why must he be the executioner too?

Goallll! And just like that he's back here and now in this beersy, blowsy, colloidal dimension infused with tequila warmth and sunshine, watching an unusually high scoring soccer match on the widescreen TV with *los guys.* By now everyone's trashed, they're laughing and shouting passionately about total nonsense, Margarito's repeatedly throwing his arm around the Snowman's shoulder and crying out, *¡Ay-ay-ayyyy, mi amigo, Snowman!*—really, it's just your average alcohol-fueled tribal guy thing, so why does he have the sense that beneath the surface of this convivial reunion he's sitting in on a war council? And is he mistaken, or hasn't he heard references to weapons, explosives? Oh wait, it's the TV. There's a trailer for the new Bobbie Rodríguez flick, the bad guys are packing enough heat to fight a war in the Middle East. Meanwhile, Helios' flaming chariot has rolled across the great blue vault of the sky and at this moment is disappearing below the darkening horizon in all its fiery red and orange Technicolor glory, shadows are spreading across the desert like unfolding bolts of indigo and lavender silk and the arrival of cooler night air is telling this merry band it's time to say *buenas noches.*

Glassy-eyed and slurring embarrassingly maudlin Y chromosome terms of endearment, *Eres mi cuate, carnal!* I really love you, man, Margarito and the Snowman drive without incident back to the house, where things briefly take another murky turn. Just before hitting the sack (apparently Maria hasn't arrived from the clinic yet), the Snowman and Margarito cross paths outside the bathroom. Their eyes meet and in Margarito's warm brown eyes the Snowman sees pain and yearning and something else that he can't define, and the thing is, he feels it too. Now what? Discover that all this time he's been closeted, even from himself? Is this leading to some kind of ménage a trois, the Snowman, Margarito and Maria in a besotted tangle of flesh and sex? Apparently not because, snapping out of his own trance, Margarito informs him that he has to return to his job tomorrow morning, he'll be gone a couple of weeks. But please, he adds with that famous bemused smile, stay here as our guest. I'm sure Maria will enjoy your company.

It's practically an invitation fraught with possibilities, which, who knows, may have come to fruition if he and Maria were ever in proximity to each other for any length of time. But that doesn't happen. Apparently there's an epidemic, sickness, disease, people dying everywhere. Early every morning Maria slings a backpack over her shoulder, climbs on her motorcycle and takes off for the clinic, only returning late at night—he hears the engine growling as she roars up out of the arroyo—too tired for anything but dinner, which he's happy to make, she, perhaps, less so to eat, and bed. (*'Night, Snowman. 'Night, Maria. 'Night, Johnboy.*)

8
Now What?

NOW WHAT? Margarito away, Maria gone all day, the Snowman's got no one to play with. *Read a book!* The house is packed with them, many in English, most technical manuals or texts on chemistry or botany or electronics, with the exception of a fairly extensive collection of political theory, including several classics on guerilla warfare: Sun Tzu's *On the Art of War*, one of the oldest books in the world on military strategy; T.E. Lawrence's *Seven Pillars of Wisdom*; Che Guevara and Mao Zedong—*Guerilla Warfare* and *On Guerilla Warfare*; *War of the Flea: The Classic Study of Guerilla Warfare* by Robert Taber; the universally acclaimed *On War*, by the Prussian general Carl von Clausewitz; the Swiss military theorist Hans von Dach's *Total Resistance*; the U.S. Army *Manual on Guerilla Warfare*; various texts on the Irish Republican Army, the Viet Cong and the Arab resistance in Algeria; Max Boot's *Invisible Armies: An Epic History of Guerilla Warfare from Ancient Times to the Present*—oh yes, and the mysterious Subcomandante Marcos' *La Historia de los Colores*. The titles are intriguing but the Snowman didn't come here to sit on his ass and read. A couple tokes of mota fogging his brain, he figures he'll go poke around in the garden, maybe pull some weeds, water some plants, but it turns out there's no need, Marg—Maria, he reminds himself—has set up various automatic systems, timers, drip irrigation, miniature insect-killing drones that mimic wasps and praying mantises in appearance and lethality, which is all very fascinating—for about two minutes. The small barn behind the garden initially seems promising but only occupies his interest long enough for him to perform a subconscious inventory: hay bales, old farm implements, rakes, shovels, picks, sledgehammer, iron digging bar, gas can, boxes and kegs of bolts and nails, as well as an array of ropes, cables, chains, come-alongs, pulleys and bungee cords—and then it's close the door on Old MacDonald. Or he watches telenovelas to improve his Spanish. There's one with this greenghost guy whose hapless clown character acts as a foil to the fearless and ruggedly handsome Mexican police detective (ironically, the Snowman mistakenly thinks the clown, with whom he kind of identifies, is the real hero).

Sometimes he drives into Chopahuac to hang out at the cyber café where, let's face it, there's a constant parade of pretty fetching eye candy from all around the globe for a lone wolf to slaver over *ow-oooo*, because despite his lone wolfishness he does need a minimal degree of human contact (sort of like Vitamin D), although he's also not the kind of fella who'll just sidle up to a gal and say howdy, Ma'am, they call me Tex, which, all in all, means his prospects for female companionship are practically nil. Or else he stops by the Hotel Cauliflornia, where Peter Lorre always manages to creep him out (ohhh, Missster Snowman, I'm so happy to see you again, *hnn hnn hnn*), to visit Professor Simianovsky, who seems increasingly preoccupied with his research, frequently muttering about a big bird, which may be a reference to a popular children's TV program, but more likely alludes to the putative giant *ignisraptor* the professor has become obsessed with. So the Snowman is not totally surprised one day when Professor Simianovsky says, What if I told you these creatures still exist? Oh, I know it sounds ridiculous, but I can assure you the locals believe it. I may have even found proof—unusual bird droppings. Very *large*. DNA testing under way as we speak. All very hush hush, of course. Don't want to crash and burn thanks to a careless mistake. You may have heard of the Hieroglyph

affair up in Texas? Bit of a scandal, what? Professor
Simianovsky aims a probing Sasquatchian eye at the Snowman
that does indeed rattle his cage, especially the allusion (or so he
perceives it to be) to some untoward sexual conduct he had
never seriously, until this moment, that is, suspected between
Judith and the great Dialectic Orthologist who, it's also true, in
the course of Judith's studies, went from the aloof *Professor
Hieroglyph* to the familiar *Hugh*. Which, while causing him a
deep although not quite mortal stab of pain, also arouses in him
again the unsettling suspicion that, albeit insignificant, no more
than a fly in the borscht (*waiter!*), he's playing a part in some
great plot or conspiracy (eerie conspiracy theory music plays in
the background ... there's no consensus on what, exactly, this
sounds like). The possibility that Professor Simianovsky really
has gone bonkers also enters his mind, except that, swearing
him to secrecy, the professor, who, if his many years in the
classroom have taught him one thing—you don't make
assertions without facts to support them—actually shows him
some mighty big bones, kind of like an enormous (think one-car
garage) Thanksgiving turkey picked clean of flesh, and not only
do these bones look real, they look pretty damn fresh. Which
may also explain why the Snowman allows Professor
Simianovsky to talk him into another trip back to the ruins to
look at some *objects of interest*.

   During the drive, Professor Simianovsky waves his arm at
an odd pair of mountains in the distance. Volcanoes, he says,
the way he might refer to a telephone pole or a fire hydrant.
Dormant, he adds in a slightly more ominous tone that suggests
they may not remain so. The Zoltec call them *hollow furnaces*,
he says. A faint bell chimes in the Snowman's memory and on
the screen we see Judith at the kitchen table in faded denim
coveralls over a chocolate brown and bubble gum pink
horizontally striped wool knit sweater, cobalt blue eyes
androidally bright, hair a black storm cloud bouncing around
her shoulders, body shedding waves of manic energy, arms
flailing Shiva-like as she cranks out white plastic cones of

varying dimensions with a 3-D printer. Professor Simianovsky digs a hairy finger in his ear as if he's trying to extract an annoying plug of cerumen or an inchoate thought. According to Zoltec mythology, volcanoes serve as portals for the fire gods at the center of the earth. On auspicious occasions they belch out molten gold—magma, actually—which the Zoltec believe is the material form of sunlight. Professor Simianovsky's beard winks mischievously. Remember? *We are stardust, we are golden?* To the professor's disappointment, the Snowman only wrinkles his brow like *maybe?*

The trek through the jungle seems much shorter and less treacherous than the Snowman remembers, but Professor Simianovsky is soon leading him on hands and knees over piles of rubble and under dense tropical foliage. The intrepid scholar pushes aside a heavy vine, pulls a flashlight out of his pocket and hops down a dark hole. The Snowman rolls his eyes like here we go again, carefully lowers himself through the opening and begins to follow the professor along a slippery, shoulder-width passage. The walls drip with condensation. The air stinks like stale urine—a combination of the damp calcareous limestone and bat guano, Professor Simianovsky explains, shining his flashlight into the darkness ahead. That's when the Snowman sees it—a pair of eyes, bright green, wide apart, the owner something large, feline. *It's a jaguar.* It is a jaguar, but not a living, breathing two hundred-fifty pound cat, all claws, fangs and muscles coiled to spring and turn him into mincemeat, but a jaguar carved out of stone, its orange and black paw print coat painted, its bright green eyes pieces of jade. It's a spirit animal protector! the professor says jovially, clearly pleased to see the Snowman has received the thrill intended. They now enter a chamber where the professor's flashlight illuminates a large grayish-white stone sarcophagus. If you would be so kind? Professor Simianovsky hands him the flashlight and carefully slides aside the heavy stone lid, revealing another sarcophagus inside painted in intricate patterns of red, blue, green and black and ornamented with gold and jade, sea shells and pieces of obsidian. It's shaped like a man but so highly stylized that it looks to the Snowman more like an extraterrestrial than a human being, and wouldn't you know it, even as he thinks this the room is flooded with a blinding light and that icy, centipedal tingler thing is climbing up his spine again. Are the Martians landing at long last? Has Professor Simianovsky discovered evidence that the pre-Columbians knew about electricity? Of course not, this is Boone Weller, not Steven Spielberg. Any fool should be able to deduce that, thanks to an incredibly complex configuration of conduits and channels conceived of by some Mayan mad scientist-cum-architectural genius, at this precise time of day on this precise day of the month a beam of sunlight illuminates the room. And just like that he's staring drop-jawed at an extremely detailed mural covering an entire wall, the central feature of which is a zoomorphic monster, dragon-like in shape, a fiery red and orange mane of scales and feathers, vertical green serpent eyes, huge fangs, a fierce warrior's face emerging from its mouth, more or less, in other words, like the stoned vision he had of Margarito. Lord Kukulkan, the professor says with genuine reverence—the *plumed serpent*. Now this is someone you'd really like to have as a spirit animal protector. Miraculous that vandals have overlooked this vault. The Snowman's been nodding his head yes, uh-huh, that makes sense, but he's not really listening anymore. His attention has shifted to the densely packed hieroglyphs surrounding this winged serpent and again that weird radio frequency thing is happening in his brain except this time he doesn't see words or Martian symbols but images, giant flying dragons spitting fire, volcanoes exploding like roman candles, a ragtag army of peasants carrying ancient weapons, halberds, matchlocks, blunderbusses, and in the middle of this chaos there's this fucking Chaac Mool sitting on top of a pyramid and it's leering at him like a hungry gargoyle as it beckons him to come closer. *Bink!* He hears a distinct sound, like a single drop of blood striking a stone slab, and the light disappears from the room. Heebie jeebies playing his spine like a speed freak on an upright bass, he sweeps the flashlight around the room and sees the professor, orange fur bristling, eyes wide behind his steel-rimmed glasses, staring at him with a startled expression. Has he been talking out loud again? Sending telepathic messages? Whatever the medium, Professor Simianovsky has clearly picked up on his odd talent for intercepting random data from the ambient airwaves. Imagine what you could do with this stuff if you understood Mayan, the professor says, screeching the lid of the sarcophagus back in place. Full immersion—probably wouldn't take you half a year to attain fluency. I might even be able to obtain some funding. Hmm, is this a new career opportunity? The *might* and *some* suggest probably not. In fact, this will be the Snowman's last excursion with Professor Simianovsky. The good prof's given all he's got to the putative plot.

9

In the Desert

BOONE SEEMS MOMENTARILY AT A LOSS. Now that he's got the
Snowman here he's not sure what to do with him. On the one
hand, this is exactly what the Snowman has yearned for—
nothing. Nothing to do but think, ponder, figure out what's
going on in his life, in his head, in the universe. Which would
also be the perfect opportunity for Boone to insert several hours
of footage of the Snowman in a loin cloth, beard grown long,
seated more or less in lotus pose beneath the great spreading
limbs of a Bodhi tree (appropriately *Ficus religiosa* or sacred
fig—fact check girl), his thoughts, shed of material concerns,
doggedly climbing up the rickety wooden ladder to
enlightenment, but even the great B-movie master knows that
navel-gazing Warholian fare isn't going to keep this audience in
their seats any longer than it takes them to eat a barrel of
buttered popcorn, a plate of cheese nachos, a tub of buffalo
wings, a family-size bag of chicharrones, a carton of cookie
dough, a couple of king-size granola crunch bars, half a gallon
of soda, a quart of chocolate chip ice—*okay, okay*, so he might
get away with it.

Early each morning the Snowman sets out into the desert,
his winter pale face shaded beneath a broad-brimmed straw hat,
his arctic blue eyes protected behind dark glasses, his oft frost-
bitten feet still adjusting to a pair of leather boots he took in
trade for his buckle-up the front, black vulcanized rubber
galoshes—not really practical in an arid clime and all that

jingling a sacrilege in this biblically barren silence. On his back he carries a day pack containing bottled water, food, and a couple spliffs of Maria's ganja. Without map, compass or any idea in the world where he's going, he trudges across miles of sandy, rocky, simmering desert, his mind simultaneously emptying itself of snow country clutter (retinal flashes of stark winterscapes in chiaroscuric black and white, streets, parks, highways, neighborhoods, houses, office buildings buried under a white blanket of snow, blinding white snowsqualls blowing out of a black night sky, the SnowBile's lights crashing kaleidoscopically against a ghostly Victorian mansion—maybe it's the light or the camera angle but it even looks like he's leaving behind wedges of melting snow beneath his boots as we return now to the present) and reservoir-like filling up with this vast desert nothingness and the various life forms that inhabit this nothing. He discovers insects and reptilian creatures that bury themselves in the sand to escape the desiccating heat, or drink up the shade and nominally cooler temperatures in rocky crevices. He learns to identify the pellet-like and lumpish spoor of jackrabbits and coyotes, the thin, winding line drawings left by rattlesnakes, the tic tac toe bird tracks made by road runners and scissor-tailed flycatchers. He is stunned by the large, waxy pink and yellow, pollen-laden flowers affixed like children's paper cutouts to otherwise spiny, austere cactus. He inhales the smells of creosote bush and sage smoldering in the hot dry air like holy incense. *Shanti.*

> *Been through the desert on a horse with no name,*
> *felt good to get out of the snow.*
> *In the desert you can remember your name*
> *cause there ain't no one for to give you no woe.*

One day, already miles into his trek, he discovers he's forgotten his water bottle. His mouth dry, his thirst quickly grown, stoned on a bud with borderline hallucinogenic properties Maria's been experimenting with, he starts to obsess.

I'm not going to die, am I? Oh Christ, am I going to die? Tongue swollen, vital organs shutting down, crawling on his hands and knees, buzzards circling overhead, weeks later a peasant searching for manna finds a pile of bones bleaching in the desert? Trying to tamp down his panic, he begins to retrace his steps, but he doesn't remember any of this. Soon he's totally lost. Disconnected shots show him wandering aimlessly through a maze of geological formations. Huge chunky buttes and towering finger-like pinnacles of pink and yellow sandstone rise hundreds of feet into the pale blue sky. Undulating purple and orange canyons cut through tabletop mesas. (If you're thinking this looks more like Utah or Arizona, you're right. Old-timers will guess correctly that Boone has stolen most of the scenery from classic Looney Tunes—Ed (Doctor Farrell to *you*).) Oddly, and this is almost certainly the pot, and maybe the angle of the sun, and the barometric pressure, and a bunch of other natural phenomena, but he has the sensation he's walking under water. Why didn't he notice before? He's standing on the ocean floor. All around him he sees seashells, red and orange starfish, purple hydras, waving blue, green and yellow fan coral. He lifts his head and sees the golden sunlight filtering down through the sparkling turquoise water. Only now does it occur to him that he's breathing water just as easily as if it were air. And just like that the salty sea shrinks back into the spikey blue-green cacti erupting out of the desert. Blinding sunlight blasts off millions and billions of grains of sand and—*what the fuck?* The sand is coming alive. Hordes of centipedes, scorpions and tarantulas scuttle and crawl around him. He's dancing on tiptoe trying not to step on the damn things, they're crunching and popping under his boots like bubble wrap. Oh shit, you *dumbass*. Now he gets it. They aren't poisonous *arthro*pods. They're dried *rattle*pod seeds that have fallen from the tree and burst open.

By now his thirst is paramount. He's convinced he's going to die if he doesn't find water soon. He spots a cactus that almost seems to be standing sentinel on a rocky hillside and a tiny, moisture-laden thought cloud appears on the horizon.

Yeah, but this isn't one of those bulging barrel cactuses you just lop the top off and it's brimming with water (if, that is, you're Porky Pig or Donald Duck in one of the aforementioned cartoons). This is a prickly pear cactus with hard green pads that look like they'd be about as juicy as squeezing blood from the proverbial turnip. But it's also covered with purple hand grenade-like fruits he's heard Maria refer to as *tunas*. He picks one and bites into it—the skin is thick, slightly bitter, but inside it's sweet, the texture something like cantaloupe. It's also dry and packed with seeds and it does nothing to quench his thirst. He also notices now that his hands are stained purple as if he had washed them in PVC primer. Worse, these small, hair-like *glochid* spines he initially dismissed as a minor annoyance—before he realized he had a bunch stuck in his lips and tongue. Now he can't stop worrying at them, until something else gives him cause for worry. He has stumbled into what appears to be a deserted village, everything scorched, in ruins, cornfields reduced to blackened stubble, a nearby stream dried up into poisonous-looking neon green and orange pools. What happened here? Some sort of catastrophe? Natural disaster? He remembers the epidemic Maria mentioned and shudders as a sudden chill wind whistles across the desert like the scream of a dying man *waaa-wah*. A church bell clangs somewhere in the distance, bringing tidings of love and death in a clunky utilitarian voice. A terrapin wanders across his path, or more accurately, he wanders across its. The yellow and black patterns on its shell look like Mayan hieroglyphs, which reminds him first of Professor Simianovsky (okay, he's not entirely out of the picture), and then of the professor's fire-breathing, flying dinosaurs. And wouldn't you know it, either it's coincidence or Boone again (same thing?), but, stopping to rest in the skeletal shade of a rattlepod tree, he hears a loud squawk and a shadow falls over him. He looks up to see an enormous web-winged creature with a huge hammer head descending upon him in a flurry of brightly colored feathers and a thunderous wind, *Thwop! Thwop! Thwop!* Wait—it's an optical illusion, the lingering psychedelic effects of a very potent *Cannabis indica*, exacerbated by the blinding sunlight and possibly some measurable telluric discharge, because it's neither prehistoric flying raptor nor even that old feathered scavenger Death decked out in carnival finery, but a helicopter's carbon-steel oars whacking their way through the hot, shimmering atmosphere (a subliminal blur of images flashes across the screen, bullet-riddled mud-brick compounds, bodies scattered on the ground, women, children, farm animals—is it a scene from the war in, um, Overthereistan?) The Snowman's instincts tell him caution is advised and he immediately drops to his knees. Through the branches of the rattlepod tree he watches the chopper land in an arroyo next to a convoy of military vehicles. A Mexican Brigadier General and a U.S. Marine Colonel with a ton of fruit salad on his chest climb out of the helicopter (the Snowman once studied military ranks, insignias and commendations for a class assignment on constructed symbolism and the hierarchy of authority). Immediately afterward a convoy of black SUVs roars up. A tall, elegant man, maybe sixty, black hair silver at the temples, perfectly tailored charcoal gray suit, gets out of the lead SUV at the same time several heavily armed men jump out of the other SUVs and swarm around him, slamming in clips and bolts, cocking hammers, tightening slings and flipping off safeties. Surrounded by this phalanx, the man strides forward to shake hands with the military officers and together they climb into a desert-camouflaged MRAP (Mine-Resistant Ambush Protected vehicle—Major John Brawn, ret. U.S. Army, 1st Cav, on the set as an advisor). The Snowman has no idea who these people are or what they're doing here but he's fairly certain if they discover him he's in seriously deep shit.

1800 hours: the Pentagon, a war room, voices speaking. Yes, sir, we have made direct contact with the party of interest. Yes sir, we are discussing terms.

10
Not the Reaction He Expected

WHEN THE SNOWMAN INFORMS MARIA of what he has seen over dinner (steamed tofu and rapini, neither of them in the mood to undertake any major culinary feat—oh, and he obviously found his way out of the desert), she releases a stream of obscenities that rattles plates and cups and nearly tears the curtains from the window sash, takes a deep breath, makes a half-hearted apology (work at the clinic's stressing her out, all these people fucking *dying*), and launches into an only slightly less impassioned tirade. When the mines came they were supposed to bring good jobs and wages. They paid us pennies for dangerous, backbreaking labor. We were supposed to have homes, schools, hospitals. We had adobe and tin shacks, the closest school was twenty miles away, the nearest hospital, fifty. Much of this land was once covered by lush jungle. The mines took out of the ground all the gold and silver, all the minerals and ores and left nothing behind but ruined dirt inhabited by evil creatures. I don't mean rattlesnakes and scorpions. I mean drug cartels, corrupt police, military, politicians. Tell me, *Snowman*, what do you think your Marine colonel was doing in the Mexican desert? Thanks to a graduate seminar in forensic orthology and rhetoric, he recognizes a loaded question when he smells one. Um, I dunno, somethin' to do with the war on drugs, I guess? (For reasons inexplicable even to himself, he's also fallen back into the Big Tex persona.) Maria sets a bottle of *El Residente* on the table, fills two glasses, knocks back hers like a sailor on her first shore leave in six months and pours another. Yes, of course, the war on drugs. How right you are, Snowman. And who is it that always gets hurt most in a war? Right again (he hasn't said anything)—*civilians*. The desert is full of graves, Snowman. It's the only thing this cursed soil is good for. Who knows, maybe if enough people die the earth will become rich again and the jungle will return. After all, it worked for your *Garden* State.

Uh-oh, is this Boone up on his soapbox again? Or is Maria's anger her own? The answer might be in what she says next. Margarito hated this poor suffering land, he raged against it, You bloody whore! You've sold yourself a thousand times! He swore he wouldn't spend his life behind a plow, wouldn't let himself be beaten down. For that reason he crossed the border into *el Norte*, for that reason they both endured the interminable separations. Not like the old days, of course, when she might not have heard from him again for weeks or months or even years. They texted regularly, sometimes skyped.

The camera tightens in on Maria's eyes, which have become glassy and distant, to let us know she's drifting into a deeper memory (also that she's getting pretty toasted). During her summers off from the university she went home to help her aunt and uncle on their farm. One night she woke with a sense of expectation. Outside her window thunder and lightning ruptured the black belly of the sky, towering cumulonimbus clouds glowed purple, ivory and rose like huge luminous clusters of grapes and the rain crashed against the house like giant wings. By morning the rain had ceased, the sun shone, the air smelled fresh and clean, and still that sense of expectation remained. She put on an old red dress, Margarito's favorite, and went out to the barn to milk the cow. She had just sat down on the stool and leaned her head against Bessie la Vaca's flank and was reaching under her belly for the teats when she glanced up and through the open barn door she saw Margarito stumbling toward her across the yard, dirty, disheveled, dead drunk or exhausted or both. She wanted to run to him, cry out, Margarito, my darling, you've come home! But she only waited, watched him come, taking in his leaner body, harder jaw, bushy black mustache, no longer a boy but a man, his glassy, bloodshot eyes filled with orange and red bands of sunrise, with neon nights of bars, clubs, cantinas in the arms of who knows how many women, and smiling that sheepish smile as if acknowledging as much. She could have spat in his face, sent him to sleep with the dogs, instead she flung her arms around him, laughing and crying. *Maria*, he whispered in her ear, his hot breath reeking of everything she suspected, and again, *Maria*, and even then, while he held her close and her tears streaked his dusty shirt, in turn soiling her dress, she knew that in his mind he was already going back.

Maria stops talking. She seems to have completely forgotten the Snowman's presence. She also seems to have forgotten the role she's playing. The clichéd narrative, the maudlin sentiments are completely out of character. It's like she's reading from a romance novel. Maybe it's Boone's new scriptwriter, the recent Smith graduate. Her (Maria's, not the scriptwriter's—she hasn't a clue) embarrassment is palpable. She apologizes profusely. Please, forgive me. I'm so sorry, those were … difficult times. He also notices that she has been speaking in the past tense with a finality that seems to preclude any present. And by the way, it's been what—two, three weeks? Wasn't Margarito supposed to have returned by now? He also has this nagging suspicion. Why is there so little of a masculine presence here? Where are the smells of sweat, cologne, the scuffed boots, worn work clothes, the tools, gadgets, *man* things? What if Margarito and Maria have split up and Margarito's actually living with another woman in another town and all this is a ruse, a charade they're putting on for his sake? Yeah, that'd make perfect sense, *Snowman*. Or what if there's something really crazy like—he vaguely remembers a past occasion, Nico, a couple beers under his belt, hinting at some *outré* escapade Margarito was involved in. What? You mean he's gay? He likes to wear women's lingerie? He has an armpit fetish? At which *los guys* broke into uproarious laughter, Oh no no no, *Snowman!* Actually eet ees a very sad story, Nico, lugubrious as a clown, started to say. Before he could elaborate, Xuan placed a hand as big as a catcher's mitt on his shoulder, the dwarf blue star flashed in a savage grin, and in a tone suggesting if not threatening mayhem, he said, We don't want to tell the Snowman something that might not be true, do we, Nico?

The next day, taking a break from his nature hikes, the Snowman makes a solo visit to *Mi Sedecita* to hang out in the cool shadows over a quiet bottle of Sol and ponder his situation. He's just sitting down at his table when two rough-looking dudes come in and sit at the bar, one short, stocky, studs in his eyebrow, barbed wire tattoo around his neck, the other tall, lean, a patch over one eye, which partially hides a jagged scar that runs from his forehead to his jaw. No doubt about it. He's seen these guys before and he's pretty sure it's no coincidence they're sitting here now, which is confirmed when the tall dude with the eye patch comes over to his table, leans down and says in English with a Tex-Mex accent and breath smelling of decay, How's it goeen', Tex? It's goin' fine, he replies (probably not wisely) in his Big Tex voice, but the name ain't Tex. Yeah? That ain't what your license plate says. So what brings you down here, Tex? You been doeen some sightseeing in the desert? That ain't safe, Tex. You might run into something bad for your health. I'll keep that in mind, he says, trying to keep up the Big Tex pose, but under the table his knees are knocking like blocks of wood.

11
Climbing the Mountain

THIS LAST ENCOUNTER he does not relate to Maria. Perhaps sensing the need for a safer diversion, however, she announces a visit to her grandfather, who lives in a kind of Spanish Colonial House of Ushers, an aging, dilapidated hacienda, terra cotta tiles missing from the roof, crumbling stone pillars, sagging stucco balconies and cracked arches, rusty wrought iron gates and railings, a walled courtyard overgrown with weeds. The heavy wooden door is opened by a little old man with snowy white hair and brows and salt and pepper beard stubble. His small black eyes gleam like raisins. Ah, Maria! So good to see you! *¡Abuelo!* She throws her arms around him. Despite this heartfelt greeting, the Snowman is immediately suspicious. Doesn't this Grandpa look a heck of a lot like the old man in Chopahuac who gave him directions? And what about the old man in the cantina yesterday? Grandpa, who obviously knows the Snowman's on to him, pointedly acts as if they've never met. What's this diabolical greenghost doing in my house? he snarls, in Spanish, of course, which the Snowman mostly gets, certainly the tone. Laughing, waving her hands for a time-out, Maria introduces him as a "friend." This in itself probably wouldn't mean diddly squat to the old fart, but when the Snowman brings out a bottle of *El Residente* and a pack of aromatic *Jaguar Ten* cigars, bought at Maria's instigation, the old man's eyes brighten like black olives and his stubbly jaw stretches into a wide grin. Ha! I knew it! You are not a greenghost after all, and so what if you are? I'll drink brandy with the devil and probably already have.

On cue (at least in the script) the camera shifts to a rear entrance and a very fat, florid-faced woman in an enormous pink huipil embroidered with red and green parrots and pink hibiscus flowers storms in shouting like a fishmonger, What in the name of Santa Agave is this *maldito* greenghost doing here?! Maria, again acting as referee, introduces the Snowman to Doña Oleinfanta, Grandpa's housekeeper, who apparently shares her employer's low opinion of greenghosts, even though Grandpa's opinion of her apparently isn't much higher. Hey! he yells. Get back in your cave you chupacabra! We don't need you interfering in men's work! Yes? And what kind of work is that? Drinking alcohol and smoking strong tobacco, and tomorrow morning you'll cry, oh Doña Oleinfanta, *boo hoo*, my head hurts too much, please make a cup of chamomile for *mi estómago*. Don't think God doesn't see! And with this final word (although not the omega), Doña Oleinfanta rotates her imposing bulk like a tracked earthmoving machine and storms out again.

Grandpa looks sheepish for about two seconds, then breaks into a fiendish grin and, rubbing his hands together in anticipation of the libations ahead, he begins to hop around like a hobgoblin doing the hornpipe, in the process very closely resembling Professor Simianovsky's God L, as Boone reminds us with the insertion of a twenty-fifth frame subliminal image of the Maya deity. Brandy quickly poured, cigars trimmed and lit, Grandpa and the Snowman initiate a conversation (Maria acting as translator when necessary but mostly staying out of the way) that progresses from the mundane, this brandy's not too shabby, the cigars are okay too, to the discursive, tell me, *señor Snowman*, is it true that soon all the ice in the world will melt and the great lizards return? Well, heck, I ain't exactly up to speed on climatology. And what is the difference between artificial intelligence and real intelligence if they both say the same thing, *señor Snowman?* Um, I ain't so sure about that one either. To the two of them slurring utter nonsense, *wazh you think bout todayzh muzhik? Crazhy, huh?* At which point Grandpa has peed in his pants and a yellow puddle is spreading outward from one shoe. Suddenly he fixes the Snowman with a hard—indeed, a quite intimidating stare, his small black eyes gleam like burning chips of coal, and he says cryptically and, yes, a little bit disconcertingly, You're the true one, aren't you? Hmm, perhaps Grandpa does have a loose transistor or two. Maria, who has more or less kept pace with the brandy but skipped the cigars, lifts her eyebrows at the Snowman like, *Don't ashk me.*

Despite or because of Grandpa's mental lapses, he and the Snowman soon establish a rapport, which serves a dual purpose for Maria. The Snowman keeps the old man company and himself out of trouble. Each time they meet, Grandpa greets him with another riddle or aphorism. They say our sun is just another star in the sky, but for whom is it a star, *señor Snowman?* Everyone wants to know if there is life after death. The answer is yes—for the living. One day Grandpa notices him staring at the yellow mountain rising above the desert, its rugged slopes and jagged peak ubiquitously conspicuous from every point on the compass, and asks *¿Qué está pensando, señor Snowman?* (What are you thinking, Mister Snowman?— Eduardo.) He confesses he's felt an urge to climb this mountain since he first arrived in Las Riquezas. Grandpa snorts, Then why haven't you? Do you think somebody owns that mountain? Or did someone tell you it is sacred—Grandpa cackles like a grackle—a *holy mountain?* The only person who owns that mountain is God and God doesn't care if foolish mortals wish to climb it. If you like, I will take you up there tomorrow morning. We will have to start early so it's best if you stay here tonight, but we mustn't say anything to Doña Oleinfanta about our plan. She'll squawk like an old hen and spill the frijoles to Maria. We'll just say we're going bird watching. Now where is that woman? I'm hungry.

Here Boone introduces another quirky element. While eating the dinner Doña Oleinfanta has grudgingly prepared for him (it's still pretty darn good, a thick spicy soup, tomatoes, potatoes, squash, beans, corn, carrots, peppers, a half round of a salty, pungent white cheese, and steaming hot fresh corn tortillas), the Snowman notices this dried-up little old stick of a woman with silver braids and tiny black currant eyes in a little brown walnut face, dressed entirely in black and seated in a little baby bear wooden chair in the corner, methodically masticating some kind of pabulum between her toothless gums. Is this yet another incarnation of Boone's perennial *little old lady in black* character Doña Hermosa? the observant cineaste might ask (same guy as above). But no, this is Doña *Añeja*, a character from a much more distant chapter in history. Her story? She served as head housekeeper of this once prosperous hacienda when Grandpa was but a child himself. Having outlived her usefulness, she has gradually transubstantiated into the generally dissipated ambience. She fades in and out of the picture like an old black and white television set with bad reception, which can be quite disconcerting for the rare guests. Whether she will appear in later scenes, perhaps even in an important role, remains to be seen.

After dinner Grandpa insists they watch his favorite TV show, *Chupa Mucha*, starring this purported sex bomb with dyed blond hair, silicone tits and collagen lips who looks kind of like a guy in drag. Of course it *is* a guy in drag but Grandpa doesn't know that and even the Snowman's not sure at first. Following an overabundance of bawdy (and bad) humor (male and female groping and cucumber jokes), at which Grandpa cackles nonstop, and an equal abundance of *El Residente*, which seems to aid the Snowman's Spanish comprehension (sorta), Doña Oleinfanta shows him to his room, lighting the way with a kerosene lantern that illuminates rusty suits of armor and hideously baroque oil paintings in gilt frames while casting spooky shadows on the creaking wooden floorboards and cracked plaster ceiling. *Buenas noches, señor*, Doña Oleinfanta says in a spiteful and even threatening tone and leaves him alone. In the darkness he can make out the luminous white mass of a four-poster bed shrouded in mosquito netting. He undresses and gets under the covers, which are dusty and feel like they're about to crumble at his touch. He has the disturbing sense that he's lying in one of those old horse-drawn hearses ornamented with crepe, curtains and feathery plumes. The air is stuffy and hot and he considers getting up to open a window but just when he tells himself, okay, *Snowman*, let's get up, he slips into a restless sleep. He hears voices whispering, steel clanging against steel, screams. Then something large, possibly feline, prowling in the hallway outside his door. Hovering on the borderlands of consciousness, he remembers the animal spirit companions mentioned by Professor Simianovsky (who, for about a nanosecond, appears in this dreamscape in a silly orange orangutan costume—or no, he *is* an orangutan, and he's addressing a parliament of bonobos, chimps, orangutans, capuchins, great apes, etc.). But whose companion is *this* thing, Grandpa's? *His?* And what if it's not companion but nemesis, and hungry to boot? Then Grandpa, who has transformed into some sort of priest in white robes, is leading him up a steep mountain. He keeps slipping and stumbling over rocks and loose gravel. Then he's lying on his back. The blinding sun burns his eyes but he can't move, he's paralyzed, he must have fallen in the climb, injured his spine. But wait, he realizes that his hands and feet are bound and now Margarito is standing over him in a feathered headdress, gold ear flares and a knee-length white loincloth. The dream shifts again and it's no longer Margarito but Maria in a much more revealing loincloth and a diaphanous band of cotton across her breasts. (Neither of which any Maya woman would have worn. No surprise, Boone, who so far has managed to escape his own **#MeToo** moment, is clearly catering to his mostly male fan base who he knows don't want to see Maria in a matronly huipil—Eduard*ito*). Even more disconcerting, she's holding a black obsidian blade over her head. Then someone is screaming. It's him. He's screaming.

He jolts awake in total darkness. (The audience hears an old man's quavering voice utter *cauchemar!* There's no indication the Snowman heard this.) Extracting himself from this four poster palanquin of dream and nightmare, he hurriedly dresses and heads downstairs to the kitchen where Grandpa and Doña Oleinfanta are filling backpacks with provisions. And some tortillas and cheese and wine. No wine! Yes, wine! And some fruit, and—did you put in the wine? Two bottles. No, one. Two bottles! Ah! You're up, señor Snowman! Doña Oleinfanta! Hurry! Make breakfast for our Snowman friend! Doña Oleinfanta gives their Snowman friend a dirty look, mutters something that sounds like *huata litl xitl!* and turns to the stove.

The sky is still dressed in its royal purple nightclothes trimmed with faint rose and lavender hues when they start out. Grandpa moves surprisingly fast, his rubber-soled huaraches barely make a sound on the hard ground, his white cotton trousers whisper through creosote and jaguar bush as he casually brushes aside the thorny branches with a polished wooden staff. The terrain climbs quickly. Roosters crow, dogs bark, lanterns glow in the scattering of houses below them. The sun appears on the horizon like a crimson-skinned hot air balloon and quickly fades from blood red to egg yolk yellow. Golden sunlight illuminates cactus, sand crystals, rocky outcroppings. Huge slabs of stone covered with pink, orange and green lichen litter the mountainside. Here and there boulders balance on hourglass-shaped columns of conglomerate rock like lapidarian polyps. Grandpa and the Snowman have been climbing about an hour when Grandpa, who has scampered ahead, calls down Helloooo! but it's not the Snowman he's calling to, but someone much farther below, a man walking behind a steel share plow pulled by a large black ox in a swirling yellow dust devil. Helloooo! the man waves back and at that moment the Snowman sees the bird, impossibly huge, wings stretched out half a mile in each direction, pinions, tail feathers, talons and beak carved into the ochre desert by years and years of the plowman's toil according to some impossible geometry planted like a seed in his brain at birth and even before, in the moment of his conception when that distant star sent its light into his mother's eyes and into her womb bearing the message of a giant bird that had come before and was prophesied to come again. What happens then? the Snowman asks when Grandpa, who has come back down the trail, finishes this rather remarkable extemporanea. (By the way, either the fact check girl's been sleeping on the job (*What?!*) or else she hasn't seen this stuff yet (*and whose damn fault is that?*)—everybody knows Boone's referring to the geoglyph in Peru, right?) Grandpa shrugs. Who knows? Maybe he'll bring back all the things that were taken from us when the false sun came. Maybe he'll shit on our heads and laugh like everyone else, and Grandpa lets out a loud and, yes, slightly deranged cackle *hack hack hack. Uh-oh.* So tell me again, *Snowman*, why are we following this old loony up the side of a mountain? What if he gets hurt, has a heart attack? What if *you* have a heart attack? It seems Grandpa has read his thoughts. Climbing this mountain won't kill me, *señor Snowman*. God will kill me. Besides, what good is life without living? And he hurries off as if he were late for a very important date.

By now the sun has arrived in all its blazing heat and glory. Sweat rolls down the Snowman's forehead and chest, his pack chafes against his back, the straps dig into his shoulders, he's panting and gasping for breath, his throat's dry as cotton and his canteen's empty. He's also lost sight of Grandpa. The sound of trickling water enters his ears like the music of some primitive instrument. A cleft appears in the rugged mountainside and there's the old shithead sitting smug as a slug on a flat stone next to a small clear pool fed by a narrow stream. Grandpa's stubbly jaw stretches into a beatific lunatic grin. We are fortunate, *señor Snowman*. The great mother has allowed us to enter her bosom, she has offered us shade and cool water to drink. We will eat our lunch and rest. The simple fare of corn tortillas, cheese and fruit (sliced pineapple and papaya) is delicious, and even better washed down with strong red wine chased with this cold, clear and strangely invigorating spring water. The Snowman's trust in Grandpa's judgment somewhat restored, his tongue loosened by the wine, he blurts out one of those profound big picture questions he's always wanted to ask some wise elder. Tell me, Grandfather, why are we here? What is our purpose in life? If he was expecting Don Juanish words of wisdom that's not what he gets. How the hell do I know, growls the grumpy gramps. I know life is hard, I know we will all die, I know you ask too many stupid questions. Grandpa gives him a fierce aquiline stare, then rolls his small black currant eyes as if to say, oh, all right, I'll play your game. Tell me, *señor Snowman*, why don't you want to be what you are, young and alive? I see it in your eyes—afraid of dying and rushing to be old at the same time. And then what? Do you think you'll sit in a rocking chair by the window for the rest of eternity looking back on yourself being old and foolish the way an old man looks back on himself being young and foolish? You don't stay old forever, *señor Snowman*. One day it all stops. Or rather, you stop, and everything else goes on without you. Grandpa, unusually voluble, and articulate (or so it seems to the Snowman, who, thanks in large part to the wine's gift of enhanced linguistic skills, has more or less gotten the gist of this speech in Spanish), falls silent, then his lips move again, his voice barely audible. *¿Mande?* The Snowman, having picked up this local colloquial for *say what?* puts his hand to his ear. Grandpa's lips move again and he says a little louder, There's a snake at your feet, *señor Snowman*. Struggling to attach meaning to these words, *señor Snowman* stares first in curiosity and then horror at the brightly colored bands of red, yellow and black draped over his boot. A confused mantra runs through his head. *Yellow and black, stand back? Red and yellow, let it mellow?* And yes, you know-it-all junior herpetologists, it is a coral snake, in the same family as cobras and therefore deadly, even though the likelihood of its being here at this elevation in this environment is highly improbable, no, Mr. Spock? The Snowman's reaction? *Nyaaahh! Beam me up, Scotty!* Shh, don't

disturb him, *señor Snowman*. I think he likes you. But what if
he bites me? He is a very poisonous snake, *señor Snowman*.
You will probably die. Best to sit very quietly and wait until he
leaves. Christ, the old man really is loony. That's his first
thought ... unless ... followed by his second, granted,
somewhat delusional, i.e., Grandpa actually is some kind of
tutelary spirit who's conjured up this serpent to remind him that
he really, *really* doesn't want to die. He closes his eyes and tries
to relax and, aided by the wine, apparently succeeds because
when he wakes from a brief but deep sleep the snake is gone
and so is Grandpa, which means he has to hurry to catch up
even though he was really looking forward to a cigarette after
lunch.

The climb has turned much steeper. He has to lift his legs
higher for each step. His thighs feel like rocks, his knees and
ankles ache. The food and wine sit heavy on his stomach, he's
sweating profusely and gasping for breath. Something feels like
it's coming loose in his chest. He bends over and coughs up a
green spongy thing. What's wrong now, *señor Snowman?*
Grandpa, visibly impatient, comes back down the trail and
inspects the green sponge. You see, that's all the poison you
keep inside. The mountain is helping you expel it. The
Snowman rolls his eyes. More Looney Tunes, right? He hears a
loud whoosh and—*what the* ...?—a buzzard that has been
wheeling high overhead drops two hundred feet in two seconds,
its black funereal feathers brushing his face as it swoops past.
Hello, Grandfather Zopilote! Grandpa shouts and waves. The
buzzard tips a wing in acknowledgement and soars upward
again into the thin blue ether, drawn on the strings of an
invisible puppeteer. If Boone has intended this apparition as yet
another omen or symbol of mortality, Grandpa pours water on
that notion when he undoes his trousers and releases a huge
equine stream, then zips up and takes off again. The Snowman,
meanwhile, having misheard Grandpa say *Soul pilot* (Zo—
pronounced *So—pilote* is Nahuatl for buzzard—Eduardo), has
gone off on another etymological goose chase: something to do

with that old soul pilot always watching over your shoulder, reminding you he's ready when your time comes, like a mortician at a funeral, gently guiding you in the right, the inevitable direction. So when Grandpa abruptly stops again, one hand on his hip, the other clutching his staff like he's bloody Sir Edmund Hillary planting a flag on the summit of Everest, the Snowman doesn't immediately grasp that they've arrived at the top of the mountain, in fact, has completely forgotten that getting to the top of this berg is the purpose for being here. There's certainly nothing to identify it as the top, no plaque or marker or unusual rock formation. A thousand feet below, he can see small white puff clouds drift by and four thousand feet below that the land stretches for what seems like hundreds of miles into a distant yellow-brown haze. Maybe it's the thinner air but he feels faint, he's almost hyperventilating. He hears a sound like a goat bleating and lifts his gaze and sees, rising even higher, yet another mountain peak. The sun gleams on its snow-blown crest and he spies something that looks like a glowing red eye. Someone calls his name, the voice is familiar and infused with Icine's icy menthol breath. *Snowmannnn.* It's those fucking angels. *We haven't forgotten you, Snowmannnn. Would you like to fly with us to that other mountain? It's easy, Snowman, just step forward and spread your wings.* He looks down and *nyaah!* sees now that he's standing on the edge of a precipice, at his feet a bottomless abyss. His body convulses, jerked awake from a brief dream-sensation of falling. He blinks, shakes his head. What about that mountain? he says. Grandpa looks in the direction he's pointing, and then back at the Snowman, his leathery brown face and small black currant eyes wary, as if *he's* staring at a madman. There is no other mountain, *señor Snowman.* He looks again and it's true, the mountain is gone. Maybe it was never there. Maybe it was the light in his eyes or a strange cloud formation.

A chill wind whistles around them. It's getting late, the sun is sinking into a pool of orange plasma, purple and black rivers of shadow spread across the land. It took them the entire day to make this climb, it's almost dark now, the trail treacherous. Obviously they'll have to spend the night. The Snowman's about a hair's breadth away from a panic attack. What if there are wolves? Bears? What if they freeze to death? He asks if they shouldn't look for some sticks or leaves or *something* to build a fire. Grandpa snorts, Well, if you really want to spend the night I suppose we can, but I was planning to be back down in time to catch Chupa Mucha, and he hurries off, the Snowman more or less blindly tripping along behind him in the fading light. Barely a minute later he stumbles into Grandpa, who has stopped abruptly in front of what appears to be a cave opening with a—stainless steel door? Grandpa presses a glowing orange button in the rock wall and the door slides open. An *elevator?* the Snowman thinks but doesn't say. The old gnome gives him a look of outright scorn. Did you think I was going to break my neck climbing back down this damn mountain at night? But why didn't we just take the elevator up? he asks, a bit peevish himself. Because you said you wanted to climb the mountain, Grandpa replies as the door closes behind them.

At first amused by this tale, Maria appraises the Snowman with a curious and then concerned look when he mentions the snow-covered mountain he *thinks* he saw. Her lips move and in her mind (the audience can hear this, the Snowman can't) she asks herself, *Can it really be true?* When he tries to draw her out, to ask in a casual manner if there's something she's not telling him, she shakes her head, laughs too quickly, says, Of course not, Snowman. Okay, now his spider senses are tingling again. A lot of things don't add up here. Like where is this clinic she's always roaring off to? How come she's never invited him to see it? Also, why is her motorcycle always covered with mud when it never rains? And while he doesn't exactly interrogate her, Maria seems compelled to explain, with copious reassurances from El Residente. She frequently rides into the mountains to treat patients who, for reasons he doesn't fully grasp, can't travel to the clinic or the hospital in Chopahuac. He pictures her on her motorcycle, splashing across rushing white water streams, charging up rugged slopes covered in dense jungle greenery. All right, that makes sense. But then there's this. Every time he has asked when the heck Margarito's coming back, Maria has repeated, soon, soon, as if she expects him any minute, but more time passes and still no Margarito. It's almost a standing joke between them. Oh, *that*, she makes a nervous little smile when he raises the issue now, but *that* she doesn't explain, in fact, says abruptly, Please, Snowman, I need to be alone.

Later that night Estragon—um, the *Snowman*—is awakened from a troubled sleep by voices. It must be Maria and Margarito, he thinks, but he's too tired (okay, trashed) to get up and see. Besides, they probably need time together—*of course* they need time together, you idiot. They haven't seen each other in weeks. They don't want the old Snowman barging in like some big, dumb, flop-eared hound dog, *Rowr, I thought you two might like some company*. What he doesn't see is this: Maria sitting alone at the kitchen table in a kind of trance, her eyes gleaming like slivers of obsidian in firelight as she carries on a conversation with herself, alternately in a huskier, throaty voice and then a softer, higher tone. But you can't tell him now, he'll leave. But if you wait longer he'll resent you even more. But it isn't time yet, the stars aren't aligned and there's still so much to do. If only I could tell him now. No, don't say it, don't think it, you know that can never happen. All you've worked for, all you've accomplished, will be lost if you violate the covenant. If not for yourself, think of your people. But it's so hard. I know, but you must endure.

Dissociative Identity Disorder (DID), previously known as multiple personality disorder (MPD), commonly called split personality, is a mental disorder on the dissociative spectrum characterized by at least two distinct and relatively enduring identities or dissociated personality states that alternately control a person's behavior, and is accompanied by memory impairment for important information not explained by ordinary forgetfulness. Norman Bates is a classic case.

12
Amanita

AND THEN THE NEXT MORNING Maria is gone and there's Margarito. Again something seems different about him. His face is pale, ashen, like he's spent the last several nights tunneling his way out of prison. He's also nervous, restless, and so fidgety his mustache seems to have taken on a personality of its own, twitching oddly and jumping about (Boone has actually inserted several frames of Charlie Chaplin's famous soup strainer the moment before the little tramp plants a chaste buss on Edna Purviance in the original eight millimeter cut of *Behind the Screen*—Edna (and don't you just love her name—*Purviance*, I mean).). Apparently Margarito and Maria have had a *misunderstanding*. Perhaps you have noticed, Snowman … Maria has *spells*, she becomes angry, intractable, another person altogether. This sounds like the definition of hysteria or some other female nervous disorder promulgated by the medical quackery of the last century. Ever the rock in the maelstrom, the Snowman plunges into melodrama mode. It's all his fault. His presence has driven a wedge between the two lovers. He's totally disrupted their home life. Margarito, taking his cue, puts on a sheepish air and suggests certain improprieties of his own. Then, either pushing his luck or proving a point or both, he proposes some diversion this evening (in uncharacteristically bad English), Maybe ees better eef we get out of Maria's hair, doan you theenk, Snowman?

Margarito mentions a club, which doesn't prepare him for *El DiscoDélico*. It's like a theme park, a sports arena, a huge, flashy Las Vegas casino bathed in neon, lasers, strobe and flood lights (the moon colonists can see the damn thing without a telescope, even the guy who got stranded on Mars swears (and he swears a lot, these days) that he can see the fucking thing *with* a telescope), and most amazing, it's sitting out here in the middle of the desert miles from nowhere. The parking lot covers several acres, it's packed with shiny new *militarized* Ford, Chrysler and GM pickups and SUVs, as well as Mercedes, Jaguars, Rolls, Lamborghinis, Maseratis, Bugattis, Lotuses and just about every other species of high performance vehicle to sail across the ocean blue from the old country on cargo ships as big as Manhattan. Oh yes, and a smattering of clearly marked rental cars, and even a small number of burros tied up at a thoughtfully provided hitching post. Inside there are multiple stages, stairways, balconies, dance cages, everything pulses with sound and light, pounding drums, sirens, whistles, gongs, smoke machines. Cadres of male and female bartenders in black ties and vests and starched white shirts with gold cufflinks sling drinks non-stop. People laugh and shout. The place is absolutely packed. Rancheros in Stetsons, pearl snap button shirts, tooled leather belts, boot-cut Levi's and Tony Llama boots with dogger heels. A fairly sizable crowd of young chopahauqueños totally blinged out in diamond and gold rings, chains, necklaces and bracelets. A small number of *indígenas* in hand-woven red and white huipils (the women) and penguin-like white shirts and black wool trousers with red sashes (the men), who, it's probably safe to venture, arrived via the burros. Also maybe half a dozen of in-the-know but clearly out of place tourists (the rental cars), thanks to *The Crowded Planet Guidebook,* whose editors might want to rethink that entry. The Snowman's looking quite dapper himself in a Hawaiian flower print shirt that defies horticultural taxonomy (*Coconuts and orchids? Pomelos and corpse flowers?*) and a pair of pleated and cuffed white linen trousers Sam Clemens might have worn on the Big

Island. Margarito steers him through the crowd to a table where he receives a hearty greeting from *los guys* who, for reasons unknown even to Boone, are wearing 1970s disco outfits, print polyester shirts, polyester pants with bells and platform shoes, they're ordering all kinds of horrible drinks, Pink Slippers, Grasshoppers, Shirley Temples (Bombástico), laughing and yakking (not to be confused with llamaing). Nico's grinning his happy sideways ferret grin, puffing on one of his rústicos and combing his pompadour into ever greater perfection. Raf-I-el's doing his levitation shtick, pretending to float in his chair, although anyone with an eye in his head can spot the trick. Margarito has good-naturedly informed the Snowman that the local women believe making love to a greenghost will fill their bellies with strange abominations, hideous *ice children,* also implying but leaving unsaid the likelihood of offended male egos, fistfights, guns, knives, etc., so he has resigned himself to a night of celibacy when a hush passes through the crowd like a winter wind, followed by a rush of whispers and a repeated phrase that, to his ears, sounds like *Chin Goddess.* A young woman in a sleeveless, floor-length dress that chameleon-like morphs from shimmering emerald to gold to crimson emerges out of a cloud of blue and green smoke. She's absolutely stunning, tall, athletic, luminous face, striking features, dark, heavy brows, high cheekbones, a black river of hair flowing down her back, and, yes, chin in the air, haughty, arrogant, which, of course, makes her even more attractive. She's surrounded by a loud, laughing caravan of male and female poseurs. They're like a pop diva's backup chorus, their every word, move and expression choreographed around her slightest gesture as they sweep across the floor and raucously occupy two entire tables, until now conspicuously empty. No, no, no, Snowman, don't even theenk about eet. Nico, who has followed his gaze across the crowded dance floor, fills him in. Her name is Amanita Mascara Valladoides. Nico waits to see if this elicits a reaction from the Snowman and when it doesn't he adds, Her father is L. Condor Valladoides, a very powerful and dangerous

individual who ostensibly (yes, Nico said that—
ostensiblemente—Eduardo) built this club for his daughter's
amusement, but also, it's generally understood, to keep an eye
on her. Nico nods at a man near the bar and then another at the
other end of the bar and then two men near the center stage
where a voluptuous young woman, naked except for a black
thong and stiletto heels, is pole dancing. They're all dressed in
black suits, they all look seriously bad (like, you don't wanta
meet these guys on a busy city street at midday, much less a
dark alley at night), and he's pretty sure he's spotted the oily
black gleam of weaponry inside their open coats. Despite these
warning signs, he's fascinated. He can't stop staring at this
Amanita creature. Suddenly he realizes she's staring back at
him. Embarrassed, he looks away. *Sssssnowmannn.* A cold
cloud of ether envelops him at the same time a stainless steel
needle inserts itself into the memory portion of his brain. It's
those damn angels again, whispering their mixed message,
simultaneously warning and come-on. But wait, it isn't the
angels. It's Nico spraying a high octane menthol-eucalyptus
breath freshener down his throat prior to requesting a dance
with Doña Oleinfanta's eldest daughter, Trombonia, a very
plump, giggly young woman in a white flouncy dress with a red
sash that gives her an uncanny resemblance to a giant soft
peppermint candy. When the Snowman looks again, Amanita's
seat is empty. Maybe she's dancing or getting a drink or she
went to the restroom. A voice, female, but with a whiskey and
cigarettes roughness, says in perfect English, Well, if it isn't
Snow White and his three, four—is it only *five?*—dwarves, not
including *you*, of course, *Margarito*. The Snowman looks up
into eyes the color of cut limes, Atlantic sea ice. Her face is
familiar. She looks like someone famous but he can't place her.
Her body, the dress she wears, her posture, is an architectural
marvel of suggestion, like a fashion designer's conception of
lines, colors and textures lifted directly from the sketch pad. Her
sensuousness washes over him like a warm buoyant wave,
knocks him around in the flotsam and jetsam of its undertow

and leaves him gasping for air when hard turns to soft and she says in a languorous tone, You *are* the *Snowman*, aren't you? The one who climbed the mountain? *Oh?* And how does she know that? In his mind he pictures himself as the seasoned alpinist in feathered Tyrolean cap and lederhosen yodeling across steep green mountains strewn with edelweiss. Until she laughs in a not particularly pleasant way. The whole town watched you and that old fool through the pharmacist Enrique Enfermi's telescope. Oh, don't look so offended. We welcome diversion in this wasteland. Speaking of which, I hear you've been wandering in the desert like one of those ridiculous prophets of old. What have you learned there, *Snowman?* Have you talked to God yet? Has *He* given you a message to bring to the people? Before he can come up with a clever riposte (and believe me, he's trying), she says, Why don't you *not* tell me about it while we dance? Her sarcasm is like a velvet gauntlet studded with razor blades, mordant and alluring, and, foolish knight, he accepts the challenge *although I'm not much of a dancer*. Amanita's almost as tall as he is and appears taller in heels. The closeness of her body, of its contours beneath this shimmering membrane, the sweet mustiness of her perfume, the strange green of her eyes immediately arouse him. Thanks to a vestige of sanity, he's also wondering why this exotic *creature* is coming on to him? His tower of self-esteem collapses, however, when she says afterwards, it's true, *Snowman,* you aren't much of a dancer. Nevertheless, she invites or rather marionette-like draws him to her table, where, all aflutter in their colorful plumage, her friends, mostly gay males, ooo and ahh over him as if he were a puppy. Discomfited by this attention (really, he's stuttering, red in the face), and never a subtle conversationalist, he says to Amanita in his Big Tex voice, I hear your father's an important fella. You're well informed, aren't you, *Snowman?* she says. Unfortunately, most of that information is incorrect. The people here do not like me very much. My father sent his precious little girl off to college in the States, my mother's birthplace, and got me in return. Now

I am an outcast among my own people. What about you, *Snowman*, are you an outcast too? Or have you found your home among these delightfully primitive people? Despite Amanita's venom she fascinates him. Everything about her screams *danger!* but of course that only makes her more attractive. He watches himself in another movie as they get up from the table and head for the door, Amanita's hangers-on calling after her in mock spiteful tones, *you bitch! you cunt!* As they pass *los guys'* table, she can't resist one last—well, *dig*. Tell me, *dwarves*, is it true that you do nothing all day but dig dig dig? And you still haven't found any gold? Maybe you're looking in all the wrong places? The guys grumble and mutter among themselves and Margarito gives Amanita a particularly dirty look that immediately starts the gears grinding in the Snowman's head. What about Margarito's long absences? And the purported fight with Maria last night? And what if *he* and Amanita … ? Naww, too crazy.

Outside, he starts for the Coupe but Amanita stares at this venerable but battle-worn product of Detroit as if she's seen a ghost and shakes her head huh-uh, no way, they're going in her car, which looks like a modified stealth fighter jet. The gullwing doors swing open and the Snowman lowers himself into the softly yielding black leather seat. The console looks like an instrument panel in a spaceship. Amanita glances at a glowing green bio scan and the engine roars to life, then settles to a low decibel scream more or less like a commercial jet, and engulfed in an arctic blast of AC, they drive or rather fly into Las Riquezas, which takes about five minutes in this rocket (the speedometer briefly tops four hundred kilometers per hour), Amanita casually steering with one hand, the rings and bracelets on the other cling-cling-clinging while she spoons coke up her nose from a gold box embossed with an emerald Chinese dragon. Don't mind if I do, he says in his Big Tex voice when she offers it to him.

Amanita lives in an exclusive condo on *Calle 34 de Octubre* in the tiny (half a square block—*maybe?*), trendy (good luck finding this place on a map) Combo District that has grown up around the equally incongruous, tourist-oriented Hi-Tone Hotel. The Snowman's senses tingle like a male black widow's as he enters Amanita's lair. She pours tumblers of hundred proof craft Texas bourbon (Old Armadillo), lights a joint that immediately envelops them in the ambience of an opium den, lays out more lines of coke, and dives into the deep end. She seems to be intentionally spiraling downward into a drunken, hyper-manic state, almost, one might think, as if she's preparing herself for an unpleasant experience. Her face looks sharper, more angular, her mouth a crooked gash. Staggering against walls, furniture, she leads him by the hand into the bedroom and begins to remove her clothes. This isn't a subtle striptease. Shoes kicked off, dress, bra and panties thrown on the floor, she's naked and under the sheets in three seconds. He more or less follows suit, drops his clothes on the floor and climbs under the covers. Other than the close contact dancing, they haven't even kissed or embraced yet. He wants to look at her body, caress her breasts, he wants to kiss and lick and taste and fix in his brain this experience as he's having it now and to remember later but she's all business. She lies flat on her back, spreads her legs. *Wait.* She sticks her fingers in a jar of lubricant, with a sharp little gasp guides him inside (truth is, he's not entirely sure *where*, he isn't even fully hard yet). She doesn't look at him, doesn't say a word. She lies almost completely rigid, eyes squeezed shut, arms at her sides. Suddenly she shudders and begins to make odd yelping sounds like a dog bitten by a snake. She utters something between a growl and a moan, bites his shoulder, and her body goes limp. She's out cold and he's, um, kinda stuck. He's essentially lying on top of an insentient body, which sorta seems like—don't say it, don't even think it—*necrophilia*. And *ping!* (there's no sound but you can almost hear it) Amanita's eyes spring open, she blinks, once, twice, makes a face like she's just swallowed a spoonful of dill pickle juice, pushes him aside more or less like an old rug in the process of bending down to pull up the sheet, reaches for a tray of coke, does a couple of quick lines, as an afterthought, hands the tray to him. They lie against the pillows and smoke cigarettes, she as if she's just survived a firing squad, he, frankly, *unsatisfied* (that's not his heart throbbing). Plus he hasn't had a smoke in days and he's expecting this to taste really good. Instead it's dry and harsh and almost as disappointing as the sex. While they smoke, Amanita, completely oblivious—or indifferent—to his distress, asks him what appear to be random questions about his life, books he's read, music he likes, films, even though most of his references are at least ten years behind the times. Kinda lost *touch*, he confesses, not that it matters because she isn't really listening anymore. His words her springboard, logorrheic release valve, she launches into dominoing chains of digressions that keep him grasping for the main point, for example, this last topic, film, has he seen any of Boone Weller's movies? He starts to say, Actually I ... but before he can boast that indeed he is familiar with Weller's work, she's quoting figures from the Bolsa, of special interest, pork shares, which, by the way, *Snowman*, are controlled almost exclusively by Sleem Pequeños, one of the richest men in the world, although very few people know this. Actually I ... but before he can say that, yes, he did read about that in the *newspaper*, she has moved on to the latest controversy stirred up by Stephen Hawking (whose consciousness, sans the wreckage of his body, continues to ponder the nature of existence in some extra-dimensional quantum state), that is, his ever evolving theory on black holes, i.e., the universe is more or less a giant Swiss cheese, the holes are all working in flux, you see, kind of like the universe's vascular system—even hurriedly sketching out exotic diagrams and equations on the glossy cover of a celebrity magazine (Amanita, not Professor Hawking), despite the fact that the Snowman understands none of this, indeed, is more interested in the *face* on the celebrity mag, which, at first glance, he thought belonged to the just referenced Boone Weller, but, reading the heading, he discovers now actually belongs to

Johnny Deep who will be *playing* Boone in the director's next project. Don't you love the way he breaks with orthodoxy? Amanita says. It's hagiography masquerading as autobiography of the living auteur—by the blessed saint himself. Entirely *metafilmic*. Of course—snorting another gram or two of coke—there's also some mutually beneficial backscratching going on. Edgy but wildly popular young actor adds another notch in his film catalogue (I did a *Booney*) while giving a boost to the B-grade master's flagging career. Or, back to the topic of physics, she once had a cat that lived in a box. If she opened the box during the day she found the cat dead but if she opened it at night she found the cat alive, kind of like a vampire cat, which somehow reminds her of this sorority she was in—it was more like a secret club, really. You know, *Snowman*, rich girls, dangerous daddies, *bodyguards*. Or, stifling a totally unexpected sob, recalling the death of a friend's pet poodle in a "tragic shooting accident" that seems to have disproportionately affected her, until, that is, she bursts into hysterical laughter and says, I'll bet you didn't know my mother was murdered, did you, *Snowman?* Umm … no, he didn't, nor does she bother to explain because now she's onto her flirtations with Satanism and Wicca but she also wants to try this telluric thing that's going around. Out of nowhere she says, Oh Christ, *Snowman*, I'm so fucking bored. You can't imagine how dreary it is to be stuck in this parochial little burg with these backwater lumpenproletariat. Just as suddenly she shrieks, *Ha!Ha!Ha! Madame Bovary c'est moi!* Perhaps it is this moment of apparent openness and even vulnerability that causes him to let his own guard down and stupidly tell her everything, the whole sad story with Judith and how he ended up in the snowbiz. Oh, she says, so are you a good snowman or an abominable snowman? Like the Snow White thing, this pun's about as stale as month-old focaccia. So, are you a good witch or a bad witch? he responds in kind (he thinks). Uh-oh, that hit a nerve. So are you a prick or just a dick? she hisses like a lit fuse. This leads to—what else?—a Mexican standoff, both act as if they've been mortally offended, neither's willing to give in, although it's mostly posturing in both camps (and all this on a first *date*). It's also now about six a.m. and they're both nodding off but Amanita doesn't suggest he sleep here and he doesn't particularly want to (something about this setup creeps him out—like the possibility of guys with guns coming through the door, and is that a camera lens in the air vent?). They rouse themselves with inch-wide lines of coke and double mocha cappuccinos served by a liveried chefbot, get dressed (Amanita is surprisingly modest, turning away from him and dressing just as hurriedly as she undressed last night) and then they drive or rather fly (the speedometer easily tops five hundred this time—Ks, that is) back to the club, still throbbing with a pounding disco beat and plenty of hangers-on loitering outside, although they've all got this disheveled, glassy-eyed zombie look. To the Snowman's astonishment the Coupe has been washed, waxed, polished and ... possibly even repainted? Amanita shrugs like don't ask me and peels out in her rocket.

About an hour later he shows up at Maria's looking hang-dogged, sheepish, one *might* even say cowed (Boone refuses to comment on the multiple barnyard allusions), and finds—not Margarito but Maria seated at the kitchen table with dark circles under her eyes and looking very grumpy (unintentional play on the Snow White thing). Apparently Margarito has disappeared again, no explanation, no goodbye. *¡Puto tramposo!* Angry, distraught, preoccupied with her own issues, Maria seems totally oblivious to his disheveled state. Despite her seeming indifference—or maybe because of it—his guilt morphs into resentment. So what if she suspects something, what can she expect? He's a grown man, a fucking *adult* (both object and modifier questionable), he doesn't remember taking any vows of celibacy. Besides, she's with Margarito and Margarito's his buddy, it's that simple (sort of).

The next time he and Amanita meet (How this is arranged is uncertain. The audience will have observed by now that the Snowman, largely off the grid, doesn't own an EyePhone®.

Smoke signals?), she hands him a flat gilt cardboard box, blinks, wrinkles her brow, suggesting something—distaste? impatience? Open it. He removes the lid, peels aside the beige tissue paper as if it were a subcutaneous membrane, lifts out a silk shirt the color of night in the desert and reeking of designer priciness. Appalled at such extravagance, his first thought when Amanita encourages him to try it on is no fucking way. Go on, she says in a flirtsy, teasey voice he hasn't heard from her before and opens the top button of her blouse. Okay, he thinks, I'll play for now, and putting his arms in the sleeves, right first, left second, he shrugs the shirt on over his T and begins to button up from the bottom. Thus the game proceeds. As he buttons up, Amanita unbuttons down until, two buttons short in her deck, her blouse comes off, followed by a lacy black bra, so that she's bare-chested as he fastens the top button at his neck. The shirt fits perfectly but, heck, that's the last thing on his mind. He's unabashedly staring at her breasts, which he somehow managed not to get a good look at during their last encounter, and which, according to some *sui generis* definition that takes into account his nursing habits in infancy, familial and social prohibitions and taboos, glimpses of soft porn at an early age, as well as the female body as presented in film and advertising, to his eyes look fucking beautiful. But if he thought there was going to be any more, *ahem*, tit for tat haberdashery here, much less *fucking*, he was mistaken. You *silly* boy, Amanita scolds him, and turning away, she takes a lacy white bra out of a drawer and fastens it on with that incredible behind the back dexterity all (*okay*, Edna—*some*) women seem to have been born with, then opens a closet and pulls a long-sleeved orange cotton top over her head.

Thus begins a strange exchange, um, relationship. Every time they meet she presents him with yet another gift or present. A narrow black leather belt with a sterling silver buckle, a sports jacket, more shirts, designer jeans, boots, shoes, silk and linen suits, an entire wardrobe, all with the name of someone infinitely richer than he could ever in his wildest dreams

imagine being stamped, embroidered, stitched, sewn or
embossed inside the collar or the waistband or boldly on the
outside breast pocket, *Armoani, Vvlgaris, Tom Frod*. Expensive
colognes in cut glass, a gold-plated, self-actualizing electric
razor with multiple apps, a solid gold necklace that feels like a
pretty good chunk of Ft. Knox, a *Rolux* that costs as much as a
new house and has as many functions as a Mars lander, even
though he can't stand the weight on his wrist, much less the
cardiological *tick tick tick* reminder of time's passage (it's
silent, stealthy, a lithium battery, but he can sense the gears
turning another notch with every blood-bulging throb of his
pulse). Amanita insists he see her hair stylist and he's gone this
far so why not? The tonsorial master Monsieur Deuxcheveux's
hands hover over the Snowman's head as if he's taking
physiognomic measurements. Every follicle has its own
individual appointment, attended to by a team of tonsorial
specialists, with a final comb-through by MM himself. He has a
facial that makes his whole body feel like it's melting into a
puddle of warm milk. Miniature Martian landers (Boone seems
to be developing another sub-theme with the red planet) rove
over the contours of his face, lightly abrading, massaging,
cleansing, moisturizing, smoothing and softening. Stainless
steel, nitrile surgical gloves and tiny infusion jets visit the
cavities and folds of his nostrils and ears, removing nomadic
hairs and unattended to traces of dirt, earwax and desiccated
snot. With the aid of personal trainers, his body is put through a
crash course of Pilates, Rolfing, Cossack dance steps,
chiropractic spinal re-alignment and balletic stretches at the
barre. He's massaged, manipulated, saunaed and spaed. His
capitulation is complete when he finds himself being measured,
fitted, groped and squeezed for the hautest of Milanese and
Parisian couture. He feels like a movie star, he sees himself in
the mirror and he *looks* like a movie star. He's even picked up
this Hollywood heartthrob Brad Pizzoccheri swagger. And in
exchange (that word *was* mentioned earlier) for allowing
himself to be turned into a high dollar clothes dummy he gets

what? Nights in bed? Wild sex? Nights in bed, maybe, following tons of coke and super stoner weed and five thousand dollar Jeroboams of champagne. When they finally get to the sex (*Live on stage! One night only!*), Amanita acts like she's giving blood at the Red Cross. She lies flat on her back, eyes shut tight, arms at her sides, body stiff, rigid, legs spread—but wait, she has to get up, she forgot the lubricant. Well maybe if we had some kinda foreplay. What are you saying? Nothing, it's just—Don't touch me! I didn't mean—Shut up and hand me the cigarettes! Which leads to huffiness, further rebuffs, a gradual thaw, Amanita uncharacteristically playing footsies under the sheets, which (Y chromosome) might lead him to believe this is finally *going somewhere*, but again he's sadly mistaken, it's only a nervous twitch, restless leg syndrome, and just like that she's off to the races again, chain-smoking and snorting more coke and drinking champagne and fast forwarding across an encyclopedic range of topics—she clearly doesn't give a shit what they talk about, only that they talk, or rather that she talk, and talk and talk and talk, which, he figures, is some kind of coping mechanism to keep her demons at bay (did she say her mother was *murdered?*), or maybe this bad girl's afraid of the dark, or she just hates to be alone, she needs someone for company. And then the *chirp chirp chirp* of birdsong somewhere and blinking against the blinding white light. Morning already? You know what that means. Amanita's mood shifts dramatically. She's irritable and sarcastic again—really, a complete bitch. Why don't you do something useful, *Snowboy*, like close the fucking blinds? (She keeps pulling the covers over her face. Maybe the light hurts her eyes or … she seems to have become oddly insecure about her appearance.) Whatsa matter, is the *Snowbaby* feeling sleepy? Can't keep up? Can't keep *it* up? *Ha!Ha!Ha!* Too bad, I was just getting ready for some action. *Really?* Dr. Jill become Ms. Hyde (maybe la Condesa Drácula is more appropriate). He knows this relationship is sick, Amanita is sick, which makes him sick (in both senses). So why is he sticking around? That impulsive, risk-taking Y chromosome thing again? There are of course the undeniable perks. An endless supply of coke, top of the top shelf booze and bud. Amanita continues to ply him with gifts. It's like libations to a god or (that tingler thing running up and down his spine)— a sacrificial victim. Despite blue-collar pretensions and a rebellious but not exactly revolutionary spirit, he convinces himself that taking advantage of this extravagance is a subversive proletariat act—certainly better than calling yourself a whore, which isn't factually true because they don't actually have much, well, *any*, sex anymore (and he's not even sure about the first time). Some kind of pattern has been established where they almost do, or at least they seem to be leading up to it, which involves the methodical consumption of considerable amounts of drugs and alcohol, Amanita leading the way and he more or less following suit, which may also be why when she suddenly puts on her tortured martyr's face and announces she's *ready*, well, *he* isn't … *quite*. Oh, well, she says, *if you aren't interested*. But wait, it'll only take a sec, I mean—too late, even as he's inching toward erection, she's reaching for a cigarette. Which means what? She's got some deep-seated sexual hang-up? Or she's bartering for higher stakes in a game he can't even begin to understand but feels compelled to play? And he does, doesn't he? Want to keep playing? Although staying at Maria's feels increasingly awkward and even more so when Amanita drops him off in yet another *Armoani, Halfinger* or *Dolce & Gibbone*.

Oh no, no, no, *Snowman*, Maria dismisses his concerns, I'm so happy for you. But orbiting the deep space blackness of her pupils he sees Saturnal rings of hurt, betrayal and resentment. And no wonder. She spends most of her life treating the sick and injured, her life is blood, pain, suffering. While you, *Snowman*—while he's living the high life. One morning he returns home drunk, wired on coke, he reeks of Amanita's perfume, he's got wine stains on an outfit that probably cost as much as an X-ray machine. Judging by the empty bottle of *El Residente* on the kitchen table, Maria too has been on an all-night binge, which might explain her unusually foul mood. Without warning or provocation her eyes flare like molten lava and she attacks. Tell me, what are you learning with that bitch, *Snowman?* That it's easier to blame the poor for being poor— and go shopping? Amanita is poison, Snowman. She will destroy you. Maria buries her face in her hands, tugs her hair up in clumps like she's struggling not to scream or say or even worse maybe do something she'll regret later. Forgive me, Snowman. I should be happy for you. You're enjoying life. You've finally found the freedom you desired. You've escaped the dark and cold and that miserable job you hated so much. You've come to the land of the sun you always dreamed of. You ... Maria stops talking. Now she's gone too far in the opposite direction. It's like she's somehow been made privy to the buried library stacks of his stored thoughts, all the justifications, the whys and why nots he has argued with himself in the small claims court of his, let's face it, not exactly rational brain, all of which she must have heard second-hand from Margarito, although, hmm, never would have figured him for being such a gossip.

One night he and Amanita encounter those two bad dudes who keep showing up on the set. In his mind he's been calling them Pancho and Flaco, so he's pretty surprised when it turns out their names *are* Pancho and Flaco, except Flaco is the short stocky guy with the tats and studs and Pancho is the tall skinny guy with the scar and the eye patch. What's up, Amanita? Flaco, who barely comes up to her neck, leers at her or rather her chest. Amanita's mouth twists into a vicious red gash and she snarls, Fuck you, Flaco. Yeah? Not sure I'm interested after you been banging this Snowman bozo. They're speaking Spanish so the Snowman bozo doesn't get all this, but he does know both his and Amanita's honor have been besmirched. He starts to object but Amanita says, Stay out of this, *Snowman.* Yeah, stay out of it, *Tex*, Flaco says. Okay, that does it. Look, buddy, I told you the name ain't *Tex*. *Let's go!* Amanita pulls him away. Glad to be extracted from what could easily have escalated into a fatal encounter, most likely his, he offers minimal resistance, but at a safe distance he demands to know what Amanita's relationship with these lowlifes is. They're friends of her father, she says. Yeah, well your father keeps some pretty creepy friends. Look, *Snowman*, I don't like it either. But they're—protecting me. Protecting you? My father has ... enemies. Yeah? Well he won't make any friends hanging out with bums like that. The very next day he sees Pancho and Flaco pushing around some dirt poor *campesino* outside *Mi Sedecita*. When they spot him they sneer and smirk and make mock fearful faces, like, look out, it's Big Tex to the rescue, but—who knows, maybe they don't like doing their dirty work with an audience—they let the guy go. That evening he confronts Amanita again. I saw your friends doing some more protecting today. Her response catches him off guard. Rather than defend her father's henchmen or even promise to have something done about them, she parries his accusation like a black belt in forensic debate. You think these people are so innocent, *Snowman*. You believe all the nonsense that mental case Maria tells you. Why don't you ask your friend *Margarito* what *he's* really up to? And, hmm, the way she says this, one, makes him think she knows a lot more than she's telling, and, two, causes him to wonder what Margarito *has* been up to? A switch clicks and the old five watt refrigerator light goes on in his head. He sees the barn at the back of Maria's garden, the door open, thin yellow shafts of sunlight gleam on hay bales, wooden beams, his mind's eye focuses on the metallic sheen of farm implements, rakes, hoes, pitchforks—or wait, is that a gun barrel? And there? And there? Naww, it's just his overly active imagination in hyper drive, right? Oh yes, Amanita continues, I know the whole story of your little lovebirds Maria and Margarito. Ha, ha, maybe I should call them Mork and Mindy? How about Mickey and Minnie? Or, ha, ha, just M&M? Isn't that *sweet?* At this pun, Amanita, who has already inhaled an ounce of coke, shrieks with operatic laughter *Ha!Ha!Ha! Hee!Hee!Hee!* Despite, or because of, these manic extremes, and just possibly something to do with his dear old mom's own mental *lapses*, the Snowman's fascination with Amanita grows rather than diminishes.

He feels like a tennis ball bouncing back and forth between different dimensions without benefit of line umpire, boundaries or net (sorry, Mr. Frost). Amanita is a sweet poison, enticing him with her beauty and impetuousness. But on her lips in their rare kisses (and more often the smoochy air kind), he tastes an alkaline bitterness. In his sleep he dreams of toothed vaginas, hissing, snake-headed clitorises. When he and Amanita do embrace, her body feels unnaturally cold in his arms, which he attributes to her greenghost mother, just as the snow in her veins has blanched the ruddy blush of Zol from her face. And then she teases him, plays with his doubts. Don't you know, *Snowman?* I'm the devil's advocate, I'm trying to win your soul, to convince you of the virtues of unfettered capitalism. She laughs, again not a particularly pleasant laugh, even a little bit, yes, *crazy*. Wouldn't that be wonderful, *Snowman*, if one soul could teach another? Maybe my soul will make your soul very bad.

13
The Coast

AMANITA ANNOUNCES SHE'S PLANNING A TRIP to the coast and
he's invited. Hmm. Why does he suspect she has more in mind
than a simple vacation by the seashore? Sensing the sticky
strands of webbing binding him ever more inextricably to a
fateful, um … fate, of course he takes the bait. C'mon,
Snowman, he reassures himself, it'll be *fun*, you'll see some of
the country—figuring they'll drive, of course. Amanita laughs.
Are you crazy? The highways are more dangerous than my
father's friends. Obviously they're going to fly. He's flown
maybe two times in his life, both as a child in the company of
his parents. He pictures himself packed into one of those dinky
little twenty-seater, twin-engine propeller planes that wobble up
into the sky over Chopahuac two or three times a day, so he's
pretty damn surprised when, after making the trip from Las
Riquezas in a ten minute blur of desert, Amanita drives right
out onto the tarmac of the Chopahuac airport and parks her
flightless stealth fighter next to an Embraer Phenom 300
executive jet, twin engines screaming, cabin door open. C'mon!
She hops out of the car and leads him by the hand up the three
or four steps into the plane and—there's no one else. It's just
the two of them in this Arabian nights flying carpet lounge,
leather sofas, ottomans, teakwood coffee table, Persian rugs,
silk curtains. He's starting to grasp just how much money
Amanita's father has. They buckle themselves up in these big,
marshmallowy seats, the jet engines scream louder and

suddenly the desert is rushing past at one, two, three hundred miles an hour. The plane leaps into the sky and not even a minute later they've leveled off and a liveried valetbot appears. A couple of exquisitely mixed martinis (it's not just ice-cold vodka with a splash of vermouth, it's like sipping liquid ether), a spliff of pot that tastes like a cross between mom's homemade apple pie and an opium smoker's dream of an opium den, and several highway divider lines of what Amanita assures him is the very finest pink Peruvian flake on the planet and the next thing he knows he's looking down on a turquoise blue bay fringed with white sandy beaches, emerald green palm trees and Mediterranean villas with terra cotta roofs (Boone's cutting costs with a cadged can of widescreen VistaVision from an unidentified 50s pic (*To Catch A Thief*?) set on the French Riviera and just hope Paramount Pictures doesn't get wind of his perfidy). A minute later they swoop out of the sky onto the landing strip of a small airport where they exit their climate-controlled time machine into a suffocating blanket of tropical heat, but rather than walk the hundred feet across the steaming tarmac to the small, humidity-stained white stucco building like the somewhat dazed-looking passengers now departing from the wobbly little twenty-seater twin engine propeller plane he had envisioned, they climb into a black Mercedes sedan that looks like it could crash through a concrete wall at a hundred miles an hour without a blemish to its finish. An equally formidable looking chauffeur with square jaw and shoulders and steel gray eyes, whose gray uniform and peaked cap shout Nazi SS officer, closes their door for them, takes his place behind the wheel and, without a word, exits the airport onto a narrow two-lane highway crowded with dense tropical foliage. They pass through a small, forlorn-looking town, clutches of electric wires drooping over shabby stucco buildings, drab shops and trashy streets, and then, *gosh, Toto*, the scene changes and they're in Oz, gated compounds, a resort, golf courses, palm trees, heavily armed cops and soldiers stationed at every intersection. Their hotel is a modern high-rise, everything bright, gleaming, stainless steel, mirrors, tiled blue and green and pink mosaics of dolphins, flamingos. Valets, attendants and desk clerks swarm around Amanita—the hotel manager himself hurries forward to greet her. (The Snowman has apparently been rendered temporarily invisible.) They all speak English perfectly, they're friendly, enthusiastic. Amanita, on the other hand, is the ice queen. Her tone is bitchy, to the manager she speaks down in high-born New England (on a frigid winter night), with the staff she insists on Spanish (of course she is *la señora,* they are *tú* and *joven*—to a man who must be forty), she complains about their accommodations before they've even seen them, she shivers dramatically and asks if there's a problem with the AC, and these sycophants love it, they clearly understand the role they're to play. They fawn, they bow and scrape and apologize profusely, they assure her action has already been taken, those responsible have been fired and very likely are being tortured to death in the basement this minute, their entire extended families and all their friends and acquaintances exiled to a barren compound in the Sonoran desert. And all that for a room and a bath? At least that's what the Snowman, who's pretty much been nowhere in his life, imagines, so he's a little bit more than surprised when their caravan of suitcases, bags and valets enters a palatial suite: mirrors, chandeliers, gilt molding and trim everywhere, master bedroom with sunken bath, guest room, separate living and dining quarters, full bar, kitchen, theater-quality media station.

After *freshening up*, which, for Amanita, means forty-five minutes in the bathroom, for the Snowman, about eight ounces of vodka on ice, they go down to the hotel restaurant where the *maître d'* personally escorts Amanita to her table and seats her (the Snowman continuing in his secondary role as the Invisible Man), all the while offering up servile platitudes that do little to thaw Amanita's arctic hauteur. Again she talks down to the wait staff, requests a *clean* water glass, this one has a spot, or a different fork, a tine seems misaligned, or there's something wrong with the salad, the lettuce looks limp, or the pheasant is undercooked, or the oysters aren't fresh, and, who knows (the Snowman certainly doesn't), maybe that's how you're supposed to act when your lunch costs enough to feed a family of six for a month. After a nap (and that's all it is, they seem to have reached some sort of understanding—that is, he understands she isn't interested, although she continues to hold out the unspoken possibility of *maybe* with unexpected little gestures, like pressing up close and tickling the back of his neck while she fussily adjusts his collar), they go to the beach. Swimming trunks (modest mid-thigh), polo shirt, sandals, shades, he's ready in thirty seconds, a minute, tops. For Amanita, preparations have just begun. Lotions, moisturizers, toners, liners, waterproof sunscreen, extra SPF facial sunscreen, antiperspirants, deodorants, hairspray. And then—which outfit, one-piece, bikini, *thong*? Oh no, not her first day. An hour later they take the elevator down and walk the twenty feet of boardwalk to the hotel beach. White sugar sand, coconut palms, umbrellas, lounge chairs, crowds of sunbathers. Seagulls laugh like inmates in an insane asylum, children scream, the chemical smell of sunscreen pervades the air. Waiters circulate with drinks. Amanita orders for them—*Tropical* somethings. A pint each of rum and tequila, bitters, tropical fruit puree, miniature pink and yellow Japanese umbrellas, plastic straws (*oh no! the sea turtles!*). It's sweet and disgusting and surprisingly addictive (Amanita, he notices, takes a sip, nothing more). Already half tanked, he watches jet skiers and windsurfers hop over small whitecaps, motorboats cross back and forth towing parasails behind them. His eyes return to shore as a platoon of Japanese businessmen, nearly identical in white short-sleeve shirts, dark blue trousers rolled above the knee, black socks secured by garters and black dress shoes, marches down the beach singing in Japanese. It's probably a company song but to the Snowman's ears it sounds an awful lot like *Do you know the way to San José?* Amanita decides it's time to take a dip. She's absolutely stunning in a string bikini, elegant, statuesque, an architectural marvel of curves and sensuality. She emits a kind of golden glow that suggests a resurgence of her vestigial Zoltec blood in the presence of the great Sun God. She strides down to the water like she's on a catwalk, barely wets her feet in the surf, then hurries on girly tiptoe back across the hot sand to the shaded safety of her lounge chair and personal umbrella, followed by practically every pair of eyes on the beach. Throughout this performance, the Snowman, alabaster white except for a pinkish, seared salmon hue on his face, stands at the water's edge, his brain steeped in alcohol, trying to decide if he should jump in and get some exercise or trail after Amanita like an obedient lapdog. Which is when he notices Condor's men, Pancho and Flaco, marching toward him, both of them red-faced and sweating profusely, completely out of place in black suits and, of all things, bowler derbies (not sure what Boone's getting at here, although Flaco does *kind* of resemble Oddjob). That settles it. He splashes into the surf and starts to swim out but it's the first time he's swum in years and he feels like a farm boy thrashing around in a stock tank. He can't get his breathing and stroke right, the saltwater burns in his eyes and sinuses. Finally he starts to relax a little and, wow, look at all these fish, they're iridescent blue and yellow, red and green, and look at that orange thing, it looks like a starfish, it *is* a starfish. And is that a fucking *barracuda?* The Snowman's having the time of his life, it's like swimming in a dream, until he feels something bump against his leg and realizes he's pretty far out and not only that but the current's gotten a heckuva lot stronger, he's actually struggling now. Panic rising, he tries to swim back to shore but he's just flailing about, his arms and legs quickly feel heavy, leaden. He wants to shout for help but he also doesn't want to look like a complete chump. His eyes lift heavenward but instead of an angel of mercy he sees this clunky-looking helicopter thing. It's a fucking drone and it's just hovering there watching him, the goddamn thing even looks like it's grinning at him, it's probably got some nerdy, bespectacled fifteen-year-old kid on the other end just tickled to death that he gets to witness this struggle between man and the natural elements. Oh boy, is that dude really drowning? Cool! Ima stream this shit. Just then a wave sweeps him across a sandy barrier and suddenly the sea is placid again and he manages to doggy paddle back to shore and stagger out of the water without looking too much like a jerk. Fortunately Condor's goons have retreated to the shade of a beach cabana (could the drone have been theirs?) and he hurries across the burning sand and gratefully collapses on his lounge chair with an exaggerated air of exhaustion (to cover the fact that he really is exhausted). By now Amanita's ready to call it a day. But instead of accompanying him back to their suite for steamy afternoon sex, she heads off to the hotel spa where she'll spend the next two hours while masseurs and masseuses, manicurists, pedicurists, personal trainers and yoga gurus lead her through a leisurely regimen of poses, stretches, modified Pilates, dumbbells, kettle bells and medicine ball, followed by fifteen minutes of steeping in a wooden vat of hot herbal tea (eucalyptus-ginger), a quick plunge in an icy cucumber and mint revitalizer bath, and the reapplication of creams, moisturizers and lotions, all of which she will relate to him later, more or less in real time (fortunately for the viewing audience, this is captured in about four seconds of film). He, meanwhile, puts these interim hours to good use drinking rum and cokes and watching TV. There's a sitcom called *This Isn't Your Life* about a maid who works for a wealthy family. The biggest joke is that in real life she actually is a dirt poor, uneducated, grossly underpaid *campesina*—she receives the same wages for appearing on TV as she does cleaning toilets. All the laughs are at her expense and there's some pretty brutal slapstick—mop handle in the face *ha!ha!ha!* falling down the stairs with a load of laundry *ho!ho!ho!* toaster oven fire resulting in third degree burns *hee!hee!hee!* Followed by an extraordinarily stupid comedy called *Burlesquoni* (apparently a knock-off of an equally boorish Italian variety show) in which a fat guy in a clown suit fondles voluptuous girls in bikinis while making lewd groping and masturbating gestures and tossing out prehistoric one liners (take my wife—*please*) to an audience of guffawing baboons, so that by the time Amanita returns to the suite totally blissed out, he's at the opposite end of the spectrum, simultaneously drunk and hung-over and decidedly out of sorts, especially when Amanita does in fact relate in excruciating detail (*Geronimo does this absolutely heavenly thing with your nipples*) the above *beauty treatment*. This is followed by lengthy deliberations over the selection of her evening wear. The pink? The beige? Strapless? Sleeves? More than enough time for some hair of the dog before they go down to dinner.

Once again Amanita is icy and aloof with the wait staff. She makes disparaging remarks about every item on the menu while the waiter and the sommelier and even the maître d' hover nearby, their pharmaceutical smiles suggesting they've geared up for some serious shit-eating. When Amanita finally orders an arugula and seared sea bass salad and a glass of champagne they praise her choice excessively. On the other hand, the Snowman's attempts at being friendly, easy-going, one working stiff to another, eh, *compadre?* are met with glowering resentment, as if he has violated an understood division between servant and master. Not helping, he's also noticeably in his cups, that aura of ugly Americanism mere centimeters from descending upon his head and proclaiming him stooge of the moment. Finally he stabs his finger at a picture of a reddish-colored fish and slurs, I'll have zhat.

After dinner, his belly full of *huachinango a la veracruzana* and a couple pints of a hopsy and potent Mexican lager (*El Brujón*), he and Amanita (electrically, magnetically attracting all eyes on the street in a low-cut red dress with spaghetti straps, probably wondering what's she doing with that drunken slob—Hey, is that Brad Pizzoccheri?! Hey, Bad Brad! Over here!) push their way through equally or even more inebriated crowds of revelers to a popular nightspot where loudly dressed, mostly fat and obnoxious greenghosts repeatedly demand that the band sing the painfully timeworn

Guantanamera, which, of course, they do, the melody anyway, to the Snowman's ears it sounds more like *Guano tan mierda* (basically *really shitty*, but not what any Spanish speaker would say—Eduardo), with the chorus going *one ton of mierrrrrda* (still in Spanish), keeping in mind that while *Guantanamera* literally means "the girl (or woman) from Guantanamo," its patriotic roots in Cuba don't exactly resonate like, say, *The Girl from Ipanema*. Which might also explain why, while the greenghosts laugh and sing along (they think), a nearby table of Cubanos, native-born Habaneros (identifiable, or at least noticeable, in their fresh off the rack (c. 1961) Brooks Brothers suits with narrow lapels and skinny ties—and either they're all wearing classic horn-rimmed glasses with fake eyebrows, nose and beard disguises, or Fidel was up to *something* (cloning?)), have begun to vocalize and then shout increasingly louder (and scarier) invectives that seem outside even Eduardo's purview of Latin American Spanish. And, uh-oh, could the fragile détente only recently arrived at between this small but tough as nails island nation and the Great Satan—er—U.S.A. already be in jeopardy?

The following morning the Snowman wakes early, no memory of how last night ended, and rather than disturb Amanita, he goes out for a stroll. The first golden sunlight is just beginning to touch the emerald green fronds of the palm trees. The streets are quiet, nobody out yet but a squad of men and women in blue jumpsuits sweeping up the detritus of last night's festivities with besoms (basically a bunch of straw or twigs tied around a stick, to the Snowman they look like the classic witches' broom—Edna), coal shovels and wheeled garbage cans. Suddenly one of them points at the Snowman's feet and exclaims, *¡Ay, caramba!* And then everyone else is pointing at his feet and exclaiming *¡Ay, caramba!* and, hmm, that's interesting because even though it must already be a hundred degrees he seems to be leaving a trail of melting snow behind his expensively shod (*Poochi?*) feet. And while the audience might presume this is Boone toying with magical realism, the Snowman surmises with some alarm that it's more likely the result of his many years of exposure to Icine, which, according to apocryphal tales heard on the job (*hahaha, ol' Nick looked like an ice cream stick*), put him at risk of two distinct and drastic consequences, the first, spontaneous combustion (cf. Dickens, *Bleak House*), the second, a more literal interpretation of *The Iceman Cometh*. He shudders as if he can already feel the ice crystals spreading through his veins. *¿Café, amigo? Está bien calentito.* An enterprising young man lugging around a large metal thermos and a stack of paper cups clearly sees an opportunity here. Ah, just what he needs. He digs a crumpled thousand peso note out of his pocket, the guy hands him his coffee and, smiling broadly, says something unintelligible while making a one-handed bell-ringing gesture, then nods up the street. Sipping his coffee, which is actually quite good, dark, rich, aromatic, the Snowman strolls in the direction indicated, expecting to see something mildly interesting, an old church or a national monument. A loud *crack* like the sound of a pine branch snapping brings him to a halt before a wrought iron gate flanked by ivy-covered stone pillars. Inside a courtyard, a burly man with a leather whip is viciously lashing the bleeding, lacerated bare back of a man chained to a post. Standing to the side, a fat man in a Panama hat and white linen suit puffs on a cigar, his free hand resting on the shoulder of a blond-headed little boy in a white polo shirt, green shorts, lacy socks and brown leather sandals. Each time the whip lands on the man's back and blood splatters everywhere, the boy jumps up and down like he's stomping a bug and screams with laughter. If Boone's trying to send a message here, the Snowman's not getting it.

Returning to the hotel, he can't figure out how the card key works. After five minutes of fumbling with the lock, he looks up to see several people recording him with their EyePhones®. *Shit!* Finally the damn electronics take pity on him and the door clicks open. He finds Amanita just waking and it's a marvel to watch. She stretches like a cat, limbs long, body sinuous, silk and satin slip over the curvature of breasts and buttocks like wind riffling across sand dunes in the Sahara. It's like a scene from a movie, like she knows she's in a movie and this is all for the camera. He even suspects she's been up for the last hour and is restaging this awakening solely for his benefit. Vamp turned blushing ingénue, she wraps herself in the bedcovers (oh, right, it's the Marilyn Monroe movie) and hurries to the bathroom, but if he was expecting her to reemerge a minute or two later wearing a sexy black peignoir or even naked, he was, yet again, sorrowfully mistaken. Instead, following a prolonged shower (sounds of water splashing, flashes of damp tiles, foggy mirrors, billowing steam, an odd, barely audible squealing or shrieking noise. Faulty showerhead? Boone foreshadowing?), she remains locked in the *powder room* for interminable applications of skin softeners, moisturizers and conditioners, depilatories, foundations, toners, highlighters, blushes and, yes, powder. Never a fan of makeup, kissing is basically like eating fresh wall plaster, he puzzles over Amanita's obsessive grooming and hygiene habits. Is this the "new feminism"? An OCD thing? You'd think she was beleaguered by random skin blemishes or she expected fur to suddenly sprout all over her body, like the kid in one of Sid Ney's more disturbing films, *The Hairy Hound,* which left the nine-year-old Snowman lying awake in bed at night, flat on his back, arms and legs splayed, terrified that if he touched himself in any way he'd feel a wooly pelt growing out. He lights a cigarette, his first of the day, and it tastes awful, nurses a preliminary scotch on the rocks he doesn't really want but justifies as compensation for enduring Amanita's obsessions. And he waits.

After breakfast (to everyone's relief, Boone skips this scene, but we have it on good account that the waiter, *maître d',* and entire kitchen staff have been promised a generous bonus), Amanita wants to do some shopping, but it's not the public market's tropical palette of papayas, mangoes, plátanos, parrots, serapes and sombreros she's interested in (the Snowman, of course, is totally fascinated by this *indigenous* stuff, his heartstrings tugged, his sympathies torn by the sight of half a dozen or so iguanas lying face down on the hot pavement, their leathery lizard hands tied behind their backs like captive bandidos, their future the frying pan). A cruise ship has just disgorged a horde of mostly obese, geriatric and phosphorescent white greenghosts who float past like celluloid revenants in ill-chosen and neon-bright casual wear that accentuates the withered calves, varicose veins, pot bellies, sagging breasts (male and female) and other signs of humanity in the ruins of time. They're gawking at everything like they just landed on Mars and their observations are equally far out. *What country did you say this is, Helen? So they speak Mexican? Lord have mercy, Elmer. What else would they speak?* A mariachi band strolls next to these dinosaurs, furiously strumming, fiddling and practically screaming at them the ever popular mariachi tune *El Querreque* while tour guides herd them in and out of select pottery, clothing and jewelry shops, which is precisely what Amanita, abandoning the rustic for the rarefied, is here for. Disgusted by this curated consumerism, the Snowman, on the other hand, is attracted to an old man's simple display of prickly pear cactus candy, which looks like blocks of slightly translucent caramel fudge, albeit (ha, ha) swarming with honey bees. It's kind of like payback time at the hive, the workers are tired of hauling the pollen for crumbs, now they're taking the cake for themselves. Brushing the bees aside with his fingers, the old man (who sure looks like someone we know, isn't that right, *Grandpa? ¿Cómo? ¿Qué dices? No hablo inglés.*) extracts a chunk of candy and encourages him to try it, and, *yum*, it's delicious, kind of grainy and chewy in an oddly satisfying way, but also sweet and caramelly. *Mi esposa*, the old man says proudly. Yeah? Your wife made it? Well it's still pretty good stuff. He hands the old man a thousand pesos, finds a bench in a small park and sits down to enjoy his confection … but, hmm, this is interesting. A couple of kids, maybe twelve-thirteen-years-old, are apparently in disagreement over the ownership of a bicycle, which both kids are holding onto tightly, one by the handlebars, the other the seat. The seat-holder has a deadly serious expression that looks far too adult for his age and he's very earnestly arguing his case (the Snowman's pretty sure it's his bike). The kid gripping the handlebars looks like a mean, scrappy little badass who doesn't give a rat's ass for rightful ownership. They've got a small audience of other kids, including one who must be the earnest kid's younger brother, he's only seven or eight but he's clenching his fists like he wants to jump in on big brother's behalf. Suddenly fists do fly and POW! the badass kid sends a Bruce Lee roundhouse kick to Ernesto's head and, *bam*, he's flat on his back, out cold, his younger brother's crying, trying to shake him awake, while the little badass, beaming like he just won first prize at the county fair, is pushing the bicycle away, followed by a small coterie of admirers.

Okay, okay, now we get it. Boone's trying to make a point about the underside of paradise, hidden poverty, violence, class divisions, etc. Maybe he'll lighten up as Amanita, wearing a newly purchased jade necklace with gold clasp and fasteners, now leads the Snowman to a conveniently located local Maya ruin, curious because she hasn't previously exhibited any interest in antiquities, and even the Snowman, who's got a couple of archaeological sites under his belt, isn't that impressed with the shabby, mildew-stained limestone platforms and temples. The view, however, is incredible. The site's situated right on the edge of a rocky cliff above the splashing ivory and turquoise surf. Something else catches his eye. A small bay nearby where a bunch of tents and thatched huts are scattered along the white sandy beach. A large red sign on a wooden pole declares this enclave *El Paraíso*, apparently some kind of hippie hangout, backpackers, low budget travelers, many of whom are lying on the beach or wading in the turquoise water, mostly, it seems, naked, which, okay, is a little startling to American eyes, but that's not what makes him stare unabashedly. Among this bohemian crowd he has just spotted the YC, also naked. They're too far away for him to really *see anything*—if, that is, he were, um, interested *look, is that a spaceship?* Why does he keep running into these two? Some minor plot device Boone has in mind? An object lesson of some kind? Truth is, he's starting to resent the male half of the YC (*asshole!*) for being with this pretty hippie chick who seems perfectly happy with their freewheeling lifestyle, while here he is, wearing way too many clothes and trailing after this uptight rhymes-with-rich (which she also is) like her fucking lapdog (minus the, um …). Which might partially justify, or at least explain, or make excuses for (alright, *denials*) the systematic belts of a very expensive single malt scotch he's been knocking back every ten minutes or so from a solid gold flask (yes, the irony is lost). He seems to be on a willfully self-destructive binge now, poisoning himself in some perverse ratio to Amanita's growing disinterest (or is it waning interest?). Largely abstaining from stimulants herself since their arrival (Is this a new health kick? Is she pulling herself together to carry out an unpleasant mission?), she does nothing to discourage him. He's even caught her giving him amused sidelong glances, the black serpent of a sneer curling her lips every time he lights another cigarette or takes another drink. That she might have something more sinister (and expedient) in mind doesn't occur to him until—a whizzing sound like the whir of tiny diaphanous wings next to his right ear alerts him to the presence of stinging insects. Something zings past his left ear and this time he suspects these pests are both leaden and lethal. Someone's trying to kill him! That dude behind the garbage can. Is that Pancho's black eye patch, his good eye sighting monocularly, and luckily for the Snowman, myopically, along the barrel of a 6.5 mm Mannlicher-Carcano rifle fixed with a silencer? Or, second glance, is it simply a homeless person digging through the trash with a stick? Not taking any chances, he crouches behind a limestone wall and, to the amusement of several children and the concern bordering on horror of their parents, duckwalks to the safety of a public restroom. Amanita seems completely unfazed by this event except for a mild look of disgust, at what, or whom, isn't clear. The Snowman's apparent cowardice (was it just a bee?)? The putative Pancho's poor marksmanship? Men in general? She abruptly announces she's tired of the beach scene, they're leaving, and he's only too happy to blow this snooty dump.

14
Tenochtitlán

FACTORIES ROAR, trucks, taxis, buses and cars honk and beep, police whistles shriek, jackhammers bang, helicopters drone overhead, jet planes thunder into the sky, people laugh and shout, cry, sing, moan and scream, and the din of civilization rises from the ghost foundation of a great city of fantastical buildings, pyramids, temples, palaces and observatories, painted brilliant crimson, yellow and blue hues. The largest city in the Americas, possibly the world. A center of trade, commerce, capital of the Aztec empire. And then they came, the Spaniards, *conquistadores*, led by the courageous and enterprising (or ruthless and conniving, depending on which side of the fence you're on) Hernán Cortés, and equipped with guns and cannons, horses, steel armor and an invisible ally, the devastating virus, smallpox, they conquered this great metropolis and destroyed it, and from its ruins they raised up a city modeled after those in Spain, loyal to the Catholic church and the Spanish crown.

Seen from space at night, Mexico City looks like a vast nebular sprawl of dirty white light. From Amanita's Embraer Phenom 300, descending through a brown blanket of smog and towering spumes of smoke and ash, the *distrito federal* looks, to the Snowman anyway, like a giant industrial motherboard, and descending farther, a pizza box diorama of high rises, sports arenas, cathedrals, factories, incongruous green polyp-like hillocks, public markets, malls, stores, restaurants, apartment buildings, tenement houses and huge sprawling megaslums (about which he knows nothing, *yet*) congregated around a sky-scraping crystal garden-like eruption of glass and steel architecture in the downtown commercial district. The plane lands and the Snowman, who had assumed they were returning to Chopahuac and in fact has no idea this is Mexico City (*Chicago?*), can see out the window that the crowded working class neighborhood jammed up against the airport chain-link fence probably isn't an optimal tourist site. Loud explosions seem to confirm this impression as he and Amanita exit the terminal. But it isn't gunshots or bombs going off. It's *cohetes*, fireworks. Bluish-white puffs of smoke erupt in the sky, followed a second later by loud booms. (In celebration of a saint's day, he'll discover, which means you can pretty much expect to hear these explosions every day, it's kind of an inside joke—Eduardo.) Again, a pretty stalwart-looking black Mercedes is waiting for them in the taxi stand, driven by an equally stalwart-looking chauffeur with granite jaw and pole vaulter's shoulders in a gray SS officer's uniform. He holds the door for them, positions himself behind the wheel and without a word transports them in climate-controlled comfort, untouched by the clamor, clang and noxious effusions of the twenty-five million or so souls who exist in the celluloid blur passing outside their windows, across town to their hotel, which, on the plus side, is rated six stars out of five, on the negative, it's surrounded by ten-foot tall concrete blast barriers (painted with scenes of children playing in fields of flowers). Also of note, scores of heavily armed guards are positioned everywhere. Meticulously groomed men in tailored suits check the undersides of arriving vehicles with small rectangular mirrors on the end of selfie sticks.

Once again Amanita is greeted with royal fanfare, suggesting just how much respect her father, by proxy, commands even here in the Big Chalupa. Their penthouse suite is the pentiest house in the joint, it's like the top tier of the Hanging Gardens of Babylon. Fountains, marble, mirrors, a sunken pool, broad leafy tropical plants everywhere, cheerful interactive chef and bartender bots on call 24/7. And then, either Amanita has a bug up her ass or else it's Boone (of *course* it's Boone), they're immediately off on a whirlwind tour. Employing cutting edge technology and his brilliant young cyber hacker—the kid's only sixteen but she (yes, *she*, Boricua, badass retro riot grrrl, *so fuck yez*) hacks like an AI raised on a steady diet of liquid coolants and algorithms—Boone splices together video feed from security cameras all over the city to give the impression of the Snowman and Amanita fluidly passing through their sightseeing itinerary in minutes (and it's pretty obvious Boone's got his Baedeker in hand—he's got something in his hand anyway). We see an overhead shot of the orange Tiffany lamp shade of the Palacio de Bellas Artes, and then the Snowman inside staring at Siqueiros' mural of a slightly deranged-looking, blue-eyed, wildly blond-haired and bearded Hernán Cortés (the discerning audience member will not fail to see a modicum of resemblance to the Snowman—nor does it escape Amanita, who is staring at him with her own creeped-out look, as if something she had not wanted to believe possible has just been confirmed). *Crunch crunch crunch.* Perversely, Cortés' face is presented in a kind of Siamese twin symbiosis with the Aztec king Cuauhtémoc, whose own face is a mask of torment. His headdress of red macaw feathers shears back from his brow like flames, vertical streaks of war paint run down his cheeks like scars or claw marks, his eye sockets are dark, empty, maybe he has been blinded, his mouth is open in a cry of rage, pain, betrayal. Judging by the Snowman's tormented expression you'd think he was personally responsible for Cuauhtémoc's suffering. *Crunch crunch crunch.* Amanita, on the other hand, exudes not pity but seething contempt for this *heathen* king. Oddly, she is visibly and uncharacteristically moved by one of Diego Rivera's rare portraits, his second wife, Lupe Marín, seated on a simple wooden chair, her long, languorous figure loosely draped in a short-sleeved, ankle-length white dress belted at the waist, her hands folded together over her crossed knees. (Her hands look huge. Some see a reference to Michelangelo's David, others simply a matter of perspective). Her head is tilted backwards, her mouth partly open, her lower jaw jutting slightly sideways almost as if she were sneering (some also see Elvis—only if Rivera saw into the future). Her eyes are pale green, like the jade beads of her necklace, and slightly hooded, which, along with the angle of her head and her facial expression, suggests either an enormous sadness (Rivera's infamous philandering?) or sense of regret. *Crunch crunch crunch.* To this observer she looks like she's been crying buckets. Nor, coincidentally, does the Snowman fail to notice a resemblance between Ms. Marín and Amanita, who has been staring at this painting as if witnessing her own gestation, and even more startling, tears are streaming down her face, startling because the Snowman has never considered empathy Amanita's strong suit and this full faucet emotional display is completely out of character. Boone's clearly getting at something because, again thanks to camera magic, Amanita and the Snowman step out of the museum and directly into Frida Kahlo's famous *Casa Azul.* We see blue walls, red lintels, green doors, tropical plants, Maya statuary, reflecting pools and fountains. The camera, along with an unbroken line of tourists, moves inside a studio crowded with wooden boxes of silver paint tubes, bottles of pigment, tin cans of brushes, easels, charcoal sketches, unfinished paintings, then on to a small bedroom with a rectangular mirror rigged over the bed that might lead the viewer to believe at first glance is for the purpose of enhanced pleasure … until you look down at the bed itself and see lying on it something that looks like a medieval torture device but is actually a leather harness and metal brace meant to contain a body broken in a horrible traffic accident and wracked until the end of its life with almost unbearable pain. After that, another bedroom and here we catch up with Amanita and the Snowman standing in a queue of tourists before a neatly made bed in the center of which is positioned Frida's polished black death mask framed by a black shawl embroidered with roses, her face smooth, strangely androgynous, the famous unibrow and mustache gone. Inexplicably, now the Snowman feels *his* eyes welling with tears, but he's not alone. The effect of being in such proximity to this great artist's personal life, her work, her suffering and her death is evident in many visitors' expressions. Amanita exhibits neither empathy nor sympathy, however, as she stands before one of Frida's most famous paintings, a woman lying naked on a bed, her body bloody, torn, brutally murdered by the knife-wielding boyfriend standing over her (*I only gave her a few nicks*, the caption says). It's almost as if Frida intended this painting as a mute witness for the prosecution, the murder victim herself pointing a bloody, accusatory finger at her murderer—metaphorically, one might suspect, the unfaithful Diego, but Boone has something else in mind as the camera tightens in on Amanita's face, which, up close, is riven with a woodblock print's stark shadows and angles that an amateur art critic might interpret as a representation of guilt and possibly remorse. To add to both the Snowman's and the audience's confusion, another image, kind of a facsimile of Frida's painting, borderline subliminal, appears on the screen, a young woman lying on—or, no, she's tied to a bed, naked. She has dark hair, otherwise her face is indistinct, the shot fuzzy, details unclear, the camera—there is a camera— focuses on a spot on her right breast, a beauty mark or tattoo in the shape of—the Playboy bunny? Highly unlikely, Jim. Mickey Mouse? Try something else. *Ohhh*, now he gets it … the *Chaac Mool?* Then … blades flash, blood splatters, the screen goes black. Students of film will later try (wrongly) to tie this scene to the above-mentioned *muralista* David Alfaro Siqueiros (A Stalinist apologist? Wannabe *sicario?*), who, life imitating art, led an unsuccessful assassination attempt, machine guns blazing, bombs blasting, against Leon Trotsky's spartan Coyoacán residence, but Boone's not going to touch that contretemps with a ten-foot papirosa (did anyone else read *priapus?*). Instead, it's off to Chapultepec Park. Trees, gardens, walkways. Throngs mill about. Children laugh and scream. Vendors hawk postcards, toys, balloons, sandwiches, tacos,

sodas, ice cream. Swan-shaped paddle boats and colorful party
barges circle the murky, famously anti-freeze green waters of
the manmade lake. Rising above it all, the rather dullish
(architecturally) Chapultepec Castle. A plaque informs the
Snowman that *Chapultepec* means "hill of grasshoppers" in
Nahuatl. Coincidentally, the man standing next to him reading
the same plaque (the Spanish version above, you can tell by the
way his eyes move) is crunching handfuls of roasted
grasshoppers between his teeth *crunch crunch crunch*. The
Snowman's spider senses tingle again. Isn't this the annoying
individual who was loudly munching fried pork skins in the art
museum despite posted warnings against food and drink?
Annoyance and a resurgence of paranoia give way to disbelief
as he reads farther and discovers that not only is this castle one
of those very *halls of Montezuma* alluded to in the famous
Marine hymn he and his fellow scholars sang with such gusto
during Ms. Winfrey's fifth grade music appreciation hour,
except that for the people of Mexico this edifice holds a far
different significance: the martyrdom of *los Niños Héroes,* the
six young cadets, some not much older than Ms. Winfrey's
wards, who died defending this very same castle against those
very same Marines during the great U.S. land grab,
euphemistically called the Mexican-American war, which Ms.
Winfrey most decidedly *did not* teach her young charges and
probably knew nothing about herself (somebody's getting
snippy). In fact, our devoted schoolmarm (sixteen-hour work
days, spends a good part of her meager income on books, art
supplies and supplemental food for her students, she's currently
saving for the down payment on a .38 special and firearms
training) has been smiling away like an inebriated goose during
this brief tutorial but in her eyes now you can see she's going,
what the fuck? The Snowman, pretending ignorance himself
even though no pretense is necessary, glances skyward like,
don't blame me, and whataya know, there's another of those
damn drones hovering overhead like a mutant insect. Is it
watching him? Naww, it's probably just some advertising

agency filming a tourist promotion. After all, the day is perfectly clear, the sun shining, the sky blue, the filthy blanket of smog scrubbed away by a hastily enacted anti-pollution campaign, which is probably why he only now notices this incredible sight. It's a mountain, it's *the* mountain, yes, the phantom mountain he saw on his vertical trek with Grandpa but also, as every citizen of the D.F. knows, the great snow-blown, sometimes fire-breathing Popocatepetl, and this is clearly Boone's doing because it's like the damn thing's right there, like the Snowman is standing directly under the volcano. All around him people are pointing and gaping. Oddly, Amanita's expression is pure horror, like the plaster cast of a Greek oracle who's just had a premonition of utter disaster. She mutters a phrase that resonates in the Snowman's brain but won't ring clearly until much later because she says it in Spanish, *horno hueco!* At which point her until now admirable patience as tour guide (pretty sure she's getting *something* out of this) gives way to exasperation and she says with a tigrine snarl, The hell with history, let's go shopping.

We now see frame grabs of the trendy, tony Polanco district on Avenida Presidente Masaryk—hotels, art galleries, shops, office towers, apartment buildings, upscale shopping malls, stores, designer boutiques and jewelers from *Armoani* to *Tzara*. While Amanita's inside a *Victoria's Top Secrets* dispensing cash like an ATM in exchange for half an ounce of silk (the weight of an average hummingbird) woven into a pair of panties comprised as much of imagination as substance (also like the hummingbird), the Snowman, who has been people-watching on a bench outside, notices two women at a cosmetics counter, one square and chunky in a beige skirt and jacket, the other tall and rectangular in a pink polyester pants suit with violently clashing yellow piping. There's something fishy about these dames. He suspects they're only pretending to examine their makeup while they surreptitiously check him out in the mirror. He's also pretty sure they're actually guys in drag. The tall skinny gal, who, he notices now, is wearing a mauve eye patch, is particularly unconvincing. Well, he won't let these thugs intimidate him this time. He's going right over there and call their bluff. Think you're pretty clever, huh, *Pancho?* He gives the tall skinny gal a fairly hard whack on the shoulder. The woman (and, yes, it is a woman) turns with a horrified look, *Pero ¿qué hace? ¿Está Ud. loco?* Slap! (My God! What's wrong with you? Are you crazy? *Slap!*—Eduard*ito* again.) Oh no! How could he make such a terrible mistake? He apologizes profusely, I'm so sorry, I thought you were this guy I know. *¿Qué? ¿Yo, hombre? ¡Cómo se atreve!* (What? Me? A man? How dare you!) *Slap! Slap! Slap!* By now several people have stopped to stare. A pair of washerwomen in shabby gray uniforms quickly shuffle past the camera, not sure what their role here is. The Snowman is lucky to extract himself from this nightmare without the police intervening. When Amanita asks why his face is red he says, laconic as a courtroom bailiff, Spicy cacahuates—*really hot.* And then they're off again, and, boy, this new film editor Boone hired (blackmailed, something to do with a porn shoot and underage *actors*) is amazing because the next thing the Snowman knows, he's riding in the back seat of a classic 1961 Lincoln Continental convertible overflowing with sprays of roses, carnations and gladiolus and packed with shrieking, screeching drag queens (DQs) in outrageous drag (ballroom gowns circa WWII are currently all the outrage). A bottle of champagne has popped in the front seat where Amanita's sitting and a tray of coke is circulating in the back where, blushing like an aw shucks eighteen-year-old Bubba just off the ranch who ain't never seen nothing like this in his entire life, the Snowman's jammed between *Fruella* in a flouncy pink chiffon gown with a creamy white silk rose in the décolletage and *Lola*, apparently the intellectual in this crowd, bucking the trend in black horn-rimmed glasses, a compact black pillbox hat, and a more subdued, scoop-necked, short-sleeved black cocktail dress. They're in a line of classic convertibles, all packed with flowers and DQs, honking, shouting and waving in the middle of an enormous LGBTQ pride parade, hundreds of thousands of people marching—well, more like boogeying, sashaying and/or strutting—beneath rainbow flags and banners the entire length of the Paseo de la Reforma, confetti, streamers and balloons everywhere, whistles blowing, bands playing. They pass the statue of Diana the Huntress, Amazon bow drawn, nakedly voluptuous, not even a naughty pair of undies to hide her bounteous buttocks. Almost as bold, the golden, gleaming Angel of Independence perched on a column high above the jostling crowd. Bare-breasted, flowing robes fallen around her hips and thighs, wings outstretched, she appears to be descending from the heavens to place the crown of laurels she holds in her right hand upon the head of some presumptive hero or victor. Pheidippides? A former president of Mexico? (It's in honor of Father Miguel Hidalgo, the father of Mexican Independence, but I don't suppose you know anything about that either, do you, *Boone?*—the fact check *girl* sounding increasingly ~~bitchy~~ pissy. And *please*, why don't you just stick with your ass kissy Eduard*ito* since you pay him twice as much as me!) The parade loops around the monument to King Cuauhtémoc, also dressed for the occasion in a full-length gown and feathered headdress that cascades down the back of his neck like a cockatoo's crest. And it's right here that Amanita's crowd somehow gets separated from the rest of the parade, pursued, the Snowman notices, by a flamingo pink 1927 Rolls-Royce Phantom Roadster, and darn if that doesn't look like Pancho and Flaco in Scarlett O'Hara sausage curls and flouncy antebellum hoop skirts. Determined not to repeat his earlier mistake, the Snowman acts nonchalant, even though he's pretty certain these *dames* are out to kill him, a surmise that seems verified when another of those pesky 6.5 mm Mannlicher-Carcano wasps whizzes by his right ear. But let's not lose our cool, Snowman. Just keep telling yourself it's only a movie, right *Boone?* And, okay, this looks innocent enough. They've driven into a huge street market, thousands of wood-framed stalls jammed together (the overhead camera shows us an enormous patchwork quilt of blue, red, green and yellow canvas and plastic tarps). Screeching, laughing, tittering, the whole crowd piles out of the Cadillac with Amanita in the lead and the Snowman in tow (you *could* even say Fruella and Lola are *dragging* him) as they plunge into the marketplace madness, throngs of people bump and bang into each other, Norteño and Tejano bands strum, thump and blare, food stands hiss, sizzle, smoke and steam. But forget the *menudo* and *pollo asado*, these gals are here to do some shopping. They swish past aisles of TVs, computers, sound systems, sashay past aisles of men's hats and boots, tools and appliances, glance *meh* at the tables of pistols, automatic rifles, crates of ammo, hand grenades and missile launchers, *coo* and *aww* over the women and children, mostly Asian, but, sure, also some Middle Eastern, African and South Seas Islanders, crammed like chickens in wire cages with price tags attached, five hundred, a thousand US dollars, ten thousand for a purportedly virginal Thai *princess* who looks maybe thirteen-fourteen *isn't she a doll?* and finally dive into the full-tilt hullabaloo of the ladies' clothing department. Endless racks of skirts, dresses, blouses. Towering stacks of shoe and hat boxes. Mountains of silk and satin bustiers, bras and panties. Women in hard hats and miners' lamps are flailing away with pickaxes. One gal's operating a Komatsu mini-backhoe. The DQs dig in like seasoned infantry armed with entrenching tools. Even Amanita has reverted to some pretty serious XX duds diving. The Snowman, of course, is bored shitless. Also, and this must be Boone messing with him again, he keeps catching liminal glimpses of men in feathered headdresses, knee-length loincloths and jade wrist, knee, and ankle cuffs dancing around like pre-Colombian gremlins. Of course he couldn't know this market has been a trading site since ancient Aztec times, or that it's more commonly called the "thieves market" because most of this stuff is either stolen, smuggled, counterfeit or a name brand knockoff. You want *Nikey, Versache, Rolux, Sonny*? You got it, sort of. If you're looking for a bargain it's the bargainest basement in town, but, *caveat emptor,* shoppers—*all sales are final*. And, *oh no*, on that sour note, here come Pancho and Flaco, and it is indeed the dastardly duo, ruffled skirts bunched around their knees like antebellum ingénues traipsing through rain puddles, only these gals are packing serious heat and the Snowman's starting to feel like dead meat, and, hmm, Amanita's got that malevolent smile again that suggests an ulterior motive for joining this slumming party. Ah, but there's something else we neglected to mention. Among the residents this place is also called *Barrio Bravo* (loosely translated as *badass neighborhood*—Eduardo, and *please*, this isn't about me) because it's inhabited by a large population of ex-cons, gang members, drug dealers, gun smugglers, traffickers in human beings, and more recently—and probably the most threatening in the government's eyes—an artist's colony. In fact, at this moment a bunch of very bad dudes in low-rider shorts, flannels, Ts, wife beaters, tons of bling, and packing a frightening amount of weaponry are chillin' with a beer and a blunt when they spy Scarlett and sister Sue Ellen charging through their turf waving heat and naturally they take an interest and the next thing you know lead's flying everywhere. POW! BANG! *Ow, ya got me!* Amanita, the Snowman, and the DQ crew take off running, but, hmm, *coincidence?* It seems this kerfuffle (eye roll) coincides with a new government crack-down on the "informal economy," ostensibly to preserve historic sites and ensure the safety of tourists (who might decide to spend their ducats elsewhere). And here Boone's got some pretty interesting footage (and no, it's not from Portland). Unmarked vans screech to a halt and dozens of men in civilian clothes emerge armed with clubs, brass knuckles and iron bars and wade into the melee, knocking people to the ground, cracking skulls, destroying stalls, pseudo, faux, sham and bogus *Vvlgari, Halfinger, Armoani* and *Poochi* flying everywhere. Then, sirens wailing, lights flashing, thank God, it's the police, right? But, ha ha, if this isn't vaudeville, what is? The men in uniform put on a big show of chasing off the *vigilantes* while getting in several kicks and punches themselves before they depart, taking a number of unfortunate *sales associates* with them for "further conversation."

Oh, this awful violence. Back in the car, Fruella lets out a sob and loudly blows her nose.

Please, let's not hyperventilate, Lola, sanding a lime-green pinky nail, says in a smoky Lauren Bacall voice.

Fruella sighs. It's this terrible Catholic guilt.

Yes, and the Catholics certainly have plenty to feel guilty about, Lola replies.

And now the intellectual really comes out of her closet as Lola warms to the topic. Keeping in mind it was the Spanish throne that unleashed the good fathers' sadistic tendencies. And might we not trace thence vestiges of the Moorish influence on the Iberian peninsula—oh, you know, turbans, steam baths, big scimitars? Lola rolls amber (butterscotch? honey? *peach?*) eyes behind her black horn-rims. And please, let's not forget those frightful blood rites of our pre-Columbian ancestors. All that slicing and dicing? *Uf!* Save it for the kitchen! Lola's argument is basically nature versus nurture, i.e., is violence inherent in humankind? Or does it have its roots in poverty, abuse, a point of view the Snowman is inclined to agree with, at which Amanita scoffs and calls him a bleeding heart. There's a sense they're just about to go for each other's throats when Boone enters the fray by resorting to an old gimmick—the split screen (top and bottom).

Los de arriba (we're in the money)

This is what Amanita sees:

She sees *Armoani* and *Poochi* coming out of high-rise condos and office buildings, *DeFlorian* and *Yves St. Courant* coming out of banks and restaurants. She sees the glitter and gleam of gold and diamonds in shop windows. She sees watches, bracelets, necklaces and earrings whose price tags exceed a doctor's salary. She sees polished leather shoes, boots, bags, wallets and purses that cost more than a nurse earns in a year. She sees a dog walker leading a dozen tail-wagging doggie dogs from the smallest Asian model to the largest mastiff exported from the British Isles and every single one of them is just *sooooo* adorable (and entitled to healthcare the average citizen will never receive). She sees the Mercedes and Lamborghinis, the Bugattis and Ferraris zooming through green lights. She sees exclusive boutiques and haberdashers where casual wear and three-piece suits cost as much as those cars. She sees restaurants that exude the climate-controlled atmosphere of private art galleries, the menus look like wedding announcements, the ingredients sound as complex as rocket science, the prices aren't listed, there's no mention of cost or payment, no money is exchanged and all transactions are conducted by bioscan debiting. This is the domain of the rich, the privileged, the elect, the chemically, surgically, orthodontically perfect, the plastically corrected, the spa and gym slim and trim, personally trained, massaged, groomed, anointed ... those (very few) who stand on the pinnacle of the pyramid.

Los de abajo (under the pavement)

This is what the Snowman sees:

He sees working class people lined up at street vendors' food carts, legions of people wearing face masks against the pollution, piles of dog shit on the sidewalk, armies of street sweepers in bright yellow rubberized uniforms, itinerant hand-cranking organ grinders (some kind of government-sponsored thing?). He hears jackhammers banging away at concrete, construction workers in hard hats whistling or shouting to each other *¡Ándale, puto!* He smells cigarette smoke and everywhere he looks he sees men, women, rich, poor, professional and working class stiffs puffing away like fire-breathing dragons. *Fumar para a ver más claro, ¿no, Snowman?* A gnarly and also familiar-looking little old hobgoblin exhales an industrial cloud of smoke in his direction and gives him a knowing wink. A gaunt, haunted-looking man who looks straight (or not) out of

Reefer Madness rushes past flashing a piece of cardboard at him
with the following message printed in black magic marker
¡FUMAR MARIJUANA NO ES MALO! ¡LO MALO SOMO
TÚ Y YO! He sees bronze, cast iron, gilt and stainless steel
statues and sculptures on sidewalks, street corners, in parks:
butterflies, elves, giant snails, lizard people standing upright in
a lizard canoe, mythical creatures, voluptuous female nudes. He
sees palm trees and purple flowering jacarandas, huge abstract
paintings ten, twenty stories tall on the sides of buildings, walls
covered with elaborate graffiti (Aztec gods and warriors are
popular). He sees throngs of people lined up outside the
fortress-like US embassy, thick stacks of documents in their
hands, a kind of droning sound, a little like a muted church
choir (think white Protestant, not black Baptist), rising from
their midst, every one of them whistling, humming or actually
singing some variation of the famous El Residente Brandy logo
as sung by Los Viejos Borrachos (Remember? *It's better to be a
resident in the US than president of Mexico*?). He sees the
Bolsa's blue glass dome with the revolving band at the base that
displays world market figures like the type ball in an electric
typewriter tapping out a message of wealth and privilege that
has nothing to do with these people's lives except to ensure
them more misery (*lalalala*). Ditto the heavily armed police in
bulletproof helmets, chest plates, shoulder pads, shin and arm
guards. He sees an older colonial city of churches, municipal
buildings and villas constructed of adobe, limestone and red and
black volcanic rock tilting at precarious angles or sinking out of
sight of the emergent new metropolis due to the unstable
swampland they were built on (Montezuma's other revenge?).
And cramming its face in among the colonial architecture and
modern high rises, in the doorways and on the street corners, he
sees Indian women in bright orange, red and yellow huipils,
shawls and scarves seated on the pavement with dirty-faced
children, hands out for whatever alms and manna that fall
providentially from the heavens which, in their case, is about
two or three above their heads. He sees homeless people

huddled under blankets or cardboard boxes or makeshift tents beneath bridges or camped on concrete islands in the middle of roaring street intersections or sprawled unconscious on the sidewalk. He sees legless, armless, blind, horribly scarred and deformed people on homemade wooden crutches or wheeled contrivances. He sees the bloody crimson tracks left in the street by pious but misguided supplicants crawling on their hands and knees behind a taxi with a portrait of the Virgen de Guadalupe on its rear bumper that enjoins them *¡Síganme!* Most noticeable, he sees kids, noticeable because shouldn't they be in school or at home with their doting abuelitas or *something?* He sees kids selling chewing gum, newspapers, candy, bottled water, soda, CDs, toys, cigarettes, pocket knives, ballpoint pens. Kids shining shoes, acting as guides, laborers, clowns, window washers on street corners. Kids dressed in ragged shorts and t-shirts, in torn and stained and ill-fitting skirts and dresses, in shoes missing heels or the toes torn open or dirty bare feet. Kids with tired, sad eyes in tired, sad little faces. Packs of mean-looking survivalist kids with knotty, muscular arms. Kids sitting on curbs and in doorways, their faces buried in paper bags, their brains buried in clouds of paint thinner, or else, heads nodding, eyes blank, squatting in pools of tarry black liquid. Members of the audience are becoming squeamish. This is a little more realistic than the usual soap opera drivel they watch with their afternoon cup of tea. Apparently Boone's inserting documentary footage he *obtained* from an unnamed source. Oh, and tell me if the narrator's German accent doesn't sound familiar. Hidden from de eyes of de casual visitor to dis teeming city der exists a subterranean community of lost boys und girls who live in doorways und cardboard boxes, in parks, in garbage dumps und under bridges, who migrate from one area to another like vild animals, copulating, fighting und killing each other, who numb demselves against de cold, de hunger, de pain by getting high on glue, paint thinner and solvents, who are brain-damaged, traumatized, ridden with tuberculosis, hepatitis und AIDS, who are constantly at risk of rape, murder, sexual enslavement, who beg, steal und prostitute demselves in order to survife … dose, in udder vords, who are crushed beneath de pyramid. And here the German narrator—Herr Zog, is it?—who has been on something of a roll, grudgingly turns the reins back over to, um, whoever's driving this train and at the moment it looks like—the *Snowman?* Most of all what he sees are Mexicans, thousands, tens of thousands, *millions* of them, their hair is black, their faces some shade of bronze, copper, terra cotta, latte, flan, their eyes, ears, noses, skin tone and physique some element of Eurasian, Spanish, Moorish, Creole, Mestizo, Nahua, Maya and hundreds of other *indígenas.* Every one of them is individual, discrete, unique (yes, we *all* are, thank you, Ms. Winfrey), and yet they are all clearly identifiable as Mexican, which means the Snowman, he of the phosphorescent hue, stands out like a dandelion in an OCD manicured lawn, or, more accurately, a mini marshmallow in a pot of café de olla (yes, redundant—spot it?). And boy, these Mexicans have got a bee in their bonnet, a burr in their britches, a *cheep* on their shoulder, they're fed-up, pissed off, tired of being the world's doormat, dissed and dismissed by everybody, especially their own *pinche gobierno.* What really sets off the powder keg is the disappearance of a bunch of students from a rural teacher's college (*disappeared* is a transitive verb south of the border—Eduardo). It's kind of like slaughtering baby seals. Right on cue (lights, cameras, action—*Boone*), Amanita and her crew get caught up in a giant protest march on Paseo de Reforma and this is the exact opposite of the joyful gay street parade. This is hundreds of thousands of very angry citizen, farm laborers, construction workers, union members, healthcare professionals, service industry employees. They're shouting slogans and blowing whistles, they're waving banners and posters, black Antifa flags with raised fists, red Communist flags with hammers and sickles, they're demanding *¡Derechos indígenas! ¡Derechos humanos!* They're shouting *¡Fue el estado!* Think of the effect on commerce! On tourism! the city's leaders plead. Perhaps someone should also inform dese leaders of de effects of poferty und disease, of drug cartels, corrupt politicians und police. Herr Zog, himself a citizen of a (tenuous) welfare state, unable to restrain himself. Der gute Herr's uncharacteristic sarcasm, at first seen as a major blunder for the purportedly impartial commentator, will later be recognized as the opening shot in a new wave of polemical documentary film-making— Ed.)

15

The Bullfight

THEN, THERE'S CLEARLY BEEN A GAP in the narrative or some
footage is missing because next we see the Snowman and
Amanita seated in an enormous bullring. The stands are packed.
A voice is speaking over the PA, the Snowman only catches
certain phrases, *Damasssss yyyyyy caballeroooosss …
Estimadooosss visitanteeesss …* Then everyone is rising for the
Mexican National Anthem, although against all federal and state
rules, regulations and public decorum it's been jazzed up a bit
(hacked?) and suddenly the entire stadium's dancing the
Macarena, it's like a genetic impulse, like they have zero say in
the matter, you can see the embarrassment and dismay on
people's faces. By the time they retake their seats they're
gasping for breath and sighing with relief, but they immediately
jump up again and break into a loud cheer *Raaaaa!* as a trumpet
sounds and a matador in a traditional montera cap and a red
satin and brocade uniform sparkling with gold and silver
embroidery enters the stadium accompanied by soaring strings,
blaring brass, thrumming guitars and clattering castanets, the
kind of music the Snowman associates with Spain and, well,
bullfighting. The trumpet sounds again and again the crowd
roars *Raaaaa!* as a wooden gate opens and a sleek, black block
of muscle with horns like medieval torture devices and testicles
as big as cannon balls trots into the arena like the baddest
motherfucker in town. There's no doubt in anyone's mind that
this bovine locomotive is capable of jumping over the wall and

into the stands in pursuit of any dumbass foolish enough to mess with his shit. Perhaps this is why the bull seems somewhat nonplussed when the matador approaches and with a wave of his red cape invites him to charge. The bull obliges, but in a flash the annoying red cape vanishes and the bull has thundered past the man who wields it. *Ooooléeee!* the crowd roars. *Hmph!* the bull snorts and stamps his hooves. Thus begins what appears to the uninformed Snowman as a kind of foreplay. The matador taunts and teases and swishes his cape, the bull stamps and snorts and charges about like a hormonal adolescent. And when the matador abruptly bows and leaves the arena, the bull shakes his head and snorts with contempt, certain he has intimidated this puny human being. But now the trumpet sounds again and again the announcer says something unintelligible and again the crowd roars *Raaaaa!* as a pair of rustically dressed (straw hats, white cotton shirts and pants, black wool vests) *picadores* armed with pink and green-ribboned lances trots in on heavily padded horses. Now what? The bull watches warily as they approach him. One of the picadores lifts his lance and the Snowman flinches as he jabs the point deep into the huge mound of muscle at the base of the bull's neck and bright red blood gushes over the animal's gleaming black hide. *Raaaaa!* the crowd roars. The bull bellows with rage and pain and digs its horns into the horse's protective padding, but the picador skillfully circles his horse so the bull expends even more energy trying to gore him and—*jab*—again the lance stabs into the bull's neck and, *ouch*, again the Snowman flinches as he feels a sudden sharp pain in *his* neck. What the heck? Out of the corner of his eye he sees Amanita smile like a sorceress pleased with the success of her spell as the crowd again roars its approbation *Raaaaa!* The bull lowers its head, raises it, its fierce gaze searching the cheering spectators for the one who did this to him. And here he comes again, it's the second picador and—*jab*—his green and white-ribboned lance bites into the bull's shoulder and more blood gushes out and *ow ow ow* a blinding red wall of pain crashes through the Snowman's brain as the

crowd roars *Raaaaa!* Again the bull bellows with rage and digs
its horns into the horse's protective padding, but once again the
picador simply maneuvers his horse around the bull and—*jab*—
stabs him again as the crowd roars *Raaaaa!* and the Snowman
gasps and stifles a moan *ahhh*. Now the picadores exit. Is the
bull's torment over? Is the Snowman's? Apparently not. The
trumpet blares and the crowd roars one, two, three times,
Raaaaa! Raaaaa! Raaaaa! as three *banderilleros* in red satin
and brocade bullfighting costumes enter on foot, waving over
their heads long darts wrapped with green and white ribbons.
One approaches the bull until he's practically standing between
its horns, rises up on his toes like a ski jumper taking flight,
raises his darts overhead like ski poles and plunges them into
the bull's shoulder and *yeow* the Snowman gasps again while
the beast lunges and snorts and stares wide-eyed at this further
affront. And here comes the second skier off the jump and
downward plunge his darts into the bull's shoulder and *ahhh!
ahhh!* the Snowman gasps again, once, twice. Now comes the
third skier and his darts too find their mark and *owwww!
owwww!* with each strike the Snowman's body jerks and
shudders. He glances around wildly, is there some kind of exit
from this torture? The bull seems in accordance. It snorts and
stamps its hooves in a frenzied rage as it tries to dislodge the
barbs stuck deep in its neck and shoulder. The trumpet sounds
again and the crowd roars *Maestro! Maestro!* as the matador
reenters the arena, his red cape in one hand, a sword in the
other, which he raises in salute first to the President's box,
resplendent with banners and bunting (the President, however,
not in attendance), and then to someone in the audience, and,
yes, to the Snowman's further distress, it's Amanita, who
acknowledges this gesture with an air kiss. (Apparently, neither
the Snowman (guy) nor the camera (gender neutral?) has
noticed until now that Amanita is wearing her hair in a style that
very much resembles the matador's montera cap, which also
reminds him, by way of a vague association, of the Chaac Mool,
another symbol of, um, you know ...) The matador now begins

to perform a number of very close and dangerous passes with his cape, the crowd shouting *Ooooléeee! Ooooléeee!* as the enraged bull charges again and again. He wants to crush, to destroy, to trample, to gore to death this puny human being, but something isn't right, the wounds in his neck and shoulders are taking their toll, he's lost a significant amount of blood, his vision's blurry, he feels tired, he can't hold his head up. The Snowman's own head is sagging, the sun is a molten golden wheel crushing him in his seat, he feels overwhelmed by a sense of loss and defeat and the thought of watching this spectacle to the end fills him with dread. Amanita scoffs at his squeamishness. Sarcasm dripping from her tongue like battery acid, she launches into an impromptu art lesson. It's an exercise in your beloved existentialism, Snowman. The arena is both canvas and stage. The charging bull is the future becoming the past. The flow of blood is the present. The matador is virile death. Watch, *Snowman*, this is life and this is art. He does watch, the crimson blood drenching the bull's black hide and the matador lifting his red cape, a lie to deceive the bull's eyes, a promise to the crowd of more blood to come. The bull gives a mighty snort and charges forward, this time certain he will destroy the wielder of the enraging red cape with a powerful thrust of his horns, but once again the cape flies away and in its place—the coup de grâce. The matador rises up on his toes as if he's about to perform an entrechat, thrusts his gleaming sword between the bull's shoulder blades and deep into its heart. The bull lets out a furious bellow that changes into a pathetic *mother help me mwaaaaa!* and like a steam locomotive built out of grass and grain, hooves churning uselessly like greased iron wheels, it plows headfirst into the sandy yellow dirt, its pizzle and massive balls dragging on the ground, its bulging eyes staring madly, dark red blood and foam gushing from its black nostrils. The magician's feat is complete, the green and white ribbons of the banderillas flutter in a welcome breeze, the crowd roars, *Ooooléeee! Ooooléeee!* The bull heaves, convulses, kicks futilely against death, against madness, against the laughter and derision, the whistles and, finally, disinterest of the crowd already rising to leave. There, *Snowman*, that wasn't so bad, was it? A small death in the afternoon? Amanita gloats like a mother who has coerced her child into eating his Brussels sprouts. He feels physically and emotionally drained, as if this *small death* he has witnessed were his own. He hears a rustling sound and turns just as the guy behind him jams his face in the sports page. Hmm, another friend of Amanita's father? Speculation that seems warranted when Amanita briefly excuses herself to speak to someone in the "front office." (According to a police report from an unrelated case this "someone's" name is Florencio Platosucio, lives in the Boca del Lobo neighborhood on *Calle 32 de Abril*, #207. By the way, Boone, out of an uncharacteristic sense of duty to veracity, or, more likely, fear of a lawsuit, has been pressing—okay, probably not the best choice of words—*encouraging* the fact check girl—*please,* we live in the twenty-first century—um, *woman?*—ditto: sexism, ageism, wageism, glass ceilings—*person?*—to verify sources with specific names, dates and other pertinent information.)

16
Nightlife

SCENE CHANGE: back at the hotel to freshen up before dinner, which means a tumbler of scotch for the Snowman, for Amanita an hour of ritual ablutions. She reappears in a short-sleeved, ankle-length white dress belted at the waist and looks stunning, the Platonic ideal of a Greek goddess, which probably explains why the Snowman, who has changed into a pink (he'd say magenta) silk shirt, white linen pants and jacket, closes his ears against his misgivings and opens them to the siren's call. Amanita's fave D.F. restaurant is *El Carnicero del Diablo*. Despite its sanguinary name, this is a hoity toity place, sommeliers, grand chef, maître d', valets. Without bothering to look at the menu (the Snowman, however, does and the cheapest item he spots is a garden salad for the price of a midsize SUV), Amanita orders two steaks, rare. After the bullfight this seems like further provocation. But the Snowman also knows that if he doesn't accept the challenge, Amanita will have won another small victory. Besides, despite the meatless diet he has enjoyed at Maria's, it's not like he's seriously flirting with vegetarianism. Only after he's eaten half his steak, and with a pretty good appetite, does another possibility occur to him, which is confirmed when Amanita gives him what can best be described as a *wicked* smile (wicked from *wicce*, the female variant of the old English *wicca*, witch—Edna *sniff*), keeping in mind that she (Amanita, not Edna, although she might consider it after this gig) *has* mentioned dabbling in the black arts. That's how it works, *Snowman*. You kill and then you eat your kill. He puts down his knife and fork, signaling that he at least will eat no more, and pouts like a child who's just discovered he does like Brussels sprouts, *so where the fuck are they?* but Amanita again scoffs at what they both know is an empty gesture.

His already sour mood packs its bags and heads farther south when he and Amanita meet up again with her DQ cohort (Classic Grace Kelly and Audrey Hepburn are trending but, really, these gals' plus sizes favor Kim Novak or Jane Mansfield. *Divine?* Oh no, that's going too far.). Fueling themselves with tablespoons of coke and *Aguas Azules* (Johnny Walker Blue, blue curacao and (*New!*) blueberry Jarritos— Eduard*ito, Hi, Girls!*), they begin what promises to be a long night of club hopping in the alternately famous and infamous gay mecca *la Zona Rosa* where the scene is already alive with a pounding disco beat and flashing strobe lights. In clouds of perfume and pixie dust, they make a grand entrance in *El Híbrido,* claim the dance floor as their own, restage *Saturday Night Fever* in its entirety (minus the cheesy and not very believable romantic scenes, and with the increasingly grumpy Snowman relegated to the sidelines as a spectator), and suck the wind out of the place upon their exit. Next up, *La Sirena Serena.* Despite its name and reputation for discreet rendezvous, Amanita's crowd barges in shouting, shrieking with laughter and overstaying their welcome long enough to leave in their wake a roomful of glowering faces. Marching, or, more accurately, mincing (but in an intimidating fashion) onward, they conquer *La Chanteuse Bleu,* take by storm *El Torón* and unabashedly crash the venerable queen of the gay scene *Jota de Joto.* No matter how loud, raucous and audacious, Amanita and her entourage (and at this point that's exactly what the Snowman feels like, part of her entourage) are given a warm welcome everywhere they go by the bouncers, staff, management and owners (all of whom, one might suspect, are under the pay, protection or threat of Amanita's *daddy*). Drums pound, synthesizers make a nonstop *RANT RANT RANT* sound, lights flash, smoke billows, people laugh and shout, bartenders sling drinks, ice chimes against glass, diamonds and gold sparkle and shine, everybody's dressed in designer, the bar tabs run into the tens of thousands, the scene is increasingly drunk, stoned, coked, frenzied, sweating madness, and this bedlam promises to go on well into the a.m., very much, it occurs to the Snowman, like the hours he *used* to keep in the snowbiz, which also reminds him of just how shitty his job and his life were then, and now somehow he's washed up on this little island of opulence (okay, decadence), while right outside the door a vast sea of suffering and poverty is lapping at the shore. But none of these *assholes* give a fuck about that, do they? Party until the apocalypse, right, *motherfuckers?* Damn the torpedoes and pass me the coke? Sentiments the Snowman only now realizes he has been *vocalizing* in an increasingly angry and even threatening animal growl, which probably explains the raised eyebrows, horrified expressions, and a general tendency to *lean away* from him, except for Amanita, who instead leans *toward* him, pushes out her lips in a pouty air kiss and says in a smarmy mommy voice, Is the widdle Snowbaby feeling sowwy for all the poor peoples? At which he calls her a *bitch* and when that gets no response a *cunt* and a *whore* and finally a *hypocrite*, which *does* precipitate a reaction, totally unexpected. Amanita shrieks with laughter and practically shouts in his face, Hypocrite?! *Me?!* And rising from her chair like a Nike missile from its grain belt silo, she strides onto the dance floor, grabs the first man she sees, kisses him deeply and drags him toward the restrooms while the Snowman, humiliated, confused—what the fuck is he *doing* here?—lurches out of the club like Frankenstein's monster fleeing the villagers' torches and pitchforks and staggers up the sidewalk, trying not to slip and fall on these patches of ice that have mysteriously begun to appear under his feet again. Granted, Mexico City's mile-high elevation makes for some chilly nights this time of year, but something more than a meteorological anomaly is at work here. Finally, after many missteps (the guy in the alley selling packs of girlie pictures from 1898, hand-tinted and pretty tame, who follows him down the street demanding in increasingly aggressive language that he buy a pack *you goddamn greenghost sonofabitch!* the bald-headed lady selling guaranteed hair restorer who digs her claws into his jacket so tightly he drags her halfway down the block before she fades into filmic oblivion, the German guy (*Herr Zog?* Oh, sorry, I thought you were somebody else ...) selling plates of sauerkraut and blutwurst from a miniature Bavarian chalet (exposed beams, wooden shutters, painted flowers), who himself confuses the Snowman with some old comrade in arms, *Ach, Klaus, erinnerst du dich wann ... ?*), the Snowman finds his way back to the hotel.

17
Mona

ALONE IN THE PENTHOUSE PLUSH and posh he sulks like Amanita's pet cockatiel locked up at home in a gilded cage. He pours himself a large scotch but doesn't feel like drinking it. He undresses and goes to bed but he's too restless to sleep. Plus he keeps hearing voices. Is it the suite below? A TV somewhere? It's annoying as hell, especially because he can't make out what they're saying, although he thinks he heard someone say *Snowman*, which is, yes, kind of alarming. Then there's something that, from what he gleans, could be the final communication between NASA and the last man remaining from the doomed Mars colony. I can't fucking take it anymore! Get me the fuck off this fucking rock! What the fuck do you mean two fucking years, you fucking fuckwad?! *We can't hearrrr you, la la la.* Followed by fragments of an extremely steamy phone conversation between a formerly hot but now faded porn starlet (it's not Stormy) and—*President Ronwald DeBoche?* (Really, how does Boone get this stuff? His super hacker girl—*I have a fucking name*—sorry, *Rosa* pulls intel from the entire spectrum: fitbits, security cameras, EyePhones® and EyePads®, the internet, satellite transmissions, police and military frequencies, home appliance bots, refrigerator apps and electric toenail clippers.)

Finally he gets dressed again, the same pink (*magenta!*) silk shirt, white linen pants and jacket he was wearing earlier, and goes down to the hotel lounge where he's surprised to find

Amanita sitting alone at the bar—or is it? At first glance, the wave of long black hair falling down her back and the short-sleeved white cotton dress *do* look like Amanita's, but a second glance reveals a somewhat dumpy, disheveled version. He can also see she's drunk, her makeup's smudged, she looks like she's been crying. Still, the resemblance to Amanita is uncanny, but there's something else ... a glossy photograph in a well-worn porn magazine, a pink gash in a patch of black pubic hair, a mouth open as if moaning orgasmically or preparing to perform fellatio or both. A name comes to mind. *Mona Moondrake.* Can it really be her? The hypothetical Mona chooses this moment to notice him. Her face sags in a sloppy mask of shock and confusion. In a whispery little girl voice on the verge of tears she says, Billy? You came back? Oh, honey, I'm so sorry, I didn't mean any of what I said. Can't we be friends again? Sensing Boone's hand at work here, he says, Look, you've got me mixed up with someone else. I don't know anything about this *Billy* dude. Oh Billy, how can you be so cruel? I said I'm sorry. Let's go back up to my room. *Please?* And what's a guy gonna do, be a chump and leave a poor girl alone in her time of need?

The still unverified Mona's room is small and cluttered, not much more than a converted broom closet, and looks lived in the way hotel rooms usually don't. Clothes strewn all over the place, empty vodka bottles, crumpled potato chip and popcorn bags, a pile of Hershey's chocolate bar wrappers, overflowing ashtrays. But it's the pictures. They're everywhere, on the walls, floor, table, couch *cum* hide-away bed, old black and whites, glossies, movie bills, memorabilia. He stares at them, his brain trying to register what his eyes are telling it. It's all pornography, huge spurting cocks, blow jobs, tits and ass splattered with cum, rectums, vaginas, *ménages à trois, quatre* and *cinq*, lesbian scenes, orgies, women with legs splayed, labia spread. There are film cans with titles like *Catholic Nuns Go Wild, Teen Sluts Suck and Swallow, Olympic Orgy Goes for Gold.* Stacks of CDs and videos signed in ballpoint pen, magic marker, lipstick. You're the best, Mona, love Rocky, love Lorelei, love Biff. And the most prominent face on all these photos, CDs and videos is the face seated next to him. With one noticeable exception, the hair. Which is when Mona bends forward and with a violent tug yanks the black raven's wing tresses from her head, revealing underneath a Brillo pad mass of shiny copper curls. What a relief to take that damn thing off, Mona groans. Identity firmly established, she splashes vodka in not particularly clean glasses, lights a joint and after passing it to him unfastens a jade necklace and places it on the coffee table. This is the beginning of a subtle strip tease. Mona undresses as if she were home alone and simply making herself more comfortable so he doesn't realize what's happening until she's nearly naked and coming on to him, which, yes, does turn him on but also kind of repulses him, I mean, sure, she may be a little out of shape but she's still fucking gorgeous, yeah, b-b-but ... *WHAT ABOUT ALL THOSE MEN SHE FUCKED?!* She's probably got enough diseases fermenting inside her body to keep the boys and girls at the CDC occupied for the next decade. Yeah, well, you know how that goes. Inhibitions lowered by drugs and alcohol, he starts to loosen—or rather, um, *harden* up. Oh boy, I'm gonna make Moona moan, I mean, Mona moon, I mean ... Oh Billy, Mona coos, you don't know how much I missed you, and she plants a sloppy kiss on his lips *smack!* at the same instant she makes a clumsy grab for his crotch and immediately announces loud enough for the entire hotel if not all of Mexico City to hear, *HEY, YOU AIN'T BILLY!* That's what I was trying to tell you, he mutters. I mean, geez, if it's only a matter of inches. *Feet?* This revelation—that he really *isn't* Billy but some guy called the Snowman—does put a damper on things. (Especially for those cinema buffs who are absolutely convinced that B-grade film star Billy "Plum" Bob Bengay and the Snowman are one and the same. Hard-core *members* (pun unavoidable) among this informal club insist the possibility still exists (something to do with prosthetics—or even penis *reduction*) and, who knows, *maybe?*) Mona gets dressed and good-naturedly suggests that, what the heck, since he's here, why don't they watch a movie together and he says sure, until the video starts. Mona kneels in front of a man with an erection as big as a baguette. It looks like she's trying to bite the end off a Philly cheese steak hoagie. If the Snowman ever had any doubts about his virility, this puts an end to it. No way could he or any even remotely normal male compete with that. The guy must have some kind of holster or scabbard for the damn thing. It's like having a third, useless leg, except when it's extremely useful, in veterinary sciences, for example (one man's bestiality is another man's animal husbandry—you lusty 4-H'ers know what I'm talking about, and it ain't exactly *artificial*), cows, sheep, horses and donkeys, larger fowl like ostriches, emus, albatrosses, spawning a new race of mythological creatures—the film has morphed into a parade of fantastic beings that combine male and female, human and animal anatomical features, breasts and wings, cloven hooves, horns and serpents' tails, clitorises as big as erect penises, erect penises as big as giant eels, double-headed penises, scrotums swinging like bowling balls in a gunny sack, huge labia stretching out like giant batwings, toothed vaginas yawning like bearded crocodiles, self-penetrating hermaphrodites. And then, in filmy Vaseline light, an amorphous pink, larval-like little body nestled in clouds of white pillows like a genderless little angel with little white wings. It turns a coy little Kewpie doll face to the camera and the Snowman clearly recognizes Mona, but still in infancy. She's already very pretty, although there's also something unmistakably boyish about her. The camera now follows her through childhood, adolescence and into adulthood. Oddly, the camera seems mostly focused on her face, which continues to look very pretty, if, yes, a little masculine, and torso, which remains very boyish, almost totally flat, and then, there they are, *breasts*, small, barely burgeoning at first, then roundish, mid-sized, then huge, balloon-like—*that was before I had the implants taken out, they were killing my back*. Then the film leaps to a hospital operating room, doctors and nurses in

green scrubs bent over a gurney. The camera draws in on the
patient's face and it *looks* like Mona, even with the oxygen
mask and tubes, but a harder-jawed, more masculine Mona with
unmistakable five o'clock shadow. *Oh Gawd,* wouldn't you
know it? I make it through adolescence with no more body hair
than a baby and suddenly the Sicilian side of the family kicks
in. It's like I'm growing a fucking rug. Just like Uncle
Giuseppe, except for the salami. The camera moves downward.
Beneath green hospital sheets a pair of legs are spread in
stirrups and between those legs is a very small erection but an
erection nevertheless (medical literature suggests erections are a
not uncommon reaction to the anesthesia but there is also the
argument that the feisty little organ is making its final salute to
the world). The film jumps again several months into the future.
A man in blue hospital scrubs takes off his surgical mask. It's
the world-renowned Dr. Sextos Plastikos. With a dramatic
flourish he pulls back a curtain and reveals a nude female, her
body is a perfectly sculpted marvel of curvilinear geometry, a
bronze Art Deco ideal of the Greek goddess Nike the Snowman
remembers seeing in a shop window. *Amanita?*

So, do you, like, have a twin or something? he asks with
understandable confusion. Mona shakes her head sadly and says
in an altered voice that is simultaneously wistful, melodramatic
and completely unlike her bimbo persona, I'm one of a kind,
Snowman. I am my own sister, my own brother, my own father,
mother, son, daughter. I conceived and gave birth to myself.
Mona examines the face on the CD case in her hand. This face
that is not my own, the face I present to the world, while behind
the mask … I only did orals at first—you know, blowjobs, cum
shots. *Tee hee,* you probably thought I meant, like, take a test or
something, huh, *Snowman?* And then, after I got my new body,
the body I was always meant to have—well, all I can say is Dr.
Plastikos is a genius. Her vagina and clitoris are as authentic,
and yes, sensitive, as any natural born woman's.
Unselfconscious as a two-year-old, she pulls up her dress and
examines herself. Imagine, Snowman, these pathetic little

openings, mewling, weeping, leaking, can produce a ten-pound,
twenty-inch baby. Not this one, of course. The science isn't that
advanced. The only thing is, her surgery cost a fortune, and
paying for her hormones is like carrying a mortgage. She was
flat broke, her beard coming out again, tits deflating. Then
Boone offered her a co-starring role in his new film, a chance to
go *straight*. The truth is, I never wanted to make this dumb old
movie—I only did it for Billy. She puts her finger to her lips
and looking slightly cross-eyed whispers, *Shhhh*, don't tell
anyone. Turns out Boone has a thing for Billy himself, sort of
an icky schoolmaster-pupil infatuation. He's done everything he
can to keep Billy and Mona apart when they're off the set. Now
he's got her shut up in this hotel, all she does is booze and eat
junk food. Boone says he won't let her back in front of the
camera until she loses weight, and what the *fuck* is that on your
face, darling, five *fucking* o'clock shadow? He called me a fat
hairy pig, Snowman, *boo hoo hoo*. Great. The next thing he's
got his arm around Mona's shoulder trying to console her even
as he's adding all this up in his mind. I mean, if *she* was a *he*
but now *he's* a *she* and *this* she and *that* she are—oh Jesus *yuck*,
does that mean that all this time *he's* been—okay, yes,
technically just once, *maybe*, but nevertheless *fucking a guy?*
The next second he's on his feet and backpedaling toward the
door like a sternwheeler going up the Mississippi while tossing
out boatloads of flimsy excuses—oh no! I left the water
running! I forgot to give the cat his worm medicine! even as
Mona implores him, please, *Snowman*, don't go! He passes a
closet with a sliding door on which he *thinks* he remembers
seeing a full-length mirror, in fact, he glances sideways and in
the dim light he sees his own reflection—or is it? He stops,
turns to examine his image more closely, which does exactly the
same thing, i.e., turns to examine *him*. Hmm, something odd
here he can't put his finger on. He raises his hand to scratch his
head, then feels silly when he sees this action perfectly repeated
in the mirror, followed by a nervous, self-deprecating, silent
guffaw that seems … just a hair off? Naw, it's his imagination,

right? He shakes his head and starts to turn away but immediately turns back, ready to say, *Aha! Got'cha!* But, no, his image turns back with the same nascent *Aha!* expression on its face. Hmm. He leans forward and examines himself more closely, frowns, as a final test raises his forefinger to touch his frowning reflection on the nose, but, mere millimeters from contact, he hears Mona call plaintively from the other room, *Billy?* Oh no, we're back to the Billy thing, he groans, and hurries out the door.

18
Neza

UNSETTLED BY THIS EXPERIENCE (he still hasn't worked out the Mona-Amanita thing), the Snowman decides to take a walk and clear his head but he soon finds himself lost. A taxi pulls over. Ride, meester? Impulsively (seldom a good thing in his case), he gets in, gives the driver the name of the hotel and they're off. Half an hour later he has no idea where the fuck he is and the cab driver's increasingly belligerent assurances that *eets only a leetle farther, güero* are starting to worry him. He waves out the window to a street cop who whistles the cab over. But rather than ordering the driver out and arresting him for kidnapping or at the very least running up the meter, the cop leans down and confers with him in a familiar tone, laughs loudly and waves him on. The Snowman vaguely remembers a couple of verses from a narcocorrido he heard driving down here that goes something like, *You call us the bad ones, but what about the rich politicians, the corrupt cops and criminal cabbies?* and figures he'll be lucky if he gets out of this with all his body parts intact. Sure enough, the cab pulls over and this doesn't look at all familiar. Where's the hotel? he asks. *Eets around the block*, the cabbie says as if it's obvious. Well why didn't you drop me there? he protests. The cabbie shrugs and says he's off duty now, and in a threatening tone adds, *I'm sorry, you weel have to exit the vehicle.* The second he steps out, the taxi's gone like a shot, leaving him in the middle of an urban wasteland. Concrete tenement buildings, broken street lamps, power lines and random wiring drooping from poles, trash everywhere, sewage running in the gutters. A piece of graffiti on a blackened brick wall looks familiar. Upon closer inspection, he recognizes it as the pyramid from the old U.S. dollar bill with the all-seeing eye in the pinnacle. Human arms, legs and heads stick out from under the base where someone has scrawled *all wretches fall under ... losers* (that's an approximation, it's in Spanish of course—Eduardo). He smells burning garbage, frying onions, rotting meat. He hears loud music, laughter, gunfire, screams. Peristaltic unease churns through his bowels and with good reason. He has unwittingly landed in the heart of Nezahualcoyotl, one of the world's largest megaslums, and despite civic improvements still a pretty rough place. Were there a historic marker or plaque to inform him, he would discover that this huge barrio was named after the Aztec king Nezahualcoyotl ("Hungry" or "Fasting Coyote" in Nahuatl). A fierce warrior, Nezahualcoyotl was also a philosopher poet, most famous for his flower symbolism and imagery of the *quetzal*, a rarely seen bird indigenous to southern Mexico and Central America:

Delight, for Life Giver adorns us. All the flower bracelets, your flowers, are dancing. Our songs are strewn in this jewel house, this golden house. The Flower Tree grows and shakes, already it scatters. The quetzal breathes honey, the golden quéchol breathes honey. Ohuaya ohuaya.
—from *The Flower Tree*, trans. John Curl

Nezahualcoyotl was also noted for expressing his personal thoughts and emotions in his poetry, kind of like pre-Columbian blues:

In vain I was born. Ayahue.
In vain I left the house of god and came to earth. I am so wretched! Ohuaya, Ohuaya!

*I wish I'd never been born, truly that I'd never come to
earth. That's what I say. But what is there to do? Do I have to
live among the people? What then? Princes, tell me! Aya.
Ohuaya, Ohuaya!*

*Do I have to stand on earth? What is my destiny? My heart
suffers. I am unfortunate. You were hardly my friend here on
earth, Life Giver. Ohuaya, Ohuaya!*
—from *Song of the Flight*, trans. John Curl

As interesting as this may be (thank you, Eduardo and
Edna—*grumbling*), poetic exegesis isn't the Snowman's top
concern as he suddenly finds himself confronted by some very
badass-looking dudes, heavy duty tats, studs, scars, massive
pecs and biceps (including an attractive young woman who also
exudes a very convincing fuck-with-me-and-I'll-carve-out-
your-heart attitude), and they're all packing a ton of heat and
cutlery, it's like a sushi kitchen and the national armory
combined. Heyyy, meeeester greeeenghost, what'choo doeen
here, *mano?* the baddest-looking badass (face completely
covered in tats and studs, name's Riki) says. Don't you know
thees ees a very bad neighborhood? Only bad peoples leeve
here. Noooo Meester Rogers. Uh-oh, this is like a scene out of a
B-grade movie (because it *is* a B-grade movie). Now what?
Disembowelment? A quick bullet to the head? Trying to act
cool, the Snowman says, *¿Qué pecho, güey?* He thinks he's
saying, What's happening, dude? (*qué* pedo—Eduard*ito*, *tee
hee*.) But he's actually saying something like, *Nice tits!* So both
the Snowman and the mostly greenghost audience are surprised
when all these homies burst into laughter. *¡Órale! ¡Mira a este
pinche chilango!* Riki says. Suddenly he shoves his Maori fright
mask in the Snowman's face and says, *¿Verdad, qué eres
chilango*, Snowman? Uh-oh, things are looking scary again. But
wait a second. Did he say *Snowman?* How do you know—? At
which point these bad boys (and girl) burst out laughing again.
Ho, ho, ho! You try to fool us, no, Meester *Snowman?* Why you
don't tell us you are a freend of *Margarito?* Before *Meester*

Snowman can ask how they know *that*, he is escorted in a vise-like grip (the young woman—okay, her name is Artemisia) to a cinder block building where it seems there's a party going on, people laughing, shouting, drinking beer and tequila, snorting coke, smoking pot, everyone armed to the teeth, gills and nines with combat knives, automatic pistols, assault rifles, *hand grenades*. The Snowman is introduced to *Neza*, a lean, intense man in a black leather jacket, with bright black eyes, an Uzi on his hip and an AK-47 slung over his shoulder. Despite his comrades' excesses, Neza apparently lives an ascetic lifestyle and at the moment he's sipping carrot juice and nibbling on a celery stick. He meets the Snowman's eyes and says, *the winged messenger of the sun, plumed in the colors of the eternal flower tree, has brought to us a cold wind from the north, and a song of snow and ice*, at which the roomful of revelers roll their eyes and give each other knowing glances. The Snowman, on the other hand, quickly parsing this parable in his head, gets the quetzal symbolism and even the reference to himself, but there's also this prophetic angle he doesn't quite grasp even as images of a snow-blanketed desert and frozen tropical foliage flash through his brain and his body experiences a mild seismic tremor as he again senses he is part of some unimaginably large and complex conspiracy. I guess you folks were expecting me, he says in his Big Tex voice, not, it seems, the metaphor and simile-loaded greeting in kind hoped for by Neza, who grimaces as if he's just stepped in a pile of dog shit and raises his hand as if to say, please, no more.

Suddenly everyone's rousing themselves, checking their weapons, jamming extra ammo clips in their pockets. Well, I'm really glad I came but all the same, I must be going, the Snowman says, but no, it seems this crowd's got a special event planned and he's the guest of honor. Don't be such a fucking *aguasfiestas* (*party pooper*—Eduardo), Riki says. *Simón*, he replies, which, he's pretty sure, means something like *I'm cool with that*, but for all he knows simply means, *I'm Simon*. In fact, some of the baddies are scratching their heads like what the fuck? But, who knows, maybe they're marveling at this greenghost's command of D.F. street lingo. Abandoning all things semantic, the revelers quickly change into catering uniforms and encourage the Snowman to do the same, white dress shirts, black bowties, vests and trousers, over which they pull on black ninja outfits and ski masks, then grab their weapons and climb into an unmarked white van and take off. Half an hour later the van stops and everyone but the driver gets out. The Snowman immediately recognizes the lake in Chapultepec Park, gleaming like black glass beneath a full moon and, uh-oh, he's getting that uneasy feeling again, especially when everybody heads for the boathouse, his body included. The muscle-bound gal, Artemisia, cuts the lock with bolt cutters and everyone hurries inside. Clearly a bunch of landlubbers, they awkwardly climb into flat-bottomed, swan-shaped paddle boats, cast off from the dock and pedal out to the middle of the lake where they don elaborate waterproof swan costumes and slip into the black water. The logic of all this escapes the Snowman, not to mention he's getting this creepy *Creature from the Black Lagoon* vibe, even though the water is barely a meter deep and they pretty much have to crawl on their hands and knees. (The eagle-eyed cineaste will see a meta-connection between the lagoon guy and James Bond in the opening scene from *Goldfinger*, where Bond swims ashore wearing a wetsuit and a fake seagull on his head and subsequently blows up an illegal drug facility.) Neza and his crew climb out of the lake and doff their swan costumes. One of the men pulls back some vines to reveal a tunnel entrance blocked by an iron grate with a rusty lock, which Artemisia again dispatches with the bolt cutters. Switching on flashlights, they trudge along the damp, dripping tunnel (the Snowman seems to be the only one who notices the skeletons chained to the walls) until they come to a narrow elevator shaft with a small door that Neza opens to reveal a dumbwaiter. Discarding their ninja costumes, the crew begins to enter the dumbwaiter in pairs and ascend. The Snowman's partner in climb (sorry) is the very attractive but also super butch Artemisia (really, she's got biceps like Franco Colombu—Italian weightlifter and champion bodybuilder back in the 70s and 80s? No? All right, forget about it.) The dumbwaiter's about half the size of a hall closet, maybe three feet tall and three feet wide, and the Snowman and Artemisia are squeezed together face to face so he can't help but stare into her bright green eyes, which gleam like slices of lime in an intoxicating beverage, and her lips, soft and plump like satin pillows, yeah, but what about that curious spider tattoo on her right cheek that says, yes, come into my web and *mucha suerte* getting out, and those biceps and triceps that could easily crush him to death in the throes of passion—if, that is, she were interested and from her expression probably not). They exit the dumbwaiter into a large industrial kitchen and a flurry of activity. Cast iron, copper and stainless steel pots, pans, skillets and kettles clang and bang, hiss, sizzle, bubble and boil. Cutlery rings, sings and zings, slicing, dicing, chopping. White toques bend and bob like pigeons pecking at birdseed. Hands that have been thoroughly scrubbed, manicured and disinfected until they themselves resemble plucked game birds, defeather and debone, taste, touch, massage, stir, whisk and tenderize. It dawns upon the Snowman that they must be in the kitchen of Chapultepec Castle even as he finds himself, along with Neza and his comrades, carrying trays and covered dishes into a large banquet hall. Gleaming chandeliers, gilt mirrors, tables laden with enormous sprays of red roses, silver candelabra, sparkling crystal and china, hundreds of guests in tuxedos and gowns, business leaders, politicians, dignitaries from all over Latin America and the U.S., and presiding over the affair, the President of Mexico, Perfidio Bolillo who, in a slap to the nation, has reconverted this magnificent edifice, once upon a time inhabited by the hapless Habsburger Maximilian, into a private residence, *his*. The Snowman's eyes are immediately drawn to a U.S. Marine Colonel who sure looks like the guy he saw in that powwow in the desert, and seated next to him is none other than Marvin Morfein, the U.S. Drug Czar in his

eighteenth-century rear admiral uniform, the whole shebang, bi-
corner hat, gold-trimmed frog-buttoned blue frock coat, ivory
vest, white knee breeches, pink silk stockings and hand-cobbled
shoes with brass buckles, who now stands up to a round of
applause and, looking slightly wobbly on his feet (maybe it's
the altitude, maybe the shoes), launches into what immediately
promises to be an interminable and rambling speech that begins,
albeit, with thunderous anti-drug rhetoric, *We've seen the
needle and the damage done! There's a little part in everyone!
Cocaine! Sweet Jane! Heroin! We've seen the needle take
another man!* and quickly devolves into an attack on gays,
women, minorities, labor unions, retired teachers, gerbils, etc.
(these loose cannon tirades are precisely why Morfein's
subordinates refer to him as Admiral Boom). (P.S. The
American audience may wonder that an event of such import
takes place at such a late hour. Well, for you provincial,
parochial, clodhopping rubes, in the best Spanish tradition, the
party's just getting started.) And—holy shit, Batman! Now the
Snowman gets it. Neza and his crew are going to massacre the
whole crowd, everyone's gonna die, including him! Oh, but
always with the drama, Snowmensch. No one's getting *shot*
here. Just change the vowel and think *bowel*. Because what the
Snowman doesn't know is that the Beef Bourguignon the guests
are already digging into with such gusto is laced with a
powerful laxative. Tomorrow morning's *Noticias con Tío
Roberto* will show an increasingly uncomfortable-looking
President Bolillo bolting from his seat and dashing out of the
hall, and immediately afterward, accompanied by volleys of
fire-at-will flatulence both explosive and liquid, the whole
crowd dashing after him, some with clearly soiled trousers and
gowns.

Meanwhile, Neza and his crew, the Snowman included,
have simply walked back through the kitchen and out to the
parking lot where the van is waiting for them and they take off.
Whoop! Whoop! Sirens, flashing lights—just like that a fleet of
police cars is right behind them. They careen around sharp

corners, run red lights, dodge a line of late-night bicyclists on the familiar red rent-a-biclas, roar up and down Juárez, Cuauhtémoc and Paseo de la Reforma, barricades are being thrown up, helicopters hover overhead, searchlights momentarily blind them. The driver screeches to a halt in a dark alley and everyone scatters. And even though Neza's crew has indeed proven to be a fun-loving bunch, the Snowman breathes a large sigh of relief to be free of their company.

19

Run!

BUT WAIT ... just when he thought he was safe, the ground begins to shake, buildings sway, the pavement buckles under his feet—it's an earthquake! Time shatters like a wall of glass and in a newly created dimension we see collapsed and burning buildings, cars crushed beneath rubble, bodies lying in the street (Boone, transgressing all boundaries of decency and natural law, has ghoulishly inserted news footage from the devastating 1985 temblor). In crudely edited and airbrushed sequences, we see the Snowman dodging falling debris, leaping newly opened crevasses in the street. The Angel of Independence teeters, totters and, wings gracefully outstretched, crashes to the pavement. Cuauhtémoc topples off his pedestal and, proud, noble even in his fall, lands on a passing garbage truck and is hauled off to the landfill of history. And—what on earth? Giant ants are crawling up out of the subway. They're crushing people in their huge claws, chewing off heads with their enormous mandibles. It seems the putative *cinema verité-er* Boone has tossed veracity to the wind. No, wait—it's the new RTF intern fucking up again, full of theories (*Eisenstein said ...*) but can't splice together a strip of celluloid. The screen goes white, we hear the metallic clatter of a film reel hitting the floor, and suddenly this huge muscular dude with a bandido mustache is charging at the Snowman with a raised machete and it's ... *fucking Rodríguez again?* The screen again goes white, there's more clanging and banging and—tell me how this is any better.

The Snowman now sees Pancho and Flaco running toward him, guns drawn, a fleet of black Peregrino SUVs circling behind them. He takes off running himself and, utterly heedless of where he's going, stumbles upon the great Zócalo. His gaze sweeps across the broad plaza, his brain struggling to process what his eyes tell it they see. Are they very large abacuses? Upright foosball tables? Now he's got it. They're racks of human skulls, thousands of them. Row after row, they stretch across the plaza, luminous, white, glowing like votive candles, and they're all grinning at him with their hollow eye sockets and bony teeth. He hears a sound, a little like the low-frequency *hummmm* of an electric motor, or maybe it's the monastic chanting of some boreal religious order that worships the abominable *SnowmanSnowmanSnowmanSnowman*. He wonders if he's having an acid flashback, or maybe it's that weird psychic interference he's been experiencing. The cables on the flag pole where a giant Mexican flag flies during the day clang and clatter. A shot rings out and another. His footsteps echo off the Presidential Palace as he takes off again in the direction of the great Metropolitan Cathedral, itself luminous and white like a giant skull in the moonlight. Desperate, he enters a small wooden door that has been left open and, lungs burning, gasping for breath, begins to run up a narrow stone stairway. Suddenly he stops, his head spinning with vertigo. In a jarring succession of cuts (observant cinephiles will notice Boone is heavily "quoting" from William Dieterle's classic *Hunchback of Notre Dame*) we see great iron bells, heavy ropes, wooden beams, patches of black sky and moonlight. He's in the fucking bell tower! He hears shouting and Flaco and Pancho appear at the top of the stairs, gasping and panting, a whole crew of murderous thugs right behind them. Reverting to survivor mode, QuasiSnowman leaps for the clapper of the nearest bell and *nyaaahhh!!!* in an amazing gymnastic feat (the judges give it an eleven on a scale of ten), he swings out over the Zócalo and in again, knocking his pursuers back down the stairs like dominos. Leaping over them as nimbly as one of the Three

Musketeers (take your pick), he dashes outside with the great iron bell he set in motion clanging furiously and L. Condor's gang on their feet and right behind him. He spots a street crossing sign with the digital figure of a green man walking faster and faster as the seconds digitally tick away *ten nine eight* ... and this is funny, as he enters the intersection running at full tilt, the green man also begins to run, in fact it's frantically trying to keep up with him because even crazier, now he's running almost impossibly fast, it's like Ratso Rizzo running down the beach in the fantasy sequence at the end of *Midnight Cowboy,* like those British guys running for Olympic gold in *Chariots of Fire,* there's even a soundtrack, a joyful and contemplative mix of piano and synthesizer (ironically, the composer's smoking like a chimney while playing this piece on the piano). And now Boone goes wild with associative digressions, the camera zooms in on a flapping, snapping flag emblazoned with the iconic Olympic rings and we hear a male voice announce in a slightly urgent, adenoidal tone resonant with whiskey and tobacco smoke *meanwhile back inside the Olympic Hall* and on the grainy, popping Technicolor screen images appear of athletes in various national uniforms marching around an arena and—oh yeah, he remembers this, it's those two track guys, the two black guys who stood on the winners' blocks with gold and bronze medals on their chests, their heads bowed solemnly, their black-gloved fists raised simultaneously in victory and protest, but then there's something he doesn't remember. As the cameras pan over the waving flags and shouting crowds, three hundred cheering fans disappear from the audience, leaving behind shadows that turn red and stream down the stone stadium stairs. What's this—an allusion to the earlier bullfight scene? A tragic outcome to the newest entry in the summer Olympics, the live ammo paintball competition? The camera returns to the Snowman. The film's in grainy black and white now, the mood's changed completely, it's beginning to rain, silver pencil marks slash the black sky. In the glare of floodlights we see an odd conglomeration of ancient and modern architecture. Aztec ruins, truncated pyramids, stairways and platforms built out of red volcanic stone and tilting at odd angles, blue stained-glass windows in a Spanish colonial cathedral, gleaming glass and steel high-rise buildings. Cold rain gusts pelt the Snowman's face. He hears shouting, voices chanting, there's some kind of demonstration, thousands of people swarm around him. Crowds have gathered in the streets to watch. People hang out of apartment windows. Suddenly flares explode in the sky. His first thought is fireworks. Then there's a helicopter and a barrage of gunfire rains from the sky. People scream and fall to the ground. The crowd begins to run but then there's more gunfire and more screaming and more people fall to the ground. The crowds run back and forth in waves trying to escape the volleys of gunfire that seem to come from everywhere, the sky and the apartment buildings and both ends of the plaza, and with each wave there's more shooting and more screaming and more people fall to the ground. The camera pans over piles of bodies lying in pools of blood, men, women and children, students, government workers, street vendors, retirees out for an evening stroll. Anxious audience members scan the carnage. Is the Snowman among them? No— there he is, running again. And—oh no!—here come the black SUVs. More shots ring out, pistols, rifles, machine guns. Bullets fly everywhere. *Help!* Just when it seems like the jig's up, a completely unassuming little figure appears out of nowhere wearing a pair of mustard yellow (*French's*) shorts over red long johns, with sproingy antennae on his head and the letters CH in red in a yellow heart emblazoned on his chest and—can it really be? Yes, it's the much beloved everyman hero el Chapulínnnn Coloradoooo! *¡Síganme los buenos!* he calls out and the Snowman and all the other *buenos* in the vicinity follow the Red Grasshopper (*Ex*spirito himself in a cameo performance—at least until the attorneys for his estate get wind of Boone's little indiscretion) to a metro station and it's completely packed, the early morning rush hour already

well under way. El Chapulín hands over ten pesos at the ticket
booth, grabs tickets for himself and the Snowman and they
hurry through the gate just as *beeeee* a train arrives. The
Snowman starts toward the nearest car—but wait! El Chapulín
holds him back, pointing at a sign that says *Sólo mujeres*. He
sees now that the car is filled solely with women and children,
but a number of slobbering, masturbating men have attached
themselves to the outside of the car like leeches. *¡Vamos!* El
Chapulín pulls him onto another car. It's also totally packed,
standing room only, everybody jammed together. Two seconds
later the Snowman feels a strange hand meaning a hand that
isn't his groping in his pocket. *Hey!* He slaps the hand away and
immediately afterward hears loud, mechanical voices as men
and women begin to push their way up the aisle, advertising
products   and   services   through   hand-held   megaphones:
electronics, driving schools, religious pamphlets, women's
lingerie. *Insurgentes!* El Chapulín says cryptically, and
disappears. The Snowman's eyes dart left, then right, expecting
bomb-throwing terrorists, gun-toting revolutionaries. *Beeee* ...
the train stops, the doors open, he spots a green plaque with the
station name *Insurgentes ... ohhh.*

   The sky has cleared, the full moon is fading and the sun
rising by the time he finds his way back to the hotel. He's
exhausted and doesn't at all relish the thought of confronting
Amanita. As he steps out of the elevator he hears a strange noise
that, to his untrained ears, sounds like a wolf howling in the
distance, but which he attributes to a glitch in the hotel's AC, or
maybe there's a plumbing issue. The suite is ominously quiet
except for the sound of the shower running in the guest quarters.
He slowly pushes open the bathroom door but freezes when he
hears a sudden *shriek shriek shriek* and spots a woman's naked
body crumpled behind the plastic shower curtain. But wait, it's
only the showerhead making a strange noise, a towel carelessly
dropped on the floor of the shower stall. He turns off the water
but now he hears another sound in the master bedroom.
Crossing the carpeted floor in the hallway on tiptoe, he goes to

investigate. Amanita is sitting in front of the mirror, hairdryer humming in one hand while she combs out her long black tresses, her face turned toward the TV flickering across the room. On the screen, the unfolding story at Chapultepec Castle. The camera now pulls in on Amanita's reflection in the mirror as she registers the Snowman's presence behind her and her benign expression twists into pure horror. It's pretty obvious to both the Snowman and the viewing audience that she wasn't expecting to see him again. *¡Pinche perdedores!* she mutters (*Fucking losers!* in English, referring, one would guess, to Flaco and Pancho—Eduardo). But why? What are you getting out of this? he says. Her response is atavistic—fangs and claws, blood red lips, *hisssss!* Why are you so fucking stupid, Snowman?! Why can't you figure it out? And when he doesn't answer (because, in fact, he can't figure it out), she says, Tell me, Snowman, why are you here? And don't give me that shit about *Margarito*, I'm not as dumb as you. Which is also totally lost on him. He's even more flummoxed when, inexplicably, Amanita starts to cry. I'm so sick of all this, I feel like I'm being torn in half. Just as quickly the tears dry up and she says in a voice so wooden Mister Geppetto could carve Pinocchio out of it. They're serious, you know, Snowman. They'll kill you if you don't leave now. He doesn't doubt that possibility at all. Still he asks, Why should I believe you? Amanita shakes her head. I've already said too much. She begins to cry again. Through her tears she improbably quotes a line of poetry that he even more improbably recognizes. *In this part of the story I am the one who dies, the only one, and I will die of love because I love you, because I love you, Love, in fire and in blood.*

A disconnected shot (Boone's favorite kind) shows a younger Amanita in an intimate embrace with a young man, flashes of their faces, her green eyes, his mustache, their mouths pressed together, lips, tongues—okay, that's more than the Snowman wants to see. A wheezy camera shutter click signals a scene change and in a black and white freeze frame we now see the same young man and someone who looks an awful lot like a younger Xuan without the facial scars. They're standing at the window of a small house, holding automatic rifles as the film begins to roll again and a convoy of black SUVs pulls up outside.

The screen goes dark.

20
Another One Takes the Bus

AFTER LAST NIGHT not much is clear except that the Snowman and Amanita can't stay together. He leaves the hotel with nothing but the clothes on his back and the few pesos in his pocket and begins to wander the streets in a fog of exhaustion. Now what? Find his way home? Where is that? Maria and Margarito's bucolic little casita? A ramshackle shack a thousand miles away in *el Norte?* His rhetorical quest leads him like a hound dog on the scent to the D.F. central bus station. The place is huge. Buses pull in and out constantly. They're modern, air-conditioned, Wi-Fi, video screens, and, who knows, maybe it's that promise of escape in comfort and hope for the best, he buys a ticket to Chopahuac for what seems like a really good price and goes back outside just as a battered old blue and white school bus pulls up and, oh shit, he just knows it's going to be his and it is, it says right there on its crumpled metal brow *Chopahuac* and below that, printed across the top of the rectangular windshield in white plastic applique, *Confía en Cristo* and out of nowhere people begin pushing and shoving to get on, old men and women, young pregnant mothers, kids— they've got zero respect for this lonesome cowpoke greenghost who is also improbably dressed in a disheveled Saturday Night Fever outfit. He's getting hit in the stomach, kidneys, ribs with shoulders, elbows, fists. Okay, now he's pissed. The hell with civility. He claws his way on board and even manages to grab a window seat, noticing in the process that, while battered and worn on the outside, the inside of this human transporter is the driver's traveling shrine. Pink and green tassels, religious pennants, banners, ribbons and strings of rosary beads hang over the windshield. The dash area is covered with medallions, crosses, votive candles, white plastic Jesuses and Marys. The ceiling is postered and painted with images of saints and Biblical figures. And this mobile church, this chapel on internal combustion wheels, is packed with believers, lead us where you will, prophet (no telling where that kind of faith will take you). The bus pulls out of the station and the driver's assistant begins working his way up the aisle, punching tickets and chatting with passengers. The driver has turned on music, which, oddly, sounds Middle Eastern (Syrian? Lebanese?) and everyone on board including the Snowman is rocking and swaying in unison. Two Indian women, nearly identical in appearance, both about four feet tall and four feet wide, big beaming pumpkin faces, long black braids tied at the ends with pink ribbons, matching red huipils embroidered with tiny yellow flowers, are dancing up and down the aisle, clapping their hands and spinning on their heels. They're doing the tango, the fandango, they're dancing sideways like Egyptians even though they have no sideways. *Finally*, the Snowman thinks, I'm back among the *people*, and succumbing to his exhaustion, he sinks blissfully into sleep. And wakes again thirty minutes later, even though it feels like it's been hours. Hot, sweaty, he yanks off his white linen jacket, rolls up the sleeves of his pink (*magenta!*) silk shirt. Apparently the bus has stopped. Outside his window kids of various ages shout for his attention while thrusting sandwiches, fried pork skins, skewers of roasted meat, candy, fruit, pastries, sodas and bottled water at him. *¡Cincuenta pesos! ¡Mil pesos! ¡Un dólar!* Some of the more enterprising board the bus and wander up and down the aisles, shoving their wares in passengers' faces. Finally the driver beeps his horn, the vendors depart and they're on their way again—for about five minutes. Every two miles the bus stops for more people to get on or off and a new round of vendors to converge on the open windows.

Taking advantage of one of these stops, the Snowman works his way back to the rear of the bus and the crudely constructed restroom with, he discovers, a non-flushing or at least non-functioning toilet that already resembles in smell and appearance the pit of an outhouse. Holding his nose in one hand, his hose in the other (yes, crude, I know, the editor was asleep—*what?!*), and staring at the ceiling, which, yuck, he realizes now is splattered with—*vomit?* he accomplishes as expeditiously as possible what he came here for. When he returns to his seat the guy who was sitting next to him is gone and now a lady who in face and form resembles Nikita Khrushchev (subliminal image) squashes against him, clutching in her arms a fat white chicken with bright orange tuberous-like feet, which results in a lot of squawking (the chicken) and cursing (the Snowman), feathers everywhere, scratches on his hands and wrists that he fully expects to fester into gangrene. Two hours later he wakes with a huge sack of garlic jammed against his ribs, his ass sore from sitting, and he's really gotta pee again and maybe take a dump, but no way he's going back *there* again. They're now climbing a narrow mountain pass, there aren't any guardrails, he can see what looks like the burned-out hull of another bus at the bottom of a ravine, and the driver, who he has observed drinking *something* from a brown bottle, is swerving all over the road. Will he make it to Chopahuac alive?

He's awakened twenty minutes later by the absence of motion. The bus has stopped just outside Chopahuac. A barricade of stones—not particularly large, more of a statement—has been placed across the highway. Several indigenous men in rough work clothes stand on the roadside or up in the vegetation, silent, faces grim. A hand-painted sign demands *tierra, justicia, pan.* No weapons are visible. The bus driver consults with the young ticket taker. Both seem nervous, unsure what to do next. A jeepload of military personnel behind them seems equally perplexed. Finally it's understood the bus isn't going anywhere soon. Everyone gets off and starts to walk toward Chopahuac. About twenty meters beyond the barricade a man in a battered white Isuzu pickup truck is offering transportation to Las Riquezas for a thousand pesos a head, exactly what the Snowman has left in his pocket. He, a young woman with a baby in a sling, and a man with a machete on his hip—possibly the woman's husband—accept the offer and climb in back. Two hours later the truck stops on the highway and the Snowman extracts himself from what has become a packed house, babies, abuelitos, entire families, sacks of potatoes, garlic, tethered chickens. Body stiff all over, butt aching from sitting so long, the urgency to pee finally remedied with a Niagaral (no, not Viagral, Dick, you prick) leak on the side of the road, he starts to walk.

21
Maria and the Snowman

AN HOUR LATER HE ARRIVES AT MARIA'S, dead on his feet, his
fancy city duds crusty with dust and sweat, and smelling like a
cowboy just off a month-long cattle drive. He's expecting a
cold-shouldered reception but to his relief no one answers his
knock and when he pushes open the door it looks as if no one's
been home for days. Maybe Maria and Margarito have
reconciled, they're off on a romantic vacation. So much the
better. He figures he'll throw his stuff in the Coupe and head
out and save everyone more heartache. But he's also tired and
thirsty and that six-pack in the fridge looks mighty attractive.
He pops open a cold brewski and, oh man, that's good. He
gulps it down in about four swallows, pops open another and
takes a seat at the kitchen table, where he notices a large roach
(and, no, it's not the inveterate invertebrate character actor
Carlitos the Cucaracha—he'll come in later) incautiously tucked
under the edge of an empty fruit bowl. An hour later, stoned,
slightly drunk, his mood maudlin, he convinces himself he
should get going, but he'd better wash up first, it's not likely
he'll get a chance on the road. Again owing to that
indeterminate male thing, rather than use the indoor facilities,
which Maria keeps spotless (maybe that's why), he grabs some
clean clothes and follows the path around the house to the
outdoor shower. Simple but elegant in design, pine, bamboo and
a wooden sluice, *la ducha* is fed by natural spring water that
splashes like liquid glass out of a fissure in the rocky hillside,

which, overgrown with bright green moss and ferns, looks
without a lot of thought about it like a verdant vagina,
suggesting, or perhaps better said, *warning* us of yet another of
Boone's endless metaphysical conceits in the road ahead.
Maybe it's the time of day, the angle of the sun, but just before
he starts to undress he notices an odd strata of stone just beyond
the spring. When he goes to investigate he discovers it's
actually a cave entrance obscured from view by a parallactic
trick of nature. Spelunking has never appealed to him, bats,
spiders, muddy crawl spaces, deadly tumbles down bottomless
chasms, drowned in a frigid subterranean river, impaled on a
stalagmite. His curiosity piqued, however, he enters. To his
surprise, the path is actually pretty good and he can see light
ahead. The cave widens into a large grotto with a bottleneck
opening at the top through which he can see blue sky. Dusty
sunbeams illuminate a sparkling turquoise pool crowded in with
lush green ferns, philodendrons and pygmy palm trees.
Iridescent red, blue and orange dragonflies flit just above the
surface of the pool. His mind and body practically vibrating
with a strange giddiness he attributes to the weed and cerveza,
he drops his clothes to the ground, lowers himself into the warm
water and begins to swim in slow, gentle circles. Almost
immediately his fatigue and all the aches and pains of the road
dissolve and fade away and in their place he feels an enormous
surge of energy and well-being. He's also getting an erection.
Without realizing it, he has also begun to swim faster and faster
in tightening circles. And then it happens. He has an orgasm and
it's really powerful, he's gasping for breath, his eyes roll back
in his head, he feels totally spent. He lets himself float face
down in the water and, hmm, that's interesting, only now does
he notice the glimmer of gold on the bottom of the pool—
jewelry? necklaces? bracelets?—and something else, bones,
human bones, entire skeletons, with small red fish swimming in
and out of ribcages and eye sockets. Oddly, it isn't even spooky,
in fact, he begins to swim down for a closer look and it's like a
dream, he doesn't even need to breathe or rather he's breathing

the water just as easily as air. *Snowwwmannn?* And then he does need to breathe—desperately. He broaches the surface gasping for breath and treading water when he spots something skimming toward him in S-shaped undulations. *Nyaah!* It's a snake! Shocked out of his post-ejaculatory lassitude, he ploughs his way back to the mossy bank, pulls himself out of the water, hurriedly dresses and starts to leave when he hears someone coming. He instinctively drops to his knees behind a large leafy philodendron and—it's Maria. She looks tired, disheveled, as if she, too, has been through an ordeal. There's also a sadness about her, an air of despondency. She begins to undress, which places him in a dilemma. He should call out, let her know he's here, but he also senses that he shouldn't be here and besides, thanks to his dithering, she's already naked and he can't help staring at her bare breasts and belly and dark pubic thatch, seeing them and not really seeing them because there's something else that makes his eyes zoom in on various parts of her body. A spot on her right breast, a beauty mark or tattoo—*Mickey Mouse?*—plucks a chord in his memory but it isn't the tattoo, it's the scars, the ragged lacerations on her thighs and abdomen, the circular cicatrices like cigarette burns in the areolas around her nipples. She enters the pool with her gaze demurely lowered, not, he senses, because she suspects she's being watched, but out of reverence for this body of water, which makes him feel even more like a cad for violating her privacy. Adding to his crime, he can't take his eyes off the tawny globes of her butt as she slowly breaststrokes around the pool. Even greater violation yet, he feels the stirring of another erection, that impetuous denizen of the nether regions unusually full of vim and vigor, which is when he also notices that Maria has stopped swimming and from the blissed-out expression on her face it looks as if now *she's* experiencing an orgasm. He hears her gasp and then she turns and floats quietly on her back for several minutes. He can see her breasts and her pubic patch but that's not what he's staring at now. It's her scars—they've disappeared. Who knows, maybe they were never there, he imagined them, it's the pot clouding his brain. He watches her climb out of the water and this is almost certainly the pot because she looks like she's surrounded by a golden aura, like she's actually glowing. He discreetly (if this word is appropriate after a blatant act of voyeurism) turns away while she dresses, and then waits several minutes after she has left before he sneaks back along the tunnel—yes, *sneaks*, like a criminal, like a thief, like he expects her to jump out of the shadows at any second and shout, ah-ha! I knew it was you! After working up a whole bunch of lies and excuses, he finally knocks at the door, feeling like a total heel, but, surprise, he's greeted by Maria's warm brown eyes (Weren't they black or more accurately *obsidian?* Contacts, maybe?) and wide smile. She asks how his trip went and when he admits it was a fiasco she says not very convincingly, I'm so sorry, Snowman. He also senses that she knows perfectly well he was at the pool, which is pretty much confirmed when, over dinner (he's given up on the idea of leaving for now), she tells him the tale of an ancient Zoltec queen who had an exclusive bathing pool that restored her youth and beauty every day. One day a man slipped into the pool. Neither she nor any of her attendants actually saw him, but she knew as soon as she entered the water. She felt like she had been raped (the Snowman groans inwardly), but even though the shaman confirmed she had not been penetrated, she conceived a child. She gave birth to a baby boy who grew up to become a powerful warrior, his triumphs thanks to the magical water his mother anointed him with before each battle. Poisoned by greed, he killed her so that he would have all the water he wanted and become even more powerful. The next day the queen's pool dried up and a great king from the east defeated the errant son in battle. An unambiguous moral tale that leaves the Snowman ambivalent about a number of things. For example, the skeletons at the bottom of the pool—are they real? And if so, how'd they'd get there? Is Maria a spider, entrapping men like flies? Has he flown into her web? And the scars—did you only imagine them, Snowman? Or was it actually, oh, I don't know, dirt or leaves or just the light? And by the way, where the heck is Margarito? A recurring question he's been on the verge of asking for the last half hour and might have except this joint he and Maria are passing keeps derailing his train of thought. Not helping, the brandy she also brought out and which they've been methodically tossing back in what appears to be an unspoken drinking contest or, who knows, maybe it's just an unbridled co-dependency thing, binge begets binge, which might also explain this prolonged eye contact that's making them both uncomfortable but neither is willing to break. It's like someone's dialing up the magnetic force field between them, he's even kind of vibrating inside. And then, what must have seemed inevitable to viewers all along finally appears to be happening. They're on their feet and kissing, it's sudden, hot, hungry, *passionate*, their mouths open, tongues probing, their arms, legs, bodies clenched together as if they were falling out of the sky tethered to a single parachute, and yes, that irrepressible Mr. Jones is acting up downstairs, if only he could pull down this damn zipper and get out of these pants. Too late. Before any chance of that happening, Maria and the Snowman break apart and stare into each other's eyes and for a moment he's staring into Margarito's eyes and then it's Maria's again and there's this animal wildness and hunger twisted up with fury and anguish *nor to know carnally nor to have sexual congress with nor by any means to violate this covenant.* Riven with guilt, or at the very least abashed, he finally asks, What about Margarito? Maria shakes her head. She seems to be struggling to speak, tears well in her eyes, her lower lip trembles. Margarito isn't coming back, Snowman. *What?* His first thought is they've split up, Maria's finally had it with Margarito's purported philandering, maybe she's even confessed her feelings for *him*. But no, that's not it. Not even close. And here it comes, that cinematic moment when Boone gives away the store. Maria chokes back a sob and utters two words.

He's dead.

The Snowman gasps. Shock and incredulity knock him backward. He asks or maybe he only forms the words without actually saying them, How? What? When? Where? Again Maria struggles to speak … Friday. He tries to remember what he was doing Friday when Maria adds … Friday, the sixteenth. Oh, wait, he thinks, that was, um, twelve days ago. Then Maria says … of June. He hears June and thinks—but that was five months ago, before I even arrived. But then Maria gives a year and it's not just five days or five months but five *years* ago. The Snowman's shock and nascent sorrow turn into confusion, disbelief. Which means what? Margarito, the Margarito he knew, never existed?

In one of those surrealist collages popular in edgy, experimental films of the sixties but now viewed as clunky, clichéd and even risible (guardians of Freedom's Gate see the influence of Soviet cinema here: no matter how serious, sad or tragic, the Rooski film director's gotta include at least one surreal episode or it's off to Lubyanka, *tovarishch*), we now see the Snowman standing in a green meadow staring up at the sun embroidered in the cerulean sky like a fiery orange marigold, but then it's not the sun, it's Margarito's smiling face and warm brown eyes beaming down at him from a pillowy, powder blue cloud like an angel in one of those "Baby's First Year" photo albums, a little brown angel with big brown eyes and a bristling black mustache (another fuck-up in the special effects department—it *is* a low budget film—Ed.). Bronze and terra cotta pigments, nose putty, plastic ears, painted-on eyes and shiny black horsehair mustache hang in space a moment longer, then curl up in a puff of flame, blacken into ash, crumble and disappear *pfft!* This is followed by a protracted shot of the Snowman staring at a rusty, skeletal bicycle contraption buried in a purple mound of bougainvillea.

A flashbulb pops and the Snowman snaps back to this moment with a *what just happened?* expression on his face (no, in the photo ID in his wallet, wiseguy). Maria, who seems just as nonplussed by these interruptions as he does, regains her

composure and proceeds to tell him the *true* true story in a voice
that suggests she has learned to remember these things the way
she remembers, well, *things*, detached, dispassionately: the
sound of a chain saw, arms and legs disconnected from bodies,
her father's head on a table, her mother's hysterical, gasping
screams as she is disemboweled alive, her younger brothers and
sisters strangled one after the other with their mother's
intestines. She remembers the smell of her own flesh burning,
the sledgehammer shock of the electric cattle prod in her
vagina, the hot slash of the razor blades across her thighs and
belly, the cigarette burns on her breasts, the repeated rape and
sodomy. She remembers being turned and handled repeatedly
like a piece of meat. She remembers the men joking and
laughing and eating cold take-out pizza. Maybe they thought
she was dead, maybe they left her as a message. Xuan found her
and carried her in his arms to the—there's a hitch in her voice,
he's sure she's going to say *pool* but instead she says—
brewhag, who nursed her back to health. When she returned
home everything had been scrubbed clean, the blood washed
out of the floorboards, the broken teeth, scrambled brains,
pieces of intestine, the decomposition of brother and sister,
mother and father into a festering chile relleño completely
erased. Margarito returned from *el Norte* soon afterward. When
he discovered what had happened he nearly lost his mind. He
wanted to take the single-shot twenty-two rifle he inherited
from his grandfather and kill those responsible. Maria
convinced him it was madness, they'd kill him too. He was
outraged that no one did anything—the courts, the police, the
people in the community—*nothing*. He hated them all, hated
their cowardice, because they wouldn't stand up and fight. As
Maria speaks, the Snowman again hears Margarito's anger
speaking—the anger of the Margarito he thought he knew. Of
course he can't know it is also the anger of the renowned
herstoricist Professor Vivian Yñaz y Ortega speaking to a small
audience of scholars and students that includes an attractive

young woman whose face looks as dark and troubled as the storm clouds roiling the night sky outside:

Yes, fine, endure pain and suffering, torture and punishment, remain silent, stoic, while their priests roast you over the fires they have built to free your soul from its corrupt body and send it trembling to God (theirs, not yours), and while they're at it to extract from you the location of the mountains of gold they are certain you possess but you do not. El Dorado does not exist. There is no golden city. There are only people, poor, oppressed, desperate. You see, it is the old people here who are the miracles, not the children. The women have babies, nurture them as best they can, grow old prematurely. The men break their backs working, die in accidents, fights. They fight God, they fight the earth, they fight each other. They get drunk and knock each other down, they shoot and stab and kill each other. They get thrown in jail, hanged, hacked to pieces with machetes, stoned to death, dragged across the desert behind horses. Their inspiration, their muse, that little spring coiled inside them waiting to be released by a bottle of booze, a woman, an assault on their masculine pride. Their passion one of constant longing and deferral, of supplanting each desire with another and another, always more unattainable, virgin, mother, queen. They crawl to her on their hands and knees until the cobblestones run with their blood, until she submits to their entreaties and becomes the wife. *And that is her undoing, because she has abdicated the throne, desecrated herself in the man's eyes. In submitting to the male's animal desires she has become little more than a dray animal herself, entitling him to beat her, cheat on her, treat her worse than his dog. As the wildly if inexplicably popular Norteño troubadour Roberto Jaslerón sings,* Oh why did you go away and leave me, my love? Just because I fought and drank and wasted all my pay chasing other women? But you are the mother of my children, my little madonna, you must come back to me *"because if you don't,* bitch, *I will kill you."* (Professor Yñaz y Ortega makes air quotes around her subtext and even imitates the sound of a badly tuned guitar for emphasis *plink plank plunk.) This is the history we have received of the oppressed people from the male narrative, which they reconstruct as one of heroic struggle. But these so-called heroes never fight back against their true enemy, which is the oppressor in all his manifestations, the mines, factories, banks, the military, police, government, cartels, landowners, the dominant male, the caudillo, el Patrón—i.e., capitalism with an erect penis. How ironic that the, ahem,* members *of PRIX refer to themselves as the party of the institutionalized revolution. How can revolution be institutionalized? Inevitably—whether through inertia, entropy or sloth—the revolution is subsumed by the institution. Well fuck that! By whatever means, the reductive, subversive, nihilistic, absurd, the sword, gun, surgeon's scalpel, alchemist's poison, writer's pen, the established order must always be challenged!* (Polite applause, except for the solemn-looking young woman, who claps loudly before she stops out of embarrassment.)

Maria has stopped speaking, her eyes are dim, her head tilted as if she's listening to an echo or a distant voice. She starts awake from her reverie, picks up her glass, finds it empty, almost knocks over the bottle of brandy reaching for it, lets out a brief, hysterical laugh *ha!ha!ha!* slumps back down in her seat, after a minute or two pulls herself more or less erect. When she speaks again her tone is distracted, her speech slurred, telegraphic. Margarito began to talk about a rezhistance movement. Maybe that was still the dreamer in him. His voice was strong, his message clear. He could have been a poet, actor. Hizh wordzh made women and men fall in love with him. But instead of *moonlight and roses, mi amor, diamonds and lilies,* now he shpoke of war, the glory of battle. He invoked the old heroes, Hidalgo, Juárez, Villa, Zapata, he mined the anger and passion latent in his lisheners' hearts. The older men may have been afraid but among the young men he found an audience. Margarito and Xuan began to train a small group of men and women. (Again the Snowman has a flash, this time clearer, of an open barn door, in the dim light, hidden among farm implements or half-buried in the hay, the gleam of machine guns, automatic rifles, crates of ammunition, RPGs.) Rumor flies on avid wings. Strangers began to ask questions. One night the black SUVs came. The fledgling guerillas fought bravely but they were up against much greater firepower. Margarito, Maria and a few others managed to escape, Xuan was wounded and captured. They tortured him, but he refused to betray Margarito. No, Xuan wouldn't—but someone else did. This time Maria is unable to contain herself and she lets out a sob as we again see a disconnected image of a younger Amanita in an intimate embrace with a young man, flashes of their faces, her eyes, his mustache, their mouths pressed together. Maria swallows her brandy, continues her narrative. There wazh an ambuzh, Xuan the bait, Margarito refused to abandon him. For that ... Maria is silent for a moment. In the chaos that followed, Xuan and *los guys* escaped, fled to *el Norte*. She cut her hair, disguised herself as a man, and followed later.

Hmm. The Snowman sees himself on the job, it's well past midnight, snow blowing, cold as hell, he's bent over a frozen valve on the SnowBile's compressor, he pushes his goggles back on his head and looks up into the mocking brown eyes of this new guy *Margarito* who's saying to him in a soft, throaty voice in heavily accented but otherwise perfectly good English with, yes, a *bemused* smile beneath his shiny black mustache, *here ees a crescent wrrrench, what deed you want the espider for?* He thinks of all the times he must have peed in front of Margarito, who always seemed bathroom shy himself. And what about Margarito's dark moods, the complaints about stomach issues? A glaring hundred watt bulb (pre-LED) goes off in his head at the same time Maria's face, the face here, now, in front of him, tears itself out of the Margarito face he still holds in his memory and he says like a child who has just discovered the truth about the man in the Santa Claus suit, It's *you. You're* Margarito. And still digesting this revelation he takes the next step. Why didn't you just tell me? Why all the lies? Again Maria seems to grasp for a credible answer. Because I thought you wouldn't believe me, Snowman. Because I didn't want to involve you in my problems. Finally, looking contrite (funny little dimples at the corners of her mouth he's never noticed before), she says, I was afraid you wouldn't come. Her face brightens. But you did come, you are here now.

(For more on this latest plot twist, be sure to check out the forthcoming documentary on the making of this film (nod to Herr Zog), in which Boone is seen with a wide and, frankly, creepy reptilian grin as he thumbs through a well-worn copy of an obscure Brazilian novel in the original Portuguese, *Grande Sertão: Sem Vergonha (The Devil Gets His Kicks and Pricks on Rte. 666*—Edilson).)

22
The Next Move

THIS LATEST DEVELOPMENT plunges the Snowman into a state of confusion. The camera shows him seated at a scarred wooden table in *Mi Sedecita*, a half empty bottle of tequila in front of him, and—where is this coming from?—suddenly his eyes are awash in a hot salt sea of tears. Embarrassed, he grabs a napkin, crushes it against his nose and blows, impregnating the pleasantly soft tissue with snot, slime and unrepentant salt water even as he inhales lilacs, lilies, the fragrance of a northern spring. Spider senses tingling, he unwads the soiled napkin and spots the PPP monogram in the lower right hand corner as a series of images begins to flash on the screen. Judith running across the snowy commons in front of Old Main, her breasts pertly bouncing beneath a brown wool sweater and a black storm cloud of hair bouncing around her shoulders. Judith in a lab coat and safety glasses, the tumult of hair contained by a green scrub cap as she works over test tubes and bubbling retorts. Judith, hair shorn into a kind of helmet, wearing a no-nonsense business suit that makes her look like a Soviet commissar. He crushes the napkin into a ball and stuffs it in his pocket. Pure coincidence, right? People all over the globe blow their nose or wipe their ass with PPP's hygienic paper products. Besides, the benign brand-name *Print and Paper Products* hardly suggests some corporate cabal or international intrigue with tentacles stretching all the way down to a dusty little desert town in Mexico, does it, *Snowman?*

The White House:
CESS?
Yes, sir. *Core Ecological Survivalist Sodality.*
Never heard of it.
Neither had we.

The Snowman's spider senses continue to tingle when an old woman enters the cantina. It's the village brewhag, turban, shawl, strings of beads, floor-length skirts, heavy makeup, big wart next to her nose—she looks like a cross between Doña Oleinfanta and a fat guy in drag (is it bruja or brujo, Snowman? Brou*haha!*) She comes and sits down at his table, glowers at him out of her cocked left eye while the right wanders like an errant moon behind a thin gray cloud, places her leathery hand on his forehead and begins to chant in a mix of Spanish and what he presumes to be Zoltec, her voice rising and falling like a squeaky pump handle, the single phrase he catches in Spanish largely nonsensical, also vaguely familiar, *when the moon is bright and the snow is on the cactus.* Abruptly the brewhag says in English, Search for the path to God, *Snowman*, and departs in a rustling of skirts.

He exits the cantina and begins to wander around the village, unsettled of mind, unsteady afoot, mostly attributable to the copious quantities of tequila he's consumed, but also due to these patches of ice that once again have mysteriously begun to appear under his feet. Slipping and sliding, he climbs a steep and narrow cobblestone street to the top of a small hill upon which sits an unusually cheerful-looking church. It's painted glossy white with bright turquoise blue and mint green arches over the windows and the large wooden front door. It reminds him of the cake his mother baked for his sixth birthday, the same year and in fact the very same day the snow began to fall in Osberg—the day the new ice age began. Remembering the brewhag's words, *Search for the path to God,* he enters the church and it's nothing at all like he expected. Large squares of cloth suspended from the ceiling give the impression of being inside a nomadic tent. The air is thick with the smells of incense, hot candle wax and fresh pine. Rows of candles flicker and glow in front of glass cases containing effigies of saints. A painted plaster statue of the Virgin Mother gazes benignly upon a crucified Christ carved out of wood. His arms and legs are long and sinewy, his ribcage pronounced, bright red blood flows from his wounds, his tormented face and forlorn eyes are raised to his putative father. There is no altar, no pews. A powerfully built young man in a coarse black wool jacket stands next to a sign prohibiting photographs. In his hands he holds a large wooden club that if examined forensically would reveal traces of human hair, blood and brain matter. Disparate groups of people kneel or sit on the stone floor, which is strewn with pine branches. Some are chanting or singing, others weep or pray fervently over an odd assortment of burning candles, incense, eggs, open bottles of Coca-Cola and dried ears of corn. The Snowman winces as a very brown, middle-aged man with thick black brows and deep lines in his face wrings a chicken's neck with his bare hands and places it in front of a burning candle. Suddenly a dark figure steps out of the shadows in front of him. *What the devil?* No, it's not Old Nick. It's Father O'Jalajan from the cathedral in Chopahuac. He's dressed in a plain black suit with a white collar and he looks like any humble parish priest. Hmm, maybe, but the Snowman senses more than coincidence here. Father O'Jalajan, who has been staring at the melting slush under his feet with a slightly startled expression, explains that in addition to his position in Chopahuac (again he refrains from referring to his lofty title of Bishop), he acts something like a circuit preacher, traveling from village to village to offer mass and perform religious ceremonies. In Las Riquezas, however, his role is more of a liaison between the indigenous people and the outside world. Nothing is as it seems here, señor Snowman. In this choorrrch the pagan and sacred are combined. Father O'Jalajan nods at an effigy on the wall, a bearded man in Biblical robes holding a

large book in his arms. He also has a lit cigar smoldering
between his lips and is wearing a cowboy hat and several
neckties. Saint Simón, rrroight? Father O'Jalajan says in his
Spanish-Irish brogue. Um, I guess so, the Snowman shrugs, not
particularly well-versed in Catholic iconography. Father
O'Jalajan shakes his head. No—Maximón (he pronounces it
Mawsh-ee-moan), a Maya god, kind of a bully, rrreally.
Definitely don't want to get on his bad side. A loud belch draws
the Snowman's attention to a man gulping a bottle of Coke. An
older man next to him, his mouth stretched in a nearly toothless
grin, clearly intoxicated, drinks from a jar of clear liquid. That's
posh, Father O'Jalajan says. At least that's how the Snowman
hears it. He figures Father O'Jalajan means something like
that's rich or even *ironic* considering the guy's getting drunk in
a church, but no, Father O'Jalajan clarifies, it's *pox*, corrrn
liquor, not exactly Kentucky bourrrbon but just as potent. The
indígenas believe the belching caused by drinking Pox and
Coca-Cola expels bad spirits. Of course the choorrrch would
prefer they chose the less destructive beverage (he doesn't
specify which that is), but we can't ask too much of a people
whose faith is already wavering, can we? Father O'Jalajan
stares into his eyes like a miner contemplating a vein of coal.
Are you a man of faith, my friend? Do you believe? Sorta, says
Big Tex, his noncommittal shrug suggesting that somehow in
some cosmic system somewhere in the universe he could
arguably be said to believe in *something,* otherwise, why go on,
right, Sam? Father O'Jalajan frowns like *who the fuck's Sam?*
then clasps his hands together. That you believe is the important
thing. Which is why I am going to tell you now that what you
are searching for is not in the choorrrch, my friend. Hmm, his
suspicions return. Like, why the hell is everyone so damn
certain he's *looking* for something? Does he have a *Quest* mark
stamped on his forehead? And since when does a priest turn you
away from the church? Is this some kind of reverse psychology
thing? Father O'Jalajan doesn't exactly disabuse him of this
notion when he asks enigmatically, How much greater are our

troubles than those of the least among us? *Huh?* How can a wealthy man who is poor in spirit understand a poor man who is wealthy in spirit? *Wha?* To put it in a nutshell, señor Snowman, your life has been pretty darn cushy so far. *Seriously?* It wouldn't hurt for you to experience what life is like for the people who here live. What I'm saying is, you should get a bloody job, *Snowman.* If you wish, I can help you in this endeavor, but keep in mind, this will be no cakewalk. You will find the life of the laborer here a verrry tough row to hoe. *Meh.* He shrugs off the warning. The snowbiz wasn't any sleigh ride either and besides, it wouldn't hurt to pick up a few pesos (very few, he will discover).

Maria seems amused and not particularly surprised when he announces he will soon be gainfully employed, but she too cautions him that this will be no walk in the park (somebody should warn them all against the criminal abuse of clichés). So why does he again have the feeling that, despite their spoken reservations, this is exactly the course Maria and Father O'Jalajan want him to pursue?

23
The Sun Lord
(Here comes the sun ... *king*)

A.M. DARKNESS pushed back by candlelight, lantern light, stove light, the pop and hiss of hot oil, the smell of frying onions, Maria, sleepy-eyed, flannel sleeves rolled up, making breakfast, the closeness of their bodies, that still electrifying touch of bare skin and even fabric as she places his dish on the table, this inconsummate intimacy of almost but not. Maybe the food is an alternate offering, maybe that explains his appetite. Huevos a la mexicana, spicy black beans, slices of papaya, fresh corn tortillas, chunky, whole-grain toast, guava jam, strong coffee with fresh cream—a sense of fatality enhances the taste of everything. Not like a man preparing to face the firing squad— no, not that extreme, of course. More like the anxious fluttery way he felt getting dressed before breakfast the morning of the first day of the new school year when he was a kid. Except for the clinking of knife and fork, they eat silently, quickly, and then it's out the door. Maria climbs on the motorcycle and he climbs on behind and they roar out to the highway, the stars overhead fading into lavender and pink, roosters crowing back and forth across the valley, the adolescent thrill of this odd embrace, his arms wrapped around Maria's waist, his chin against her shoulder, his crotch practically against her butt, and not a single word spoken other than maybe good morning and now goodbye when she lets him off. A truck comes and he climbs in back among a dozen other men. Some grunt and nod but none speak. For the non-viewing audience, the Snowman doesn't seem as terribly out of place as one might think. Maria has dyed his hair and eyebrows dark brown, his face and hands have acquired a passable tan, he wears a long-sleeved shirt, baggy trousers and work boots like the other men, if anyone asks, he has a fairly credible story about an auditory defect, illustrated with hand gestures, to explain his limited language skills. At Maria's suggestion he has also taken on a Mexican name, *Hilario Lacrimoso*. The truck arrives at a large metal gate. Chain link fence, concertina wire, security cameras perched everywhere like robotic hawks. Large signs warn against trespassing. Men armed with automatic rifles wave them through. They pass sheds, corrugated steel buildings, farm machinery. Gravel crunches beneath the truck's tires. Thin yellow light has begun to spread over the wide valley. Endless rows of huge, spiky plants, like artichokes on steroids, stretch into the hazy distance. *Agave*, he hears the other men refer to them. Large spoked aluminum wheels, like carnival rides without seats, are spaced at ten meter intervals, connected by metal pipes that serve as both axles and conduits for water to irrigate the plants. Here and there work crews are getting down from trucks, stretching, yawning, gathering up tools and starting into the fields. The sun is just appearing on the horizon like an enormous red ball and it's already hot when the Snowman's truck stops. He and the other men get down, attach machetes in canvas scabbards at their hips, throw round-bladed hoes over their shoulders and trudge into the furrowed field. The hoe's hard wooden haft feels as alien as if he were marching with a rifle on his shoulder, a reminder that he knows nothing about plant cultivation and even less about these monster vegetables. The agave are huge, six feet tall at least, with giant, grayish-green, sword-shaped leaves armed with fishhook spines on the edges and gleaming black needles at the tips. The foreman of his crew, Gilberto Favor, a lean, leather-faced man whom he will hear the other men refer to as Gil, pronounced alternately as *Geel* or *Heel*, barks ¡*A trabajar!* and the guy next to him unsheathes his machete, whacks off the outer leaves of an agave like they were blades of grass *whack whack whack*, sheathes his machete, takes up his hoe, jabs the shiny round blade *chop chop chop* at the base of the plant, severing it from its roots. He then methodically chops the remaining leaves off the bole until all that's left is something like a giant pineapple, which he tosses onto the pile the other men have started. Whole operation took him about five minutes. Ohhh, so that's how it's done. The quick study Snowman approaches an agave, unsheathes his machete and takes a wild swing, hacking off part of a leaf with a metallic *zinnng* and poking himself in the arm with an agave needle, producing a sharp, deep pain and raising a small red blossom in his chambray shirt. He awkwardly chops off a few more leaves, sheathes his machete, picks up his hoe, aims at the base of the plant and *jab, clang, wonk*, his blade nicks the agave hide, ricochets off a rock and plunges into the dirt dangerously close to his right foot. And so it goes. An unfamiliar twinge announces itself in his lower back. The friction of his hands sliding up and down the wooden handle of the hoe chafes his skin and raises blisters. The agave spines hook themselves in his flesh like cat claws so that blood mingles with the sweat trickling down his wrists. Heat waves rise around him in trembling liminal curtains. The sun simmers in the sky like an egg yolk in a frying pan. Apparently breaks aren't on the agenda. The men raise the water jug overhead for a drink, or turn away to pee, but that's it. They speak little or in a low electrical hum that buzzes in his ears like the sound of a meadow full of apian wings. He recognizes Zoltec but its meaning is totally lost on him. Occasionally his eyes meet the other men's. They look at him from a thousand years away, their gaze not hostile but indifferent, *alien*, except now he's the alien. What the fuck are you doing here, *Snowman?* Is this some kind of penance? Further penance? Penance upon penance and never acquitted, pardoned, paroled? What did you so that was so *bad?* Murder someone in a drug and alcohol frenzy you've washed from your memory? Lied to a girl and said you did when you didn't? Has God marked you as one of his chosen ones? Unchosen you? *God?*

Lunchtime comes around one o'clock. The men eat sitting on the ground or squatting on their heels in the shade of a corrugated iron storage shed among mind-numbing petroleum and chemical smells. He's famished but also exhausted and rather than gobble down the food Maria packed for him he eats with slow, thoughtful bites. An old man with rheumy eyes and a bristly lower jaw like a rough pine box sits across from him. How old is he? Sixty? Seventy? *Forty?* His body aged two years for every one lived? Is that what this idealized bucolic life does to you, Snowman? He notices a small man in maroon polyester pants and a faded, banana custard-colored western shirt with brown piping and pearl snap buttons, squatting on the heels of his heel-less boots. To the Snowman's amazement, he's reading a book, a beat-up paperback. Occasionally someone speaks in a lowered voice. Mostly they're silent. Heads sink forward, chins rest on chests, the black Lethean waters of sleep slip among them. *¡Ándenleee, putooos!* Gil's voice whines like a chainsaw and they pull themselves to their feet.

The Snowman figures the afternoon can only be worse and it is. The sun is an unrelenting heat lamp, hot air boils around him. His sweat-dampened clothes chafe in his crotch and under his arms. The blisters on his hands tear open and burn from the sweat. The muscles in his arms cramp and contract spasmodically. His back aches. His work with the hoe and machete has become increasingly ineffective. He wants to sink to the ground and die. He actually feels like crying. Finally the sun sinks on the horizon like a nuclear core melting into the earth and Gil barks *¡Ya!* The men sheath their machetes, throw their hoes over their shoulders and trudge out of the fields. The Snowman's so beat he can barely climb up in the truck. Every bump in the road sets off a barrage of aches and pains throughout his body.

Heigh-ho, heigh-ho, it's home from work we go!

Home. Quicksilver twilight dissolving into indigo, crickets chirring, warm, herbal-scented air. It hurts to undress, it hurts to bend over, to stand up straight, to open and close his raw, torn hands. He stands under the shower and the cool water splashing over him is like bathing in rubbing alcohol. Dirt and sweat and traces of blood flow from his naked body. He thinks of the queen's pool and then Maria's naked body, but he's too beat to feel anything but the slightest stirring. Maria has prepared a large meal but one beer and he's falling asleep in his soup. He remembers collapsing on the bed, and then Maria at his side, working some kind of salve into his hands, which she tells him comes from the aloe plant and is a little sister to the agave. Maria's voice slips into a distant drone and he falls asleep with the vague notion that she's putting a spell on him. Then he's climbing a steep stone stairway. His thighs ache, his back is sore, but he struggles upward toward the orange ball of fire burning in the cerulean sky as a black obsidian blade rises and the angels call out to him *Snowmannnn*.

Snowman? Maria's voice wakes him.

If yesterday was bad today is much worse, not only due to the abuse his body has already sustained, which he is reminded of every time the truck hits a bump on the way out to the field, but because he knows exactly what's ahead of him for the next twelve hours. Somehow he survives those twelve hours and twelve hours the next day until the twelve hour days compound themselves into weeks. And here we see a montage of the Snowman, or rather *Hilario*, and the other men in the fields, the hot white sun blazing down on their sweat-stained backs, the gleam of their machetes rising and falling, the shining silver blades of their hoes chopping the leathery, gray leaves from the agave boles, which the men call *piñas*. Sometimes he looks out across the field and thinks he sees agave spikes poking up through a white blanket of snow and then he reminds himself that it's not snow, the snow was then and there and this is here and now. Throughout the day he lifts his head and stares up at the sun burning in the sky like a thousand watt incandescent bulb, trying to calculate what time it is and how much time has passed since he last looked. *Mah K'ina,* the old man next to him smiles broadly, toothlessly. Later he learns this means *great sun lord* and is a title given to Maya kings, but now he hears *máquina* and thinks, of course it's a machine, a molten dynamo roaring through space with a tiny blue-green planet tethered in tow by a wisp of gravity. *Because no matter what you are doing, working in the fields or eating dinner or taking a shit or making love, it's all the sun, not just an object you can point to in the sky and say, there, that's why, that hot ball of gas burning in the thin blue ether, but the sun as another dimension that knows no here nor there, a dimension that surrounds, engulfs and inhabits you, you breathe the sun into your lungs, you eat and drink the sun, you sweat and your body expels hot, swollen drops of sun like melted butter, you make love and you are consumed by the sun.* Hand-written in smudged lead pencil, in Spanish he mostly understands, on a crumpled piece of paper he's pretty sure he saw fall out of the back pocket of this guy Pedro who's always got his nose buried in a book during their brief lunch break. Which makes him wonder what the fuck *he's* doing here.

By now he's accustomed to the intense labor, the aches and pains have disappeared, his hands are callused, his body harder, leaner, the flab he accumulated around his gut from his gigolo lifestyle gone. He can't remember when he stopped smoking. He hardly drinks. The audience can see from the golden cinematic aura surrounding him that he's entering a purer state of being. Something else is happening. Before, when the other men spoke Zoltec, he only heard your fundamental "the natives are restless" mumbo jumbo. Now they open their mouths and tools come out, hoes, shovels, machetes, the things around them, rocks, dirt, trucks, mountains, the agave plants. He feels like Konstantin Levin swinging a scythe with the peasants—keeping in mind he's more of a peasant himself than a wealthy landowner and they aren't harvesting wheat (nor are they speaking Russian). The men call the agave *xoc,* which they pronounce *shock* but he hears as *shark,* which figures, right? The agave's leathery hide is like shark skin, their spines are like shark teeth. So he will be *shocked* when he also discovers that xoc actually does mean *shark* in Mayan.

And here the great documentarian Herr Zog—Werner, isn't it? Ach, Fritz? *Entschuldigen Sie mich bitte*—so urgent to educate the audience about the agave's unique properties that he's practically soiling his lederhosen, butts in again. De agaffay's botanical name is *Agaffay americana,* but another name giffen to de agaffay iss *century plant* because dese plants receive so little rain in de desert und grow so slowly dey seem to live a hundred years. Finally dey push up fifteen to twenty-foot asparagus-like stalks, which should come as no surprise because de agaffay iss in fact in de *Asparagaceae* family, ha, ha, ha, *ahem.* Silently und through de miracle of time-lapse photography, dese stalks explode into carillons of waxy white flower bells. After putting on dis incredible floral display, de agaffay turns yellow und black at de base und collapses in on itself like de withered claw of some strange prehistoric creature. It almost seems an act of self-immolation, as if de agaffay would never die otherwise. Herr Zog—if we may, *Fritz*—pauses a minute, then continues. So fearsome iss dis plant dat no predator dines on its clawed leaves, no foraging herbivore iss foolish enough to test its mettle, und yet, as threatening as dis warrior vegetable iss, it iss undone by a small insect, a half-inch long black beetle called de agaffay billbug because of its bill-like proboscis with which it cuts a perfectly round hole, very much like a cigarette burn, into de bulb-like base of de plant. It den tunnels into de heart of de agaffay und lays eggs dat develop into larvae, which in turn consume de plant's center und cause it to die from within. To prevent dis premature expiration, agaffay growers send out crop-dusting drones to drop insecticide on de plants, which de growers say only kills de harmful insects. But research has shown—Thank you, Mr. Zog. But I am not finished. I wanted to say dat—*THANK YOU,* Mister Zog! But—*mmph!* (In the unedited cut, a shepherd's crook can actually be seen reaching out toward *der gute Herr* from off-screen. The Snowman would kind of like to hear him out. No such luck.)

While the growers say the pesticide only kills the billbug, the men complain that it kills the xoc's spirit, it makes the xoc sick, it makes *them* sick. On top of this, the growers force the xoc to drink more water than it needs so the plants looks bloated and swollen. To supply this water, growers drill deep wells, depleting the aquifers so the villagers have no water for their crops or livestock. The Snowman's informant on these matters is Pedro the poet, as he has begun to think of this poor wretch who comes to work every day in the same faded banana custard-colored western shirt and torn maroon polyester pants, with the heels missing from his boots and often times nothing to eat for lunch (the Snowman only recently convinced him to accept part of his own meal—*mi esposa*, she makes too much, he said, patting his belly). And still he finds the energy and wherewithal to read books and even scratch out lines of poetry, although it has also occurred to the Snowman that Pedro may simply have copied the verse from the books he reads. There are other complaints. The men used to take a siesta in the middle of the day. They ate their tortillas and beans and drank pulque, and then they slept until the hottest part of day had passed when work was worthless anyway, and then they worked again. Now they work all the time and earn barely enough to feed their families.

Inexplicably, a woman wearing a bowl of tropical fruit on her head and a full-length blue flamenco dress with white ruffles at the ankles sambas her way through the agave fields singing,

> *I'm Chiquita Banana*
> *and I'm here to say*
> *I work like a donkey*
> *and I like eet that way.*
> *Ride me all night*

*and ride me all day
in the heat of the sun
without any pay.
I'm Chiquita Banana
And I like eet that way.*

The Snowman soon learns it isn't just the agave plant or the workers who cultivate it that have suffered from a disruption in the order of things. In the crepuscular light of evening bats flutter and swoop over the men's heads. At first the Snowman—*Hilario,* he still has to remind himself—ducks and dodges or swings his hoe at them, but the others admonish him. Noooo, Hilario. Do not hurt the bats. They are our friends. And so they are. Herr Zog—*Fritz*—steps in again: In natural circumstances de long-nosed bat, genus *Leptonycteris*, iss de primary pollinator of not only de agaffay but desert cacti and succulents in general. Before de new ice age, millions of dese flying mammals migrated north to the United States every spring in columns dat stretched across de sky like enormous black shrouds. Now dey can no longer traffel to *el Norte* because it iss always cold der and der are no insects for de bats to eat. Or, as Pedro dolorously concludes, Poor bats. Now they stay here all the time, they are slaves like us. Which sounds pretty heavy-handed, but considering the long hours, lousy pay and lack of *career alternatives*, the wage-labor exchange is clearly weighted in favor of you know who. Some of the more cynical among our viewers have suggested that the *right to work* concept, a mainstay of worker ~~exploi~~ *rights* throughout much of the United States and especially the south, has simply been more stringently interpreted down ol' Mexico way. And, true, the Snowman has wondered why such threatening-looking plants require such heavy security. Guard posts, chain link fence topped with concertina wire, cameras, searchlights, foot patrols with psychotic Rottweilers and Doberman Pinschers, surveillance drones armed with miniaturized, body heat-seeking missiles, military convoys, truckloads of soldiers—it doesn't take too much to imagine a high security prison or even a concentration camp.

One day he spots a Humvee in which he recognizes American uniforms. Hmm, what's up with that? That same night on SNN, Tío Roberto hosts a panel including General Urgencio Tabasco, Chief of National Internal Security, and visiting Americans, Louisiana Senator Strumplin Snoops, Senate Armed Services Committee Chairman, and U.S. Marine Colonel Stewart P. Ditto, and yes, it is the very same Marine Colonel the Snowman saw at the Chapultepec Castle debacle and, therefore, also the same colonel he remembers from the powwow in the desert. Tío Roberto starts off the program with a pretty blunt question. So why the heavy military presence here, General? These soldiers are protecting the men working in the fields, of course, General Tabasco responds. Doing due diligence, Tío Roberto persists, Protecting them from what, General? The general is equally straightforward. Bandits, hooligans, self-purported revolutionaries who want to destroy this important cash crop and ruin these honest workers' lives. Tío Roberto turns to Senator Snoops and the American officer. And the American presence? General Tabasco smiles broadly at Colonel Ditto. Our very good freends from the north are assisting us in training and logistical support. Tío Roberto raises a skeptical brow, but not only does he know which side his tortilla is buttered on, he also knows how easily such a rich diet can kill you. So, gentlemen, he lobs his guests a softball, there's no reason for the public to be concerned? General Tabasco, Senator Snoops and Colonel Ditto all scoff and shake their heads vigorously. *Nawww. No way. Absolutamente not!* You heard it here, Tío Roberto says. The soldiers are our *freends. No olvides, un pueblo informado es un pueblo cálido* (which actually doesn't make much sense in this climate). And here Boone (brilliantly, some would say, amateurishly, others) makes a chasmic segue. Forgoing any transitional device, he splices in several frames of archival film footage, it's black and white, scratchy, jerky, but you immediately get the picture—

U.S. troops in turn-of-the-century (twentieth) uniforms firing on crowds of gaunt-looking peasants, bodies lying in pools of blood, a partially burned sign on which one can make out *Un ted Fru*. It's over in an instant. Barely suprasubliminal.

Of course this charade does nothing to alleviate the Snowman's suspicions. Yeah, sure, he can buy the business about the cash crop, back in *el Norte* everyone and his abuelita's brewing craft and boutique tequilas and fighting for market share, although when he gazes out over the endless rows of agave stretching across this vast, hazy valley, he also thinks, that's a lot of tequila. That evening the truck takes a different route out of the fields. He's just nodding off but he immediately sits up straight when they pass a huge processing plant. Semi-dump trucks are lined up, waiting to drop their loads of *piñas* onto a growing mountain of agave boles, but what really catches his eye is another line of semis. These are snow white tanker trucks and they all have a familiar big blue I on their air foils. A feeble flame ignited with iron and flint flickers in his brain and he makes the following caveman calculation. Not tequila? *Icine?* Made from agave? Which is the question he more articulately poses to Maria over dinner that night and it's pretty obvious she's done her homework. Turns out these aren't your everyday desert variety agave. These are AgaveX®, a patented GMO originally developed to augment the production of biofuels. Thanks, however, to one of those serendipitous accidents by which science sometimes advances in leaps and bounds, researchers discovered a more profitable use for this plant than fuel for internal combustion, much less alcohol consumption. Maria rolls her eyes as if to say, yes, I know this is more than you wanted to hear *but* ... She then explains that the distillate from the fermented AgaveX® is processed through osmotic filters that, for functional reasons, look exactly like giant communion wafers down to the cross in the center. Maria's right hand clutches reflexively at her chest and she takes a deep breath. It so happens that these filters are manufactured from recycled paper by—and here she makes a shoulder-shrugging *sorry-but-what-can-you-do?* expression and says—*PPP*. And sure enough, the second the Snowman hears that plosive, tri-partite aspiration, the bells chime in his head and he again pictures Judith, but this time in full corporate battle gear, lethal-looking jewelry (very pointy, possibly explosive), black leather jacket, bustier and skintight pants, stalking a boardroom of mostly men (and mostly trembling) like a professional assassin. But before he can wallow in self-pity and remorse at what once was, much less entertain the possibility of some big, crazy, *maybe* conspiracy involving not just Maria and Judith but pretty much the whole world, that train leaves him at the station as Maria forges ahead on her own track. This filtration, or *bleaching* process, produces a liquid—as you surmised, Snowman, *Icine*—while leaving behind a crystalline precipitate. He sees himself in the front office of the Ice Factory, staring at an invoice and the words *waste product* printed in fire engine red one second before Evelyn, ever the exemplar of secretarial efficiency, snatches it from his hands, her bright blue bird eyes simultaneously threatening and pleading for complicit silence. So what happens to this waste product? he asks, assuming it to be the crystalline precipitate. Maria gives him her classic bemused look (the dimples again) and says, Icine *is* the waste product, Snowman. *Huh?* For a moment he's totally flummoxed. He performs a slightly more advanced primate equation in his mind. So if Icine is the waste product, that means the precipitate is the primary product? Which means—? Another feeble flame flickers in his brain but this time the question is slower in coming. Just thinking about it gives him a hot, burning sensation, kind of like squeezing out a big fat brain turd. You mean *Ice?!* he practically shouts, referring to the highly addictive street drug. Maria nods and he continues his own train of thought, but the conclusion he's barreling toward like Casey Jones at the throttle of the Old 97 seems utterly preposterous. So in other words what we're really talking about is government involvement in the drug trade? Maria looks at him as if he really is an idiot, then pushes aside the dishes and plops down next to him like the good-hearted varsity cheerleader who has volunteered to tutor the class dunce (who, any hope of a boyfriend-girlfriend thing apparently hopeless, still gets an adolescent thrill out of this close contact *bzzzzt!*) and flips open her laptop. It's not for nothing this guy is called the drug czar, Snowman. On the screen we see Marvin Morfein in his Admiral Boom naval costume speaking to a bunch of government suits.

It's a win-win situation, gentlemen (there are no ladies). We've got the entire religious establishment with us on this. Catholics, Protestants, Jews, even the fucking ragheads—no offense, Mandeep. Oh, Sikh? Sorry. Drug use is a violation of God's will, a defilement of the body and spirit, blah blah blah. We've got the courts, the police, educators, the medical establishment. And the irony is, even Big Pharma's down with this. We don't *take* business from them. We *share* business with them. Overpriced prescription drugs, overpriced street drugs— as long as the public's addicted to *something* we all profit. And here Marvin actually breaks into an awkward little song and dance—you can tell he really wants to cut loose (there's this wild a-guy's-just-gotta-tap gleam in his eyes), but he makes do with a two-second simulated top hat and cane routine (word is that Boone's considering a remake of *Guys and Dolls* as a tragedy, others suggest a Pynchon thing).

Ohhh ... we make your life so lousy,
you just wanta get high,
you wanta get low,
you wanta get drowsy-wowsy.
We've got drugs to get you up in the morning
and drugs to get you through the day,
drugs to ease the boredom, the tedium, the pain.
Drugs to mellow you out at night
and turn the lights down low.
Drugs to help you sleep and eat and fff ...
well, you know

(oh, and even to pee and poo).
Drugs to stop taking drugs
and drugs to fill the void when you do.
Oh, and here's the rub—

Even the Snowman can guess that *rub* is probably rhymed with *gov* but Marvin breaks off in mid-step to say in a more sober, well, *gloating* tone, It's simple, gentlemen. We tax people to pay for the war on drugs at the same time we tax them to subsidize the production of drugs. We tell them to say no to drugs when we really mean say yes to drugs. And when they do as we want them to, we punish them for their drug abuse. We raid their homes, seize their property, take away their children, put them in jail, destroy their lives—and here's even better news: every step of the way we make another dime. Gentlemen, it's the perfect cri—*system*. Maria gives the Snowman a look like, *I know, what a snow job, right?* (Not sure how she acquired this video.)

Not long afterwards he's out in the fields, playing the prole, chopping away at an agave with his machete, dripping sweat and pondering these latest revelations, when he hears the haunting hollow notes of a pan pipe and this time clearly recognizes the Peruvian classic *El cóndor pasa* as a shadow falls over him and he looks up and sees a buzzard circling high in the pale blue sky. Old Grandfather Vulture, of course, his ragged black haberdashery crawling with fleas and mites, reminding us that the tediously inevitable but always unique experience of Death is, indeed, omnipresent. And then, soaring higher still, a much larger buzzard, and, hmm, this is interesting because he's seen this buzzard before, it's a kind of raptorized buzzard that spends hours in the gym hitting the weights and munches steroids like M&Ms, a fierce samurai buzzard that both kills and eats its kill, in this case a B2 stealth bomber painted exactly like a buzzard, down to its scabrous red head.

When the Snowman reports this latest sighting to Maria, she again plops down next to him, triggering another barrage of warm tinglies throughout his body, and flips open her laptop. On the screen he sees grainy satellite images of enormous jet cargo planes painted like giant vultures lined up on an airfield in a shimmering yellow strip of desert (military enthusiasts will recognize these as Russian Antonov An-124 *Ruslans,* one of the largest military transport planes in the world, designated by NATO, coincidentally, as *Condors*). Know where that is? Maria asks. He shakes his head. Northern Tamaulipas mean anything to you? Um ... that one stumps him too. Maria gives him another clue. Near the southern part of Texas? Ohhhh, he says, like *now* I know, even though he doesn't. And guess who owns those planes, Snowman? No idea? Recognize the name L. Condor Valladoides? Yeah, *him*. And would it also interest you to know he runs the biggest drug cartel in Mexico? Holy shit, and he was—well, *did, once, maybe*—boffing this guy's daughter? He doesn't actually say this aloud but Maria looks at him like *mm-hm* and continues. Truth is, Snowman, Condor's dirty business is good for the economy. He provides employment for *millions* of people in every profession. Airline pilots, aviation technicians, structural and mining engineers, chemists, agronomists, CPAs and lawyers, lots and lots of lawyers. Maria ponders this for a minute. Not to mention blue collar and clerical workers, construction, retail sales, truck drivers, common laborers and, of course, your rank and file hit men, henchmen, foot soldiers, mules, couriers, etc. Keeping in mind—Maria rolls her eyes—that much of federal, state and local government, including the military and police, are also in his pay. Also keeping in mind that accepting employment with señor Condor isn't always a choice. Sometimes entire villages, men, women, children, are forced to abandon their jobs, homes, schools—their own crops to harvest marijuana or opium poppies or work in the agave fields. Maria's eyes meet his. Refusal is met with—well ...

From time to time he notices large plumes of smoke rising in the distance. At first he assumes it must be farmers practicing their age-old slash and burn agriculture but this is the wrong season and besides, the smoke is unusually black, with odd sulfurous yellow and Paris green streaks, as if it were produced by burning paint, plastic, synthetic materials, the kind of stuff you might expect to find in, oh, say, houses? One day a black Peregrino SUV pulls up to the jobsite and a couple of beefy guys in street clothes get out and ask for Pedro. No one says anything but their eyes inadvertently identify the poet. The beefeaters immediately grab him and start dragging him back to the SUV. Hey, what's going on? the Snowman blurts out and immediately regrets it because, yep, one of the beefeaters turns with a menacing expression and says, Who's this guy? Gil rolls his eyes in the Snowman's direction and makes a gesture that indicates he has some mental deficiencies. Yeah? Well he'd better learn to mind his own business if he knows what's good for him. A couple days go by and Pedro hasn't shown up on the job site. When the Snowman inquires, the other men shrug and stare at the ground. Finally one says Pedro fell off a ladder and hurt himself. When he mentions this incident to Maria, she insists they get in the Coupe and drive to Pedro's house, which turns out to be a one-room, dirt-floor shack. The wife, who looks sixty but can't be more than thirty-five, bare-foot, frayed brown wool skirt, faded and stained pink blouse, worn face, dazed eyes, bad teeth, makes excuses about the state of the house, the work she has to do, but finally lets them in. Half a dozen skinny kids in ragged clothes and dirty bare feet stare at them from a simple wooden table. There's no sign of food anywhere. Pedro's lying on a mattress on the floor and it's immediately obvious he didn't just fall off a ladder. His face is bruised and swollen, his nose crooked, and from the pain in his blackened eyes and the way he's lying he's probably got some broken ribs, at least a broken arm and possibly a broken leg. When Maria asks what happened the story remains unchanged. Through missing teeth Pedro mumbles that he fell off a ladder. He refuses to look at them when he says this. Maria, who has brought along a medical kit, methodically begins to treat his injuries and, contrary to the Snowman's recent doubts, it's pretty obvious she's had a lot of experience in this business. Sometimes Pedro grimaces or flinches but otherwise he shows no sign of pain, even when she sets his arm with the help of the Snowman, who nearly passes out. Fortunately the leg isn't broken, just badly bruised. When Maria finishes, she gives the wife antibiotics, pain killers, a bag of food and a small wad of cash. The whole way home she stares straight ahead, but she grimaces and twists her lips and mutters incoherently as if she's carrying on an angry conversation with herself or at the very least channeling an angry god. At one point she turns to him as if she wants to make what he can only guess is a terrible confession. Her face looks both tormented and murderous. Before she can get a word out, Boone cuts away and her face is replaced on the screen by a man's face, brutally beaten. The camera draws back so we can see that he's tied to a tree. His clothes are torn and bloody. A sign on his chest says *soplón* (informer—Eduardo, I'm closing my eyes now). A man approaches him with a metal can and douses him with gasoline. Another man tosses a match and he's engulfed in flames. His screams are horrible, heart-rending. In the background vendors sell candy, soda, bottled water, balloons. People laugh and chat and fan themselves (not much different than your typical lynching back in the good old Jim Crow days). The images are captured on cell phones and instantly go viral. The following day peasants storm a freight train hauling corn and fill anything handy, chamber pots, cuspidors, sombreros, with golden grain. Stores are looted and burned in Chopahuac. A hundred peasants armed with machetes and clenched fists invade a luxurious mansion in a gated estate, forcing the wealthy owners to abandon their brunch and the mansion to the peasants. These acts are followed by reprisals and counter reprisals. A convoy of SUVs drives into a mountain village in the middle of the night and slaughters all the inhabitants except for a baby girl who crawled into a clay pot. A mass grave is discovered in the desert. Human heads are stacked like soccer balls outside the police station. Dead bodies hang from a bridge like marionettes.

Every day the news is worse. The game of tit for tat grows ever deadlier. Fear encircles the village of Las Riquezas like a pack of starving wolves. The Snowman senses an undercurrent of hostility directed at him. The skinny guy on the corner glowering at him over a cigarette. The fat taco lady who shoves his taco at him and takes his money without a word. Raúl, the new guy on the crew, who watches his every move like a, well, cat with a mouse. On a couple occasions he glances up just as a drone zips away.

One night he's driving back from Las Riquezas where he has gone to buy cigarettes to feed his recently revived habit (the pharmacist Enrique Enfermi, himself a heavy smoker, recommends Faros, a very strong, unfiltered cancer stick). The Coupe's headlights sweep over a troop transport parked on the side of the road, illuminating a platoon of soldiers armed with lethal-looking FX-05 *Xiuhcoatl* carbines, the famous *fire snakes*. Their youthful faces look like burnished copper masks beneath their steel helmets, their eyes gleam like distant watch fires, and, *oh shit*, they're signaling him to pull over, they're approaching the Coupe. But—*what the fuck?!* It's *los guys*, Nico, Bombástico and Xuan, and they're grinning from ear to ear. *¡Hola*, Snowman! Nico calls out with a friendly wave. He starts to wave back but just then Boone of all people jumps out of a Humvee dressed in a Mexican army colonel's uniform (apparently he's rented an entire battalion of Mexican soldiers for peanuts—well, a couple thousand bucks and a crate of Kentucky's finest bourbon) and man does he look hot under the collar, which possibly has something to do with what appears to be a growing insurrection among his own ranks, the editorial staff, for example, and this impudent fact check *person* (that's *Glenda*, to you, *Boone*, single mom, two children, three jobs, four including part-time *bitch*. And, no, I won't get you a goddamn cup of coffee. And furthermore—*fuck you!*), oh, and that punk-ass blogger kid who referred to him as *Boob* Weller. He throws his hands in the air and practically screams, No! No! No! You aren't doing it right! To which Nico replies like a smart aleck schoolboy (oddly in perfect English), I thought we were supposed to extemporize. I'll extemporize your ass! Boone snarls. Suddenly the guys are all business. They yank open the doors of the Coupe and drag out the Snowman. Nico slams the butt of his fire snake into his shoulder. Xuan's fire snake lands in his lower back and sends him reeling toward Bombástico, who bends him double with a blow to the stomach. Why you are so stupeed, *Snowman?* Nico hisses in his ear, his accent returned. Why do you get meexed up in sometheeng that's none of your fokking beezness? The Snowman stares at him in pain and confusion. What the fuck's going on? Aren't these guys supposed to be his friends! He's just about resigned himself to an early grave when Boone yells *cut!* and the guys immediately start joking with him again, oh ho ho ho, Snowman, we had you going, no? But no professional thespian he, he can't shut off his emotions so easily. Nor can he suppress the sense that he has become a thorn in everyone's side. Plus this skewed Dorothy of Kansas mantra keeps running through his head, What the fuck are you *doing here*, Snowman? Maybe it'd be better for all parties involved if he got his ass out of Dodge and headed home. When he broaches this possibility with Maria, she laughs it off. Nonsense, Snowman, stick around, the fun's just about to begin. But in her eyes he sees something—desperation? *madness?*—and his suspicions return. What if this is all part of an elaborate scheme to trap him here? But why? What does he have to offer anybody? Yes, he knows Maria has probably been using him to gain info from Amanita about L. Condor, just as Amanita was almost certainly using him to gain info on Maria. And somehow all that ties in with Judith and PPP. Which makes him what—an unwitting double, triple and possibly even quadruple agent? But that's just your paranoia talking, right, Snowman? *Right?*

24

L. Condor

AND THEN, AS IF SUMMONED by the mere mention of her name, who else but Amanita roars onto the set in a cloud of dust, screeches her fighter jet to a halt half an inch from the Snowman's right foot, lowers her window, engulfing him in a wave of arctic air, and says, You look thinner, Snowman. What have you been up to? Not hiking in the desert again? Oh, spare me the drama. I know all about your little peasant charade. Amanita extends her hand as if she's showing her driver's license to a traffic cop and with unexpected tenderness caresses his scarred fingers and callused palm. So, it's true, Snowman. You've become a member of the proletariat. First a prophet, now a peon. What are you trying to prove? Do you think you can expiate your white Protestant guilt through *honest* labor? Or fill empty bellies? Or change corrupt laws? Or right past injustices? You'll break your back, you'll grow old and bent and consumed with resentment. He hates her guts, he hates that what she says is true, he hates this twisted mechanism inside him that, proportionate to his own impotent rage, elevates her power over him that much more. Don't look so hurt, Snowman. I don't care if you play your little game. Think of it as research. Maybe you'll learn something useful. Oh, by the way, my father is hosting an event this weekend. You're invited. I hope you will attend. But please, Snowman, not in your rustic costume. As much as she pisses him off, and despite all kinds of warning sirens and bells, in fact, because of these very things, of course he'll attend. He even has this delusional idea he'll discover something useful he can pass on to Maria (flash of James Bond in a white dinner jacket and black bowtie, Walther PPK 7.65mm in hand, stealthily entering a darkened hotel room), although it might have been wise to let her in on his plans.

The screen fades into penumbral black and then, briefly, blinding white again to suggest we've entered a new day and indeed the Snowman has obviously had more than just a shower and a wardrobe change as we now see him seated behind the wheel of the Coupe, shaved, groomed and cologned in a white linen jacket, pale blue oxford shirt, dark blue trousers, and a belt with monogrammed buckle (yes, it's an S, but finely etched parallel lines render it a very subtle dollar sign), vestiges of Amanita's largesse, of course, probably cost about as much as *pobre* Pedro earned in his lifetime (just saying). He's following a tortuous track of switchbacks, overhangs and hairpin curves up into the rugged, cactus-strewn mountains, the Coupe making strangely sentimental whinnying and neighing sounds the higher they climb. And explain this: he comes to a concrete bunker, razor wire, heavy iron gate, armed guards. These are some seriously bad cats, tats, scars, studs, gold bling, and they're armed with an arsenal, Glocks, Uzis, AK-47s, sawed off shotguns. This older dude, rock-hard physique, black guayabera, gray fedora, trim salt and pepper goatee, too many deaths in his eyes to keep track of, reflexively snaps to attention and salutes as the Coupe rolls up to the gate, then does a *say what?* double take, leans in the window, gives the Snowman a very hairy eyeball, takes out a cellphone, scrolls, stops, glances at the Snowman again, sighs as if he's been interrupted in the middle of strangling some traitorous son of a bitch with his bare hands, rolls back the gate and waves him through. The camera now returns to the Snowman and we can see from his expression that he's struggling with his own confusion as he remembers the one time Amanita consented to ride with him in the Coupe. It was early morning, already hot, but Amanita insisted they keep the windows closed, she didn't want to ruin her hair (new do, he couldn't tell the diff). The sunlight was blinding and she said, Push that button, Snowman. But it doesn't do anything. Just do it. Now turn it to the right. A dark green tint began to suffuse the windows. How'd you know? Amanita shrugged. Lucky guess. And, who knows, maybe, but he also remembers now the time Amanita, thoroughly trashed on booze and coke, alternately crying and laughing hysterically, told him the story of her mother's murder. Her father was out of town on business. On a whim her mother took his car for a spin, an American classic—like *this*, sort of. Amanita wrinkles her nose at the Coupe's dilapidated interior. Another car pulled alongside, one of her father's *business rivals* leaned out the window with a machine gun. He couldn't see that her father wasn't behind the wheel because of the tinted windows. Amanita was five-years-old, asleep in the back seat. She woke with her mother's bloody brains splattered all over her. *Boo hoo hoo!* A week later the business rival received a package at his office. Ribbons, fancy wrapping paper. Inside, his wife's head. *Ha ha ha!*

A few hundred yards farther he comes upon an incongruously lush green cleft in the mountainside and another gate, black wrought iron ornamented with cut copper palm trees and flamingos and crowded in on both sides with purple mounds of bougainvillea. A pair of security cameras is perched on top of the gateposts like watchful little gargoyles. On the soundtrack we (and apparently the Snowman from his expression) hear the hollow, breathy tones of the panpipes playing the haunting *El cóndor pasa*. His every instinct tells him to turn around, go back, *flee*. Too late, the gate rolls aside and before he even presses his foot on the gas the Coupe surges forward of its own accord, like a horse eager to get back to the stable after a long ride. He has to stomp the brake to keep from crashing into a large marble Venus de Milo that even to his untrained eyes looks pretty damn authentic (remember that scandal at the Louvre?). Ahead of him lies a Mediterranean villa, pink stucco, black wrought iron balconies, sugar frosting columns and marble staircases half-buried in banana and palm trees, bougainvillea and large, leafy philodendrons. A fountain splashes in the circle in front. A brutish looking individual with a low forehead and gorilla arms bulging out of a dark blue suit appears and in a polite but insistent tone about two octaves below normal human range offers to park the Coupe. The Snowman's first reaction is no way, he's never let anyone else behind the wheel of this baby, and besides, what if he decides not to stick around or he needs to, you know, make a fast getaway? In the end, of course, he relents. Ringing the bell next to a sturdy wooden door that looks like it could withstand a Roman battering ram, he is greeted by Clive Hedgeworth Yañez-Urrutia, L. Condor's valet. Despite his copper skin and Indian features, *Clive's* British accent is perfect except for his "s's," which come out like "th's," so that Clive addresses the Snowman as *Mithter Thnowman* as he shows him into a palatial foyer. On the walls the Snowman recognizes Picasso, Modigliani, Dalí, Pollock, de Kooning, and he's pretty sure these aren't reproductions. *Snowman!* In a theatrical entrance Boone unabashedly stole from an old black and white TV series (colorized), Amanita floats down a curving marble staircase in a pale yellow flounce of satin and chiffon and the Snowman remembers again just how striking she is (apparently he's shoved the Mona Moondrake thing into an old steamer trunk in the basement of his subconscious). Amanita asks Clive to bring her a dry martini—the Snowman requests a mango margarita, which elicits a raised eyebrow and the suggestion of a sneer from Clive, who returns with their drinks just as a tall, handsome man in a gray *Armoani* suit strolls in. Sixtyish, black hair, steel gray at the temples, square jaw, trim athletic build, perfect white teeth, bright black eyes. He smiles broadly and excuses himself for being late, and no doubt about it, this is the guy the Snowman saw in the desert. He is also, as Amanita confirms when she says in mock exasperation, *Ay papi!* none other than the notorious drug lord, L. Condor Valladoides. Harvard-educated, business, economics, his English impeccable, his conversation replete with allusions to art, music, literature, travel to exotic locales, he seems anything but the unflinchingly cruel monster he is reputed to be. Even the way he welcomes the Snowman to his *little retreat* with a humble nod of his head. To which the Snowman, thinking himself quite clever or maybe not thinking at all, blurts out in his Big Tex voice, So what're you retreatin' from, pardner? L. Condor gives him a curious glance, which could be read as *seriously?* but also *hmmm, what does this guy know?* then takes him by the arm. Come, my friend, let me introduce you to the other guests, among whom, the Snowman is more than a little discomfited to discover, are included the State Judicial Police Commissioner, in full uniform, the state Attorney General, the state Governor, as well as all five state deputies and all four state senators. Also in attendance, L. Condor's *good* American friends, Senator Strumplin Snoops, who gives the Snowman's hand an oily squeeze and grins like an inbred hillbilly who's just been caught fondling one of the hogs, Drug Czar Marvin Morfein in his Admiral Boom uniform, who greets the Snowman with a jaundiced eye and an unsteady handshake, and an American military officer, also in uniform, whom the Snowman clearly recognizes as Marine Colonel Stewart P. Ditto. Jug-eared, five o'clock shadow, leering grin, bear-like slouch, he seems easy-going and friendly but his bone-crushing grip suggests he's probably broken at least a few necks with that mitt. In addition to this crowd of powerful and, it goes without saying, dangerous people, the Snowman also notices a number of less cultured-looking dudes in expensive but ill-fitting suits, as well as several precariously underdressed young women whose combined IQ, he's guessing, is less than that of a fifty dollar bill (although, who knows, maybe they're all high school teachers, college professors, the skin trade just pays a helluva lot better). He also spots an adolescent boy, fifteen, sixteen tops, perfectly groomed, sports jacket, open collar, trying to act cool but clearly nervous, whom he hears referred to as the *prince* and (stupidly) thinks to himself, oh, they must still have some kind of royalty here. Meanwhile, Amanita has become totally absorbed in a strikingly handsome guy with movie star looks and aplomb and manages not to notice the Snowman's lame attempts to catch her eye.

In the middle of this scene Clive appears to announce dinner. A half dozen valets seat the guests at a large table, antique Spanish lace and linen, silver candelabras, gold leaf china and crystal, bouquets of yellow gladiolus with flower spikes like Gaudían church spires and strangely transsexual orange anthuriums, both membranous and phalloidal (the attentive florist might see some sort of theme for the evening). L. Condor makes a brief speech, during which he introduces his guests of honor, with a special mention of *our other American friend*—nodding in the Snowman's direction—who, if I understand correctly, represents *the snow industry*. Condor then raises his drink in an esoteric toast to *Mexico's future in winter sports*. Following the chiming of glasses, the servants begin to serve a succession of dishes and everyone digs in. Unhappily, the Snowman sees that Amanita has been seated next to the movie star, while he, not uncoincidentally, he suspects, has been placed between two Neanderthals whose bulging muscles threaten to Hulk-like burst out of their monkey suits.

Following dinner, drinks and dancing to music provided by a small easy listening combo whose identically dressed members (white leisure suits, black velvet lapels and piping) look like they're ready to grab their instruments and run at the drop of a bod—*hat*. Their trepidation seems unwarranted. The action on the dance floor's pretty lame, it's like an episode from American Bandstand, the guy at the mike even looks like Dick Clark, at least from the Snowman's vantage point, which is at the back of the room trying to blend in with the wallpaper. Decorum quickly gives way to debauchery. Champagne corks fly. Trays of cocaine circulate. Soon all present, police, politicians and high-ranking dignitaries included, look as if they've been eating powdered donuts. People laugh and shout, the suited thugs join in some pretty rough horseplay, the *prince* is getting sick in a wastebasket. Various couples are, well, coupling and even engaging in oral sex in not particularly discreet corners of the party. Amanita and the movie star are nowhere to be seen. The Snowman is feeling completely out of place as well as pretty toasted when L. Condor appears at his side and invites him into his private office, which they arrive at by stepping through a door into some kind of elevator that, judging by its motion, travels both vertically (though down or up the Snowman has not a hunch) and horizontally (though east or west he couldn't guess), so yes, more or less diagonally, while whisking them away very far very fast, so that for all he knows they could be several miles underground or out in space when they step through another door into a large room that does in fact resemble the cockpit of a space ship with multiple wall screens, computers, consoles and communications equipment. This is the brains of L. Condor enterprises, the man for whom this organization is eponymously named says with the restrained pride of an English lord giving a tour of his castle. He then proceeds to discuss mostly arcane business matters, the difficulty of obtaining certain raw materials, the billions (*billions*) of dollars he's saved thanks to falling oil prices, the diversifying market for recreational drugs in the U.S., along the way earnestly soliciting the Snowman's opinion as if he were a professional consultant even though he's already consumed the full tumbler of very smoky and potent single malt scotch L. Condor offered him and, let's face it, he's pretty fucking blotto. He's slurring and, God knows why—probably because he assumes that a powerful *businessman* like L. Condor would naturally harbor conservative sentiments—blurting out obviously rightwing and even fascist dogma (really, it's utter nonsense, the Pope is a Zionist agent, the President is in cahoots with the Rooskies—okay, that might be true), but he can't stop himself, he feels compelled by this handsome, older, self-assured and powerful presence to say the right thing. But what is the right thing? An edge of anger has entered his voice. He gestures wildly and begins to shout all sorts of absurd statements that essentially endorse torture, genocide, mass murder. An eye for an eye! Kill them all! Exterminate the brutes! (Who *them* is isn't at all clear.) Oddly, L. Condor doesn't seem the least bit disturbed by this outburst and even appears amused, until, that is, the Snowman, perhaps still stung by the slight he received from *los guys* the other night, incautiously mocks the military for allowing itself to be infiltrated by a bunch of boobs. At which L. Condor raises a simultaneously inquisitive and threatening eyebrow, assuming (incorrectly) that he, the Snowman, must be referring to his, L. Condor's, own men. Regaining his poise, Condor claps a tan, well-manicured hand on the Snowman's shoulder. Well, my friend, I see you are a man of passion. I confess, your conservative sentiments surprise me. You and I must continue this conversation later, but for now—Condor spreads his hands and evaporates in a flash of light. Bela Lugosi in *Dracula*, right?

The next thing the Snowman knows, he's lying in his bed (each guest has been assigned a room), trying to extract himself from an uncomfortably realistic dream in which he lolls between pink silk and satin bedcovers while L. Condor caresses him and makes crude sexual suggestions. He wakes with an urgent need to pee and a piss hard-on he selectively disconnects from his dream. In search of a bathroom, he passes a door that has been left slightly ajar (another flash of James Bond in white dinner jacket). Inside he sees Colonel Ditto rocking back and forth in an Ikea Poäng spring chair, masturbating furiously (and, sorry, for you armchair Freudians who may have hoped otherwise, he does have a pretty big whang) and muttering incoherent nonsense … thish is my fucking country, by God … I'll show thesesh gook bashtards who da big boy is … and even reprising some of the exact language the Snowman himself had used with L. Condor, *Kill them all! Exterminate the brutes!* while his personal secretary, Fallacia Hardwicke, turns the pages of a porn magazine for him and says with feigned enthusiasm and the classic, eye-rolling, bored secretary expression, Give it to 'em good, Stew, baby! The Snowman passes another room with the door ajar and *what the fuck?!* danged if he doesn't see—and, yes, this does cause him considerable heartache—Amanita down on all fours, being fucked doggie style by the putative movie star, but there are also cameras, lights, Mylar reflectors, it's a fucking (what else?) porn shoot and—wait, doesn't Amanita look a bit pudgy? And are those copper curls a wig or—*Mona?* Simultaneously trying to decipher and wipe this image from his mind, he hurries on and—okay, this is clearly Boone pulling one of his juvenile stunts because next we see, through yet another open door, Marvin Morfein sprawled on a couch and, folks, we'd be remiss if we failed to report that he looks completely whacked out, his eyes are going *boinga! boinga!* his bi-corner hat's hanging off a chandelier, his frog buttoned jacket is unfrogged, revealing a dirty white t-shirt stretched over a pot belly, bottles of booze and pills lie everywhere, giggly, scantily clad young women are snorting mountains of coke from a gold tray, the *prince* is passed out on an ottoman, pants down to his knees and his butt in the air. The Snowman passes another partly open door and inside he sees several fat, thuggish men fucking, sodomizing, penetrating and violating every orifice and fold of flesh imaginable in a young woman who, despite a clown mask of makeup, doesn't look older than fifteen. (A video will appear on the black market shortly afterward showing a young woman—okay, *girl*—being disemboweled, arms and legs hacked off, head cleaved from her neck with a single blow of an axe. Is it real? Is it fake? You decide.)

L. Condor's mountaintop retreat is a house of horrors, a rookery of wraiths. Outside another door the Snowman overhears L. Condor, apparently the only person here who has retained his sobriety, speaking to Senator Snoops. I am certain you remember from your school days, Senator, that cold air is denser than warm air, which gives airplanes greater lift, permitting them to carry heavier loads? Senator Snoops, who's already got about a quart and a half of Kentucky's finest under his belt, nods away yup, yup, yup like a Bible—oops, *bobble* doll, his face twisted into a sloppy, slack-jawed rubbery grin, although it's pretty obvious he has no idea what the fuck Condor is talking about and this better not be on the test. Condor continues. It has long been my dream, Senator, to see this poor country of mine become—shall we say, *climate-controlled?*—as is your nation. Ironic that the Icine we would need for such an enterprise we export to your country. One can only imagine what a tragedy it would be for all concerned if insurgents disrupted this supply. And with a complicit wink (the camera zooms in on an eye as black and shining as a lump of coal in the center of which burns an orange flame), Condor raises his glass to the Senator, who, splashing whiskey everywhere, lifts his glass in return, even though he has zero idea what kind of devil's bargain he's agreeing to.

The following morning, that is to say around noon, after lots of coffee, trays of cocaine and platters of jelly-filled pastries, L. Condor, casually dressed in a white guayabera and tan twill trousers, leads his generally hung-over but totally wired guests on a stroll about the grounds, which unassumingly boast (if that's possible) an eighteen hole golf course, riding stables, a car barn housing two dozen classic automobiles, including now the Coupe, which seems quite at home (indeed, the grill, the Snowman observes with a stab of betrayal, actually looks like it's grinning at him), a heavily guarded helipad (and you're right, that isn't a Sikorsky S-76 VIP or Eurocopter Mercedes-Benz EC 145 or other top dollar executive chopper parked on the tarmac, but rather a U.S. military HH-60G PAVE Hawk, bristling with .50 caliber machine guns and both air to air and air to ground missiles, and featuring a full complement of cutting edge communications and navigation systems, as well as a radar warning receiver, infrared jammer and a flare/chaff countermeasure dispensing system that, taken as a whole, suggest the need for sudden, evasive and combat-engaged flight-plans—the sticker price at last glance came to a cool forty million), a large Japanese garden, and an orchard where the

Snowman immediately notices the enormous, and familiar, he thinks, black monkeys climbing in the branches of the mango trees overhead. Apparently they have been trained to pick the large, reddish-orange fruit and place it in canvas bags they carry over their shoulders. Something odd about these monkeys, though—they kind of look like *men* wearing monkey costumes, and, indeed, so they are. L. Condor says to the Snowman, After our conversation last night, I'm certain you will approve of our methods. Seems these men have violated certain *company policies*. As punishment, they're put on a restricted diet, water, and sent up into the trees to pick fruit, which they are absolutely forbidden to eat. Any violation of this edict and their *trainers* shoot them out of the trees with beanbag guns. Day after day they climb the trees, their hunger growing greater, their arms and legs weaker, the temptation stronger. The Snowman hears a *bang* and a sickening thud and sees a monkey man writhing on the ground. A trainer stands over him, beanbag gun crooked in his elbow, the proud air of the accomplished sportsman on his mustachioed face. This isn't exactly what I had in mind, the Snowman, who only remembers disconnected fragments of last night's conversation, thinks but doesn't say. Despite his reservations, he will soon discover that firearms and the sporting life are a large part of L. Condor's planned entertainment.

After a late buffet lunch (Maine lobster, Alaska king crab, a barbecued side of Texas beef—apparently the Mexican chef has an inferiority complex), and enough alcohol to float a small yacht, the sportsmanship continues poolside where last night's eye candy are now lounging next to the turquoise water in thongs, string bikinis and mostly topless. But Condor and his guests aren't here for aquatics. The Snowman now notices a rack of shotguns overlooking a wide green lawn surrounded by towering palms, leafy banana trees and red, pink and purple mounds of bougainvillea. Apparently there's going to be some skeet shooting. The Snowman has an ominous feeling about this, but, at L. Condor's insistence, he takes up a shotgun along with everyone else. Other than snow guns, he's never fired or even held an actual firearm in his life. It's like clutching some kind of venomous creature capable of spontaneous murder and mayhem. Although, true, as he examines the natural mottling of the burnished black walnut stock and the gold plated receiver engraved with a bucolic scene of pheasants hiding among tall grass and leafy vines that extend along the steel barrel, he has to admit this weapon is also a thing of beauty. Condor nods in respect. You Americans make some very nice firearms. Noting the Snowman's unfamiliarity with the weapon in his hands, Condor says, Allow me to demonstrate. He turns, faces the lawn with his shotgun resting in the crook of his right arm and barks *Dale!* Out of nowhere a black and yellow clay disk flies over the green lawn and, in a surprisingly casual movement, Condor raises his shotgun to his shoulder and—*Bap!* A loud, flat retort and his shoulder jerks backward at almost the exact instant the disk disintegrates in midair. *Dale!* Condor barks again and *Bap!* another clay disk explodes in midair. *Dale! Dale! Dale!* he says in quick succession and *Bap! Bap! Bap!* another one, two, three yellow and black disks disintegrate against the clear blue sky. Now it's the Snowman's turn. He swings the shotgun to his shoulder in a wild arc and horrified faces duck for cover. *Dolly!* he croaks and a clay pigeon flies over the lawn. *Bap!* The shotgun slams against his shoulder and a coconut crashes down from the palm tree overhead while the black and yellow ceramic disk sails intact toward a patch of green jungle foliage. *Bap!* An instant before the disc disappears, it disintegrates and Amanita, who has appeared in a short-waisted black leather jacket, designer jeans and gaucho boots, lowers her shotgun. The others now take turns proving their prowess with smoothbore firearms, but after Condor's and Amanita's display, it's all moot and the guests soon retire for more drinks under the beach umbrellas where L. Condor again broaches the subject of his business. Come, come, señor Snowman, I know your true sympathies lie with the poor, but I think you misunderstand my motives. Your country's thirst for Icine has put us in an unfortunate situation where we in turn must put our own people in an even more unfortunate position. It is not I who wish to see the people suffer. I am only protecting my interests, which are also the interests of my country. What's good for L. Condor is good for Mexico, no? Which the Snowman says he can kind of understand, I mean, when you look at it that way. But L. Condor is not in the mood for condescension. He seems impatient, even annoyed, like a chess grandmaster sentenced in hell to play the same incompetent boob (how many times can you fool's mate someone before they catch on?) for eternity. Nevertheless, he's built this weekend production around the grand finale, so let's get on with the show.

L. Condor leads the guests, drinks in hand, to something that looks like a small stone coliseum with very steep rows of seats, also built out of stone. At the center is a small bullring, thirty feet in diameter at most, encircled by a wall of vertical stone slabs, perhaps five feet tall. It feels very constricted, formidable, suggesting little room to maneuver for man or beast. An out of tune, off-key brass band made up of a tuba, trombone and two trumpet players in saggy, ill-fitting blue uniforms with red epaulets and piping down the legs, marches, or more accurately, staggers around the ring, producing a squeaking, squawking, unintentionally lugubrious version of the Ballad of the Lonesome Bull, and, oh no, the Snowman groans to himself when a wooden gate opens and the bull appears. He's been through this before but not this close. The bull seems reluctant. Men are yelling at it and trying to drive it into the center of the ring. There's something odd, ungainly about this rickety, bony creature with its moth-eaten hide and folds of loose skin and that, um … silly bull mask? Ohhh … now he gets it. It's a joke, right? Comic relief? Not a real bull but a couple of men inside a bull costume. Another man appears in a rather tawdry matador outfit no one would be surprised to learn has been worn in some pretty sordid porn shoots. He's wearing a sword at his side and in his hands he holds two tasseled banderillas that actually look like barbecue skewers and which he unceremoniously raises over his head and plunges into the bull's shoulder blades. It looks very authentic and the man wearing the bull's head even bellows like a bull and what appears to be real blood trickles down the shoulders. The bullfighter now draws his cape and his sword and approaches the bull. There is none of the finesse, the *pas de deux* between man and beast, the elegant cape work and breathtaking near-death encounter. The matador waves his cape, once, crudely, his blade rises, plunges, rises and plunges again. Blood splatters everywhere, the stone walls, seats, the audience. It's like tomato sauce. The Snowman discreetly wipes a hot red blot from his cheek as the silly bull sinks to the ground, writhing and convulsing and twisted in the middle like a rag, blood gushing out, head and tail struggling desperately to go their separate ways, escape this thing that relentlessly pursues them, death. The bull's head has fallen off, revealing a man, his mouth wide, empty, except for the black stump of his tongue, his dazed, bloodshot eyes mad with pain, unable to cry aloud, only bellow like an enraged beast. But Snowman, Snowman, what are we doing here? This is madness. These are very bad people. Hey, Boone, what's going on? This was supposed to be a joke, right? But not a peep out of the great director to suggest he's the least bit concerned about his numero uno thespian or even anywhere on the set. This is seriously scaring the Snowman. He's practically hyperventilating, his heart's tachycardial, he desperately wants to get up and run like hell but he's packed in with all these gangsters. L. Condor seems to have read his mind. You look a bit pale, señor. My men will escort you back to your room for a *rest*. And a pair of enormous goons take him by the elbows and literally lift him off his feet. Amanita, the movie star standing so close behind her they could be having backdoor sex, gives him a little *ta-ta* wave of her fingers and makes a comic grimace like, aww, does the poor Snowman not feel well?

The next scene shows the villa at night, a man's silhouette pacing back and forth in front of a window. Norteño music plays somewhere. A car engine starts up. The Snowman—it is the Snowman—hears a key in the lock and thinks, uh-oh, this is it, but the door opens and Amanita slips into his room and somewhat breathlessly tells him she wants to help him escape. Why are you doing this? he asks. She shakes her head as if to cast away tears or deny an unspeakable truth or both. Then, verifying what the audience has already suspected, she confesses. She and Margarito had a "fling"—Amanita air quotes this risibly dated term but her eyes are wet, her voice tremulous. You know what they say about opposites attracting, Snowman? Like that. Unfortunately for all parties involved, she fell in love with Margarito. When he rebuffed her, she betrayed him. At the last minute, she changed her mind, tried to save him—too late. Amanita finishes her tale with a kind of goofy, loopy, cross-eyed, what-can-you-do? expression that, damn, does kind of remind him of—*Mona?* but when he says, I don't believe you, her ire flares like a skyrocket. Don't get huffy with me, *Sleighman.* Your beloved Margarito fucked anything that moved. Anyway, I don't hope to redeem myself, just avoid past mistakes. Amanita tells him to wait ten minutes, and then leaves as the camera pulls in for a close-up the Snowman's eyes, which are understandably bright with anxiety.

The scene changes. The camera has moved outside. We see a door open and a dark form slip into the shadows. Then we're in the jungle, following the Snowman's breathless flight through the dense undergrowth. It's almost dawn. Quicksilver seams of twilight pierce the dark tropical foliage. Patches of fog drift here and there. He's tripping over tree roots, getting tangled up in vines, and then—what the *fuck?* It's like a cheap sci-fi flick (it *is* a cheap sci-fi flick) where the scenery is painted on canvas and suddenly it's torn away and just like that the jungle ends in a perfect demarcation and the ghostly white desert begins. But right when he thinks he might have escaped one nightmare, he stumbles into this, another B-grade horror film. Rotting corpses lie everywhere, half-buried bodies rise out of the sandy soil like ghouls from the grave, arms, legs and headless torsos are scattered around like parts of mannequins. The air is so rancid he gags violently, staggers forward and plunges into a pit of strange jelly-like substance mixed up with hard white sticks and *ai-yi-yi, please god no*, he's neck deep and treading water so to speak in a stinking potpourri of decomposing flesh. Vomiting everything in his guts, whimpering and moaning and possibly even shitting himself, he crawls out of this human muck on his hands and knees and dripping protoplasmic goo rises to his feet and staggers forward like, yes, one of *those* zombies, his mind a house of horrors he desperately wants to escape, flee, run as far away from as possible, and that's basically a given zero. Worse, dawn cracks and just like that, the sun's up and it's immediately brutally hot. He stinks and he's wretched and coated with this foul shit and now what? He has staggered into something like an ancient Greek theater with a macabre Christian touch. It's a cemetery set in a broad and perfectly round natural concavity with concentric rows of mostly fresh graves marked with crude headstones and wooden crosses, and now he's running past them, faster and faster in a mad ecstasy, and even crazier he's leaving behind icy tracks that hiss and steam like dry ice. Suddenly he stops and stares at one grave in particular with— what else?—his name on it. We hear the rolling thunder of a timpani, a single strike of a triangle, and then a neurotic piano roaming around middle C, followed by an adenoidal and melancholic oboe. In the second row of the woodwind section we see the Snowman playing the bassoon. Oh. The buffoon. Really, what's he doing there? He's like the court jester at the Queen's ball. He's dancing around and playing the mouth trumpet, completely out of tune. Fortunately his mike's off. The martial *rat-a-tat-tat* of a snare drum returns our attention to the orchestra and an incredible voice, female, singing notes without words that soar among the clouds and touch the hem of the celestial realm, reminding us that the human voice is also an incredible musical instrument. How can a human being produce this sound and not be inspired by the angels, by love—by God?

(Ha! scoffs the perennial cynic Boone, who knows full well ol' Beelzebub has crooned his sweet tune in the pious ears of many a sweet maid.) Against the barren white desert the Snowman now sees Amanita riding toward him on a black horse. She's wearing a black leather Stetson, black leather vest over a black western-cut shirt, black kid-leather pants and gloves, black dogger-style cowboy boots with silver spurs, and a pair of Colt .45s in tooled black leather holsters on her hips. She reins in her horse, unholsters a pistol and aims it between his eyes. My father's men will be here any minute. Once again he asks, But why, Amanita? I don't know why, Snowman. Because it's my nature. Because you are a greenghost and sooner or later you would betray me, the way your people have always betrayed us. The Snowman's not sure who this *us* is but it doesn't matter. A convoy of black SUVs is approaching. Struggle is useless. Amanita dismounts and without warning pushes a wet cloth against his face. I'm sorry, *Snowmannnn.* He makes a clumsy, pawing attempt to resist but, too late, the angels have taken him by the arms and are carrying him away.

25

A Snowball in Hell
(or Hieronymus Bosch Does Grand Guignol)

THE ABATTOIR.
Why not just kill him now?
Because he may know something he doesn't know he knows.

HE REMEMBERS BEING DRAGGED along a bare concrete hallway, dazed glimpses of naked cow carcasses suspended from metal hooks, human heads crudely sewn on their necks, their fore and hind legs extended like a macabre Rockettes chorus line. Naked men's bodies with pigs' heads clumsily stitched to their shoulders arranged in a semi-circle like a garnish of giant prawns. Chainsaws rev up like angry, internal combustion hornets. Screams smothered behind duct tape, torture victims grunt and squeal through their nostrils like pigs. The soft *thud thud thud* of limbs hitting the cement floor. The hard *conk* of heads. A red haze hangs in the air. Bright red blood with stray bits of flesh and tissue and even an occasional organ gurgles and slurps around the workers' rubber boots. In places the crimson liquid is congealing into black blood pudding (it should come as no surprise that some of this stuff is sold in the meat market near you). Here and there naked women are locked in form-fitting wire cages that push up their butts doggie style or spread their legs for the conventional missionary when the workers need a diversion. Their toothless mouths are wired into perfect Os for sodomizing without the risk of their biting off a worker's penis. Their eyes reflect a dazed celluloid horror of madness and absolute surrender of the self. Outside the door of this slaughterhouse, a line of victims hobbles forward, wrists and ankles bound with rope, wire, chains, plastic ties, their mouths covered with duct tape. Some have their entire heads wrapped in duct tape. They all want to scream out to their mothers, to God, *help me!* But they hobble forward like cattle because of the paralyzing fear, because of the workers screaming at them and jolting them with cattle prods, *¡Muévete, puto! ¡Chíngale!* They kneel in rows, staring into each other's terrified eyes, gasping for breath through their nostrils, some weeping silently, tears streaming down their greasy pallid faces. Workers walk behind them, methodically swinging sledgehammers, *thud thud thud,* sometimes a glancing blow has to be repeated, or the sledge sinks into a skull and has to be extracted, covered with bloody brain matter. Faces crumple like grotesque rubber masks. Hair, skull, blood, brains splatter everywhere. Most of the workers wear surgical masks over their nose and mouth, protective glasses over their eyes, but this bloody gunk still gets in *everywhere.*

The Snowman sinks into unconsciousness and wakes again to shouts and laughter. Through a metal grate he sees a bunch of guys kicking a battered human head up and down a field in an impromptu game of soccer. He appraises his own situation. He's in a small cement block building, tied to a swivel chair naked, not a position he'd like to be in even with a urologist or other medical practitioner with the right to such intimacy. It's safe to say he's never really considered until this minute what a woman must feel like with her feet up in stirrups. Heat rises from a black iron frying pan placed on a hotplate on a wooden table. On the wall next to the door hangs a human head with a penis sticking out of its mouth, a large jalapeño pepper where its nose used to be, a human tongue stapled to its forehead and ping pong balls in its eye sockets. The Snowman's attention shifts to a cockroach on a windowsill, its beady eyes gleaming brightly, its antennae waving madly, almost as if it were trying to communicate with him. Whatever message it wants to convey is lost when Amanita's *protectors*, Pancho and Flaco, and a man in a Judicial Police uniform (the Snowman will hear Flaco and Pancho refer to him as José) enter the room. Pancho cocks his good eye parrot-like at the Snowman and snarls, *mira, puto!* Then swivels his chair around. Across from the Snowman another man, also naked, is tied to a metal chair, his mouth duct-taped shut, his pink, pudgy body covered with burns, bloody wounds. Without ceremony, Pancho takes out a straight razor, bends down, slices off the man's penis at the base and tosses the quivering organ in the hot frying pan where it sizzles and writhes while the man squeals and snorts and blood spurts from his pubis. Pancho turns the penis in the frying pan a couple times with his knife, then spears it, tears the duct tape from the man's mouth, shoves the seared penis between his teeth and fastens the duct tape back in place while the man shrieks though his nose and Flaco and the cop laugh and mock him, *¡Joto! ¡Mamón!*

Okay, the boys have had their fun, given the Snowman a preview of what's to come, now it's time to get down to business. You are an agent provocateur! You are here to interfere in our country's affairs! Who are your friends, Snowman? Tell us their names! What are they planning? Tell us now and it will be easier for you. But what can he tell them? He doesn't know anything. Pancho and Flaco shake their heads in disappointment. Have it your way, Snowman. They start in slowly, a few love taps, a cigarette burn or two, an extracted pinkie fingernail, a couple of superficial lacerations with the razor. He's just a regular guy, he hasn't been trained in esoteric spy techniques to resist torture. He screams, he begs, he repeats, I don't know anything! Or wait—again he sees the barn behind Maria's garden, the door open, hidden in the hay and among the farm implements, automatic rifles, machine guns, crates of RPGs, something that may be a surface to air missile. He's just about to say *b-b-b-barn* when a blow to the side of his head knocks the word out of his mouth. The police officer, *José,* snarls at Flaco and Pancho, *Este pinche cabrón* is tougher than you thought. *¡Oye, Snowman!* Now we're going to give you a little treatment. Maybe you will change your mind. A man in a white smock enters and without preliminary plunges a large hypodermic needle in the Snowman's neck. He feels a searing pain and a deep ache and then his whole body is on fire, it's like a rocket engine igniting, and here comes Flaco with an electrical cord and—*hssst! zzzt! pzzz!*—like the fangs of a poisonous snake the exposed wires strike the Snowman in the face, in the chest, in the scrotum. His entire body constricts each time the snake strikes and the surge of electricity incinerates the highways and byways of his nervous system. His eyes bulge, his brain feels like it's going to explode out of his head, a hot yellow stream gushes down his legs. He's peeing electricity. The frequency increases to an ultra-high pitch, a dentist's drill boring through his skull and into his brain. Someone is prying his eyelids open with surgical clamps. Flaco bends over his face with a small leather pouch. One teaspoon or two? he says and dumps a cascade of the infamous red powder, rumored to exceed one million on the Scoville Chart, into the Snowman's *eye-yi-yi-yiiiiís* and through those impossibly delicate portals of sight twin lightning bolts explode into his brain. His entire being is consumed in a fiery matrix of pain that can't even be quantified as pain in human terms. This is God's eternal wrath, Satan in all his flaming glory, the neutron bomb of the Alpha and Omega having fun at the expense of a lump of clay. Then he's crawling on his belly in the desert. The scorching sand sears his naked flesh. Cactus needles pierce his skin, razor sharp rocks shred his hands and feet. He wants to roll over and die but wise old Grandpa Mexico (not sure who he is) leads him on, teasing and mocking him, *ándale, Nievito*, if an old man like me can climb this anthill so can you. High above him he sees flames roaring from the mouth of a volcano at the same time he hears the angels screaming at him in shrill operatic voices, *Snowmannnn! Snowmannnn!* Then he's lying naked over a stone altar and—he's seen this before—Maria, in an elaborate headdress with long blue, green and red feathers, scanty white loincloth and a diaphanous band of muslin across her breasts, stands over him holding a black obsidian blade and, uh-oh, he knows what's coming next. She plunges the blade into his solar plexus, slices it open and, in a preternatural act of intimacy not described in most medical journals, reaches inside his chest cavity and squeezes his beating heart in her hand. He feels her twist and tug, then watches as she raises his still pulsing heart up to the sun. She then takes the sun out of the sky and places it inside his chest.

But what if he identifies you?

I doubt if he can see anything now. Besides, our Snowman friend won't be talking to anyone again.

Through molasses and fog he recognizes the voice of Marine Colonel Stewart P. Ditto.

He wakes again with a pile driver banging in his head. His eyes feel like they've been marinated in kerosene. He can't tell if they're open or closed. He must be blind. No, there's something. Through a red film he sees black specks circling above him. A thousand feet up in the milky blue sky, two solemn old morticians ride the thermals with barely a flick of the pinion feather. They've been in this business so long their insouciance has become a kind of vaudeville shtick. Smell that, Fred? What is it, Ralph? Rabbit, mile and a half over yonder, next to the barrel cactus. Oh, right, I see it now. But it isn't a rabbit, is it? It's the Snowman. He's staked out on the hot sand, naked. His mouth is as dry as the desert around him, his eyes burn like pools of gasoline. Out of nowhere an ugly mongrel mutt trots up, lifts its leg and pees in his face and, oh God, thank you, it actually feels good. A mechanical-looking little arachnoid backhoe he recognizes as a scorpion scurries across the sand and onto his face and *yow!* plunges its stinger right in his nose and that *doesn't* feel good. The red-hot venom slams into his already ravaged nervous system and in seconds he resembles Jimmy Durante. A dry whisking sound grows in his ears and, by kind of scrunching his face sideways, he spots a yellow and black box turtle creeping toward him. What kind of insult is this little Nazi helmet going to heap on him? But wait, in the mottling on its shell he recognizes the Zoltec character for *help*. You need help, buddy? What about me? And really, what an understatement because just then he smells gasoline and hears a chain saw whine and here come Flaco and Pancho, kicking the naked fat guy along the ground on his hands and knees. There's someone else. The Snowman recognizes the *prince*. The kid's face is contorted with fear and he's crying. In his hands he's holding a running chain saw. *¡Vamos, chico!* Flaco yells at him. The boy's face transforms into a mask of anger and determination. He revs up the saw again and jams the spinning chain against the man's arm. Blood, flesh and bone fly everywhere and the arm plops onto the ground at the same time the boy drops the whining chainsaw and pukes. *¡Cagón!* Pancho kicks him in the ass, grabs the saw, revs it up and cuts off the man's other arm, causing him to fall forward flat on his stomach. Pancho now grinds a boot into the man's lower back and methodically saws off one leg, then the other, leaving the man a heaving, bleeding torso with a head and Pancho's about to take care of that. Letting out a strange, yelping laugh, he ploughs the saw into the man's neck and off topples his *cabeza*. Throughout this ordeal the Snowman has been lifting his own head and craning his neck trying to see what's going on even though he really doesn't want to see what's going on. Now it's his turn. Pancho bends over him, their eyes meet triangularly and, no doubt about it, Pancho looks like he's going to enjoy the hell out of this. He revs the chainsaw and aims it right for the Snowman's crotch. On the screen there's a flash, maybe three frames at most, of Sean Connery spread-eagled on a stainless steel table, a neon red laser beam eating its way through hard metal toward soft and vital flesh. The camera zooms in on the Snowman's eyes and we see his terror turn into bewilderment as white hoarfrost blooms over Pancho's face and body and the chain saw abruptly dies in his hands. Hey, Pancho, whatchoo doeen, man? Flaco (who didn't have an accent earlier, maybe it's his confusion) gives Pancho a shove and—what the heck? Frozen solid, Pancho falls over and shatters into tiny pieces that immediately begin to thaw into a watery pile of pinkish-white crabmeat. At which point Flaco and the prince both take off running. Flaco doesn't get ten feet before his body sprouts a fuzzy white growth and his arms and legs undergo a strange transformation between the blur of running and frozen stasis and he too crashes to the ground and shatters like glass. The prince, meanwhile, has continued to run, every second glancing over his shoulder in abject terror, although you can see he's starting to feel like he's home free, and he is—for now. The camera shifts to a small gray cement block building. A voice— it's the cop, José—calls out, hey, Pancho, Flaco, what hoppen to the door? Eet's stock. I can't open heem. Come on, man, open the fokking door! Eet's too cold in here! I'm freez—not another word comes from José. The building is completely covered in frost, it looks like a giant sugar cube. Again we hear a crash and the sound of shattering glass. Followed by silence. The Snowman strains to see what's going on. Then Xuan is standing over him, holding in his hands a cryogun. (And for those in the audience who don't know what a cryogun is, here's *Fritz* to fill us in—*Halt mund! Du kannst mich nicht* Fritz *nennen. Ich heisse* Herr *Zog! Verstehst du?* Herr *Zog!* Oh, well, I guess we won't be hearing any more on that subject.) The Snowman notices a large cockroach perched on Xuan's shoulder, waving its antennae. Lucky for you Carlitos was still on the set, Xuan says, bending down to untie him. Before Carlitos came to get me, he sent Tomás to tell you help ees coming. Tomás? the Snowman whispers through cracked and swollen lips. The turtle, Xuan replies. That almost makes sense. Where's José? The sapphire gleams as Xuan grins. José? He mayonnaise.

The Snowman wakes again bouncing in the bed of a pickup, his head, apparently, cradled in Maria's lap. He passes in and out of consciousness. At one point he hears Maria say *it would have been a terrible loss if he had died.* Her tone sounds flat, oddly dispassionate, as if by *terrible loss* she does not mean his death. He can't tell to whom she is speaking. The following is all dream-like, maybe it is a dream. Maria and Xuan are carrying him through a tunnel. Then he is suspended under water, but instead of panic and drowning he feels a tremendous sense of relief and well-being as he breathes the water deep into his lungs. When he wakes again Maria is bending over him, her face a shadowscape of fatigue and worry. Behind her Xuan says in a comically lugubrious tone, Is the Snowman dead? Sleep draws over him again like a heavy wool blanket.

26
The Fiesta

ALL NIGHT HE HEARS THUNDER or maybe it's horses' hooves or the tramping of thousands of feet. Barbarian hordes? Harbingers of the apocalypse? Despite this disturbance he wakes feeling profoundly rested. Golden sunshine pours in the window. His ears fill with joyful birdsong and a sound like honeybees swarming over a field of clover or maybe it's the murmur of voices, lots of voices. Curious, he gets up from the bed and begins to dress but stops in amazement. There are no wounds on his body, nothing to indicate the torment he has been through. Did he imagine the whole thing? Did that bastard Boone cut the scene after making him endure all that? Here's another surprise. Maria appears in the doorway in a bright red, green and blue feathered headdress, gold filigree necklace, jade ear flares, and a bright red huipil cinched at the waist with a green sash. She takes his hand and leads him outside and—*what the fff... ?* Banged-up school buses, RVs, pickup trucks, donkey carts and horses are parked or tied up as far as he can see and crowds of people are milling about, many of them in indigenous costumes decorated with feathers, animal skins, pieces of mirror, bells, bangles and beads. People are erecting tents, building fires, stirring huge cauldrons, roasting entire sheep and goats. Into this commotion stride *los guys*, Nico and Carroteeno, Bombástico, Xuan and Raf-I-el, who are also dressed in colorful ceremonial garb, bright red, green and blue feathered headdresses, gold and jade ear flares and nose plugs, robes made of feathers and animal skins. They're greeted with cries of *Aha! Aha!* which sounds Japanese to the Snowman's ears but Maria says is Mayan for *lord.* She gives him an amused look and explains in an off-handed, betcha-didn't-know tone that *los guys* are actually descendants of Zoltec kings, leaving him to speculate what that makes her—princess? queen? She and *los guys* now escort him (cordially—they're all back on good terms, doesn't hurt that he can't remember much of anything) into a lodge constructed of pine poles and animal hides. Men and women are seated around a fire pit. Incense smolders, clay pipes are being passed. The Snowman alternately inhales sweet, spicy cannabis and a very powerful tobacco that he guesses must be the native *Nicotiana rustica.* Pox, pulque and mescal are also being imbibed freely. At some point Maria begins to address the gathering in a mix of Spanish and Zoltec. She seems to be in a trance, even her voice has changed, as if she's speaking through one of those old traffic cone megaphones or, who knows, channeling a spirit, albeit one with a bitter wit.

We have heard the people of Mexico referred to as la Raza. *Perhaps* eraser *is more accurate. Efface personal identity, culture, ethnicity, submerge all in the cauldron of humanity, in the successive waves of invaders, immigrants and slaves, spun together with all the hundreds and thousands of indigenous peoples in a DNA centrifuge, and out of this produce a single entity, homogenized,* pasteurized. *But is this triumph? Survival? Or is it loss? Betrayal? Are we sacrificing our identity and the identity of our mothers and fathers before us? Their faces hammered out of molten bronze, out of gold and copper, out of the terra cotta, the coffee and chocolate and abundance of fruit that blossomed and swelled out of the fertile earth of this ancient land. The land we ruled from one ocean to another. The land upon which we built great cities, empires. Then they came, the* conquistadores. *Perhaps they were the first to practice reverse engineering. In order to understand our architecture apparently it was necessary for them to take it apart. But why waste time and energy on meticulous deconstruction when gunpowder will do the trick in an instant? They said they were bibliophiles, they liked a good read, they wanted to brush up on our culture. Too bad for us, we trusted them. All our ancient records, our codices, parchments and scriptures, destroyed, immolated by the good church fathers. In this way they thought they had destroyed us. But we have sent dream messengers into the underworld to retrieve the words as they were first spoken. Now that we know our beginning we can also see our ending.* Admittedly most of this is lost on the Snowman, but he glances around with interest when Maria mentions a special guest seated among them, until he realizes everyone is looking at *him*. Maria then speaks of a unique role he has to play and an all too familiar *uh-oh* feeling floods his body like ice water when she finishes in a voice both solemn and rousing, Today we feast! Tomorrow we fight! *Fight?* She means figuratively, right? And what's this *we*, Kemo Sabe?

He remembers music and singing, laughing and dancing and even attempting a few clumsy steps himself at the invitation of a fairly stout, seventy-something lady with tortoise shell glasses and a ruddy red apple face. He remembers drinking and eating, tables covered with food, carne asada, smoked pork, chicken steamed in banana leaves, simmering pots of beans, baked squash, roasted corn, tamales, enchiladas, empanadas, moles, chorizos and chiles relleños. His senses heightened (*dulled?*) by cannabis and several jars of pulque, he imagines himself quite the gourmand as he samples increasingly exotic fare. The *huitlacoche* sounds great, looks kind of like cooked blueberries, who'd ever guess this gloopy stuff is corn smut fungus, or that the Aztecs good-humoredly called it *crow shit?* And why not give those famous *chapulines* a try? Hmm, salty, kind of nutty, legs get stuck in your teeth, but *yum*, delightful little buggers. And crickets? *Mmm*, sort of like Chex® party mix with an unusually high ratio of government-allowed insect parts. Oh, and who could pass up the roasted ant larvae? A little gooey, gluey, like overcooked rice, but, sure, all right. (FYI: the International Cafeteria Ladies' Guild does recommend that you include more insect protein in your diet.) The shadows are lengthening, the sun setting, bonfires are being lit. The Snowman finds himself seated among a small group of men who are methodically eating gnarly green cactus bulbs that look something like pin cushions. Their tongues are stained dark green, their eyes are unnaturally bright. The man next to the Snowman raises his fingers to his mouth, indicating, eat, eat. He pops a bulb in his mouth and crunches it between his teeth, anticipating a fresh, herbal taste, maybe a little minty, or even, detecting the initial assault on his tongue's papillae, something like the bitter green liqueur distilled and consumed by grim, silent monks in fortress-like monasteries. It's at this moment that an alkaline locomotive slams head-on into both his taste buds and his guts and good God, this stuff is awful! It tastes like bile. It's like eating vomit. No more for me, he thinks, but the man next to him encourages him to eat another and this is even worse, he can barely get it down. A bottle of mezcal comes around. Ahh, there is balm in Gilead. But alas, the bottle's almost empty and to his horror a large, yellow, segmented worm is lolling in the liquid remaining at the bottom. *Eat! Eat!* the other men encourage him as if he has received a great honor. By now his stomach is churning like a food processor but he's also in the spotlight and you know what they say about finishing what's on your plate when you're in Rome. He upends the bottle with the intent of swallowing the worm whole but there isn't enough alcohol and the damn thing lodges at the back of his throat and, oo, yuck, it's rubbery and squishy and only by a perverse effort of willpower can he make himself swallow it. But now he can't stop obsessing over this damn worm he's eaten. He knows it's dead but he can feel it wriggling around in his belly. It feels like it's gnawing at the lining of his stomach. Now he's certain of it—the worm's alive! And it's eating him from the inside. He can feel it growing. It fills his belly, his intestines, it's pushing up into his esophagus and out his asshole. And just like that he's on his feet and hurrying into the underbrush in search of an appropriate spot which is pretty absurd because the whole fucking desert is essentially a toilet. It's also dark now and not likely anyone will see him. He barely gets his pants down before unleashing a cannonade that would have felled Santa Anna's army, after which he falls forward on his hands and knees and begins to vomit violently while making oddly onomatopoeic retching sounds *Ah Puch! Ah Puch!* unintentionally invoking the skeletal, corpse-like Maya god of death, into whose clutches he seems to have fallen. He's never felt so sick in his life, he wonders if he actually might die. He's projectile vomiting and shitting all the entomological delicacies he consumed with reckless abandon only a short while earlier and even worse, *they're all alive!* Iridescent red, green, purple, the insects wriggle and writhe on the bare earth and in the midst of this swarming, swampy Katrina bouillabaisse he recognizes the mescal worm and even more monstrous, it pushes itself up on its final segment and in a high-pitched dental drill voice screams, *I am Juanito el gusanito and I accuse you of murder!* And it breaks into shrill, ear drum-shredding laughter *hee!hee!hee!heeeee!* Horrified, he draws up his drawers, never mind the besmirched bum, and with a sense of icky discomfort staggers off, in his haste stumbling over a piece of deadwood that before his eyes transforms into a coiled snake, but this isn't just any snake, it's brightly colored and feathery, kind of like a Chinese dragon, and it lifts its head and speaks. I am Lord Kukulkan and I have a message for you *Sssssnowman*. And— *zzzzt!*—the snake's fangs sink into his ankle and it's just like getting slammed with a sledgehammer. An electrical shockwave ploughs through his nervous system and explodes in his brain. The snake's mouth stretches into a wide smile, its tongue flickers in and out and it says, Now we shall sssseeee if you are the true one, Sssssnowman. May the godssss of healing be on your sssside. Later he'll wonder what this snake guy meant by the *true one*. Later still he'll remember that someone else referred to him as the true one. And even later he'll wonder if he didn't just scratch himself on a jaguar bush and imagine the whole thing. Right now, he's absolutely convinced he's going to die, his stomach heaves and convulses, he's sweating profusely, his body aches all over, he's … and just like that the terrible sickness has passed, it's like something that happened a long time ago, like Tinker Bell scattered pixie dust over him and now a warm tingling is spreading through his body and in his brain, he feels like he's vibrating and, look, the stars in the sky are vibrating, they're like glass chimes ringing *ting tinngg tinnnggg* in a maudlin, sentimental Hollywood Christmas classic of heartbreak, loss and redemption, indeed, he feels a sense of reverence and love for all of creation and at the same time a soul-crushing nostalgia and remorse for all those who have suffered and been lost, hot tears are streaming down his face and he's sobbing uncontrollably and blubbering *I'm so sorry, it wasn't my fault, I didn't mean to, I didn't know.* By extraordinary coincidence, he has also wandered into a cemetery. The air smells of smoldering copal. In the flickering candlelight he sees gravestones and crosses decorated with mounds of marigolds, red amaranth, gladiolus and calla lilies, religious icons, portraits of saints, photographs of deceased loved ones, bottles of beer, soda, tequila, packs of cigarettes, trays of sugar skulls, cakes, pies and cookies. And then shadowy figures. Men and women in Edwardian costume parade past him, the women in gauzy, wide-brimmed hats and loose, ankle-length gowns with frills and ruffles, the men in top hats, wide cravats and black morning coats with tails. Their clothing is covered in cobwebs, their faces are painted like skulls—they *are* skulls. *Booooo!* The Snowman shivers as if someone dumped ice water down his back. He's totally spooked. He has no idea where the hell he is and his instincts tell him things are likely to get a whole lot scarier. And, hocus pocus, in a finger-snap instant he's thrown himself right back on top of the Bald Mountain of his worst nightmares. Shrouded wraiths shriek past him. A horrible wail draws his attention to a woman dressed all in white who is wandering along a sandy arroyo, weeping and calling out in a plaintive voice, *¡Niños! ¿Dónde están?* Her face is twisted with torment, the bags under her eyes overlap like lava flows. He speaks to her, *¿Señora?* But either she doesn't hear or she's ignoring him. She wanders away, continuing to wail and call out, *¡Niños!* Glad to be rid of this nuisance (frankly), he ducks behind a boulder (Styrofoam) at the sound of heavy footsteps and breaking branches and an instant later a large hairy form appears out of the scrub. Flames flicker in its cavernous eye sockets, blood drips from its huge fangs, it's got a gutted goat carcass slung over one shoulder and it's taking huge bites out of another. He hears a loud groan and peeping out from his hiding place he sees the Frankenstein monster lurch past, furiously puffing on a cigar and clutching a violin by the neck like a tennis racket. The wings of a very large creature beat the air around him and Dracula in a tuxedo and natty red cummerbund briefly appears, before transforming into a bat and fluttering away. He hears a terrifying howl and a man in a cheesy Wolfman costume appears in silhouette against a full moon before bounding off. What's going on here? Is this Boone diving head first into a colossal monster mash? Wait— did someone say *colossal?* It's *The Amazing Colossal Man! The Colossus of New York! The Attack of the Fifty Foot Woman! The Giant Claw! The Giant Behemoth!* (redundant?) A giant ear of corn marches past, or no, it's a carrot—wait, it's Marshal Matt Dillon playing a monster vegetable from outer space. Odd calliope-like music enters his ears. It seems to be coming from a grove of organ pipe cactus, played by the night, by the fingers of ghosts, by, more prosaically, the breeze that has sprung up, blowing across holes birds and rodents have pecked and clawed into the cactus. The whole universe resonates like plucked harp strings and, sound transformed into light, the aurora borealis hangs its green and red draperies across the black membrane of night and out of this celestial plasma Boone's face appears in a greenish aura looking supremely wise like the Wizard of Oz before his embarrassing wardrobe fail. Boone, is that you? the Snowman calls out. Silence. Are you God, Boone? he cries. Again no answer comes. Boone continues to look wise, indifferent, unperturbed. Then there's a pop and a hiss and

Boone's image melts and curls and bursts into flame like a celluloid frame jammed in a movie projector and the funny thing is—something *is* funny, suddenly he feels like laughing, he is laughing. *Ha!Ha!Ha!Ha! Now* he understands! It's perfectly clear! It's all a joke! *It's a joke! It's a joke! It's a joke!* And just as he thinks this the entire universe roars through him like a diesel locomotive. *Look!* he shouts. *Look! Look! Look!* But now he can't remember anymore. What was clear? Who is he shouting to? Which is when he realizes he's sitting on the ground naked with a bunch of people, most of whom are also naked, and this is interesting, they must be in a corral because horses are nervously pawing and whinnying around them, and no wonder, some of the men are laughing and shouting and trying to mount them, bareback and, yes, carnally, which is when the Snowman also realizes he's sitting in horse manure, in fact, he's clutching lumps of horseshit in his fists and fervently saying to somebody, but that's exactly it! That's what I'm talking about! There's no difference between this shit and God! It's all the same stuff! Later still he hears himself roaring exuberantly, I like snow! I like making snow! And even later, in a transient fit of lucidity, in a subdued voice verging on melancholy, *I am snow.* Across from him sits an old man with a leathery face and thoughtful, wise-looking eyes and in fact he says something that sounds wise and profound in its simplicity. After all, you *are* the *Snowman, ¿verdad? Don Juan?* he says. *Hahaha*, the old man cackles through salt and pepper beard stubble and stalagtitic teeth. *Grandpa?*

And then he has no idea how this happened but he's in the back seat of a car, it may even be the Coupe, it *is* the Coupe, and he's squeezed between Bombástico and Xuan, Raf-I-el's shoved in on Xuan's right, up front Maria's driving, Carroteeno's in the middle, Nico's riding shotgun, all of them still in ceremonial garb, all laughing and singing. Warm, humid night air pours in the windows. The Snowman sees now that they're driving through the jungle. Giant toads as big as VW bugs hop past. Snakes the size of oil pipelines droop from tree limbs. Creamy white night-blooming flowers as big as dinner plates flood the air with the scent of roses. Vines and tendrils hang everywhere. Luminous and iridescent winged creatures flit past them. Then they're standing at the base of a pyramid. They begin to climb the steep stone stairs. Drums beat, flutes shrill and shriek, torches flicker and flare. A stone balustrade carved in the shape of a giant plumed serpent seems to twist and writhe beside them. The Snowman feels like he's wearing lead boots. Each step requires an enormous effort. But even as he thinks this he sees that they've arrived at the top of the pyramid, maybe they took the elevator. A bright red Chaac Mool reclines on its elbows, leering at him. Then he's lying across the Chaac Mool, naked (the camera is discreet). His arms hang lifelessly at his sides, maybe they're bound. He hears Maria say, We know you have suffered a great deal, but now we must ask you to suffer more. Do you willingly submit to the tenets of the covenant, *Snowman?* Maria's eyes gleam in the flickering torchlight and in them he sees desperation and pleading and possibly a glint of reassurance. He has no idea what he's agreeing to but he nods his head and whispers *yes*. A single ray of sunlight, brilliant, sharp as a scalpel, slices across the dark green jungle and gleams on the black obsidian blade Maria has raised over her head.

27
The Pot Boils

0900 HOURS: Washington, D.C., the Pentagon, a military operations room. Colonel Ditto stands in front of a wall screen, briefing the President, select congressmen and a bunch of military brass: Mister President, Gentlemen (again there are no ladies). Operation WhiteOut will begin on or about the 24th of December when a massive polar vortex is expected to drop down out of Canada into the southern plains. At this time our technicians will synchronize a broad band of internet repeater and radio transmission towers, radar dishes, satellite antennas and randomly placed propane-fired barbecue pits stretching across the entire southwestern United States, in turn producing a powerful electromagnetic force field with which we can catch this arctic mass and, kind of like a surfer riding a wave (shout out to Col. Kilgore!), send it skipping deep into Mexico via the high desert plateau separating the Sierra Madres Oriental and Occidental. With the assistance of friendly assets in-country, we'll turn the whole damn pissant place into an icebox for at least a month, excuse my English, Sir, which will give us plenty of time to put a major damper on these commie-loving Che Guevara wannabes. President DeBoche nods his approval. Of course, Colonel Ditto continues, the general populace will suffer some discomfort, extremely harsh conditions, bitter cold, devastating crop loss, starvation. *However*, President Bolillo agrees this is an acceptable risk (thanks to the transfer of ten billion dollars to an off-shore account Colonel Ditto doesn't mention). And I have your assurance, Colonel, that should a worst case scenario occur, the actions of my office, cabinet, the esteemed members of Congress, the military and all interested parties shall be found utterly unimpeachable? Absolutely, Mister President.

The camera draws back and, accompanied in quick succession by subliminal images of the Wicked Witch of the West peering into her crystal ball and then Saruman the White gazing into his palantir, we now see Maria seated at a desk, watching this scene on a computer screen. Behind her stands the Snowman, apparently alive and in fine fettle, although his memory of the fiesta and the ritual on the pyramid and just about everything else over the last several days is foggy at best. (By the way, the live feed they're watching is thanks to Maria's own super hacker, none other than Raf-I-el, whose extraordinary cyber skills have gone unrecognized until now, clearly a bald-faced attempt to assuage his disgruntled fan base, who feel Boone has sorely slighted Raf's character—you know, Raf the space cadet, Raf the ditzy Rastafari, Raf the fakin' fakir?). Nico, who just walked into the room, is making rabbit ears over Ditto's and the President's heads and even more impetuously he grabs an ink marker and draws mustaches on their faces, fortunately erasable. Despite these attempts at jocularity, Maria is distraught. This is worse than I thought, Snowman. We won't be able to develop the enzyme in time. *Enzyme?* Maria sighs and the whole story comes out. We now discover that not only are *los guys* descendants of ancient Zoltec kings, they're pretty fair scientists. Nico makes a sideways ferret grin like, who would've guessed, right? Hmm, the Snowman ponders, so is it Zoltec or Zol*tech?* Maria rolls her eyes and continues. In a sort of mad dash (years in terms of medical research), they've been working to create a unique enzyme that will irrevocably alter the molecular structure of the AgaveX® so that it no longer produces the active agent in either Icine or the street drug Ice. Maria takes a deep breath and uncorks the real shocker. Due to a fluke of time and place, out

of all the ten billion or so people on the planet (Big growth
spurt in the last few years. The religions of the world have
engaged in a friendly procreative competition. Not surprising,
the Catholic church, recently returned to strict doctrine, the
evangelical Christians (always big on family), the Muslims
(ditto) and the Hindus (it's an upper caste thing) are essentially
running neck and neck, and the Chinese (Um … Confucians?
Buddhists? Don't give me that *no preference* crap!) have upped
the ante to three children per family. Of course the Jains and the
Shakers and their ilk are at a terrible disadvantage here.) … um
… uh … *Line!* Glowering at someone off camera, Maria takes
another deep breath and starts again. Out of all these billions of
people, Snowman, you alone carry a specific gene that has
traveled down the ancestral highway of Hernán Cortés's
descendants over the last half millennium. *Oh?* His ears perk up
like the little priss in sixth grade who's just been told in front of
the whole class that he/she/they is/are *gifted.* On the one hand,
this information provides him a huge ego stroke (if simply
inheriting a gene merits any accolades, especially when it
comes from a notorious … *lalala*). On the other, it begs a
number of questions: 1) What is the significance of this
discovery? Maria's shoulders slump briefly as she realizes she's
getting in much deeper than she'd intended, but she straightens
up again and explains that a sample of this Cortés gene is vital
for the anti-Icine enzyme. He ponders this response before
asking his second question: 2) How did she and *los guys*
identify him out of all the people on Earth? Simple, Maria says,
although the answer is anything but. Thanks to the Galactic
Cloud as well as exponential advances in nanoprocessors, they
were able to crunch essentially all of human history, genealogy,
birth and death records, municipal ledgers, written
correspondences (*Mi querida hija*), and finally, the ultimate
determiner, DNA, into a single strand of code with the
Snowman's name on it. Once they had a positive ID, they began
to *cultivate* him with the help of farmers. *Farmers?* Yeah, you
know, *Snowman*, friends, intimates, people close to you. Hmm,

that's interesting because he never really had many of those except—once again sirens scream, klaxons blare and a red neon sign in his brain flashes *CONSPIRACY! CONSPIRACY! CONSPIRACY!* as he sees Judith running toward him like a TV commercial, her hair bouncing like a black storm cloud around her face and shoulders and her breasts bouncing pertly beneath a brown rag wool sweater. But before the tidal wave of emotions (hurt, anger, betrayal—*does that mean it wasn't love? that it was never love?*) swelling in the Snowman's gullet can erupt into some sort of histrionics he'll regret later, Maria gives him her classic bemused look like, oh, Snowman, are you really so dense? and continues. When conditions seemed right, *los guys*, as you call them, traveled north to secure the asset. *Huh?* his expression says. *You*, Snowman. (Boone had envisioned something like Tolkien's Fellowship of the Ring but instead of a bunch of hairy and, to be perfectly candid, smelly, unwashed hobbits (well, okay, before the bath at close of day), it's Nico, Raf, Xuan, Bombástico and Carroteeno who set off to deliver the ring (i.e., the Snowman) to Mordor (not clear on the analogy here), accompanied by a host of Middle Earth super heroes, as well as the great wizard Gandalf (whom one can't imagine putting up with that dreadful Harry Pothole's shenanigans for one minute), but none of that's going to happen with this budget.) And 3) (the Snowman's third question, that is, and this is of particular interest to him): How do they extract this gene sample? Maria stares at him as if she's judging just how much more of this mumbo jumbo she should divulge. Finally she shrugs like oh what the heck and explains that, according to an ancient Zoltec covenant, the *chosen one*, i.e., *you*, Snowman, must willingly shed blood and a *precious offering* of a human heart be made to the gods. The covenant, however, does not specifically say how much blood must be shed or *whose* heart has to serve as the precious offering (their attorneys were pretty good even back then). Maria then gives him what must seem to the audience an improbable story about an extremely important person desperately in need of a heart transplant and a brain dead donor patient—a sixteen-year-old girl who died in a heart-breaking (well, not technically) accident involving a cucumber and a tennis ball cannon. As Maria speaks we see a short flashback, the silhouettes of doctors and technicians in scrubs working inside a lamp-lit medical tent set up on top of a pyramid—a human hand in a blue nitrile surgical glove raises a beating human heart up to the hot white slice of sun as it edges above the horizon (it's just an instant, not long enough to cause damage to this most vital of organs). Maria concludes her story: While the medical staff were at it, they extracted some of your blood, Snowman, ten milliliters, not a drop more. Since then we've been working 24/7 to develop the enzyme. Unfortunately, the initiation of Operation WhiteOut means we'll have to take action now.

Hmm ... he adds all this up in his brain. So it's true. There really is this great big mega-conspiracy in which he plays an integral role. Which means what? The thing between him and Maria was just part of the plot to get him here and take his blood and not—he doesn't say *love,* not even to himself, but it's pretty obvious that's what he's thinking, which also means that once again, stupid *Snowman,* he's been a total dupe. Maria's face expresses sadness, compassion, and yes, maybe there is a trace of love. But then the camera draws in on her eyes, which are murderous and bright, and she says, I knew the time would come when I would have to face this darkness again, and now it has. And then she laughs, and it's not at all an attractive laugh, more like the manic, disturbing laughter of a hyena that actually bends her over and leaves her gasping for breath. Don't worry, Snowman, she says, recovering. I haven't lost my mind completely, and she now relays to him the following piece of information. Unbeknownst to Col. Ditto's crowd, the date they've chosen to initiate Operation WhiteOut corresponds precisely with a date determined by the Zoltec calendar two thousand years ago, more or less around the birth of Christ *your* savior, Snowman. And what happens then? he croaks like the straight man waiting for a sixteen-ounce Everlast punchline to smash him in the face. The world ends? Don't be ridiculous, Snowman. *And then* (Maria makes air quotes) *the lord Quetzalcoatl shall return and the ancient fires shall burn through the earth*. Maria gives him a sideways glance. Yeah, I know, silly superstition, right?

Now we hear tramping feet, voices singing, iron bells clanging. Luminaria flicker and glow along cobblestone streets and narrow roads like strings of cowry shells. A procession of people, most in simple peasant garb, among them the Snowman, head bowed piously (or else he's avoiding the camera), wends its way past adobe and stucco houses and faded colonial buildings. At the head of the procession a man lights the way with a kerosene lantern. Behind him a man in biblical robes leads a donkey on which rides a woman, similarly attired. Here and there the procession stops at homes whose brightly lit windows and open doors invite them inside to eat and drink, laugh and sing in front of elaborate altars decorated with pink and green papel picado, brightly colored Mexican blankets, huge sprays and bouquets of roses, carnations, gladiolus, plastic skeletons in mariachi costumes. Candles and incense smolder and glow among ceramic and plastic statues and framed pictures of Jesus, the Madonna, famous singers, matadors, movie stars, piles of sugar skulls, candy, fruit, baked goods, bottles of tequila, beer and soda. The camera briefly catches the Snowman cramming an enormous orange sugar cookie down his throat and glugging what is probably his second bottle of beer before he discreetly wanders out back where a group of blindfolded children who have been taking turns whacking a red and green, star-shaped piñata now scream with delight as toys and candy shower to the ground. (As everyone on *this* side of the border *knows*, *Las Posadas* are part of a nine-day religious celebration representing Mary and Joseph's search for an inn. As everyone on *that* side of the border *thinks*, this is just another in an endless succession of festivals, saints' days and miscellaneous holidays the inhabitants of this torpid clime invoke to avoid an honest day's labor—Eduardo.)

On the morning of December 24th the sun sprawls on the horizon like a pile of bloody gauze before it disappears altogether behind a purple and gray slump of clouds that appears in the sky like a giant leviathan. An unfamiliar breath of cold air descends on the region and like a wraith slips through villages and towns and into large cities, invisible and insidious and therefore all the more startling in its grasp. It's like a hard slap to the face, an insult to bare flesh. People pull on unfamiliar sweaters, jackets, coats, wool caps. They shiver and commiserate, *Pinche frío ¿no, güey?* But this isn't just a brief cold snap that passes in a day or two and people talk about it for another day or two after that before it slips from their memories. In a matter of hours the temperature has fallen well below freezing and continues its plunge to unheard of territory. The cold is like a vice that crushes everything in its frozen grip. Rivers, streams, lakes, wells, ponds and cattle tanks freeze solid. Life in the desert comes to a halt. Snakes cease their slither in mid-sssibilance, encased in S-hook skins of ice. The mechanical-looking scorpion stalls in mid-sting, silent, unmoving, waiting for the return of the sun to reboot its tiny, insensate electric motor. Then it begins to snow. Many locations see their first snowfall in over six hundred years of recorded history (the previous six hundred years' history having been destroyed by that *hijo de puta Hernán ... lalala*). Snow blankets cactus and yucca and turns the desert landscape into a thorny white comforter. Huge swaths of tropics wilt and blacken overnight, crops die, people freeze to death, or succumb to carbon monoxide poisoning from ersatz attempts at home heating, in some cases whole families, entire villages. Melancholy and gloom pervade everything. The Snowman digs his parka out of the closet, pulls it on as if it were a used body bag and sinks into an all too familiar funk (& *Wagnalls*, look under: the blues, depression, despair, doldrums, dumps, gloom, hopelessness) that soon finds him huddled under the covers like a neglected child, clutching a rapidly emptying bottle of tequila and puffing on a joint of Maria's potent but dwindling stash of marijuana. He feels helpless, defeated. He's convinced the cold and snow have followed him here from *el Norte*, and even more than that, the cold is actually emanating from him, as if he, his body, were some kind of zero K generator that reduces everything to absolute stasis, which, sure, fine, he is the Snowman. But it's not just about him, is it? What about your *friends*, Snowmensch? What about everybody else who lives here, not just Las Riquezas, the whole fucking country? Your presence has put a curse on all of them. *You* did this, *Snowman*. It's in your blood. You are *Cortés!* By now, of course, he's totally trashed, blubbering like a baby, snot running from his nose.

Poor deluded Snowman.

The scene changes again and we see something that could be a very large whale's spout on the horizon or a plume of smoke or—an erupting volcano? And not a volcano spewing red-hot magma but—*snow?* And here the camera takes the audience along for the ride as it plunges into a towering geyser of frozen precipitation and down, down, down we go, slamming into huge clots of snow, chunks of ice, we're being buffeted about like an Apollo space capsule returning to earth in a meteor shower, like a brave but misguided little spermatozoon salmon-like fighting its way back upstream annnnd ... *pop!* Well, actually there's not even a pop. It just feels like it as the snow squall stops and the camera emerges in a cavernous space that looks kind of like one might imagine the inside of an enormous hollow Hershey's kiss or ... the empty shell of a mountain, which is exactly what it is. Suddenly the sound returns, a loud roar punctuated by the intermittent *whoosh* and *hiss* of large bursts of steam. And—okay, Boone has definitely lifted this from a Bond film. We see huge stainless steel tanks, iron ladders and catwalks, floodlights, hundreds of workers in hazmat suits, a control room in which men in hard hats and white coats monitor valves, gauges, computers and wall screens. Live video feed shows a column of supercritical fluid pouring out of a fissure in the earth and rising up a cylindrical shaft studded with giant, jet engine-like injector heads that infuse the hot fluid with thousands of gallons of Icine per minute, creating a frozen white mass that explodes from the mountaintop like an endless wad of jism and shoots several miles into the sky before it bells outward, disintegrating into individual snowflakes that fall to earth in vast white swaths. Another screen shows satellite images of similar *snow volcanoes* bursting like gigantic pimples all over a map of Mexico. And who is this elegant, sixtyish gentleman observing these activities in the control room with obvious satisfaction? L. Condor, of course. Nor is his delight any less evident when another screen shows a fleet of enormous, ungainly-looking airplanes that pretty closely resemble giant white geese rumbling down an extremely long runway and lumbering into the air as if they were tumbling off the edge of the earth (you just know the pilots are gritting their teeth and muttering trench (cloud?) prayers), until finally they rise into the sky and slowly trundle off toward their destination, each aircraft's eight 3000 horsepower Pratt and Whitney engines dutifully dragging these winged monstrosities through the atmosphere like Pegasusian draft horses. For reasons unfathomable even to those closest to him, L. Condor has ordered these aerodynamically unsound flying machines to be built more or less according to Howard Hughes' original design for the infamous Spruce Goose, a giant wooden airplane that rose from terra firma (the sea, actually), circled over the water at an altitude of about seventy feet for a distance of approximately one mile, and never flew again. A quick fact check (thank you, Glenda ... what? No, I'm sorry, a raise is out of the question. *What?!* That's blackmail!) tells us that the original goose was actually built primarily of birch, but Condor, in yet another slap in the face to his patria, has constructed his, oh, shall we say *iteration?* from the sole surviving forest of rare highland spruce in the mountains of northern Mexico and, in one fell swoop, depleted the winter nesting habitat of a large colony of monarch butterflies. (Apparently the wood makes the planes less detectable by radar. Condor is also counting on the

snowfall to provide additional cover for his *aeroflota blanca.*
Regardless of his motives, Condor has proven Mr. Hughes
correct. The damn things will fly.) Condor's primary interest, of
course, is not the history of aeronautics. His *aerogansos* also
happen to be loaded down with hundreds of tons of pure crystal
Ice. The forward-thinking Condor, sensing fate closing in on
him in the form of rival cartels, the impending election of an
unsympathetic government, and unfortuitous policy changes in
the U.S., has some of his own policy changes in the works.
Unbeknownst to his American associates, he's taking advantage
of the window of opportunity created by this arctic aberration to
move all his commercial assets north of the border to an
abandoned U.S. military base (those pesky budget cuts, sorry,
you pork barrelers) in south Texas at the same time he's also
covering his own assets.

Meanwhile, SNN reports that entire convoys of Icine tank
trucks have been destroyed, although it does look suspiciously
like they're just showing the same burning truck over and over
again. Later Maria will provide video of very intact columns of
Icine tank trucks snaking their way along narrow mountain
passes, accompanied by fleets of black SUVs packed with
heavily armed men. Right now, however, blame falls on
insurgentes and it looks like things are playing into the hands of
Ditto (although less so than he thinks) and L. Condor (more
than Ditto knows). North of the border Icine shortages result in
furloughed workforces, eviscerated municipal budgets, and a
rare thaw that isn't pretty. All across the nation worn-out
appliances, abandoned cars, piles of household garbage and
mountains of just plain shit immediately start to appear out of
the melting snow. On top of which, the tequila industry, riding a
wave of popularity on the yanqui palate, has been devastated by
a nearly one hundred percent loss of the Mexican agave crop,
further destabilizing the economy. And the constituents are
pissed. The Tea Potty is pissed. The Snowflakes are pissed. Old
Granny Donut across the street, Mrs. Harper from the PTA and
John Barley the elementary school custodian who fought in two

poorly conceived and executed wars and wears a prosthetic arm
and leg are pissed. In response, President Bolillo stands before
the Mexican congress to announce a new offensive against what
are now being called terrorist elements. At the same time his
U.S. counterpart President Ronwald DeBoche addresses
Congress to request additional funding *to aid our friends and
neighbors south of the border in training and logistical support*
(and yes, we've heard this song and dance before).

Just when it seems things couldn't get more complicated, a
powerful rumble rolls across the Valley of Mexico. Folks can
feel it all the way out here in Las Riquezas. Live from the snow-
blanketed D.F. we now see the great Popocatepetl spewing its
primitive message. Any time, any place, without rhyme, reason
or apologies from God, total chaos can explode like one of
great-uncle Ramón's legendary bouts of flatulence (beans, beer
and red-hot chile peppers). Reports soon come in from around
the country of more volcanoes erupting. Red-hot lava pours
down mountainsides, hot slag and ash sizzle and steam and turn
the thick blanket of snow into melting slush. Apparently L.
Condor's scientists did not take into account de destabilizing
effects of de *controlled release* of geothermal gases. Just as de
petroleum industry did not know dat fracking caused soil und
ground water pollution, sinkholes, earthquakes und other
geological events, iss it not? Oh ho! What's this? *Herr* Zog
butting in again? Guten Tag, mein *Herr*. Wie geht es *ihnen*,
mein *Herr?* Was wollen *Sie*, mein *Herr? Fick dich, Klaus!*

Speaking of petroleum, most of the country's pipelines are
aging, corroded and riddled with illegal taps. It doesn't take a
genius to imagine what might happen if—uh oh, looks like
somebody's been playing with matches. All across Mexico
improvised napalm bombs explode into orange flame and black
smoke. Adding to the conflagration, the country's huge
proliferation of fireworks factories, legal and il-, explodes in a
chain reaction. Even more incredible, citizens in remote areas
claim to have seen *fire-breathing dragons* attacking a fleet of
huge wooden airplanes, which, saturated with pitch,

immediately burst into flames and fell out of the sky. Unfortunately, there is no photographic evidence, no cell phone images. *Esa gente es pobre. No tienen nada, ni comida, ni papel higiénico. Y decididamente no tienen celular.* (These people are poor, they ain't got diddly squat. Definitely not cell phones— Eduardo.) The combined effect of these various pyrotechnic events is a sudden and unexpected warming trend. Balmy breezes begin to blow and like a time-lapse film in reverse, the snow melts away and evaporates and things miraculously begin to turn green again, corn grows, flowers bloom, banana trees bend beneath the weight of their fruit, the tropics turn tropical again and—oops, *miraculous* is right, someone's obviously jumped ahead to the next reel. Yeah, sure, the worst is over, the snow's mostly gone, the temperatures are rising, but the whole goddamn country's a mess. Thousands are dead. Human and animal carcasses lie rotting everywhere, most of the agriculture is in ruins, hunger and disease are epidemic. Clearly someone's gotta pay for all this havoc and once again blame falls on the usual suspects: dissidents, liberals and leftists of every stripe, as well as LGBTQs, the handicapped, elderly, mentally challenged, poor, sick and infirm, that gossipy Doña Chismosa next door who I've always despised, Juan's cousin Arturo who stole his girlfriend Legumina, Fernanda's niece Fluvia—*stuck-up little fresa beetch.* You get the picture. Black SUVs, police vans and army transports rumble over the roads day and night. People disappear from homes, schools, job sites. It's like the bloody effing French revolution all over again, except with the monarchists in charge. And you never know in whose name Madame Defarge will knit a stitch next.

28
Revolution

*"We are sorry for the inconvenience, but this is a
revolution."*
—Subcomandante Marcos, January 1, 1994

ONE NIGHT THE SNOWMAN SEES a shooting star zip across the
sky like a bottle rocket at the same time he hears a strange cry.
It thrills in his chest and in his head like a great G major chord
on a pipe organ. It echoes across mountains and valleys,
throughout tiny towns and villages and big cities. It's the urgent
clanging of an iron bell, the fervent voice of a parish priest, it's
the cry for freedom of an entire people and all of humanity
since the beginning of time. This is *el Grito*. The following
morning Nico enters Maria's house dressed in a plain olive drab
uniform and cloth military cap and the Snowman thinks, oh no,
here we go again, and prepares himself for further physical
abuse, but instead of pummeling him with a gunstock, Nico
announces solemnly (he's always a whisker away from
breaking into a mad cackle) that the *Subcomandante* has
arrived. The Snowman goes outside to see who this
Subcomandante is and in a scene Boone has clumsily lifted
from a Hollywood classic, Maria (who briefly appears to have
sprouted a bushy mustache—it's an odd shadow, dusty film
stock, something like that) rides up on a white stallion. She too
is wearing an olive drab military uniform and cloth cap, as well
as a red bandana around her neck, bandoliers loaded with

copper-jacketed bullets across her chest, pistols on her hips, and in the crook of her left arm an AK-47. Her whole being seems transformed, her body leaner, her cheekbones more severe, the obsidian gleam in her eyes more ardent, the red slash of her lips harder. Behind her, also on horseback, appears the rest of *los guys*, also in military outfits (Bombástico's mount is a retired Anheuser-Busch Clydesdale, who might have preferred the glue factory to this late-life gig), followed by Father O'Jalajan in a black surplice with military gold braid and epaulets, leading a boisterous crowd of kilted and tamo'shantered Irishmen sporting green shamrocks on their vests and hoisting aloft knotty shillelaghs and frothy pints of Guinness stout as they repeatedly shout in a heavy Spanish-Irish brogue, *Hasta la victorrrria siempre!* Ah, sure and 'tis that green grow the lilacs-oh! chortles the normally reserved Father O'Jalajan, whose uncharacteristically cheerful mood suggests he's been sampling a wee bit of the old sod himself, probably explains the sentimental tears welling in his eyes and the arm thrown familiarly over the Snowman's shoulder as he relates a slightly muddled history that Boone wisely skips over (are you out of your fucking mind?). (Apparently a large number of disaffected Irishmen—you get tired of being called *mick, shamrock, green nigger, tuber eating pig*, etc.—facing conscription into the U.S. Army to fight in the previously mentioned land grab aka the Mexican-American war, instead fled south of the border and joined their putative enemies.) Father O'Jalajan's anecdote is only the first note in what promises (or threatens) to become a chorus of uniquely Mexican ethno-his-and-herstories as we now see approaching a fleet of Cadillac convertibles packed front seat and back with African-Mexican-Americans (can they do the can-can? I can't say), sporting braids, fades, twists, dreads, retro-, half- and full fros, and they're chanting in hip hop-inflected Spanish, *¡Hey José, chíngale! ¡No queremos más de tu mierda apestosa! (Hey José, fuck you! We don't want any more of your stinking shit!*—Eduardo (Not sure who this José is).) Leading this delegation is a noble Nubian prince in red and purple robes, lion skin (faux) and King Tutankhamen beard, whom the Snowman recognizes first with incredulity and then a wide open Tom Sawyer smile as his former workmate, ~~Huck~~ M'Shaka N'Baka. (Once again Boone skips the back story, which the Snowman was made privy to during a memorable but barely remembered night that began with top shelf booze and a brief romance at the Blue Heart Beat in east Osberg and ended the following morning in the pews of a Black Baptist church rocking in the bosom of Abraham. Twice removed from the greenghost's world of snow and ice, M'Shaka is descended from escaped slaves in Vera Cruz. His Spanish-speaking great grandparents crossed into the U.S. with the *Braceros* program and stuck around after the U.S. Government kicked everybody else out. No one noticed except for a census worker who referred to their broken English as that *Negro jive*. They settled in the notoriously segregated east side of Osberg, Texas and in one generation they were as American as any other African-American—know what I mean, *Snowman?*) This history or rather its lacuna is interrupted (supplanted?) by the droning of two-cycle internal combustion engines and everyone's attention shifts to the fleet of ultra-light aircraft circling like giant dragonflies in the skies above. Enveloped in clouds of blue smoke, engines whining like angry cats, they touch down in a perfect V formation and out of the lead aircraft steps another of the Snowman's former workmates, Moll Flowers, a big strapping gal with a ruddy, outdoorsy face and a tousled blond shock of hair. Looks kind of like a trans Joe Palooka. The first snow*woman* in the snowbiz. Two tours in Overthereistan as a combat helicopter pilot. But, yes, here she is again, leading a squadron of overachieving teenage Mennonites (some kind of family connection), all of whom are freckle-faced, white as snow (*Edelweiss, Edelweiss*), hair some shade of blond (platinum, lemon yellow, flaxen, wheat straw, strawberry, etc.), and dressed identically, the boys in aw-shucks farmer John straw hats, red and blue checked shirts, denim coveralls and brown leather work boots, the girls in nineteenth-century sun bonnets, ankle-length, gingham granny dresses and button up shoes. These enterprising youngsters are piloting DIY ultra-light aircraft constructed out of baling wire, barn wood, canvas and recycled lawnmower engines. Granted, there is some confusion over the role they will play. The sound of tramping feet cuts short this narrative and up marches an army of Zoltec farmers in black balaclavas and red bandanas, wielding rakes, hoes and machetes. A creaking armored vehicle made out of corrugated tin bolted to an antiquated pick-up truck with a Civil War era Gatling gun mounted on the cab and the bed packed with masked Zoltecs grinds to a halt. Lastly, a plaid-skirted contingent from the Girls' Dialectical Christian Academy springs forward batting badminton birdies, albeit with lethal speed and accuracy. If the Snowman had expected a more formidable army—nope, this is it. Is Maria totally deluded? And all those devoted to her? (For viewers in the audience who detect a faint reference to the classic *Magnificent Seven*, you are absolutely *correct-o*. Listen closely to the film score riiiight ... *here* and you'll recognize a few bars from the Marlboro theme. We even see (some of us, anyway, it's either drug abuse or Boone doing his sub-subliminal thing) the iconic shot of the titular characters riding toward us across the desert on horseback, a few frames, nothing more.) Even the term of endearment Maria's followers have anointed her with, *la Sup* (pronounced *soup*. OMG! *Caldo tlalpeño* is to *die for*— Eduardito), suggests some confusion. (The title *Sub*comandante serves the dual purpose of identifying the individual as merely a subordinate figure, and, therefore, a less attractive target, in a much larger organization than actually exists—Colonel Jedidiah Sutpen, in a lecture on guerilla warfare at the United States Army War College in Carlisle, PA.) The Snowman's hopes soar, however, when Maria speaks in a loud and resounding voice. Many of our people have been falsely imprisoned in Chopahuac, many have been tortured and murdered, many more driven off their land. The dark forces have sought to extinguish the fire of the sun. Now the children of the sun will fight back!

The stallion rears up and Maria leans forward in the saddle, raises her rifle overhead and shouts, *¡Hasta la victoria siempre!* *¡Hasta la victoria siempre!* everyone shouts back, including a couple of croaking adolescent male Mennonite voices.

The revolution begins and it *is* televised. (Both SNN and FUCHS News have drones on the scene within minutes and everybody in the world's got their EyePhones® in hand.) It's like a dream, maybe it *is* a dream. Everything seems thick and molassesy. The Snowman sees himself running in slow motion through the streets of Chopahuac with what appears to be a fifteenth-century matchlock in his hands. He has no idea how or even *if* it works. Next to him Doña Oleinfanta, rolls of flesh bulging out of a heavy wool WWI British foot soldier's uniform, is carrying a Natty Bumpkin flintlock musket. Running ahead of them, *los guys*, Nico, Xuan, Bombástico, Carroteeno and Raf-I-el, are armed with much more modern and lethal looking weapons (Xuan is toting his cryogun—no idea what model that is). Then, shouting, gunfire. Maria's forces enter the zócalo, taking cover behind palm trees, garbage containers, stone walls, the bandstand where a small orchestra is energetically playing Los Tigres Del Norte's *Crónica de un Cambio*. Bullets whack into soft crumbling stucco and limestone. pocking wedding cake friezes, columns and porticos. The solid, stolid Carroteeno takes a slug in the shoulder but soldiers on. Xuan grins savagely, the blue sapphire in his front tooth gleaming like a death star as he bats aside bullets like horseflies and fires off icy blasts from his cryogun. Trying to hit the wiry Raf and Nico is like shooting at fettuccine. Even the barn-sized Bombástico remains untouched by the fusiliers on the opposing side. An organized tour group in identical pink *Teddy's Tours* t-shirts tramps through the mayhem, cell phones extended on selfie sticks like monocular eyestalks, and for about five seconds it's all part of their movie and their fiction stitched into Boone's narrative, before they exit stage right, unscathed by bullets or the carnage of civil unrest in this third world cesspool (thanks, Prez) that, let's face it, holds zero interest for them or anyone back home. Finally the gunfire dies down as Maria's forces overrun the small military post and the local constabulary, liberate the jail and free the prisoners. The rebel flag, a golden starburst on a red field, flies over the Palacio Municipal. One speaker after another steps forward to demand land reform, human rights and justice for the indigenous people. Bonfires burn all night in the zócalo. There is a great deal of drinking and jubilation, which the Snowman experiences more or less on the sidelines. To put it bluntly, this isn't his fight and he isn't really much of a fighter. Plus he feels kind of excluded. Maria, *los guys*, delegates from the Zoltec Agricultural and Oral Hygiene Committee, M'Shaka and Moll are involved in an intense *tête-à-tête*, planning for what inevitably must come next, with kibitzing from Father O'Jalajan, who seems unconflicted by the conflict of his priestly and military duties.

The following morning emerges gray and misty, a chill pervades, fires smolder, men and women sleep on mats, or huddle against each other wrapped in blankets. Now we hear the creaking, clanking and growling of military vehicles, armored cars, Humvees, deuce-and-a-halfs, tanks, followed by the *thwop, thwop, thwop* of helicopters. Then explosions, machine gun fire. The odds are overwhelming, the army is getting the upper hand, the rebels falling back. In a desperate counterattack, M'Shaka's Cadillac contingent rolls up lobbing watermelons from catapults mounted in their trunks. These giant fruits of the Cucurbitaceae family (pumpkins by far grow the largest, the current record, 2,624.6 pounds, is well over a ton, followed by a descending hierarchy of melons, honeydew, musk, Persian, Santa Claus, cantaloupe, etc., as well as a broad range of squash and, to a lesser extent, cucumbers—Glenda, and don't give me that check's in the mail bull, *Boone!*) crash through the windshields of military vehicles and smash down upon dazed Mexican soldiers' heads. A loud buzzing sound cuts through the gunfire. What follows will leave cinephiles arguing for years. One camp calls it a tribute to the classic scene in *Goldfinger* when Pussy Galore leads her Flying Circus of lesbo-piloted Piper Cherokees in a poison gas attack on Fort Knox to a thrilling Henry Mancini score with shrieking woodwinds and pounding timpani! No! their opponents cry. It's a critique of the scene in *Apocalypse Now* where Robert Duval as Colonel Kilgore leads a squadron of Huey attack helicopters in an assault on a suspected Viet Cong village accompanied by the rousing brass (have tubas ever been used so effectively?) and fluttering woodwinds (think angels' wings *Snowmannn*) of Wagner's "Ride of the Valkyries" from the Ring Trilogy! What it *is* is this: to strains of Rimsky-Korsakov's "Flight of the Bumblebee" performed by the Bay City High-Steppers Marching Kazoo and Ukulele Band and the whining drone of 2-cycle gasoline engines, Moll Flower's teenage Mennonites (*I was a ...*) zoom in (well, kind of), launching rounds of chewy white string cheese, loaves of sourdough bread and sweet, cinnamon-flavored snicker doodles at government troops on the ground. The low speed ultra-light aircraft would seem like easy targets, but they also fly erratically so that, like mosquitoes, they're almost impossible for the Mexican forces to hit. Besides, most of the soldiers (grossly underpaid and mostly underfed) have stopped shooting and are stooping down to pick up cookies, bread and cheese. And that's when it happens. An enormous SQUAWK rends eardrums left and right and a giant creature with vast leathery wings, a head like a huge claw hammer and tufts of iridescent gold, green, red and blue plumage drops down out of the sky, cranks open its huge beak and releases a blast furnace roar and a sheet of flame that incinerates a Humvee a mere instant after its occupants dive for safety. Is it really possible? Can this be the great *Quetzalcoatl ignisraptor* Professor Simianovsky spoke of? And ¡ay, Dios mío! now a whole flock of these giant flying lizards is engaging the Mexican helicopters. Tracer bullets and sheets of flame fill the sky. A helicopter goes down in a fiery crash and an ignisraptor crumples and falls to earth. There's a loud shout and Professor Simianovsky himself, dressed in a samurai uniform (actually, it's the traditional classic era Zoltec warrior garb, which does bear a remarkable resemblance to the samurai uniform of the Edo period), swoops out of the clouds on the back of one of these quetzal-whatchamacallums, his blue eyes gleaming madly behind his rectangular spectacles and his orange beard grinning widely as he yells down at the soldiers on the ground *THIS IS WHAT ACADEMIC ACTIVISM LOOKS LIKE!* A helicopter fires two missiles and, *boom*, a ball of orange flame erupts in the sky. For about two seconds we see an image of a bearded skeleton riding on the back of a giant roast turkey and then it disintegrates into falling ash.

Despite this heroic but foolhardy and ultimately futile flanking maneuver by the ignisraptors, the soldiers continue their advance and the rebels fall back. The scene is total chaos. Boone himself seems to be losing control of events. A gasp of astonishment and then dismay goes up from the audience when the sesquicentenarian Doña Añeja fades into view and in a reference either to Mother Teresa or the Pietà, we see her cradling Grandpa's limp body on the pavement in a pool of blood. Another loud gasp goes up when Bombástico goes down with a crimson rose blooming in his chest. The mighty Xuan Carlode (a family name, apparently—Eduardo) slings him over his shoulder as if he were a feather pillow and along with the Snowman, Maria and the rest of *los guys*, they retreat into the cathedral where a large number of people have already gathered. Babies are crying, the wounded groan and scream, candlelight flickers on the gallery of tortured saints and prophets. Father O'Jalajan moves among the exhausted rebels, consoling, giving last rites, tending to the wounded. Monks in brown habits offer food, water and medical assistance. Outside, gunfire continues. There are reports that the soldiers are executing the wounded and fallen in the streets. Father O'Jalajan goes out to face the army. This is a sacred place! Leave us in peace! Maybe it's only the remains of the daylight, of God's light, the light of tourists' cameras and cell phones sending viral images all over the world that prevents an all-out onslaught on the church, but an attack seems inevitable. After midnight Father O'Jalajan rouses the rebels. Lifting a stone panel in the floor, he lights a kerosene lantern and leads them to escape through a secret catacomb clotted with cobwebs and dusty *momias* that even the Snowman's too preoccupied to notice, finally exiting in the wooded outskirts of Chopahuac. Maria informs the Snowman that she's taking the wounded to the hospital (the audience will be happy to know that Bombástico is among them). Afterwards she and her troops will disappear into the mountains. She doesn't say this is goodbye or I hope to see you again someday. She doesn't say anything. She simply gives him her bemused smile and then she's gone.

29
Trapped!

WE NOW SEE THE SNOWMAN standing in front of a large TV screen in the lobby of the Hotel Caulifornia (Oh Missster Snowman, I'm so happy to see you again, *hnn hnn hnn*), watching the latest events on SNN with a bunch of very nervous tourists and ex-pats who couldn't begin to guess what he's been up to. Heavily armed soldiers patrol the streets of Chopahuac, helicopters swoop over green mountains, firing rockets and machine guns, jets drop bombs, orange flames and black smoke explode out of dense jungle foliage, peasant huts disintegrate into splinters (by now it shouldn't surprise anyone that the penny-pinching grave robber Boone has unabashedly inserted old Nam footage here). Reports continue to come in of reprisals, counter reprisals, atrocities committed on both sides. Police officers slaughtered in an ambush, the Deputy Attorney General murdered, attacks on large land owners. Paramilitaries massacre an entire village. In one of the most egregious acts, we see graphic footage of soldiers executing wounded rebels in the hospital, hacked from the EyePhones® of the soldiers themselves, recorded for later *viewing pleasure*. A special newscast announces that Father O'Jalajan has been assassinated and the whole lobby goes up in a cry of despair. The Snowman feels especially despondent. What should he do now, try to find Maria? Stick around until someone taps him on the shoulder, *Come with us*? And, oh no, that seems to be exactly what's about to happen as two men, dressed, oddly, in WWII French

gendarmes uniforms, approach him while in the background we
see Colonel Ditto and the State Judicial Police Commissioner,
also both in uniform, seated at a table, nodding and smiling in
approbation. (And yes, it is very much like the scene in
Casablanca when the gendarmes come to Rick's nightclub to
arrest Ugarte, yes, played by *that* Peter Lorre—very much like
because it *is* the scene from Casablanca, with a few
modifications by Boone's new CGI guy. In this version, for
example, it isn't Ugarte who's going to be arrested, it's the
Snowman, which is probably why the present day Ugarte—er,
Peter Lorre—can be seen on the sidelines, wringing his hands
with pretty obvious schadenfreude and going *hnn hnn hnn*.) The
audience is on the edge of its seat (very small audience or very
big seat). Is the jig up for the Snowman? He's turned pale, he's
broken into a cold sweat, he's actually shaking. Will they shoot
him on the spot? Drag him away and torture him to death? But
wait a second, looks like Boone's overly eager special effects
guy completely fucked up. The gendarmes stride right past the
Snowman and just as in the original scene head straight for
Ugarte—or rather Peter Lorre—and haul him off as he yells,
*Snowman, help me! You must help me! Do something,
Snowman! Snowman! Snowman!* And just as in the original,
Rick—*ahem*, the Snowman—saves his own ass. In an instant
he's out the door and—is this a final goodbye gift from
Maria?—in the courtyard he finds her motorcycle. He's never
driven a motorcycle in his life but he knows that in about two
minutes the cops are going to figure out their mistake. He hops
on and, more or less remembering how Maria operated the
damn thing, hits the starter, lets out the clutch and takes off.

What happens next is unclear. Either another wrinkle in
time has occurred or Boone's getting his chronology confused
again. Inexplicably we now see the Snowman behind the wheel
of the Coupe, we hear the tires going *click clack, click clack,
click clack* over a stretch of broken pavement, and then, *click
clack, click clack, click clack*, we see train wheels rolling down
a track. Separated by maybe fifty meters of desert and a string

of leaning telephone poles, the Snowman's running parallel to a long passenger train. The camera zooms in on one compartment in particular and danged if he doesn't recognize the young couple (YC) sitting at the window. Maybe their battered little car finally pooped out on them or, alarmed at current events, they thought it safer to travel by train. At least they've still got each other, they're happy, or so he thinks (that unquashable sentimental streak). Which is when Boone, who can never leave well enough alone, takes the camera inside the YC's compartment and, boy, they don't sound happy at all. They're bitching and complaining and sniping at each other. It's hot and it smells. The toilets are completely stopped up *I'm not going back there again*. There's no AC. They haven't had a decent meal in two days. They're both suffering some kind of stomach distress, his the worst. And now this goddamn train is just *fucking* creeping along. Cool it, there's nothing we can do about it. Cool it? You're not the one who's shitting his guts out. I told you not to drink that stuff. It wasn't the booze, it was the food. Christ, we won't even reach the goddamn border until midnight, and then we still gotta find a way back to fucking Osberg. We'll get a hotel. I don't wanta get a fucking hotel, I wanta get *home*. Which is when he looks out the window and sees the Snowman behind the wheel of the Coupe. The camera draws in on his eyes and we can see exactly what he's thinking. *That lucky bastard, he's totally free, he can go wherever he wants to go, do whatever he wants to do, instead of being stuck in this roasting tin can with this unsympathetic bitch!* Which, in addition to making him come across as a total asshole, contrary to our earlier impressions, is a perfect example of the neighbor's grass looking greener. The camera now returns us to the Snowman and, uh-oh, his good fortune seems to have flown out the window as he glances up in his rear view mirror and sees a fleet of black SUVs hot on his tail, and that's not peanuts they're shooting at him. He hits the gas and speeds up but what's that ahead? A military convoy is blocking the highway. A platoon of very hostile-looking soldiers has taken up position and they're pointing their deadly Xiuhcoatls directly at him.

The screen goes black. The tension in the theater is palpable. What sort of deus ex machina does Boone have in store for us now? Will the cavalry ride to the Snowman's rescue? Will he be taken somewhere and executed and no trace of him ever heard or seen again? To a loud gasp of dismay, the credits begin to roll over disconnected images: a child's snow sled bursting into flames, the wheels of a baby carriage bouncing down a broad, snow-covered stairway, a man suffering a heart attack on a trolley as he tries to catch the attention of an attractive young woman in the street. Totally befuddled, the audience (what remains of it—there's maybe half a dozen diehards and they're staring at each other like, *what the fuhhh ... ?*) begins to get up and leave. And that's it. We're left with this inconclusive conclusion. Who knows, maybe Boone's already planning a sequel for Christmas release.

ESCAPE FROM ZOL!

ABOUT THE AUTHOR

REYoung was born in Pittsburgh, Pennsylvania and currently resides in a limestone cave deep beneath the city of Austin, Texas. He is the author of the novels *Unbabbling* (Dalkey Archive Press, 1997), *Margarito and the Snowman* (Dalkey Archive Press, 2016), *Inflation* (TageTage Press, 2019) and *The Ironsmith* (TageTage Press, 2020).

UNBABBLING

A NOVEL

In the tour de force called America, one of the tired, the poor, the huddled masses struggles upward to the penthouse of God, discovering too late he's taken the elevator marked down. Resurrected from the rubble of dreams as a messiah and accidental revolutionary, his cry for freedom echoes like a broken record as they lower him into the ground. Like a hopelessly lost coal miner, he digs on, deflating the gloom with slapstick, pensive as a clown, gathering strength for the next round.

MARGARITO AND THE SNOWMAN

REYoung

Margarito and the Snowman

A NOVEL

A nation buried in snow and ice in an obligatory 365 days a year Christmas celebration, a tribe of Mayan warriors in comedy troupe disguise, an existentially challenged hero known as the Snowman on a quest that takes him south of the border down ol' Mexico way, and a B-grade movie director named Boone Weller with his own agenda. Is it a book? A movie? Told in a shoot from the hip Texas style, *Margarito and the Snowman* is loose, rangy, battered with an attitude and bound to offend everybody.

INFLATION

A NOVEL

Martin "Marty" Grasso (think Mardi Gras) wakes to find the world turned into a Dantesque "carnival of bloat." Excess consumption is patriotic, high fat and cholesterol diets are good, exercise is frowned upon, the price of fuel ticks upward by the second, and giant virtual billboards, or VRBLs, bombard citizens with advertisements for consumer products. As a mysterious vortex sucks up rapidly dwindling energy reserves and civilization faces famine, chaos and collapse, the impending catastrophe is blamed on a subversive element known as the sappers. Marty's quest for the truth intersects virtual worlds, utopian societies and ever-morphing nightmares—in a wild vaudeville cyber-punk noir romp that crosses into the twilight zone of "sic"-fi where nothing is ever what it seems.

THE IRONSMITH

A NOVEL

Born out of myth and fairytale, in particular the tradition of the wise old wizard mentoring a bumbling apprentice, and told in language echoing Homer, Beowulf, biblical scripture and John Coltrane, among others, *The Ironsmith* evolves into a surreal Bildungsroman of a self-perceived "monster," a painfully introverted young man whose obsession with the ancient sport of weightlifting causes him to withdraw into an increasingly delusional world that anachronistically intersects classical Greece, the Middle Ages, the Industrial Age, WWI and II, the tumultuous sixties, and the age of the Internet.

www.ingramcontent.com/pod-product-compliance
Lightning Source LLC
Chambersburg PA
CBHW031553240626
47153CB00002B/492